YOU'RE MAKING ME SIX

For Dick Robinson

ISBN 978-1-338-77023-0

10 9 8 7 6 5 4 3 2 1   21 22 22 24 25

Printed in the U.S.A.   40

First edition, November 2021

Edited by Michael Petranek and Conor Lloyd
Book design by Salena Mahina

graphix

AN IMPRINT OF
MSCHOLASTIC

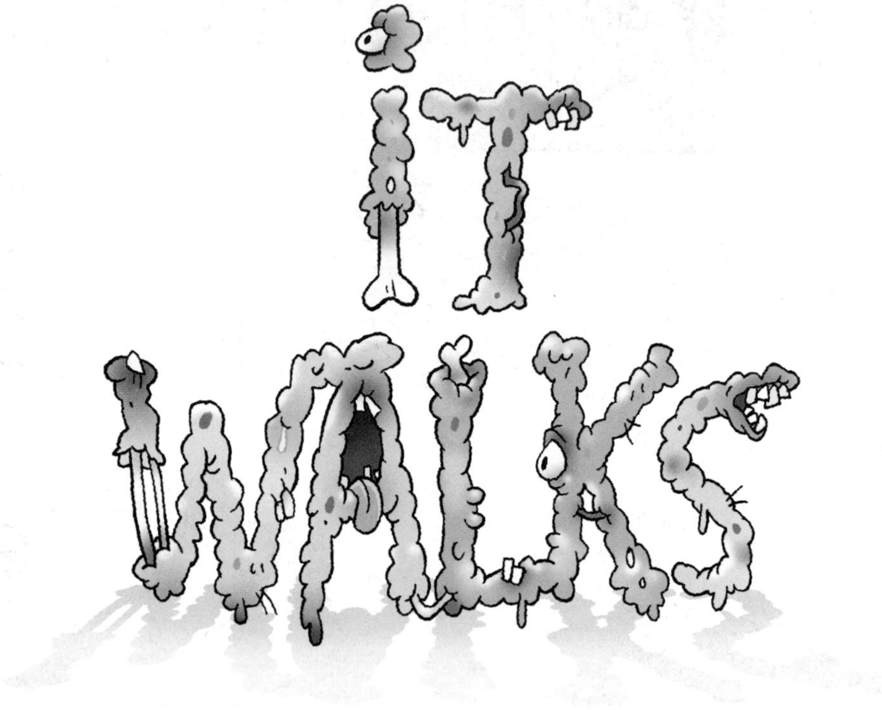
IT
WALKS

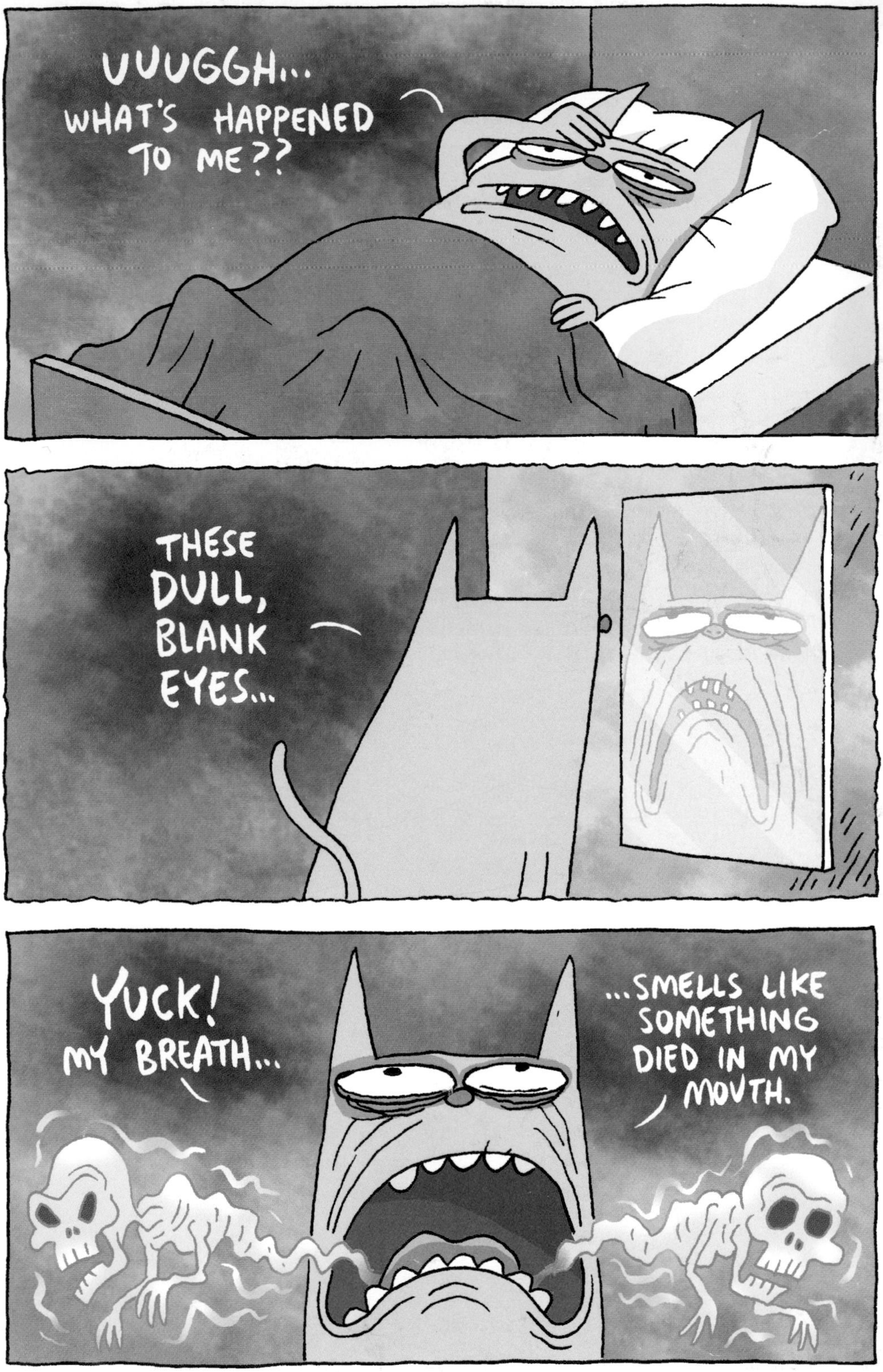
UUUGGH...
WHAT'S HAPPENED TO ME??
THESE DULL, BLANK EYES...
YUCK! MY BREATH...
...SMELLS LIKE SOMETHING DIED IN MY MOUTH.

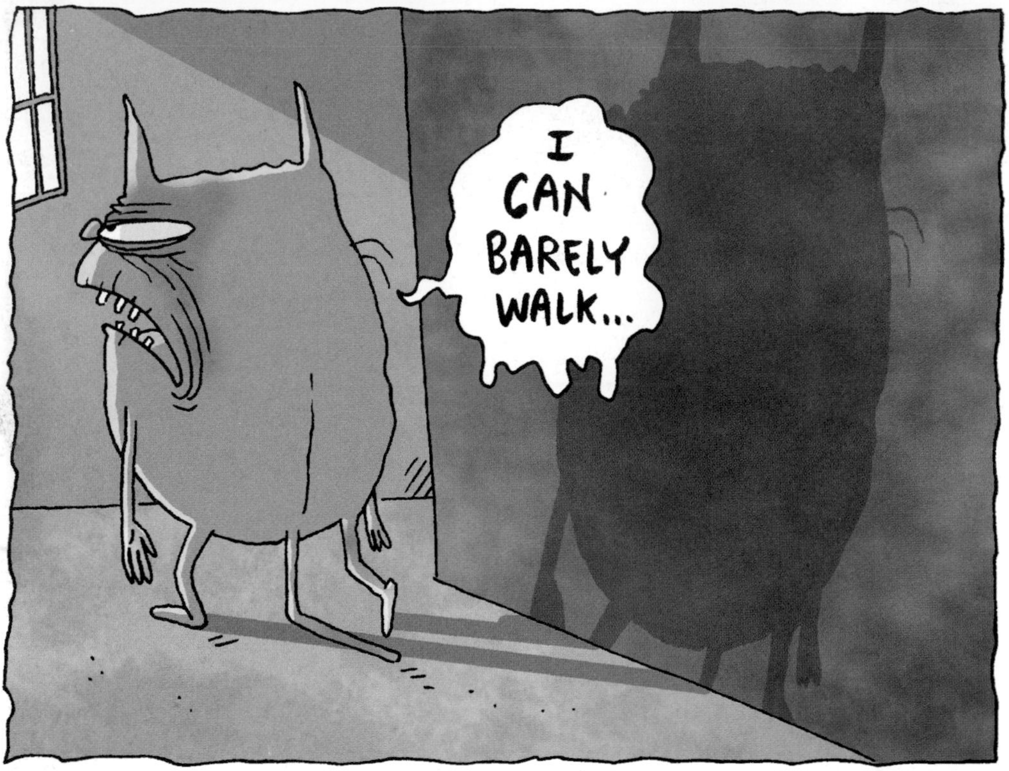
I CAN BARELY WALK...

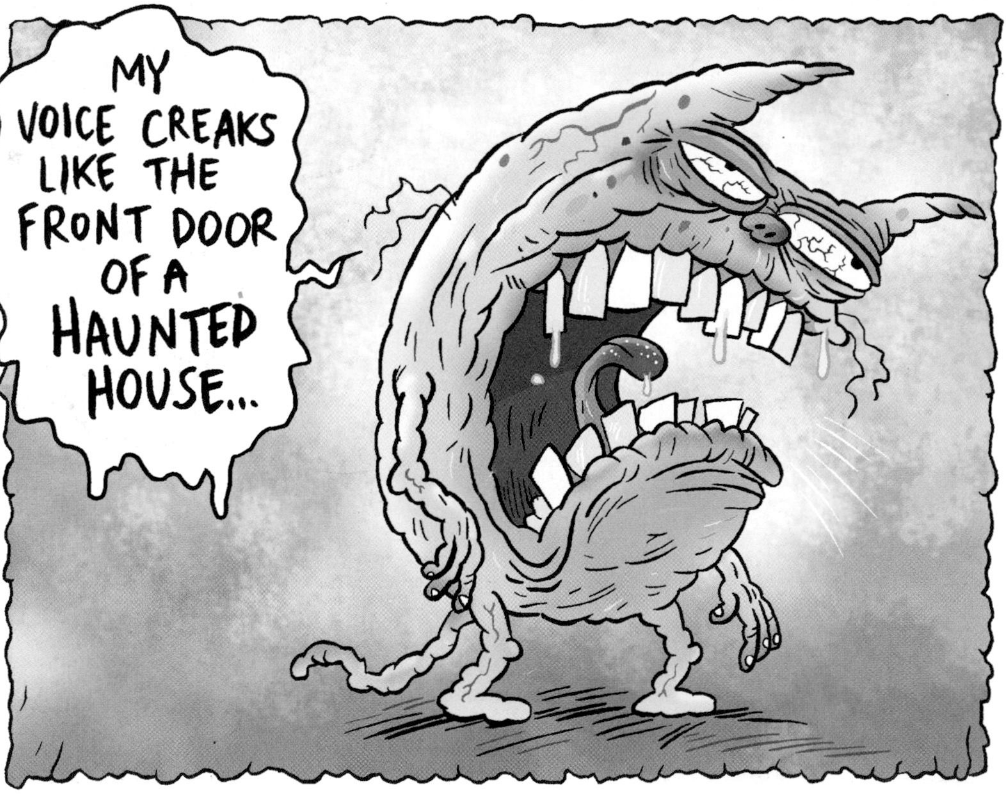
MY VOICE CREAKS LIKE THE FRONT DOOR OF A HAUNTED HOUSE...

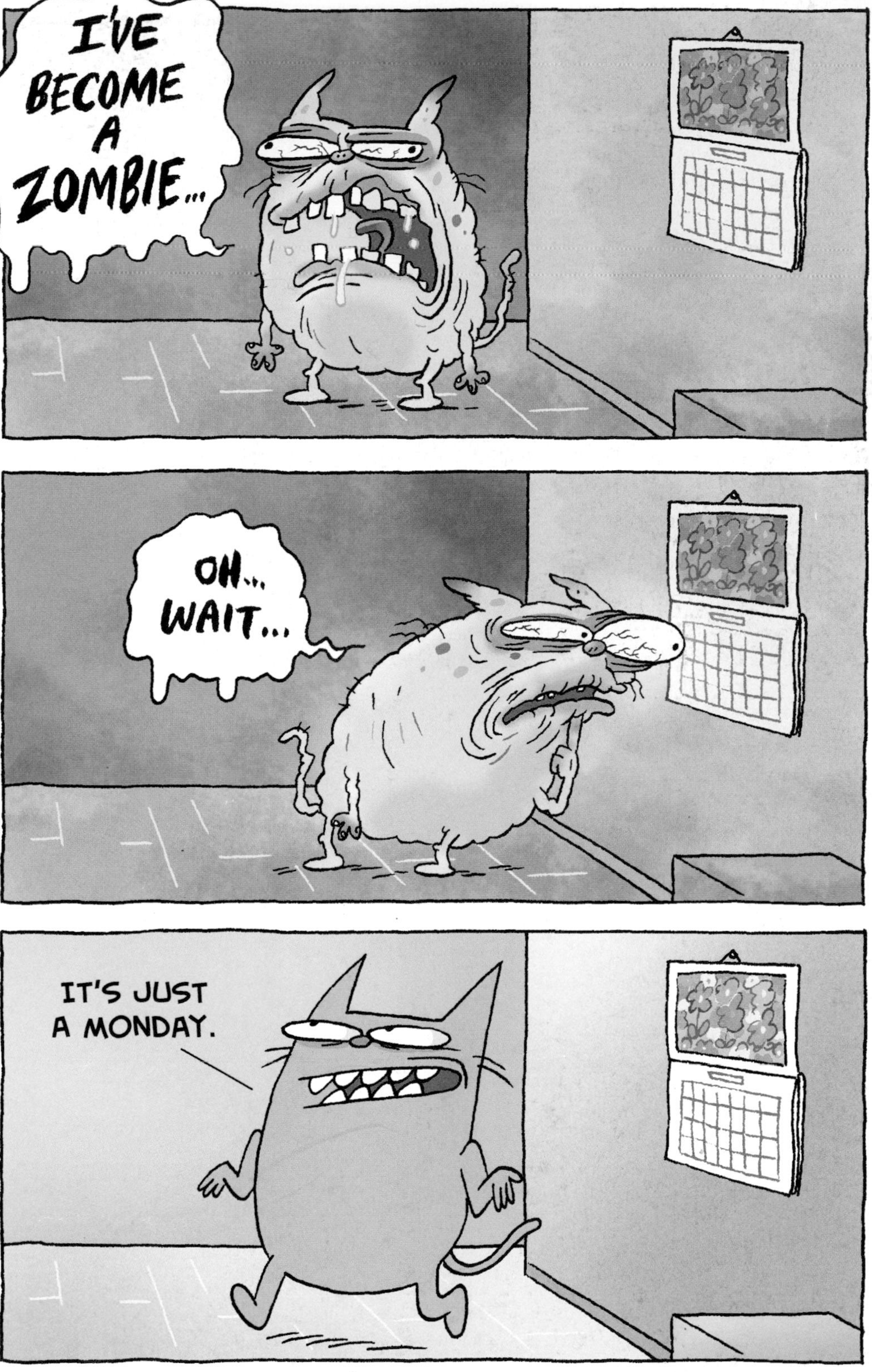
I'VE BECOME A ZOMBIE...
OH... WAIT...
IT'S JUST A MONDAY.

the
MAGICAL
UNiCORN

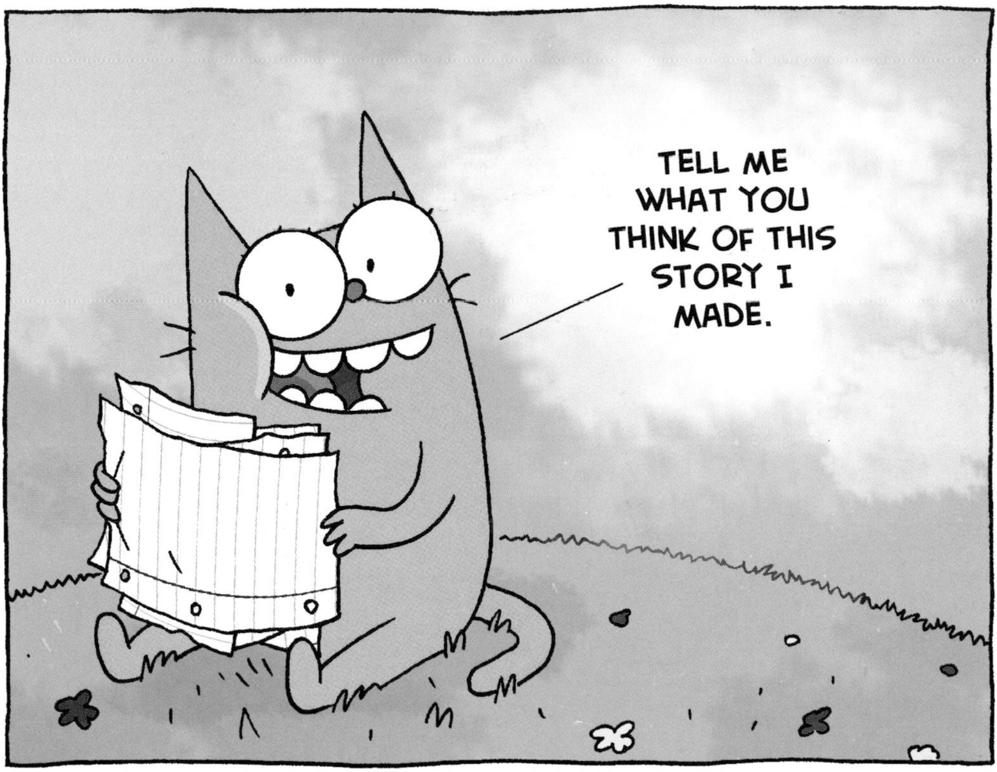
TELL ME WHAT YOU THINK OF THIS STORY I MADE.

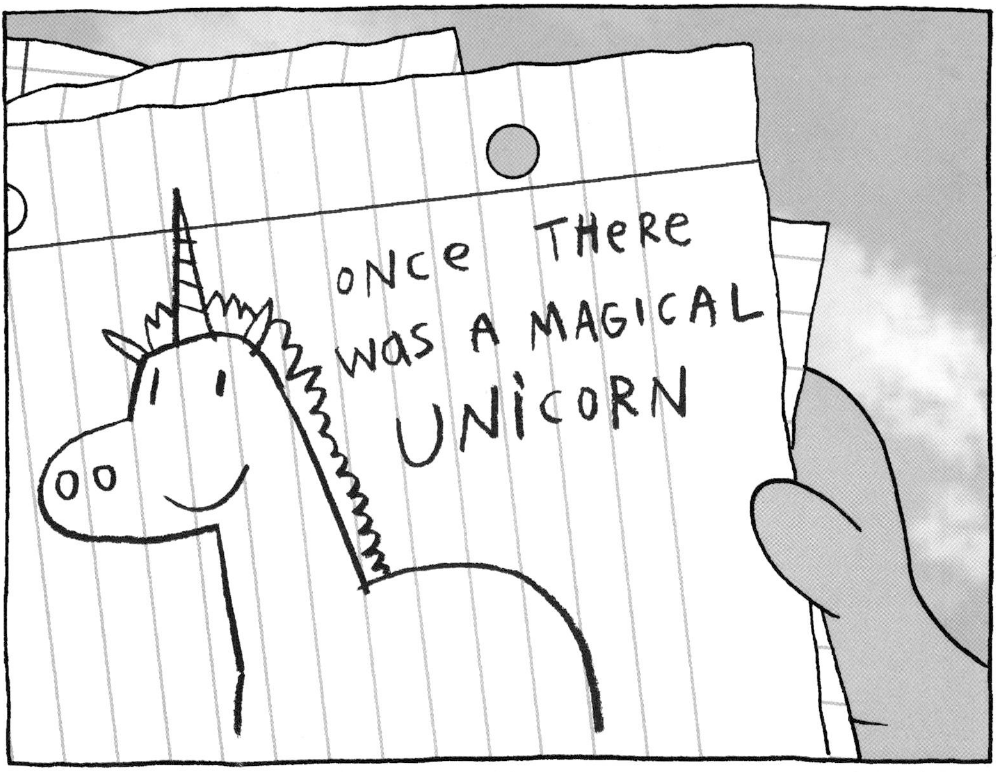
ONCE THERE WAS A MAGICAL UNICORN

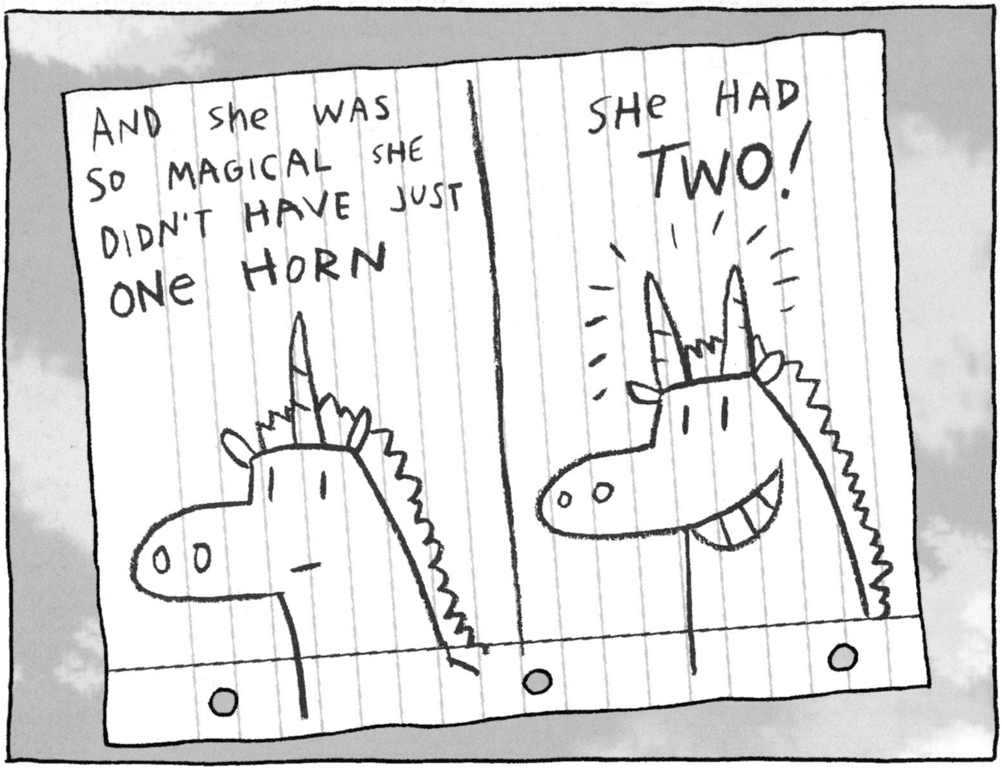
AND SHE WAS SO MAGICAL SHE DIDN'T HAVE JUST ONE HORN
SHE HAD TWO!

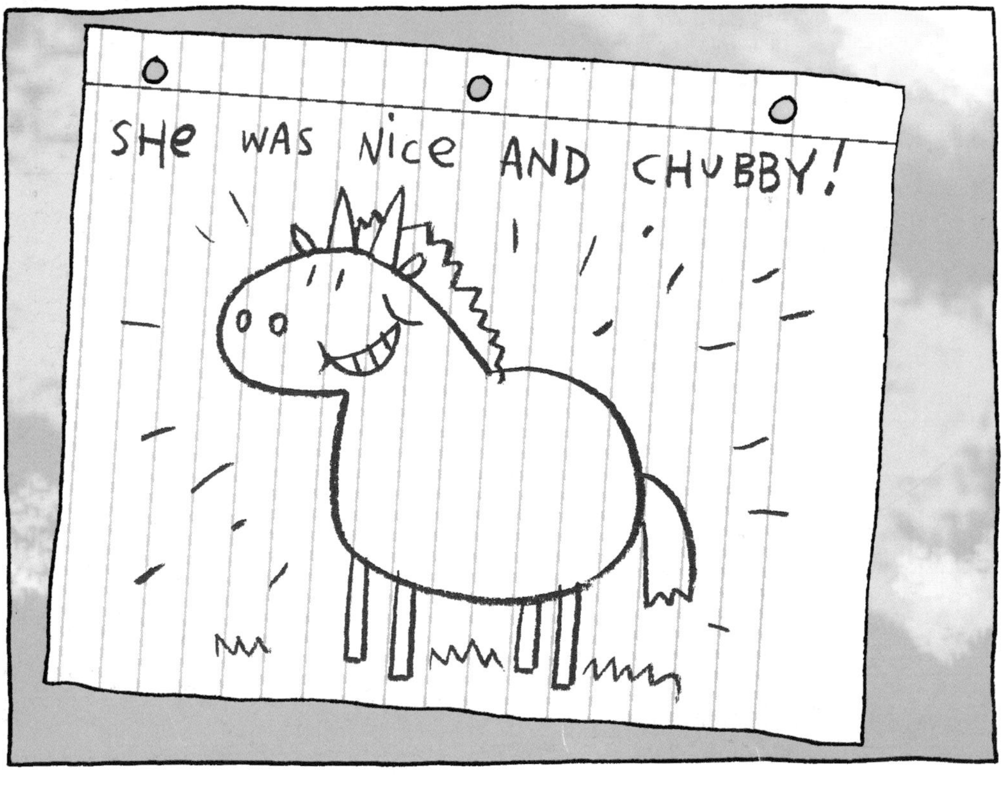
SHE WAS NICE AND CHUBBY!

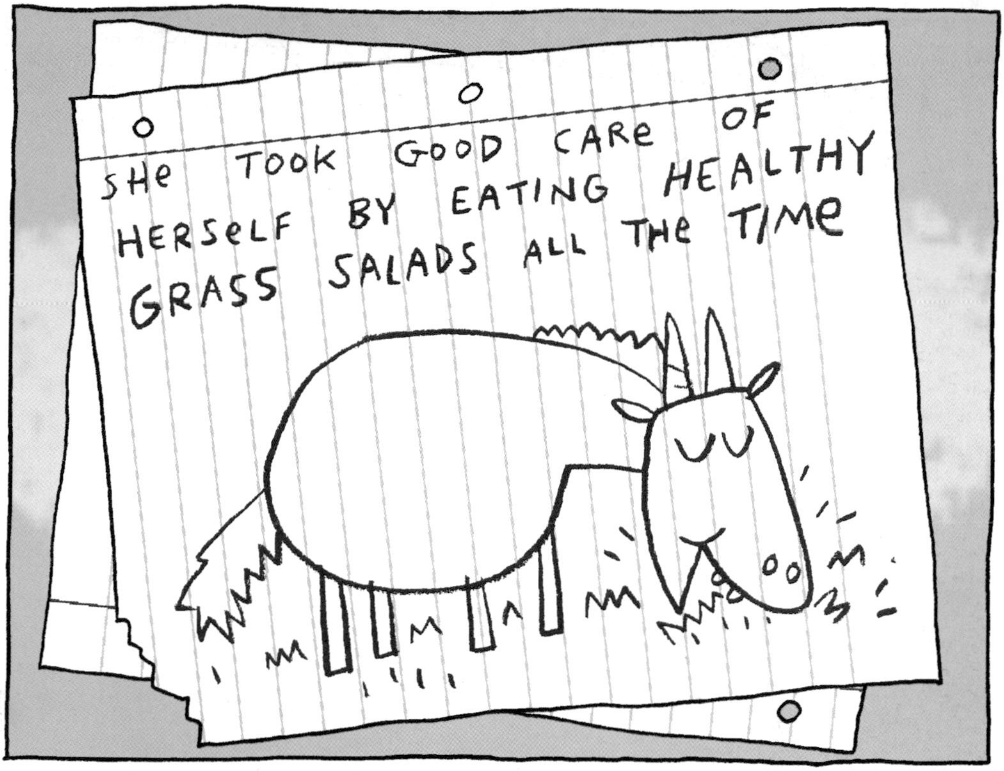
SHE TOOK GOOD CARE OF HERSELF BY EATING HEALTHY GRASS SALADS ALL THE TIME

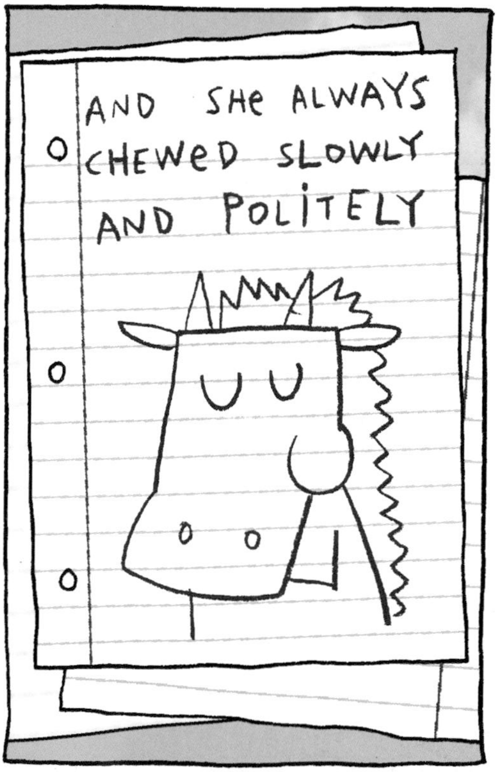
AND SHE ALWAYS CHEWED SLOWLY AND POLITELY

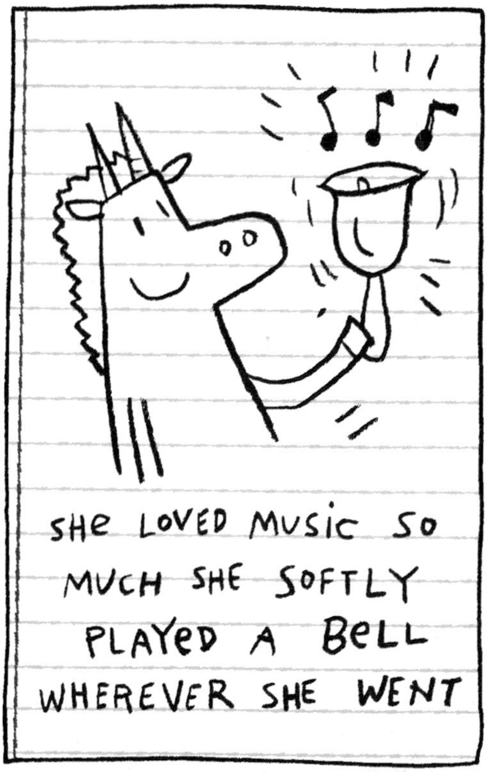
SHE LOVED MUSIC SO MUCH SHE SOFTLY PLAYED A BELL WHEREVER SHE WENT

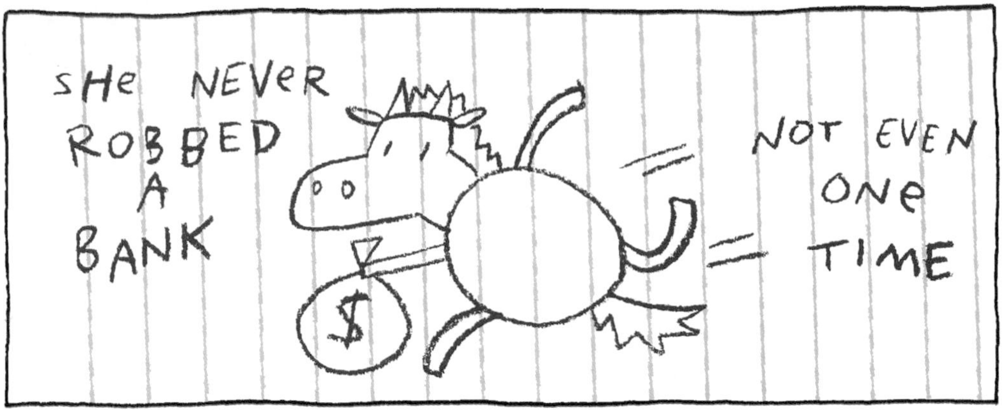
SHE NEVER ROBBED A BANK
NOT EVEN ONE TIME

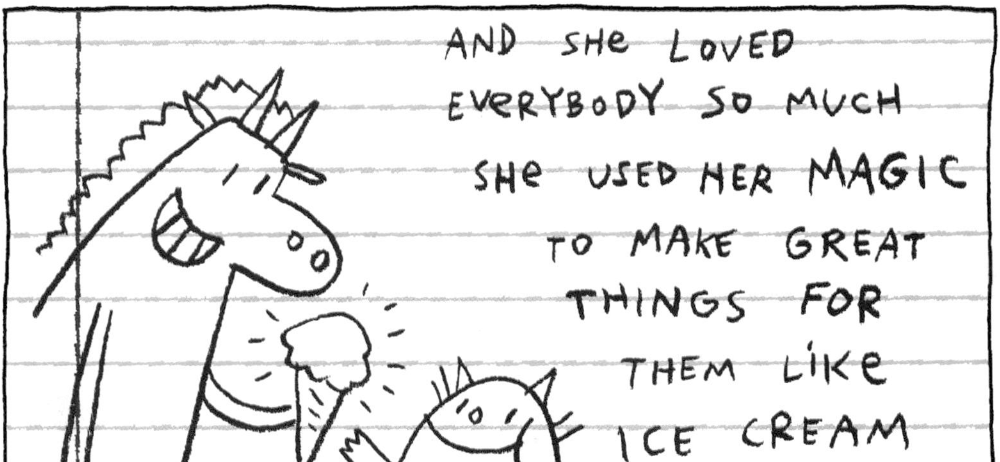
AND SHE LOVED EVERYBODY SO MUCH SHE USED HER MAGIC TO MAKE GREAT THINGS FOR THEM LIKE ICE CREAM
THE END

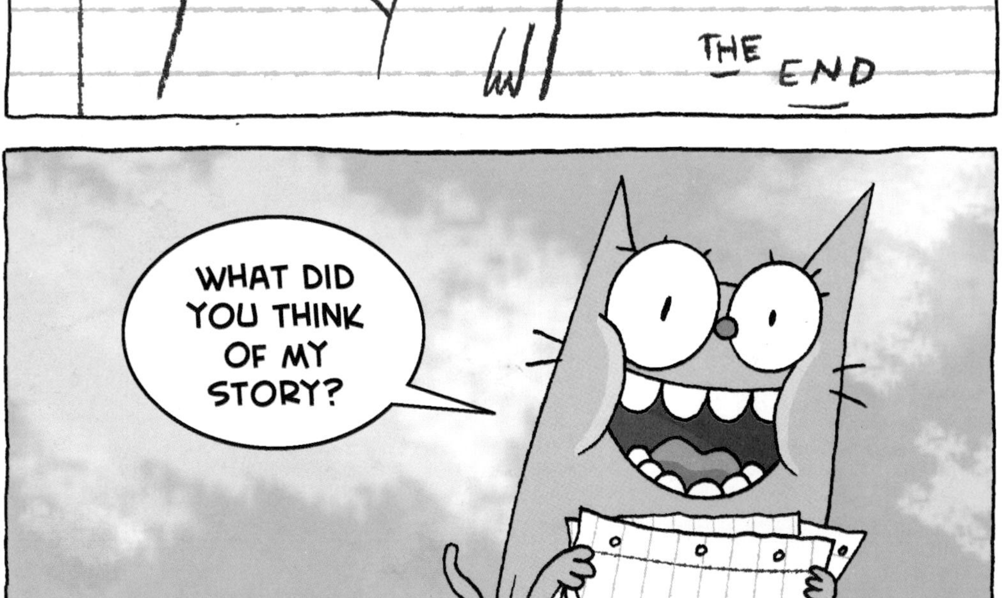
WHAT DID YOU THINK OF MY STORY?

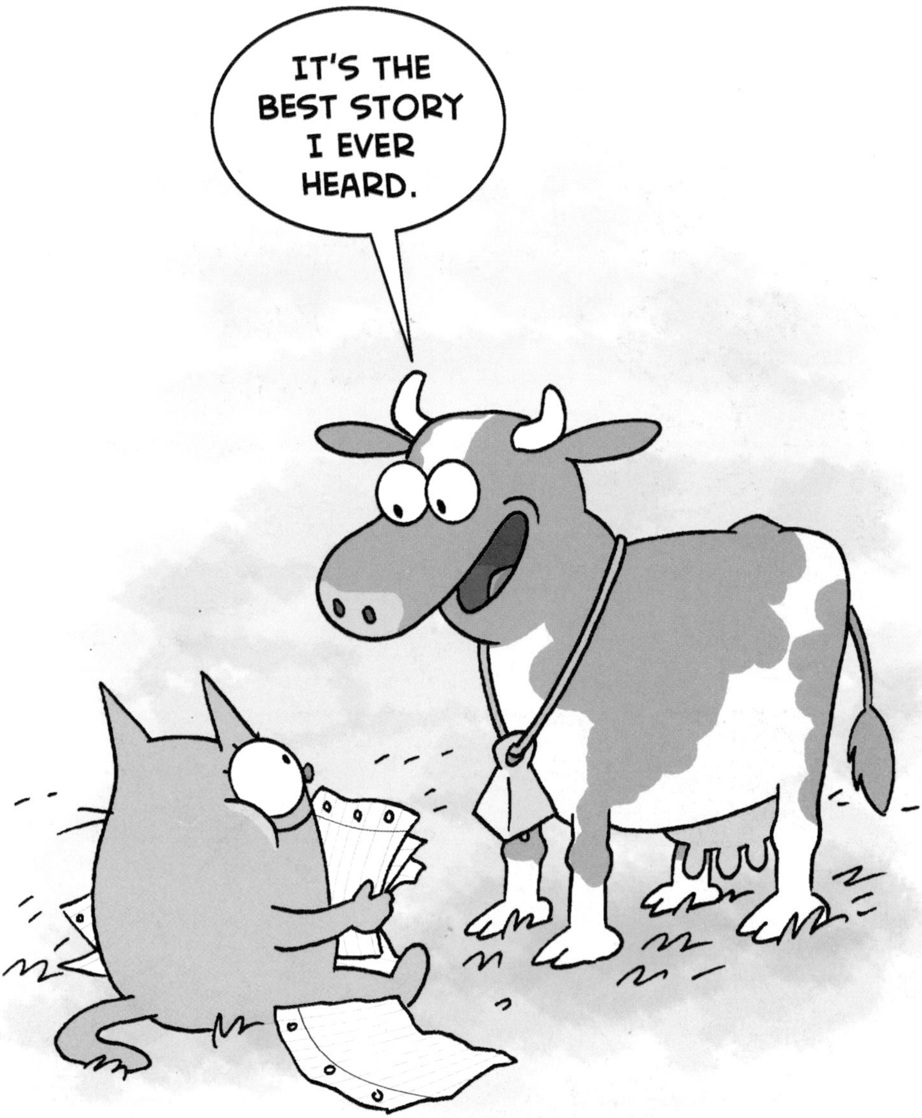
IT'S THE BEST STORY I EVER HEARD.

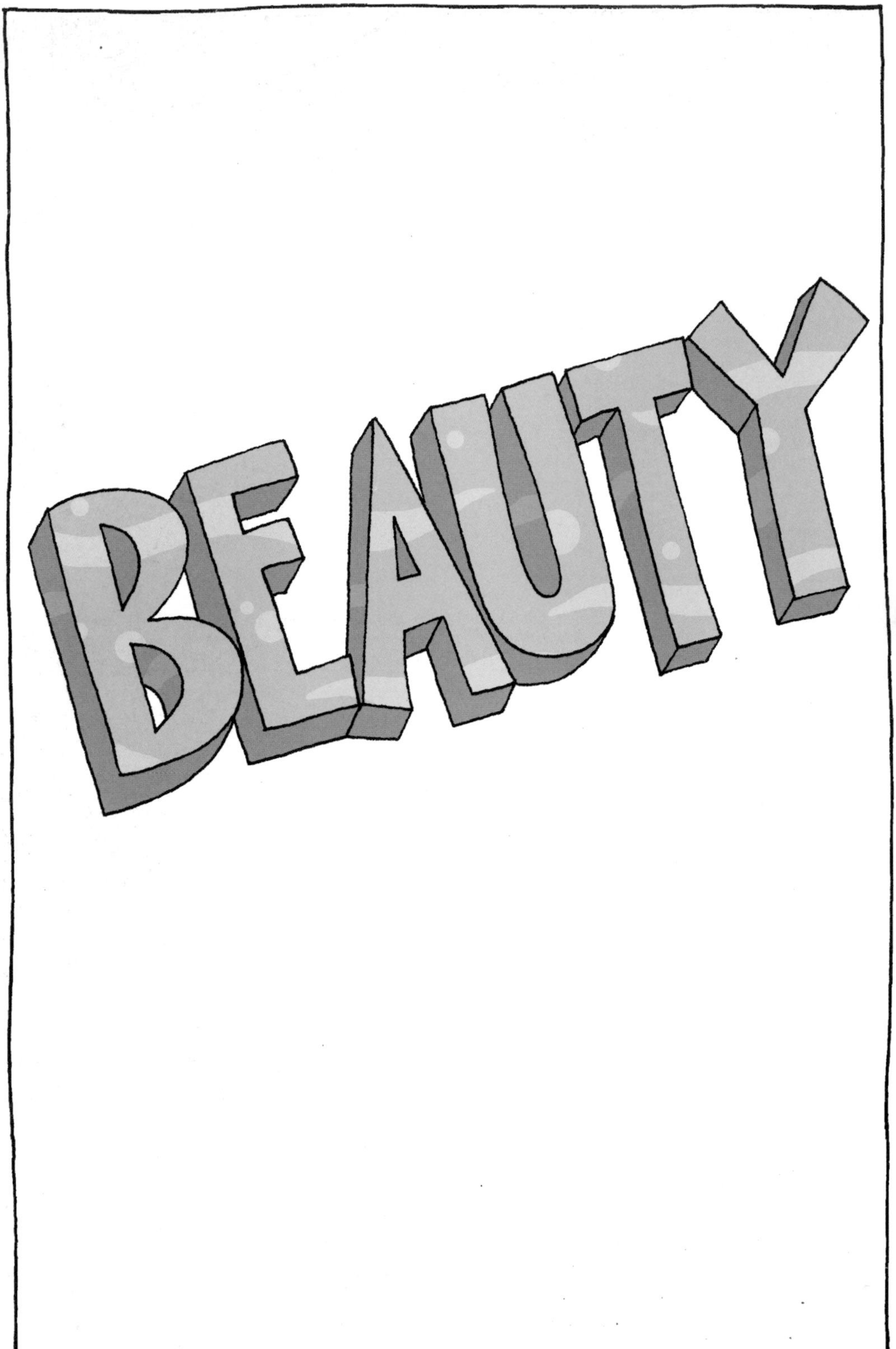
BEAUTY

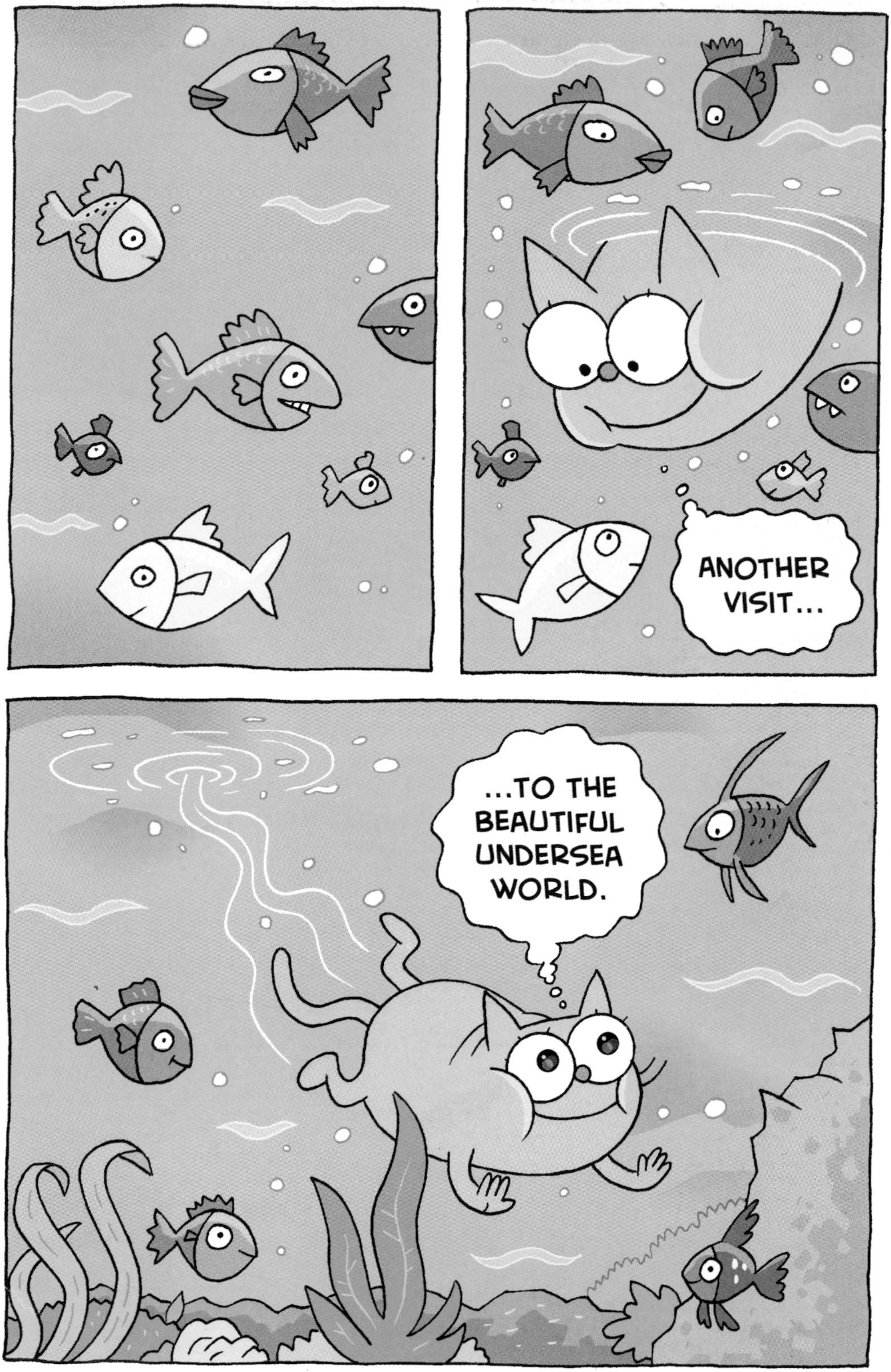
ANOTHER VISIT...
...TO THE BEAUTIFUL UNDERSEA WORLD.

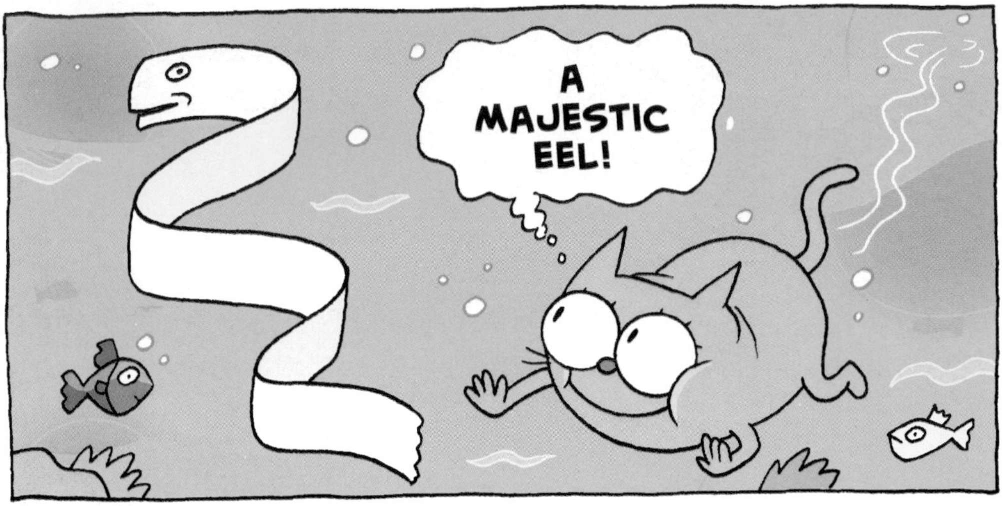
A MAJESTIC EEL!

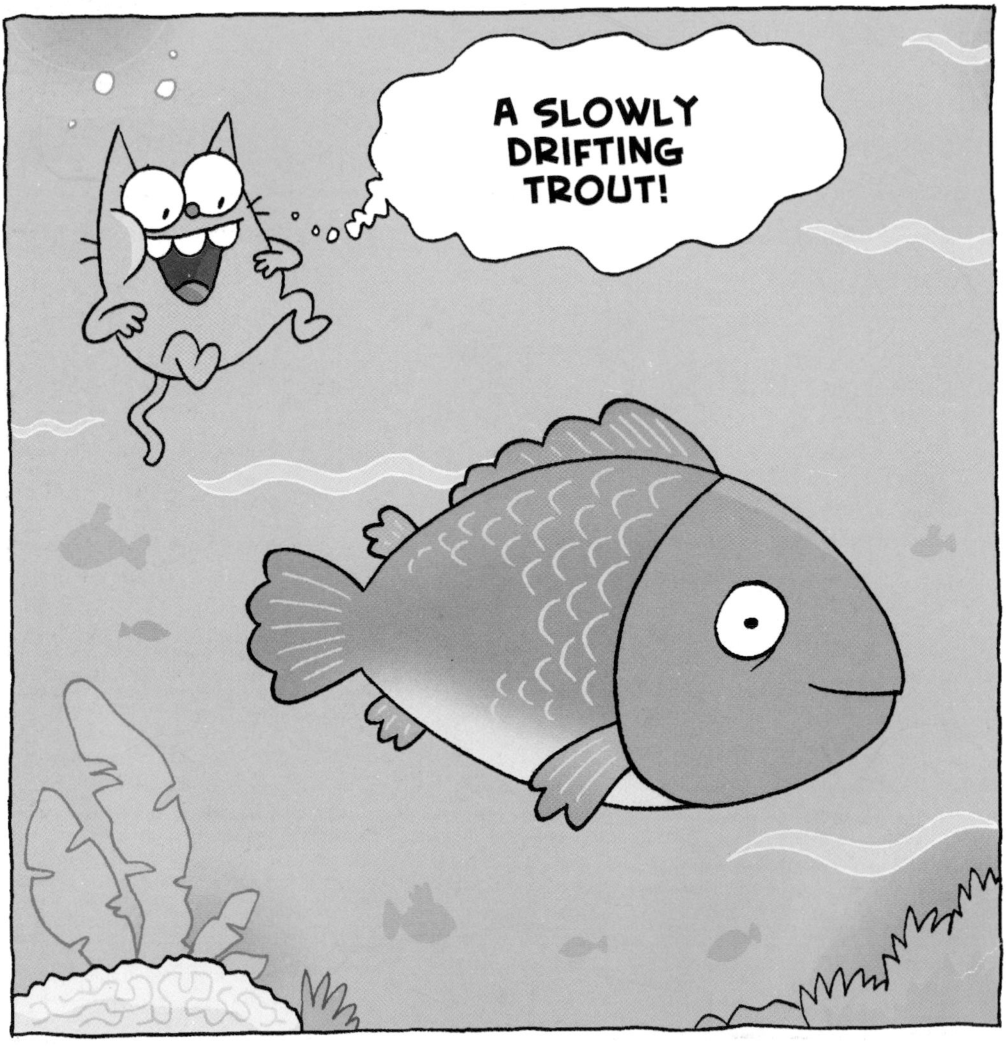
A SLOWLY DRIFTING TROUT!

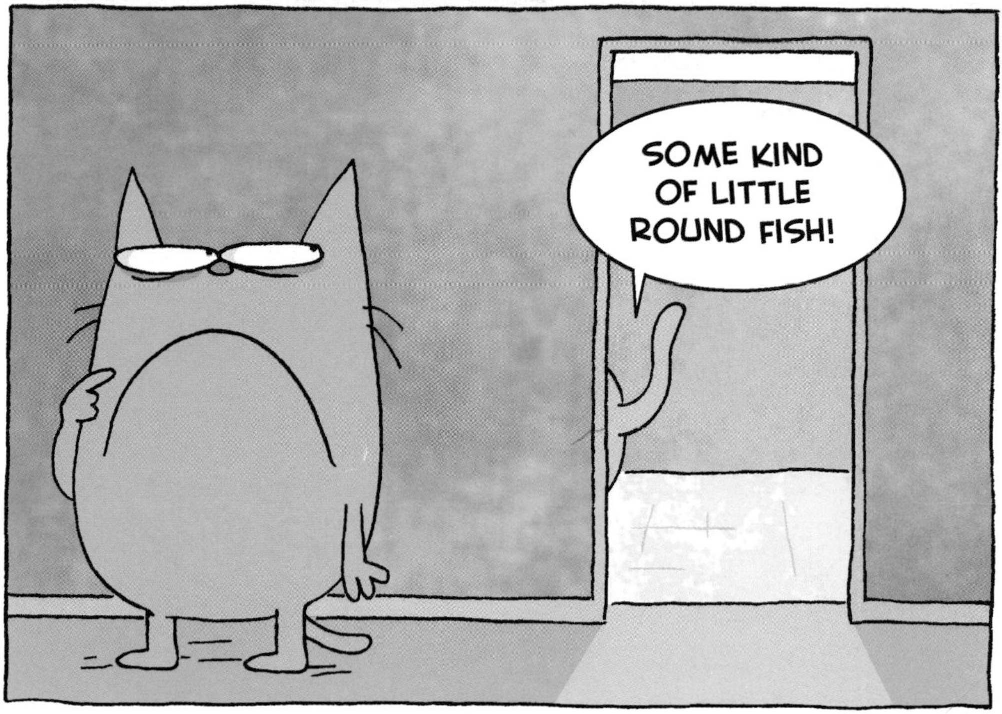
SOME KIND OF LITTLE ROUND FISH!

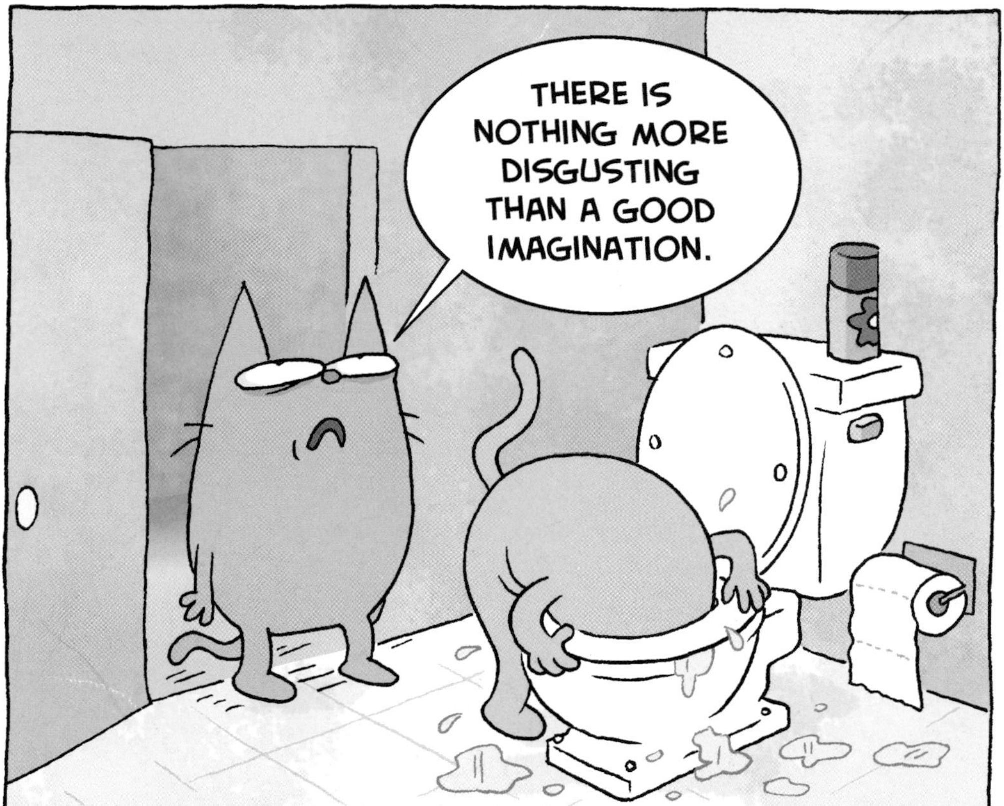
THERE IS NOTHING MORE DISGUSTING THAN A GOOD IMAGINATION.

eyes

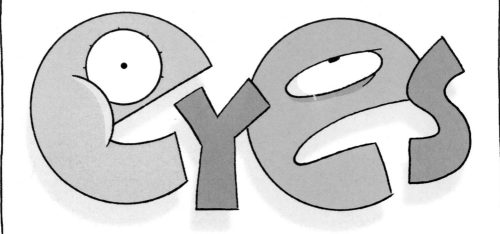

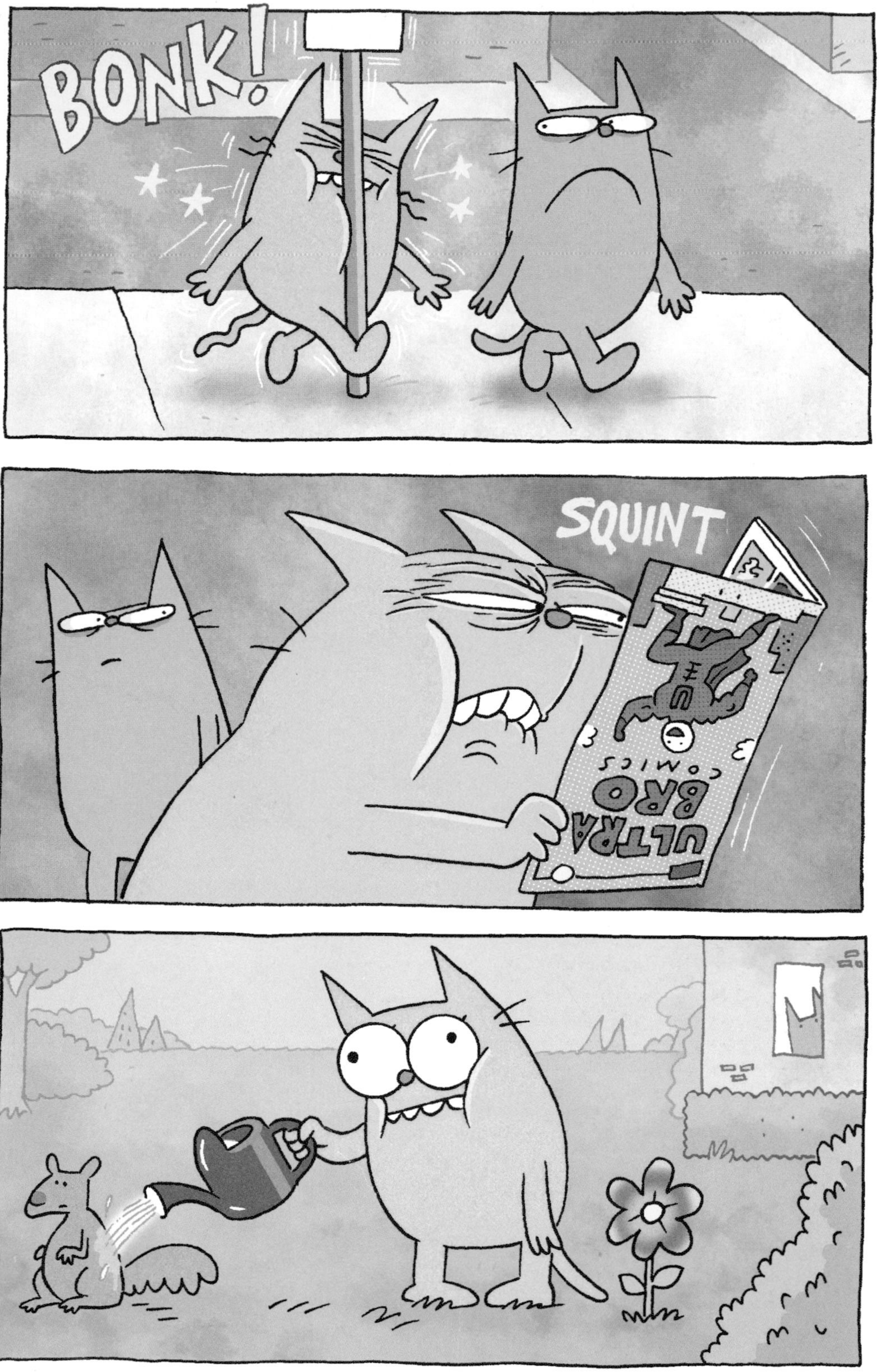
BONK!
SQUINT
ULTRA BRO COMICS

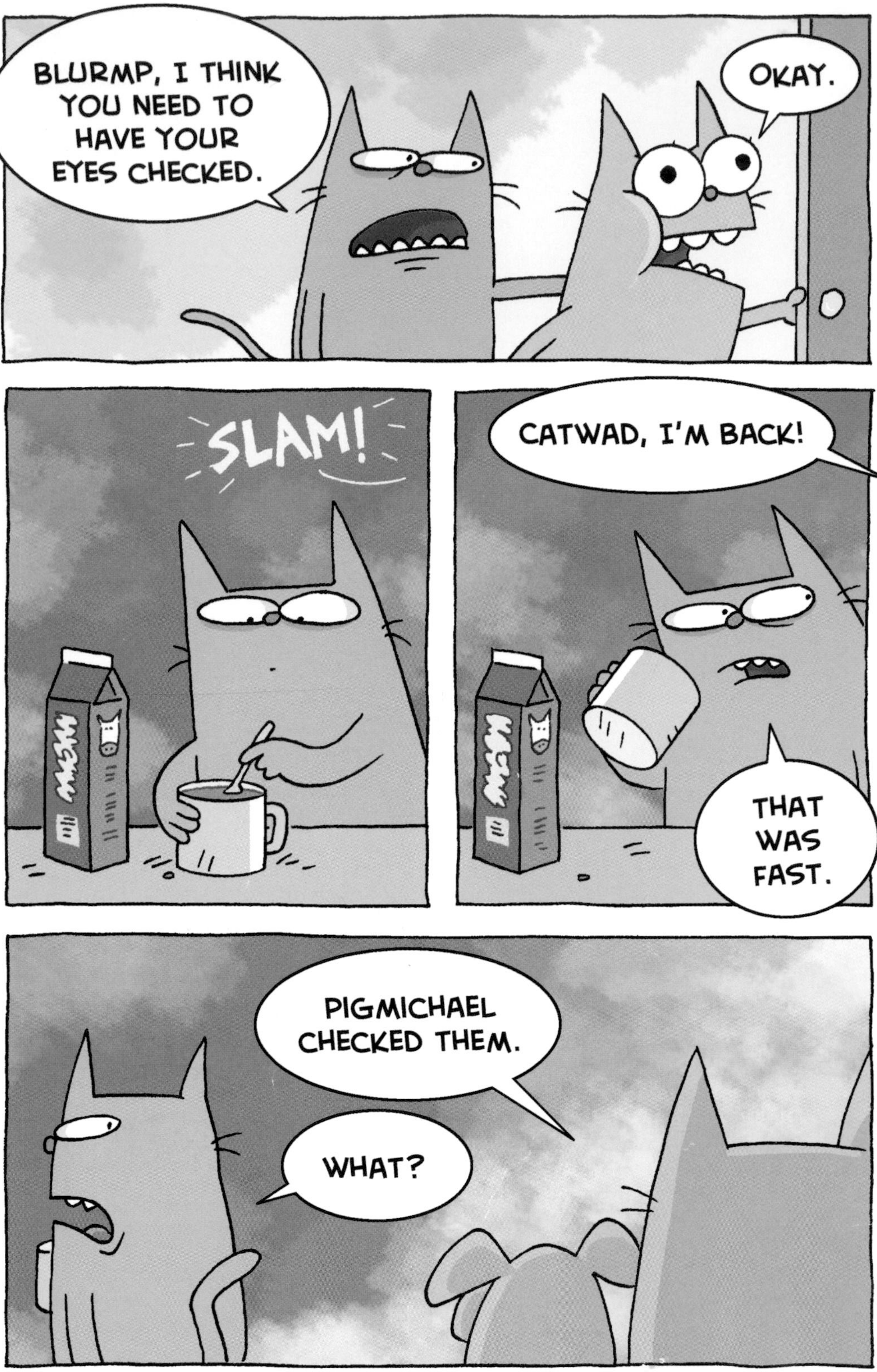
BLURMP, I THINK YOU NEED TO HAVE YOUR EYES CHECKED.
OKAY.
SLAM!
CATWAD, I'M BACK!
THAT WAS FAST.
PIGMICHAEL CHECKED THEM.
WHAT?

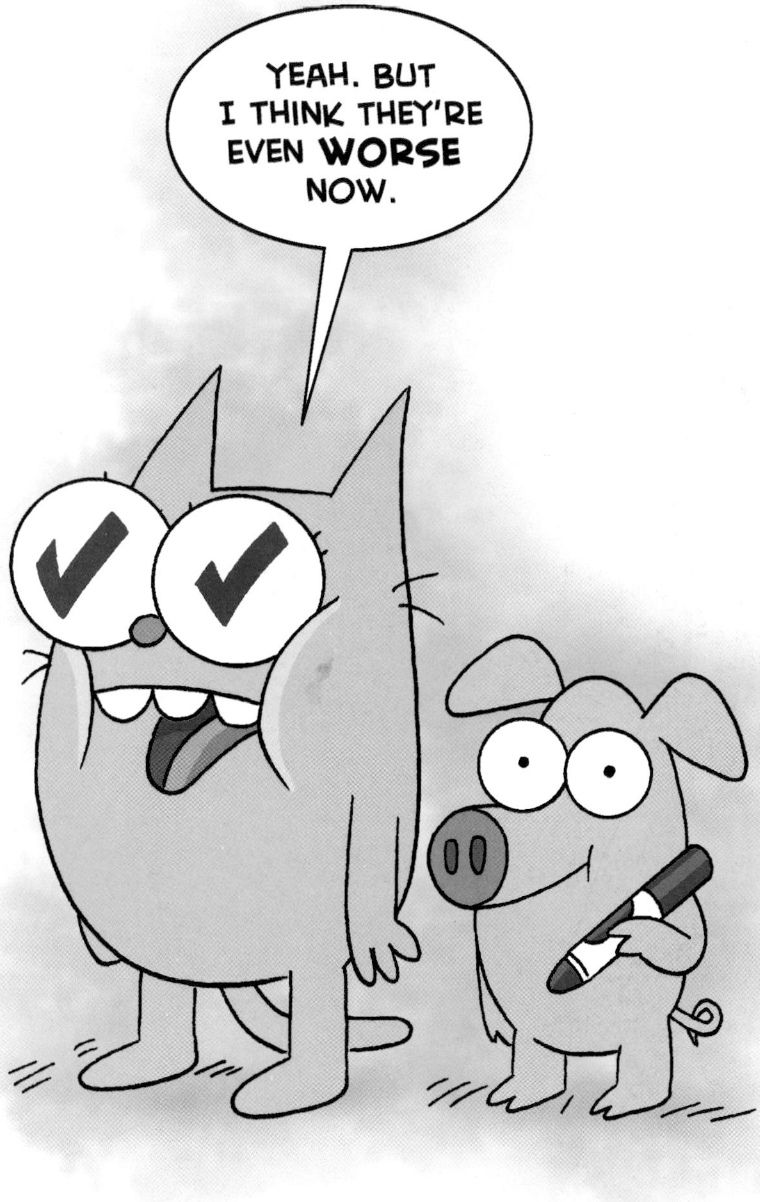
YEAH. BUT I THINK THEY'RE EVEN WORSE NOW.

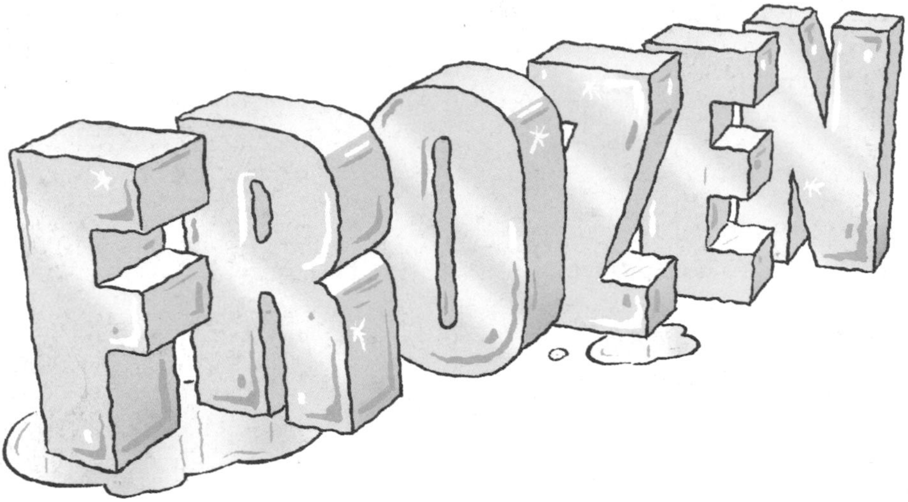
FROZEN

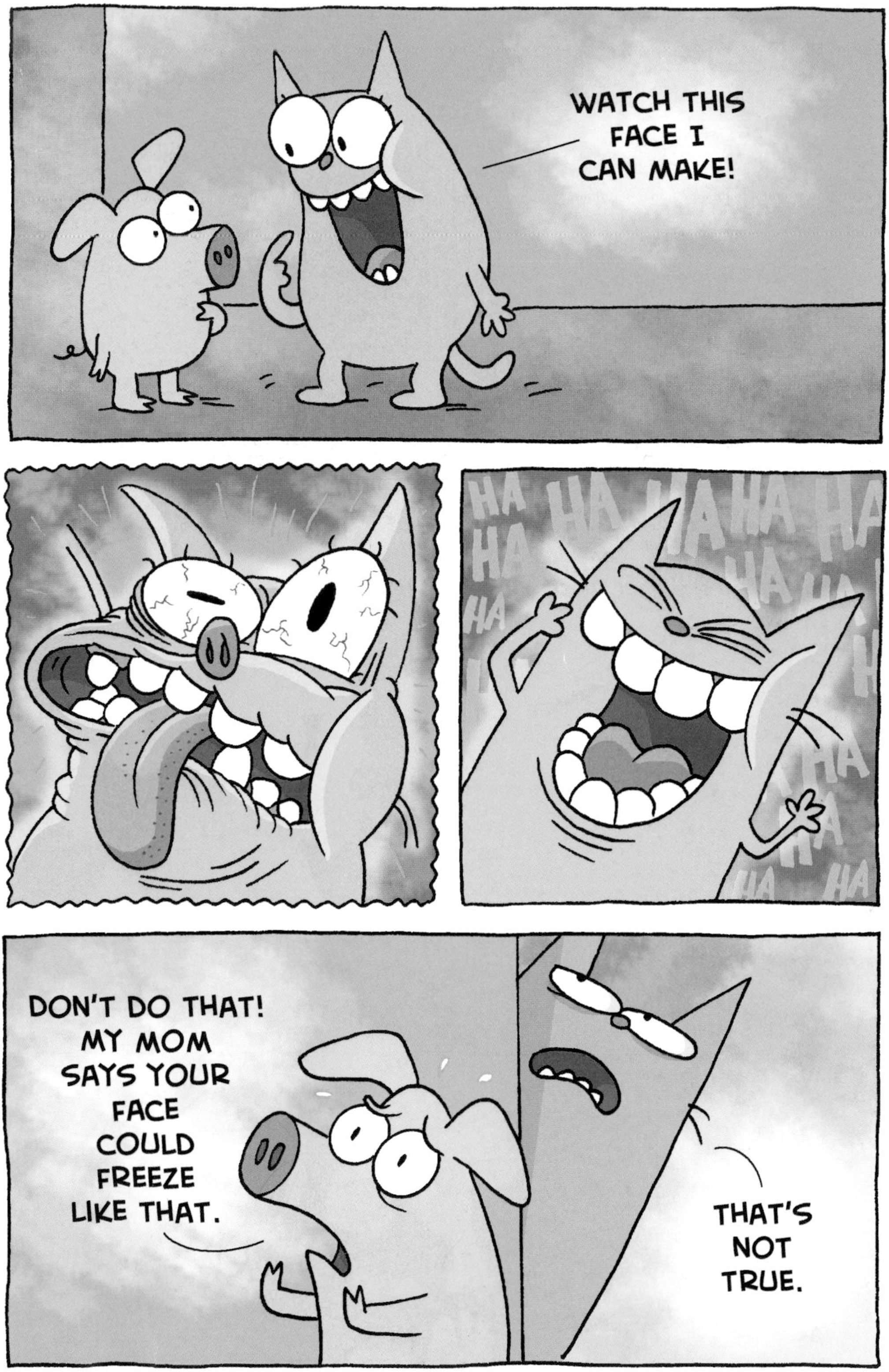
WATCH THIS FACE I CAN MAKE!
HA HA HA HA HA HA HA HA HA HA HA HA HA HA HA HA
DON'T DO THAT! MY MOM SAYS YOUR FACE COULD FREEZE LIKE THAT.
THAT'S NOT TRUE.

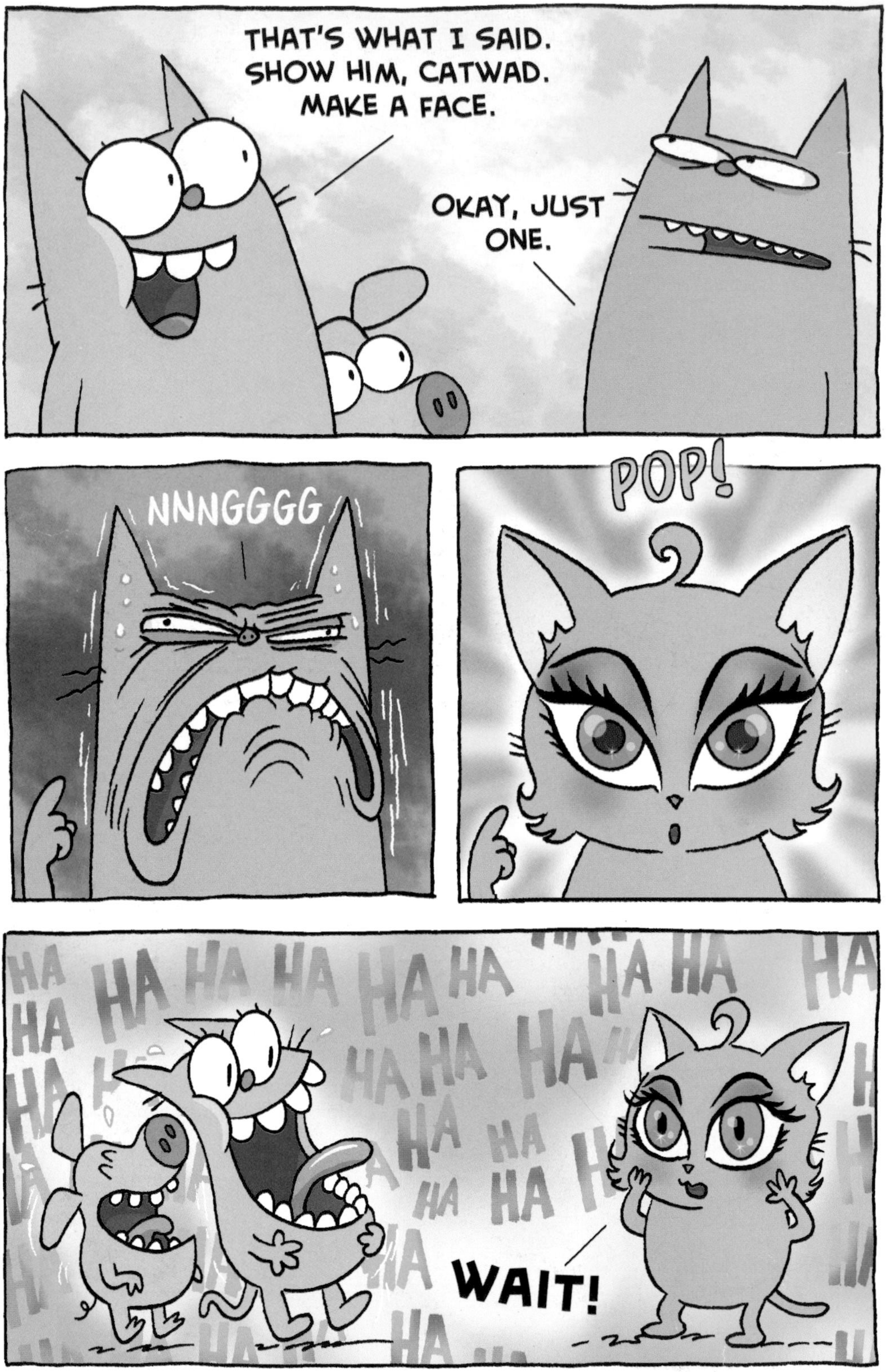

THAT'S WHAT I SAID. SHOW HIM, CATWAD. MAKE A FACE.
OKAY, JUST ONE.
NNNGGGG
POP!
HA HA HA HA HA HA HA HA HA HA HA HA HA HA HA HA HA HA HA HA HA HA
WAIT!

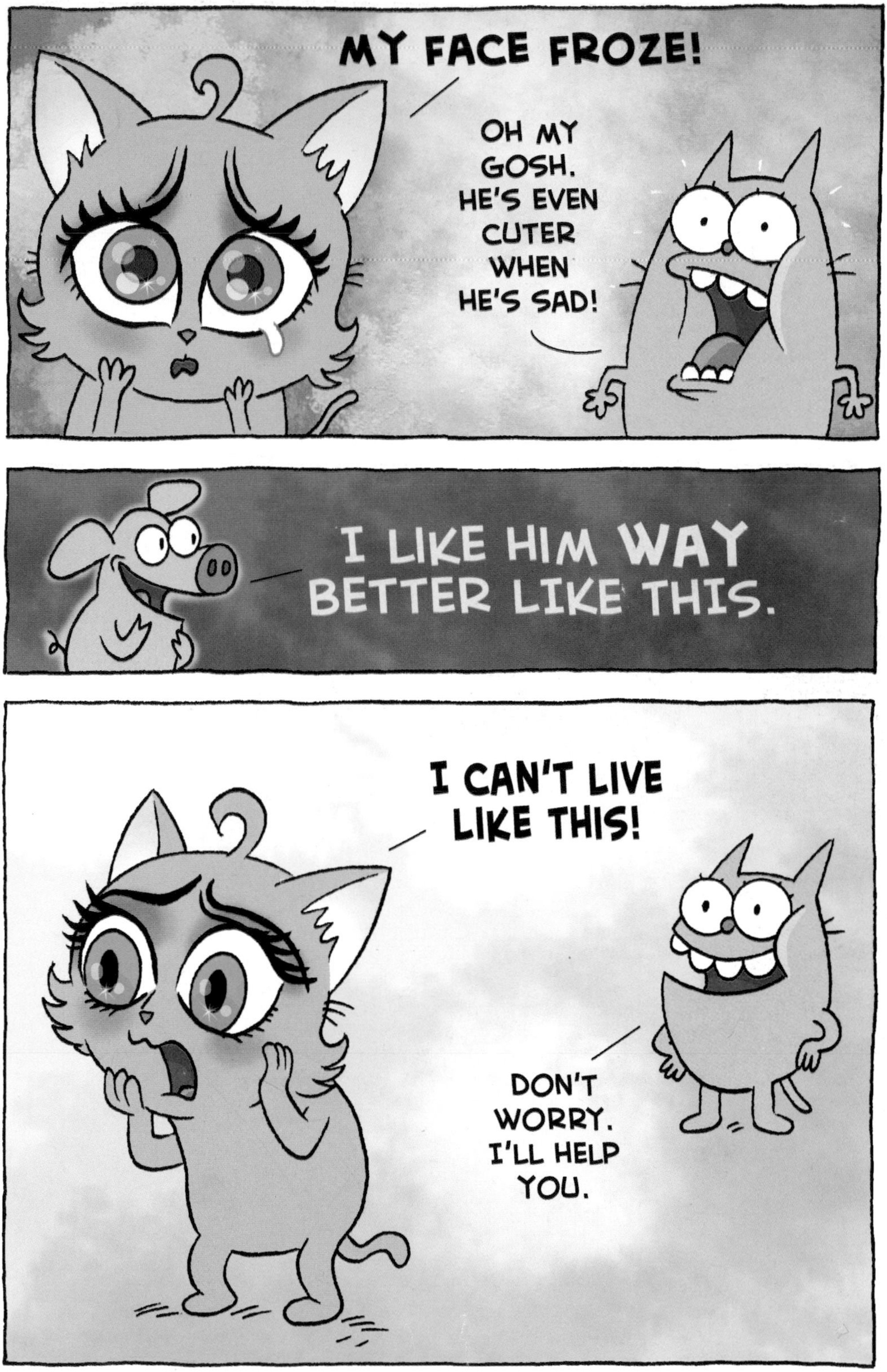
MY FACE FROZE!
OH MY GOSH. HE'S EVEN CUTER WHEN HE'S SAD!
I LIKE HIM WAY BETTER LIKE THIS.
I CAN'T LIVE LIKE THIS!
DON'T WORRY. I'LL HELP YOU.

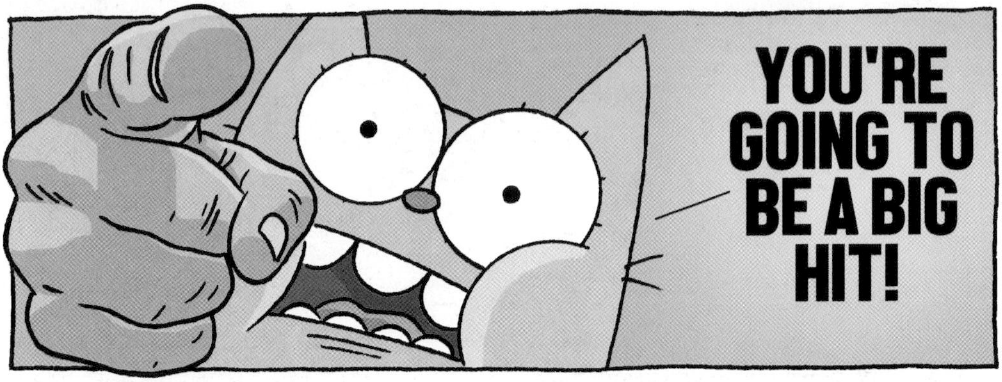
YOU'RE GOING TO BE A BIG HIT!

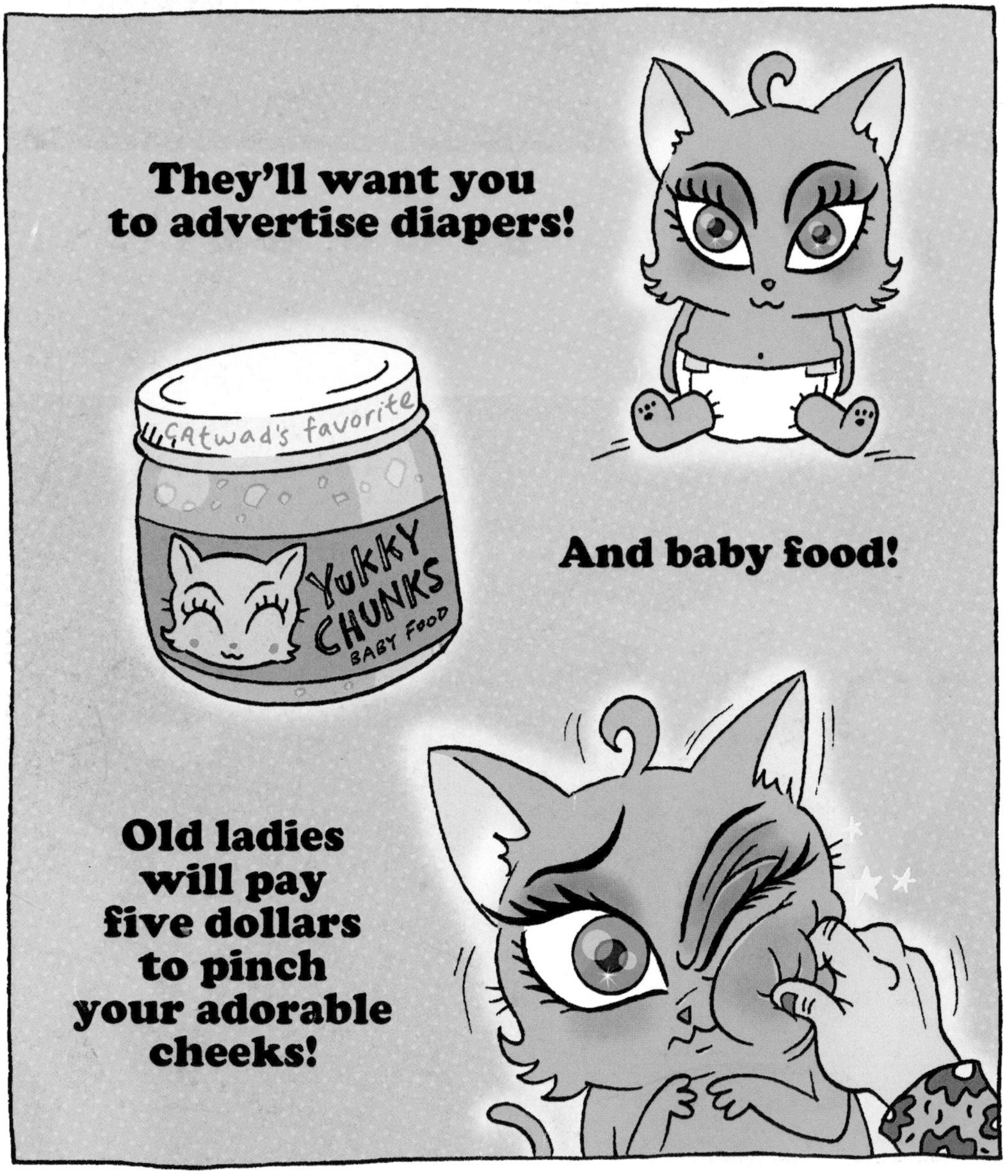
They'll want you to advertise diapers!
CATwad's favorite
YUKKY CHUNKS BABY FOOD
And baby food!
Old ladies will pay five dollars to pinch your adorable cheeks!

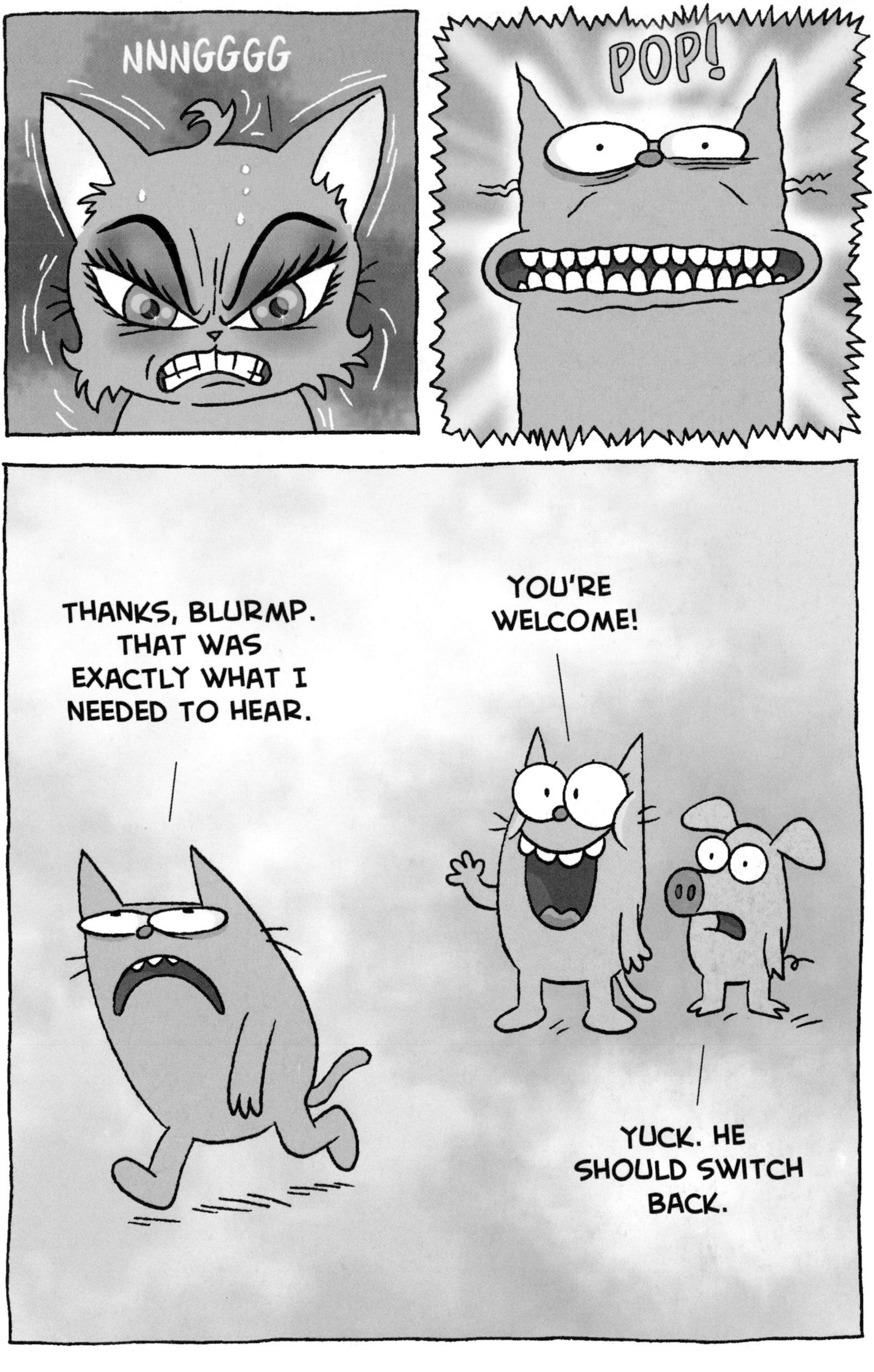
NNNGGGG
POP!
THANKS, BLURMP. THAT WAS EXACTLY WHAT I NEEDED TO HEAR.
YOU'RE WELCOME!
YUCK. HE SHOULD SWITCH BACK.

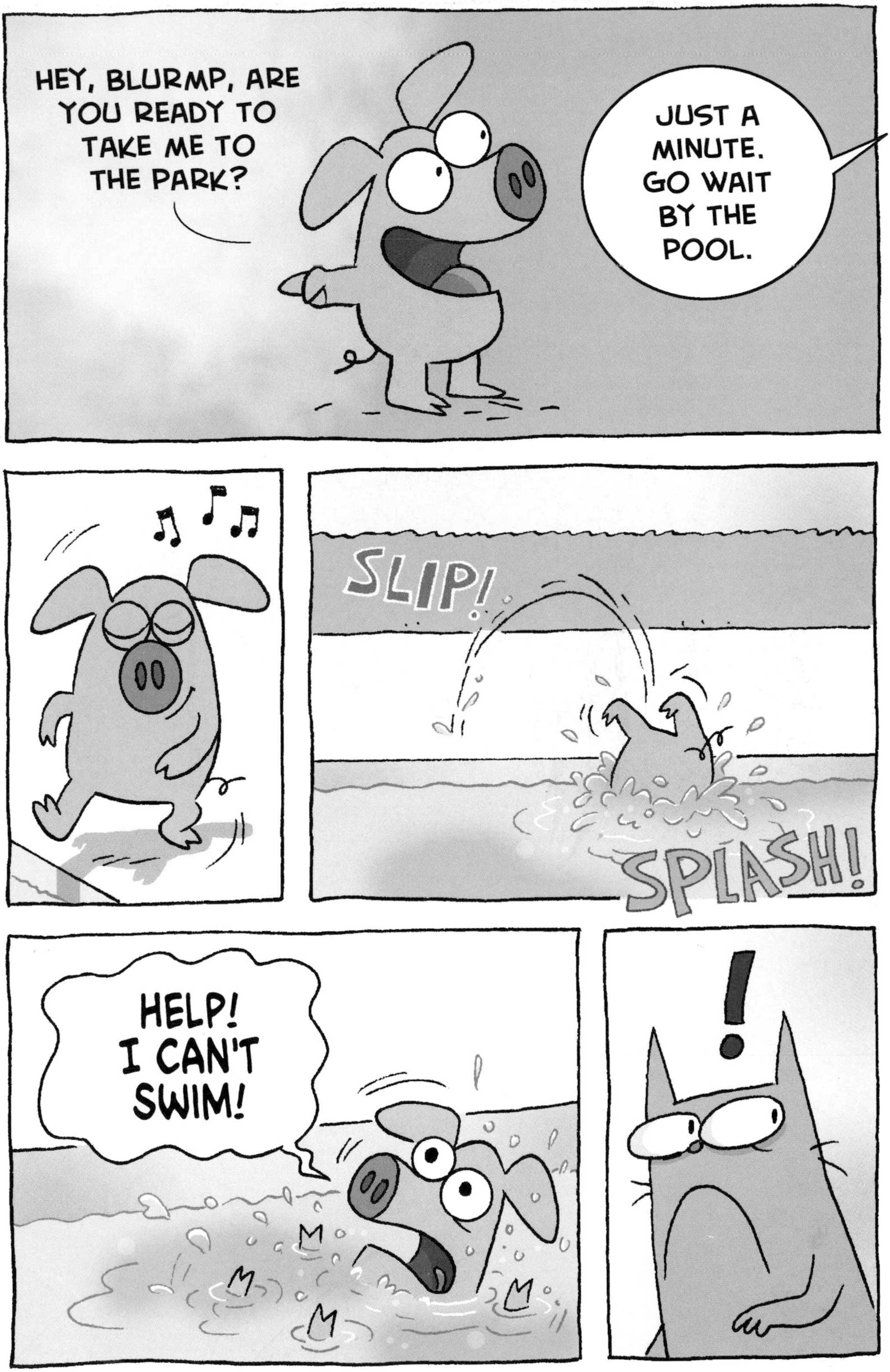
HEY, BLURMP, ARE YOU READY TO TAKE ME TO THE PARK?
JUST A MINUTE. GO WAIT BY THE POOL.
SLIP!
SPLASH!
HELP! I CAN'T SWIM!
!

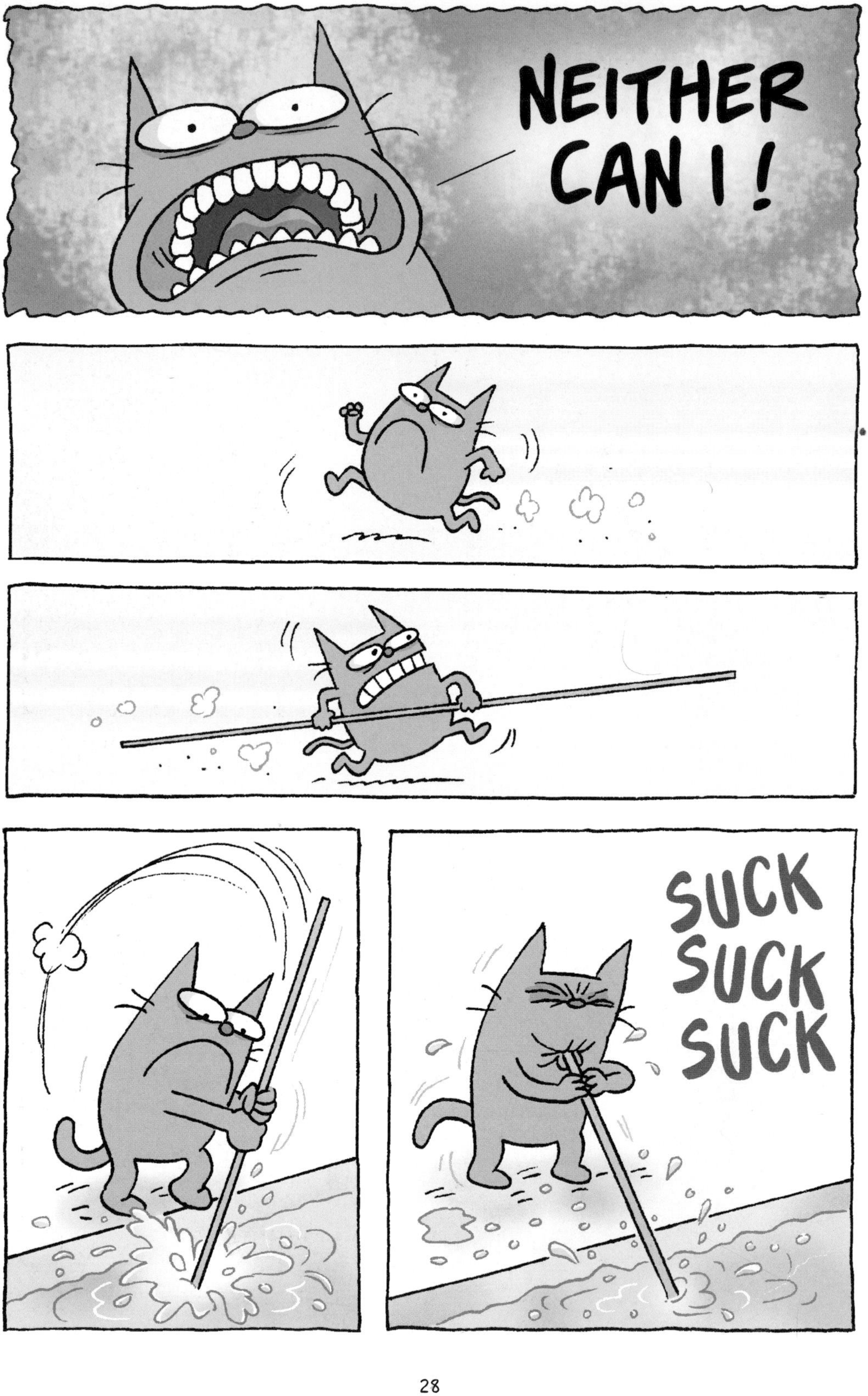
NEITHER CAN I!
SUCK SUCK SUCK

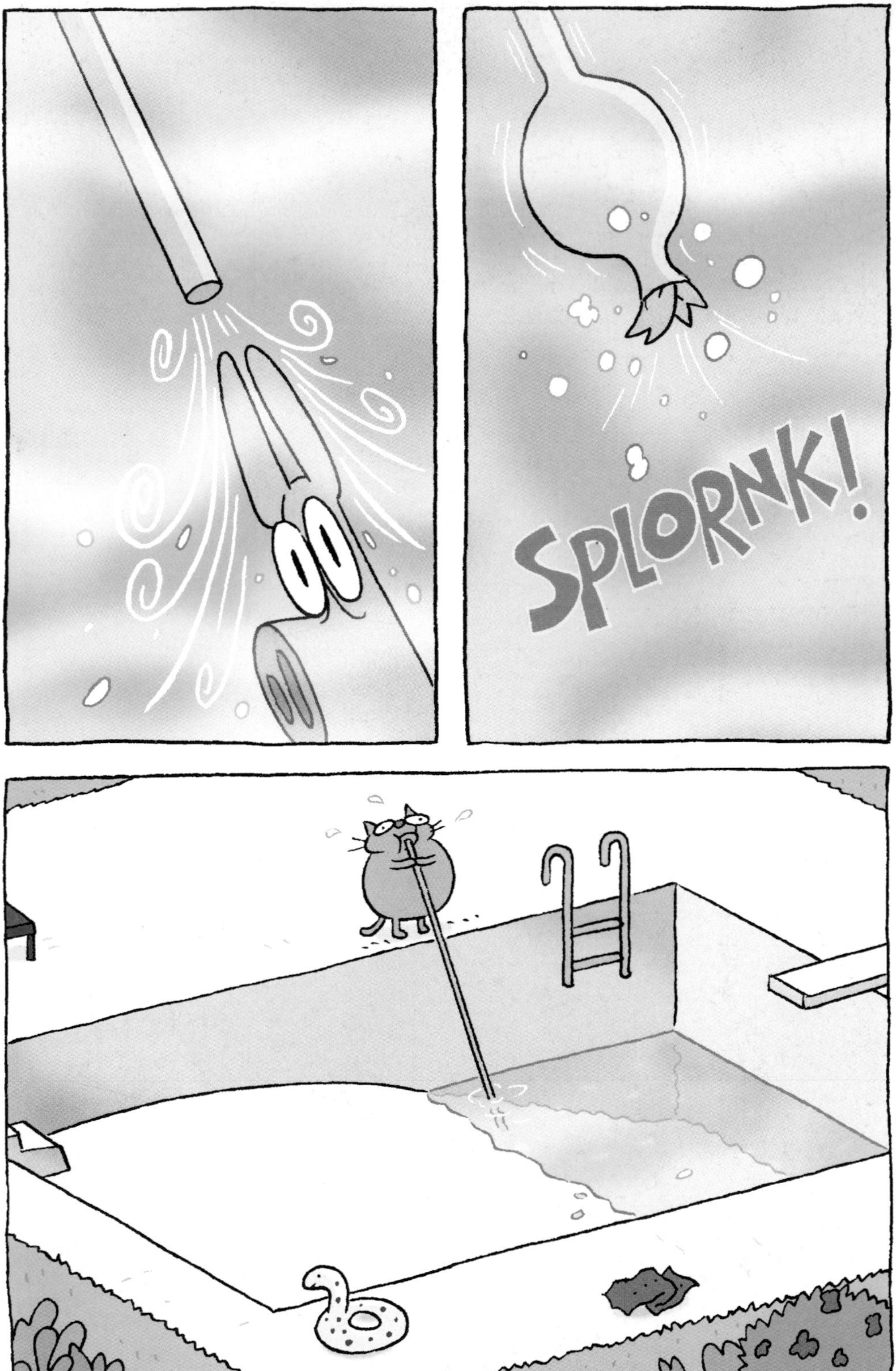
SPLORNK!

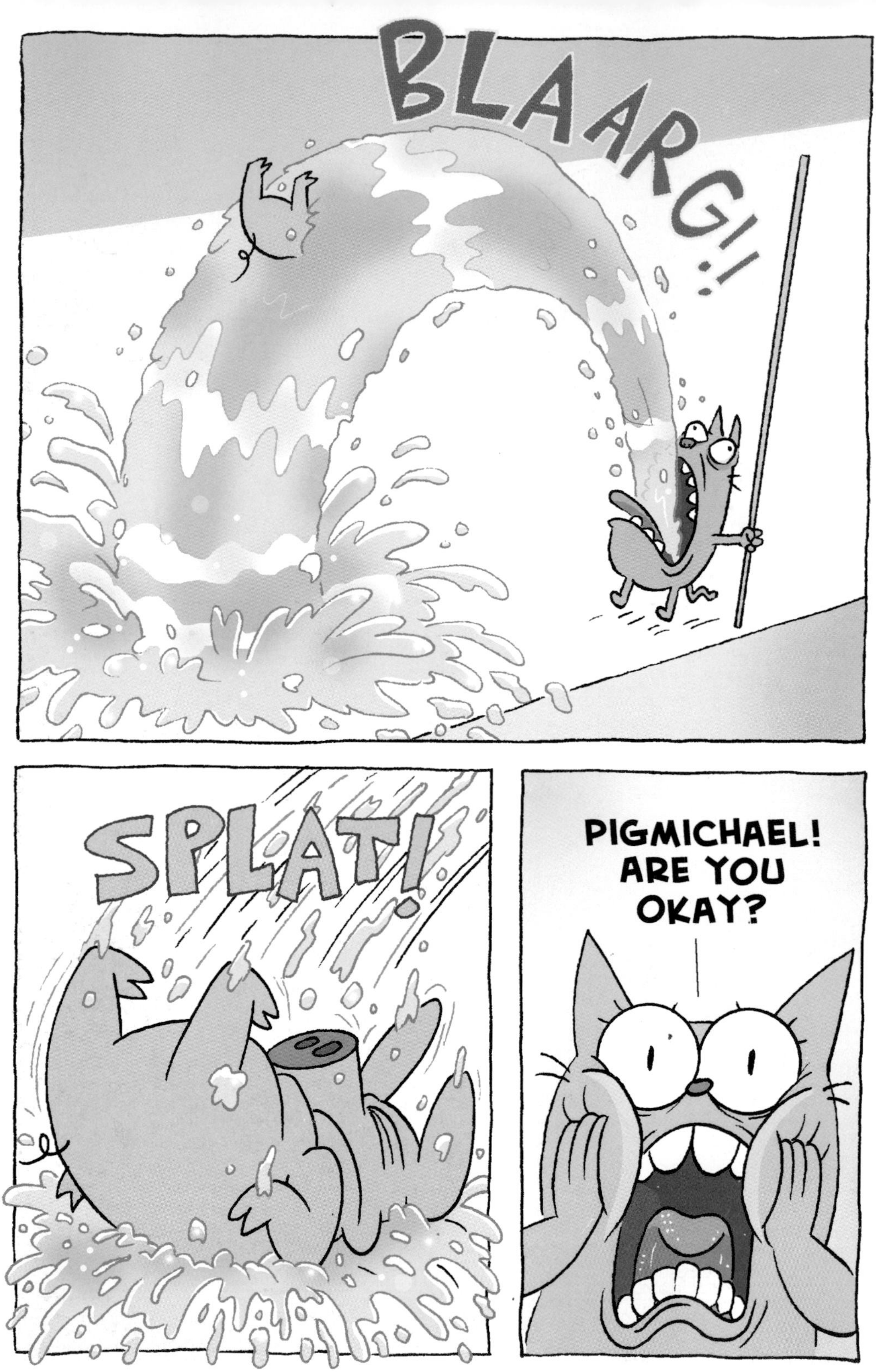
BLAARG!!
SPLAT!
PIGMICHAEL! ARE YOU OKAY?

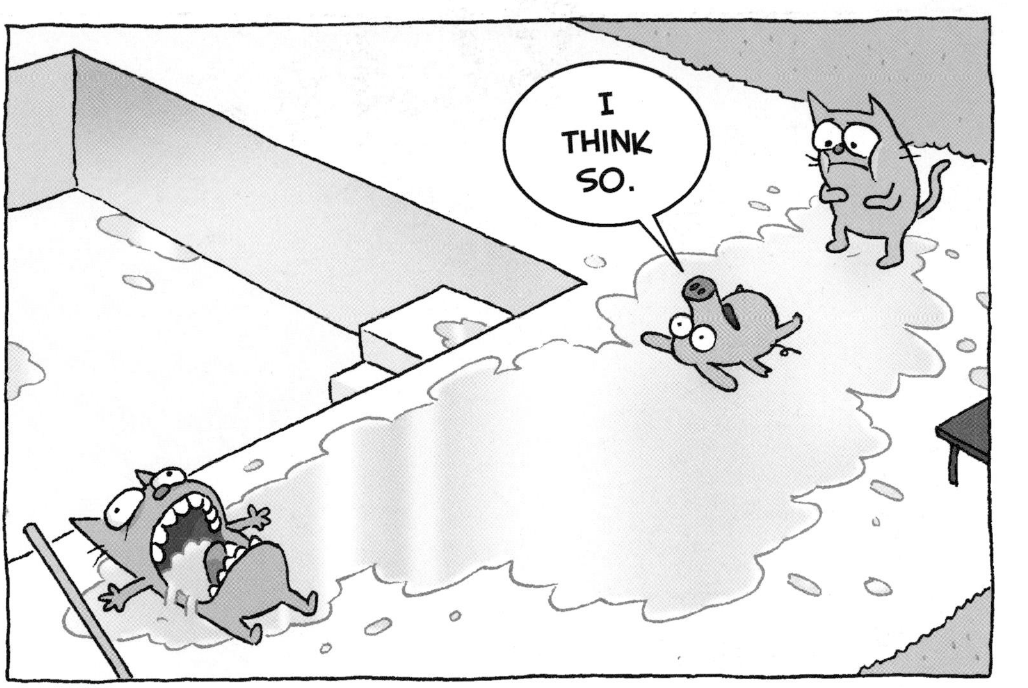
I THINK SO.

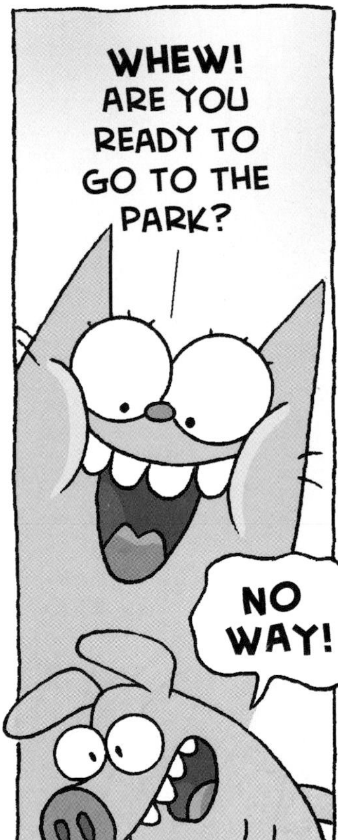
WHEW! ARE YOU READY TO GO TO THE PARK?
NO WAY!

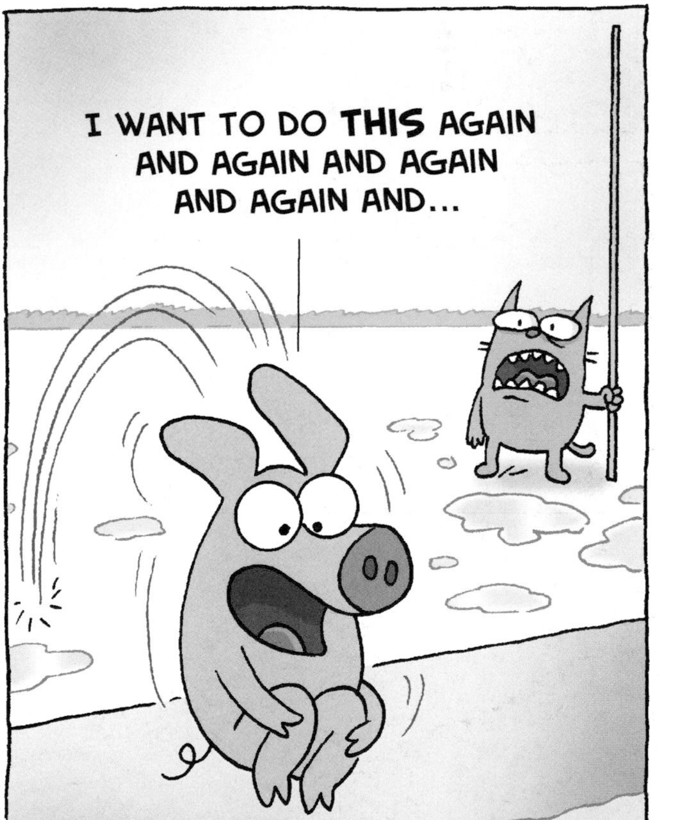
I WANT TO DO THIS AGAIN AND AGAIN AND AGAIN AND AGAIN AND...

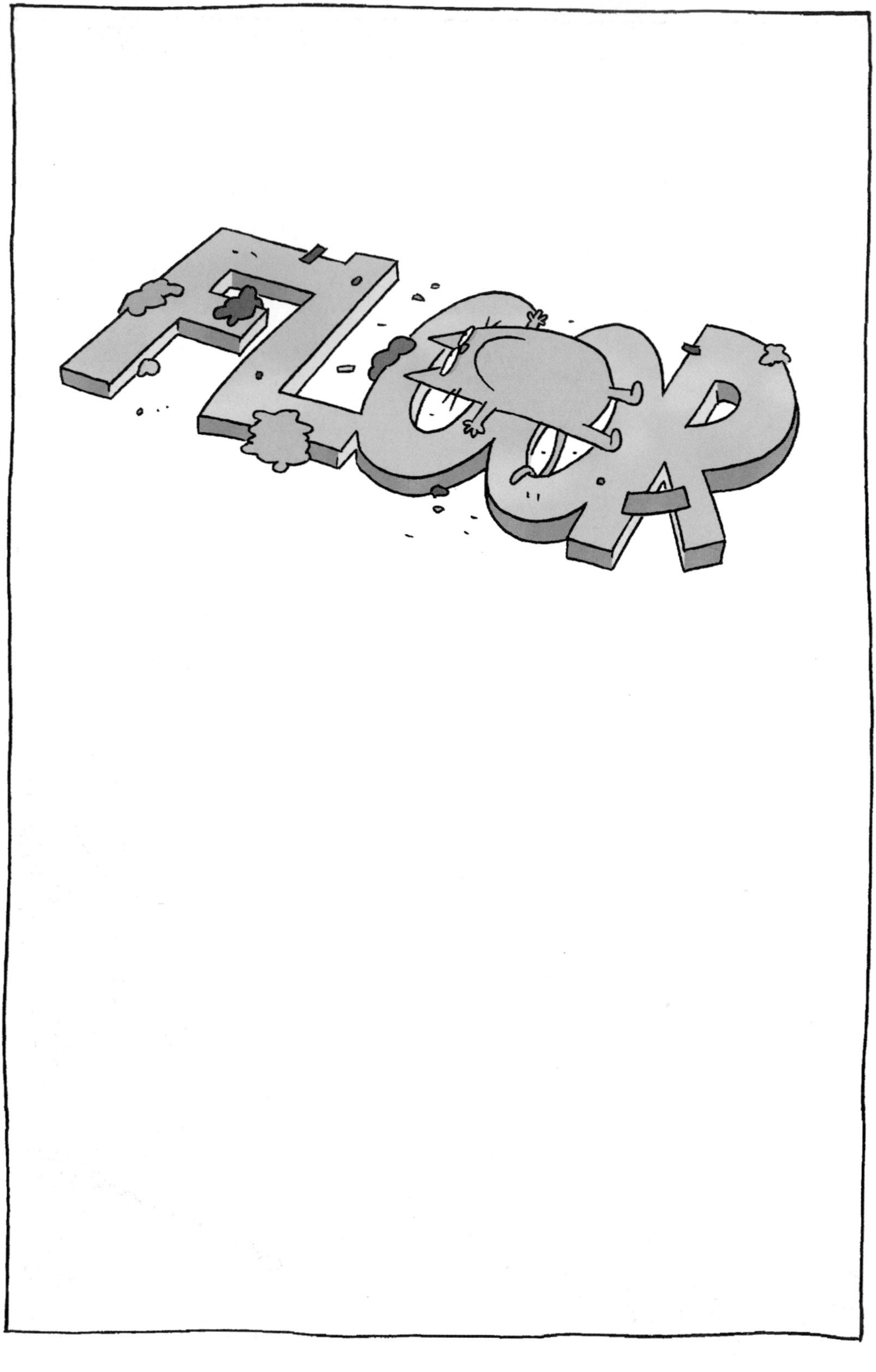
FZLOOP

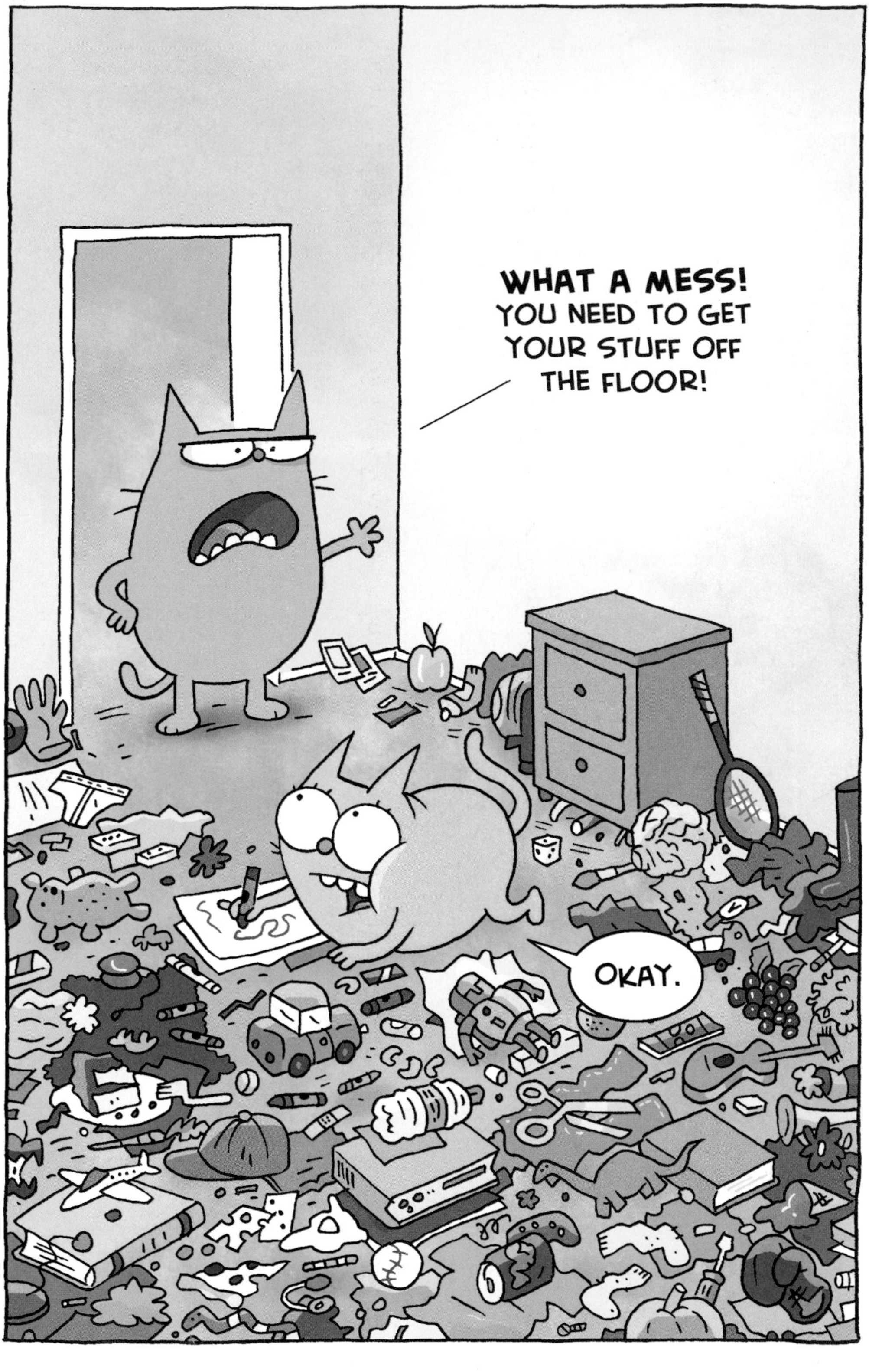
WHAT A MESS! YOU NEED TO GET YOUR STUFF OFF THE FLOOR!
OKAY.

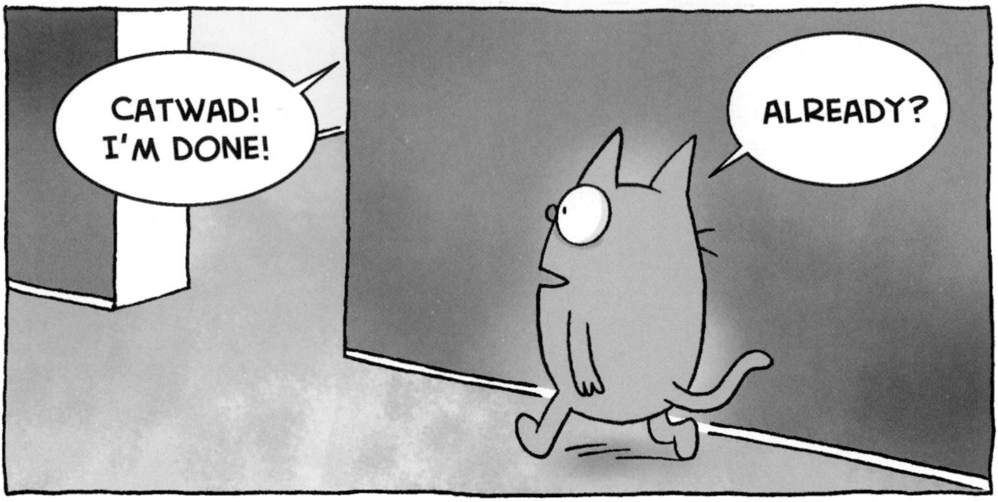
CATWAD! I'M DONE!
ALREADY?

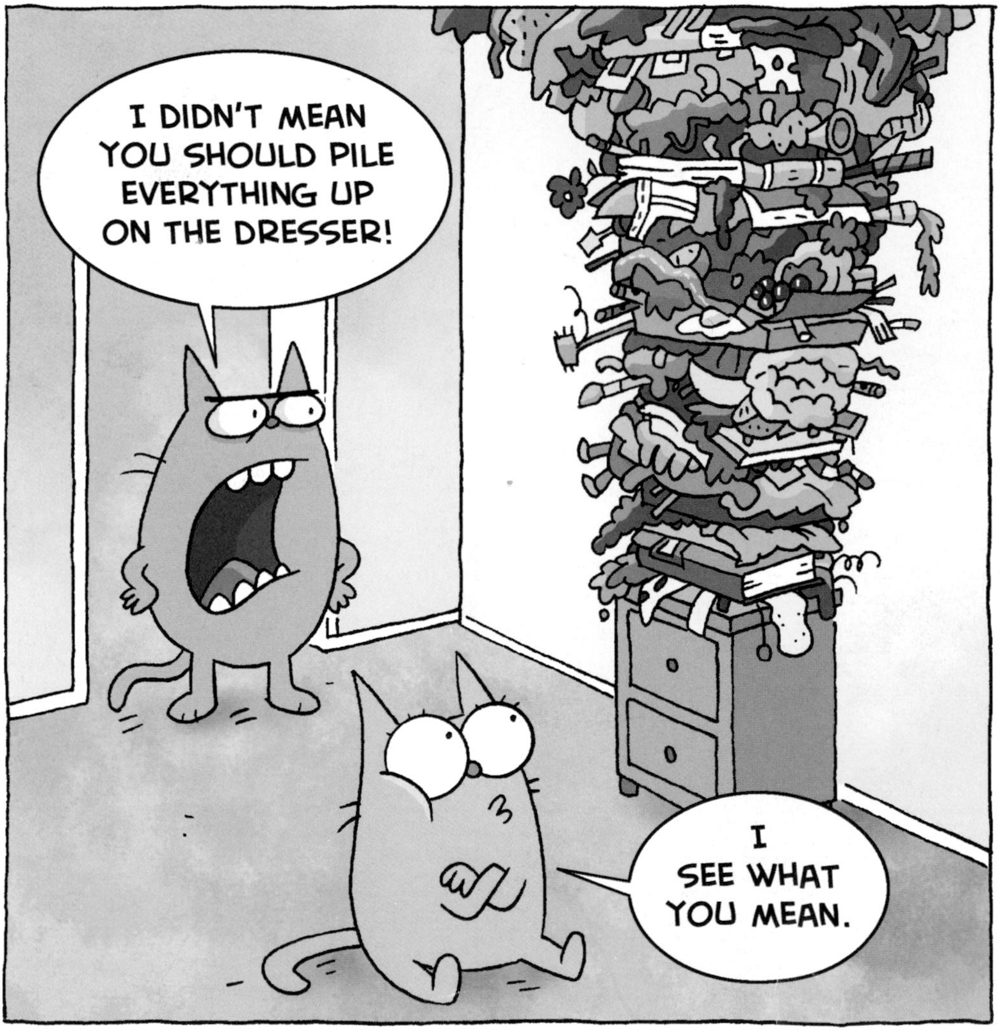
I DIDN'T MEAN YOU SHOULD PILE EVERYTHING UP ON THE DRESSER!
I SEE WHAT YOU MEAN.

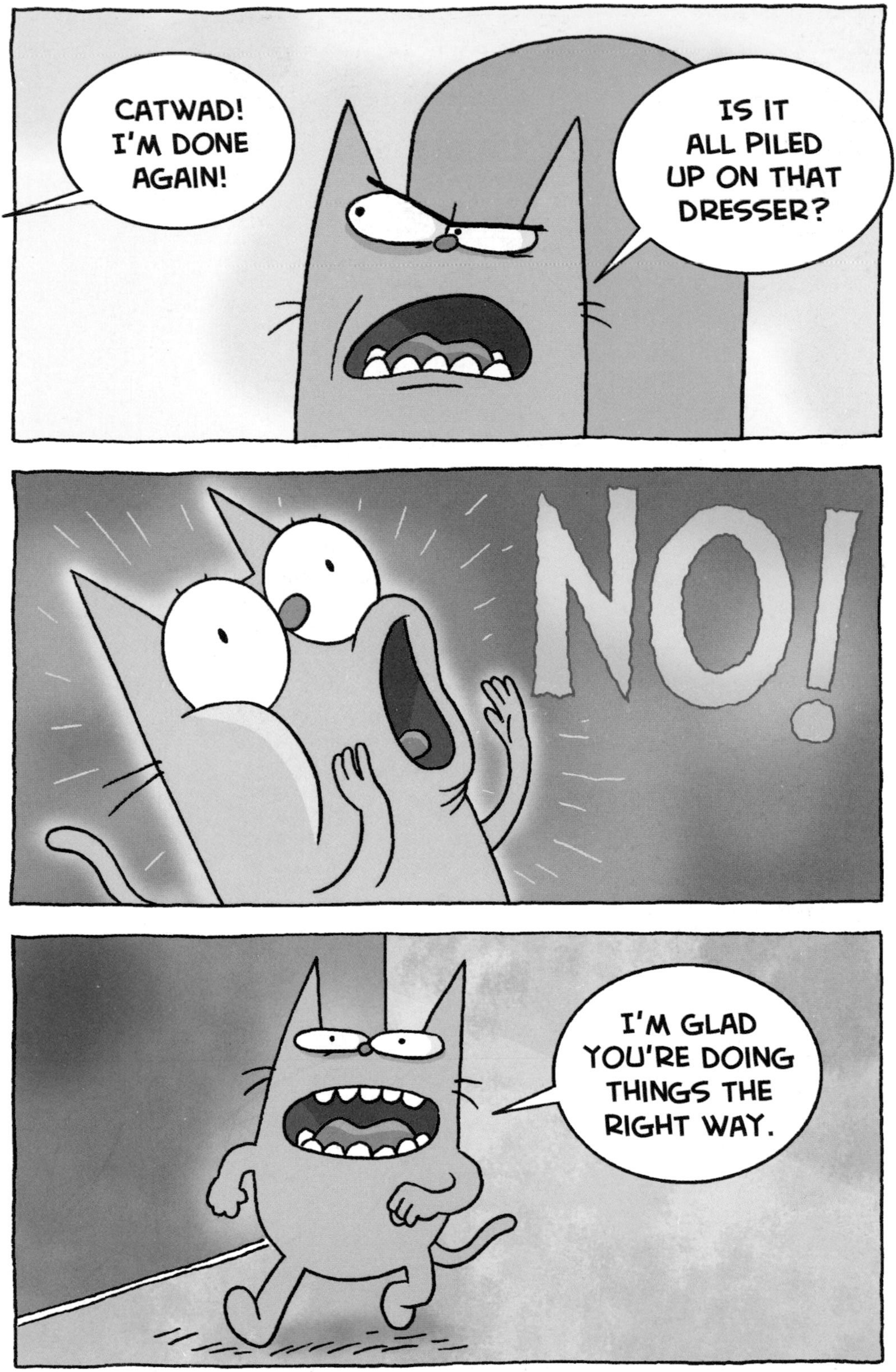
CATWAD! I'M DONE AGAIN!
IS IT ALL PILED UP ON THAT DRESSER?
NO!
I'M GLAD YOU'RE DOING THINGS THE RIGHT WAY.

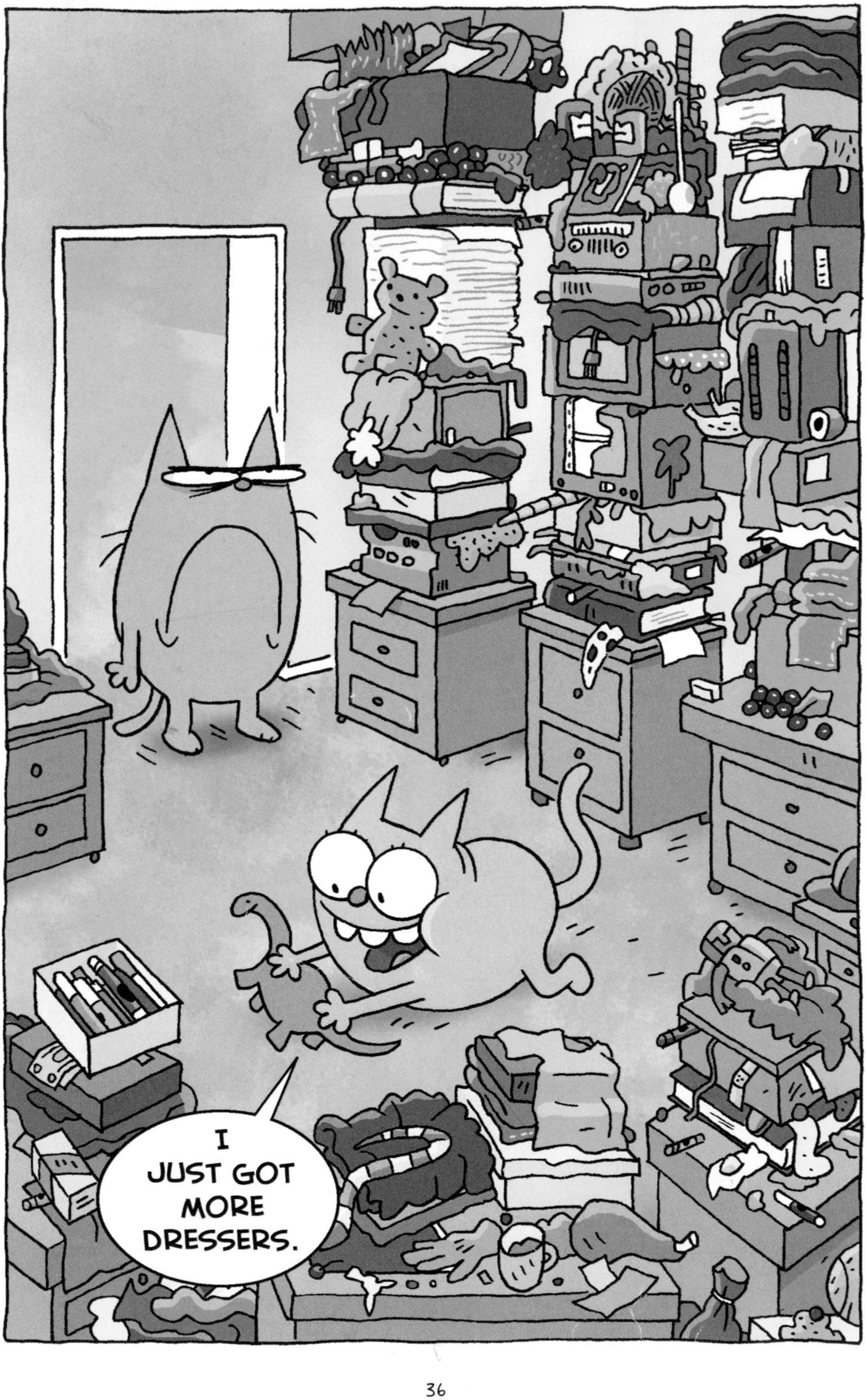
I JUST GOT MORE DRESSERS.

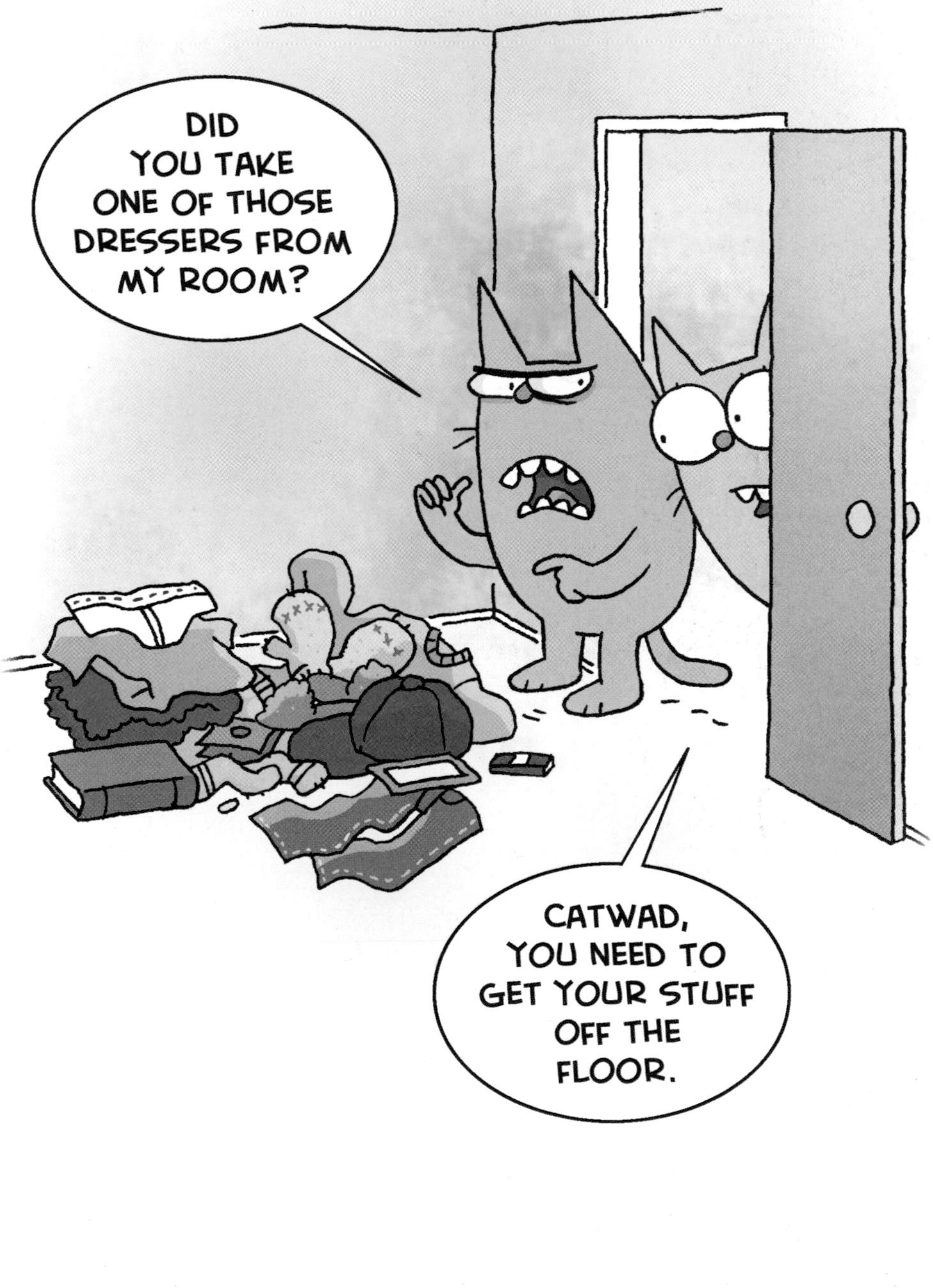
DID YOU TAKE ONE OF THOSE DRESSERS FROM MY ROOM?
CATWAD, YOU NEED TO GET YOUR STUFF OFF THE FLOOR.

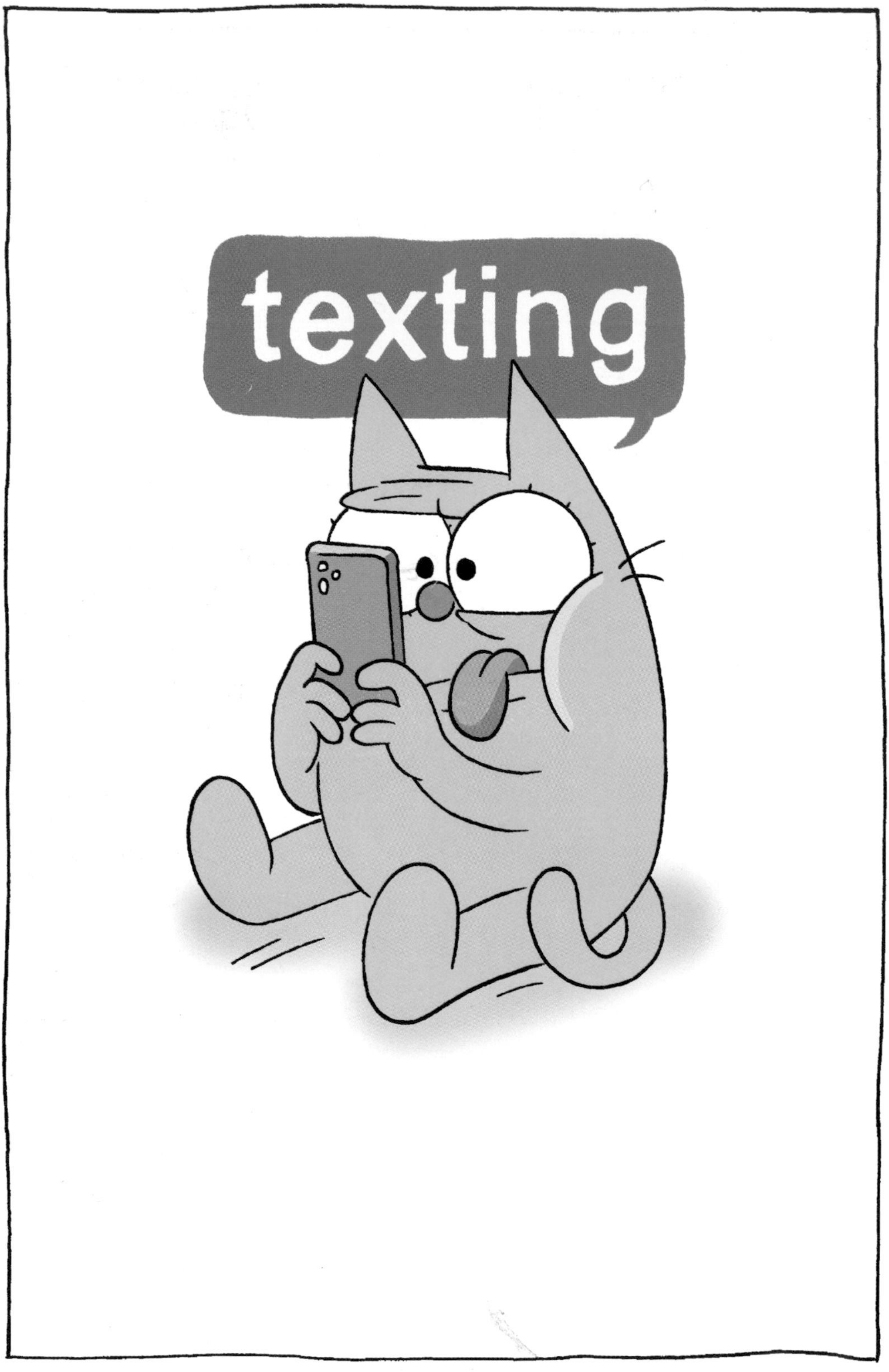
texting

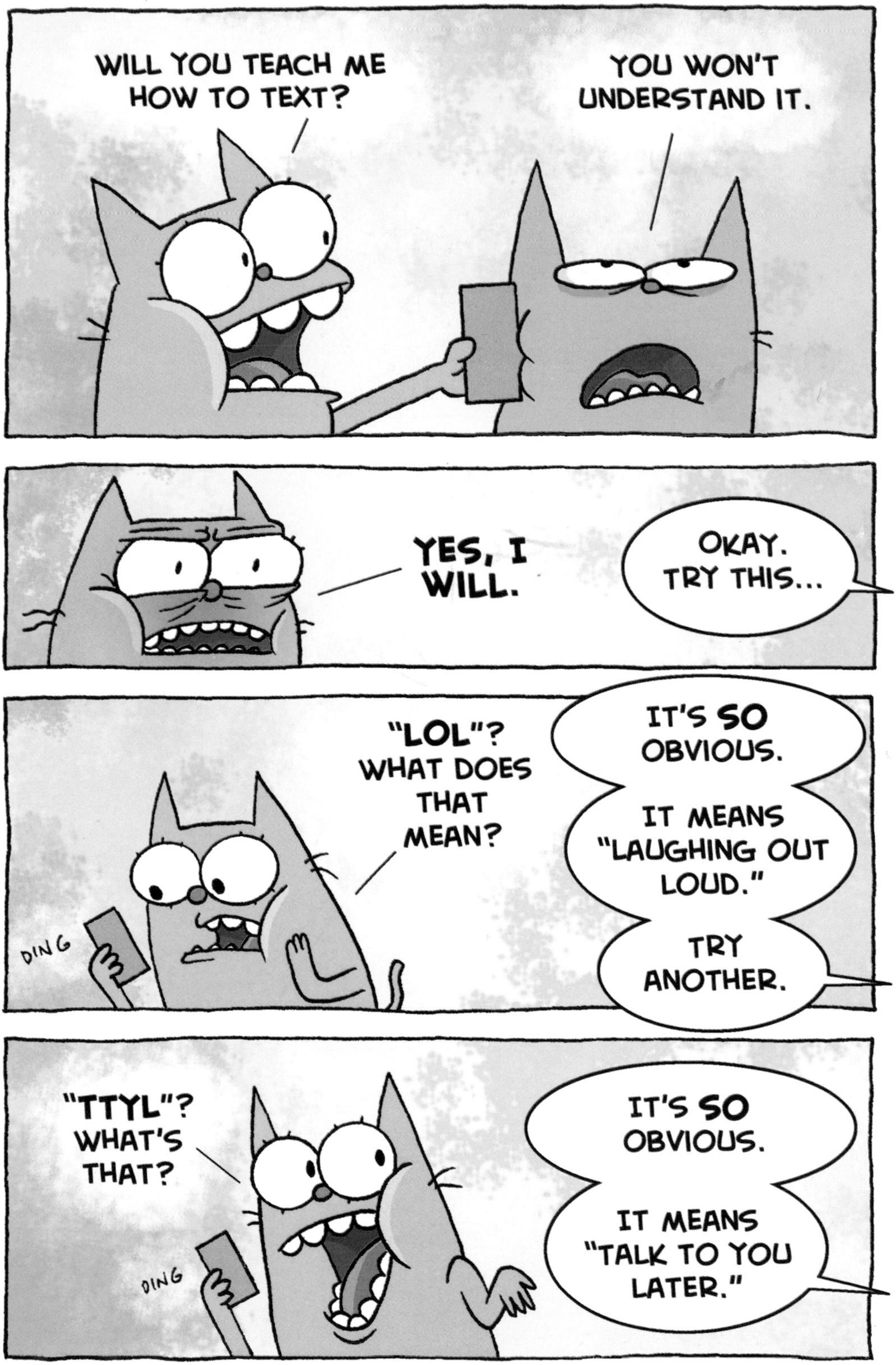
WILL YOU TEACH ME HOW TO TEXT?
YOU WON'T UNDERSTAND IT.
YES, I WILL.
OKAY. TRY THIS...
DING
"LOL"? WHAT DOES THAT MEAN?
IT'S SO OBVIOUS.
IT MEANS "LAUGHING OUT LOUD."
TRY ANOTHER.
DING
"TTYL"? WHAT'S THAT?
IT'S SO OBVIOUS.
IT MEANS "TALK TO YOU LATER."

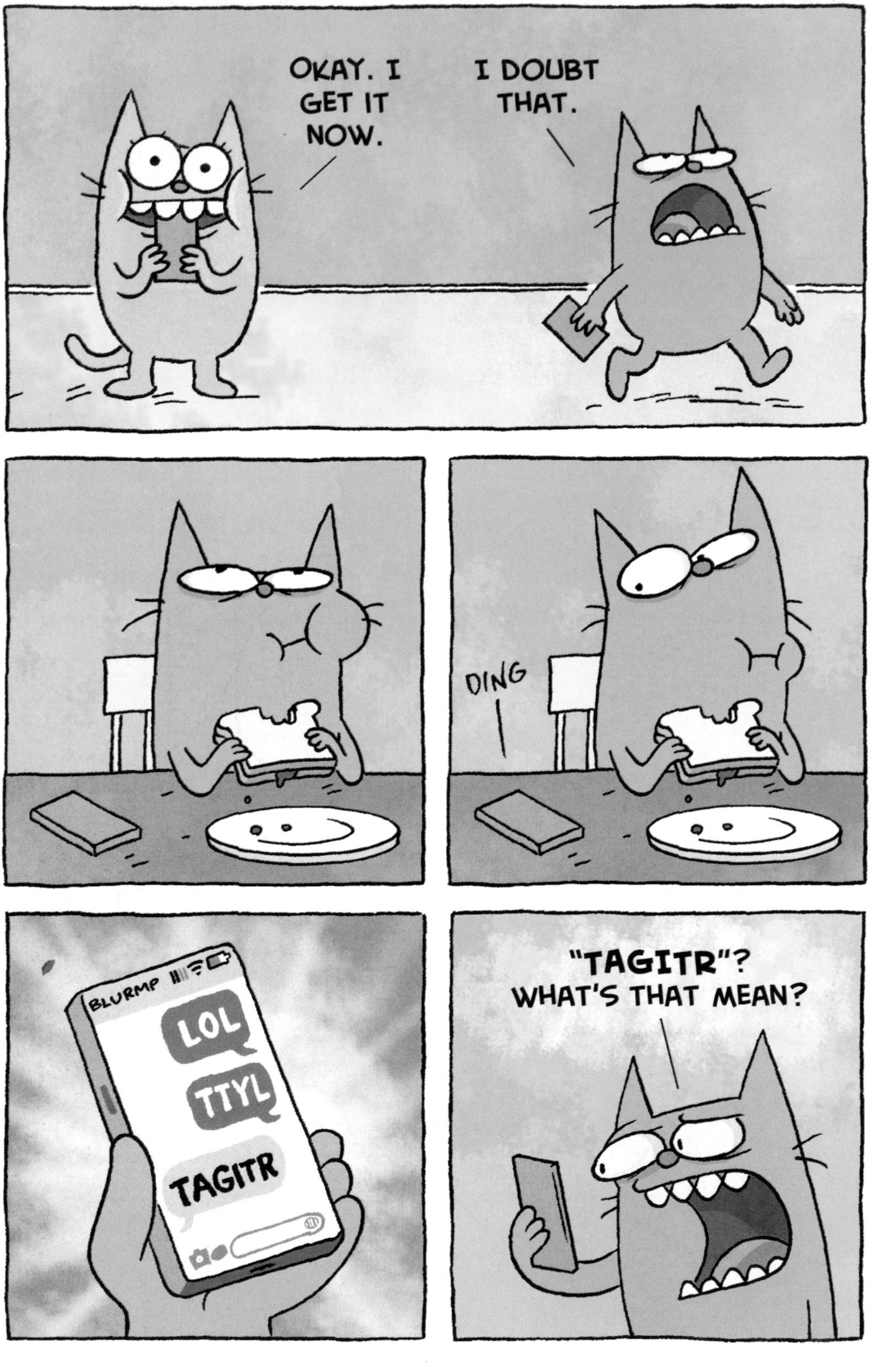
OKAY. I GET IT NOW.
I DOUBT THAT.
DING
BLURMP
LOL
TTYL
TAGITR
"TAGITR"? WHAT'S THAT MEAN?

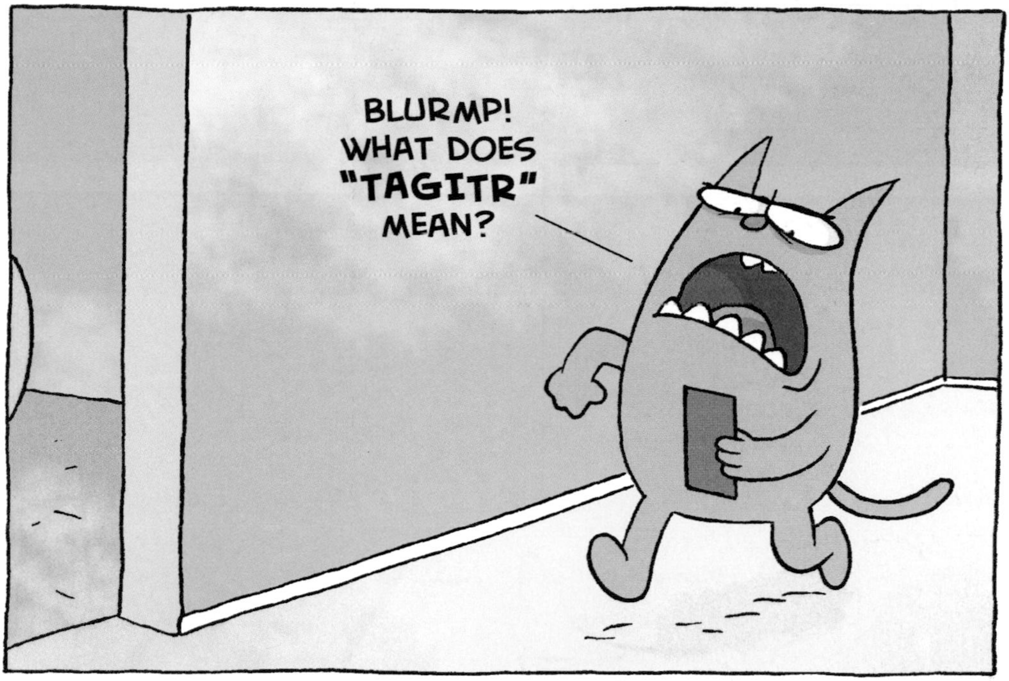
BLURMP! WHAT DOES "TAGITR" MEAN?

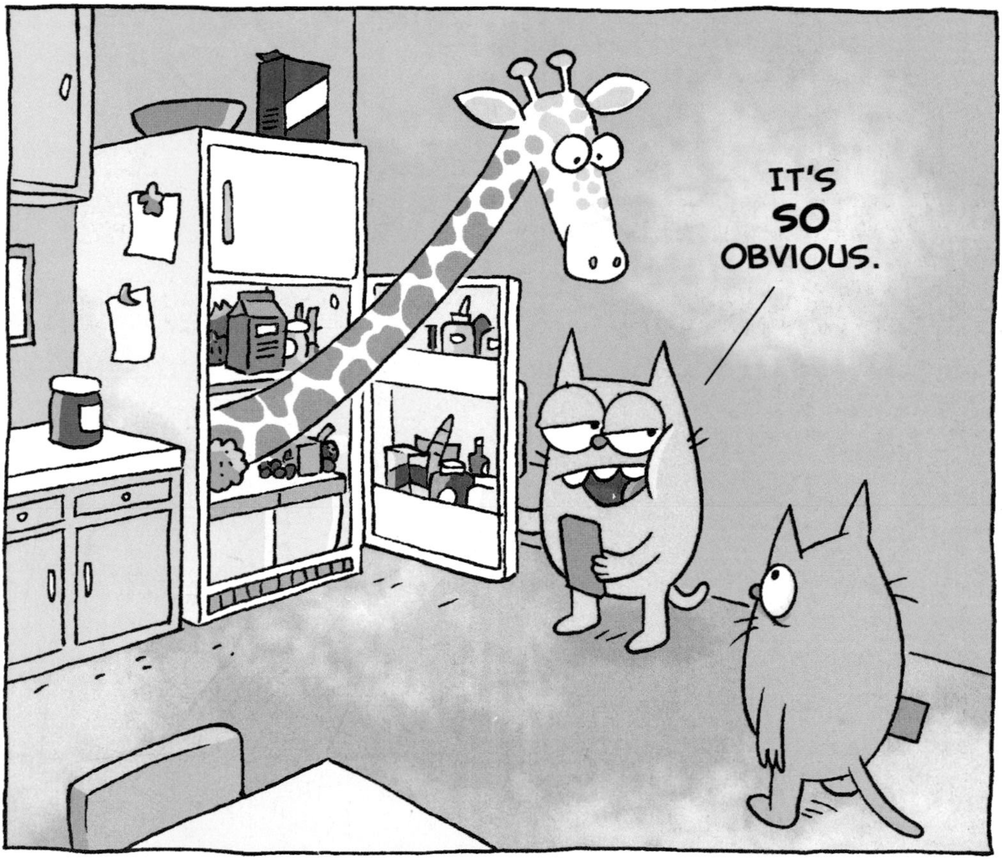
IT'S SO OBVIOUS.

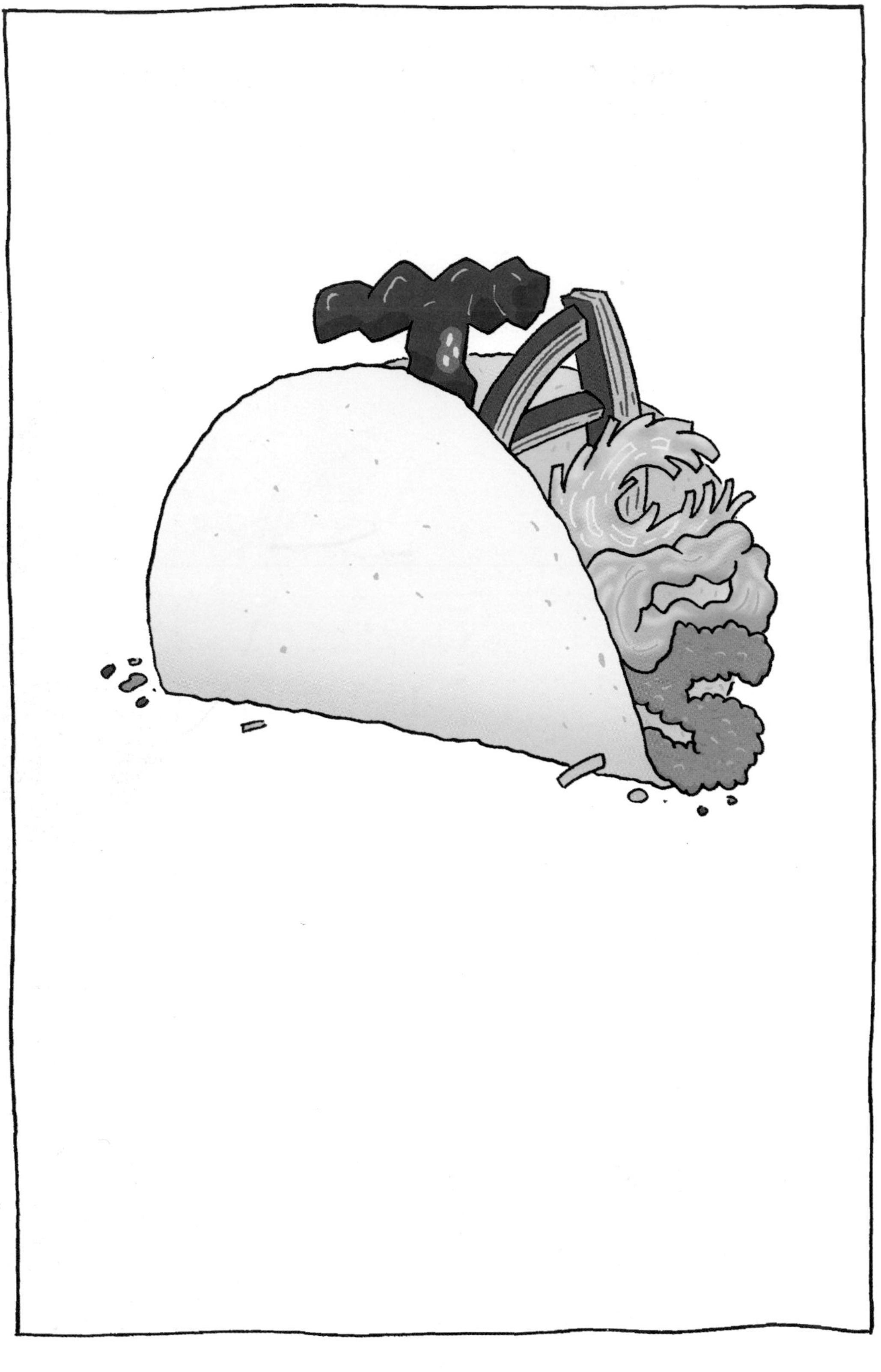
TACOS

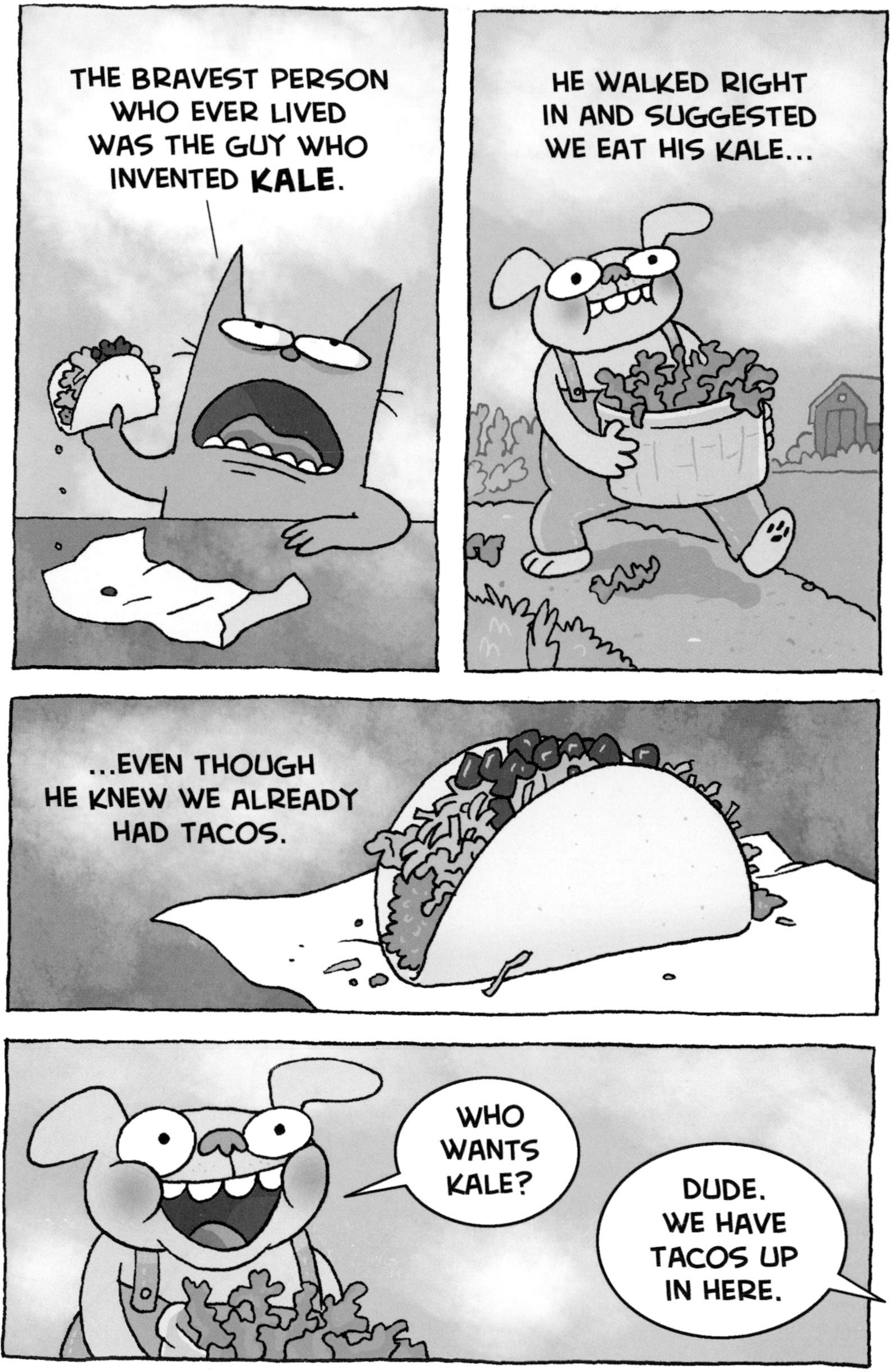
THE BRAVEST PERSON WHO EVER LIVED WAS THE GUY WHO INVENTED KALE.
HE WALKED RIGHT IN AND SUGGESTED WE EAT HIS KALE...
...EVEN THOUGH HE KNEW WE ALREADY HAD TACOS.
WHO WANTS KALE?
DUDE. WE HAVE TACOS UP IN HERE.

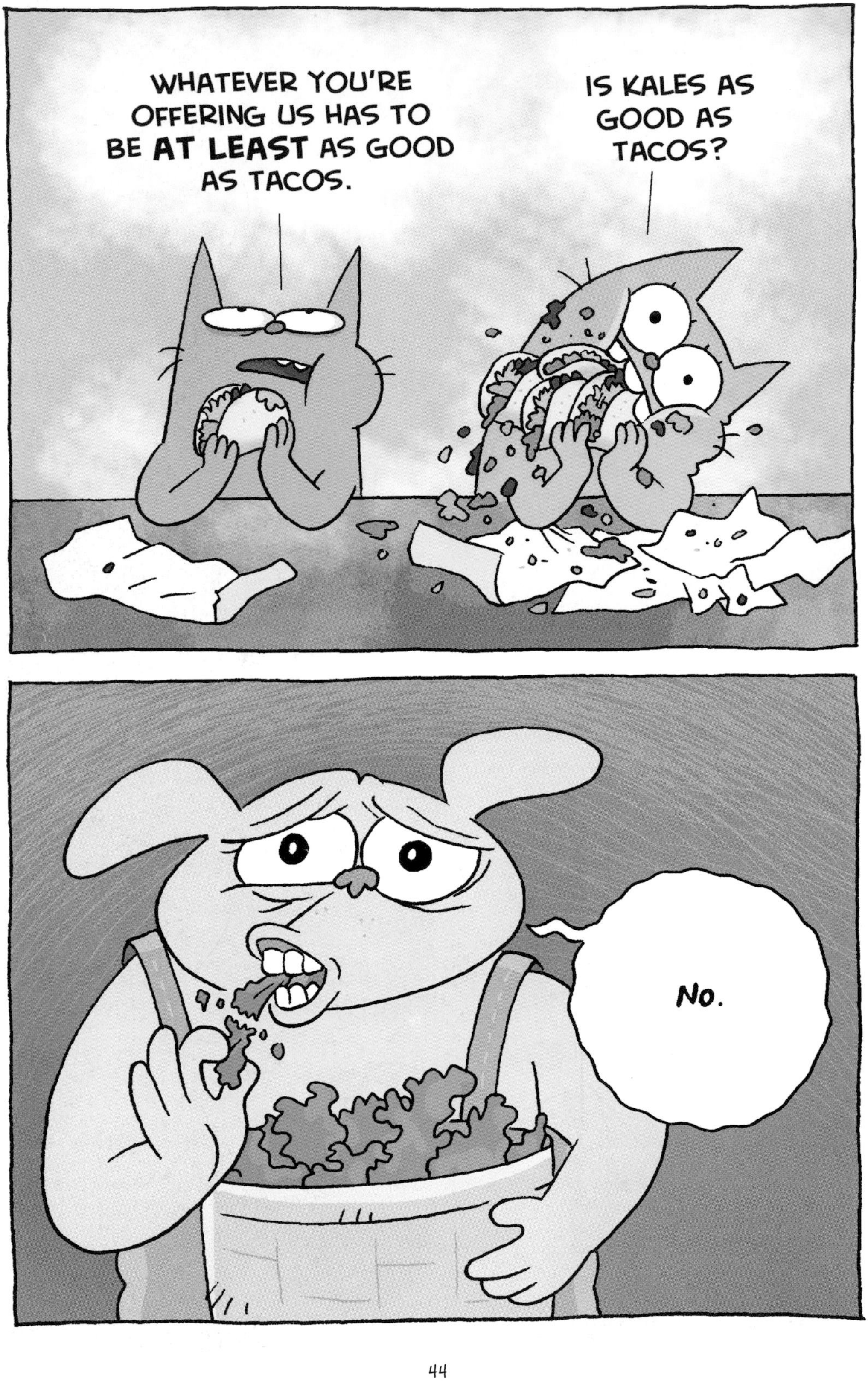
WHATEVER YOU'RE OFFERING US HAS TO BE **AT LEAST** AS GOOD AS TACOS.
IS KALES AS GOOD AS TACOS?
NO.

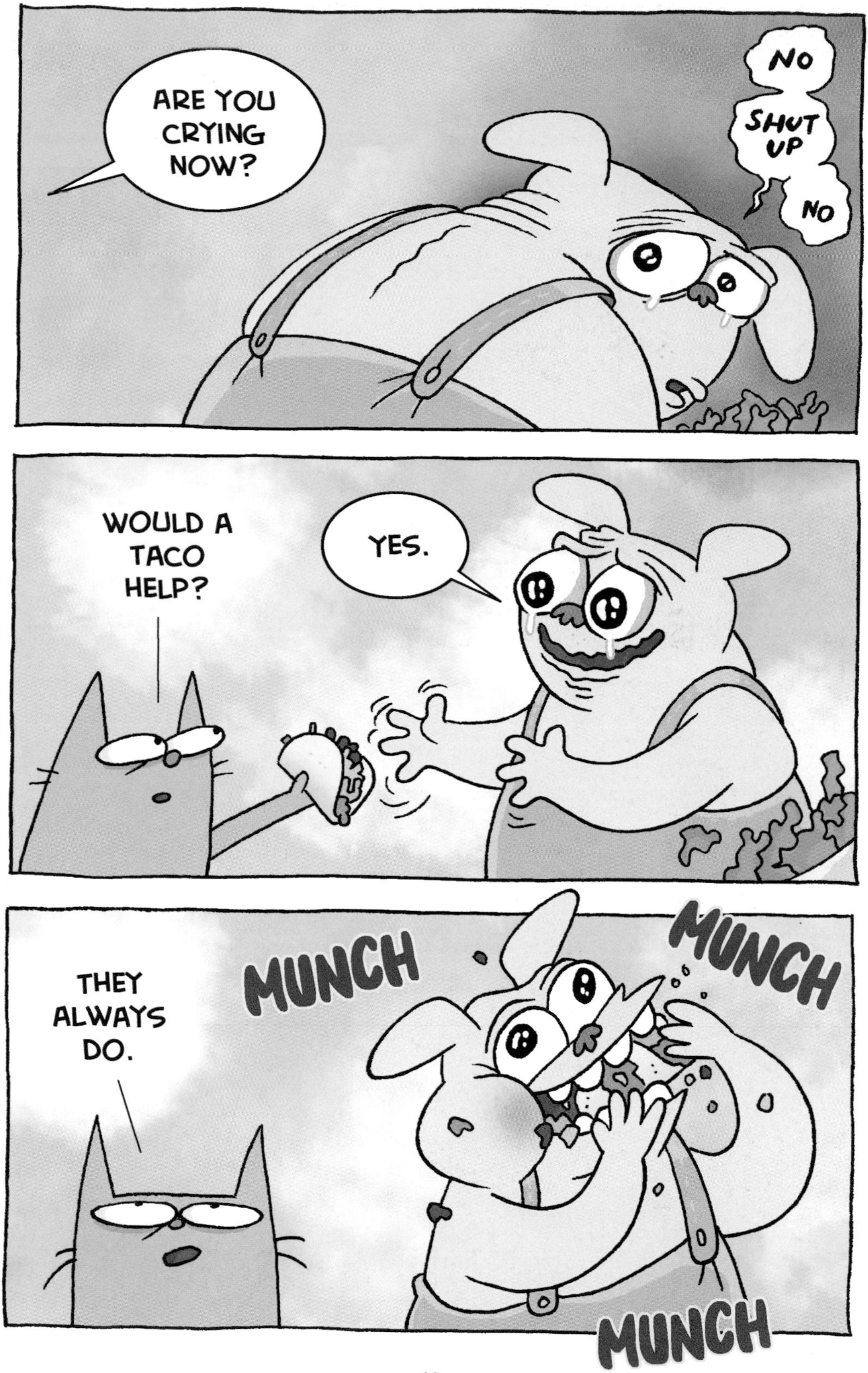
ARE YOU CRYING NOW?
NO
SHUT UP
NO
WOULD A TACO HELP?
YES.
THEY ALWAYS DO.
MUNCH
MUNCH
MUNCH

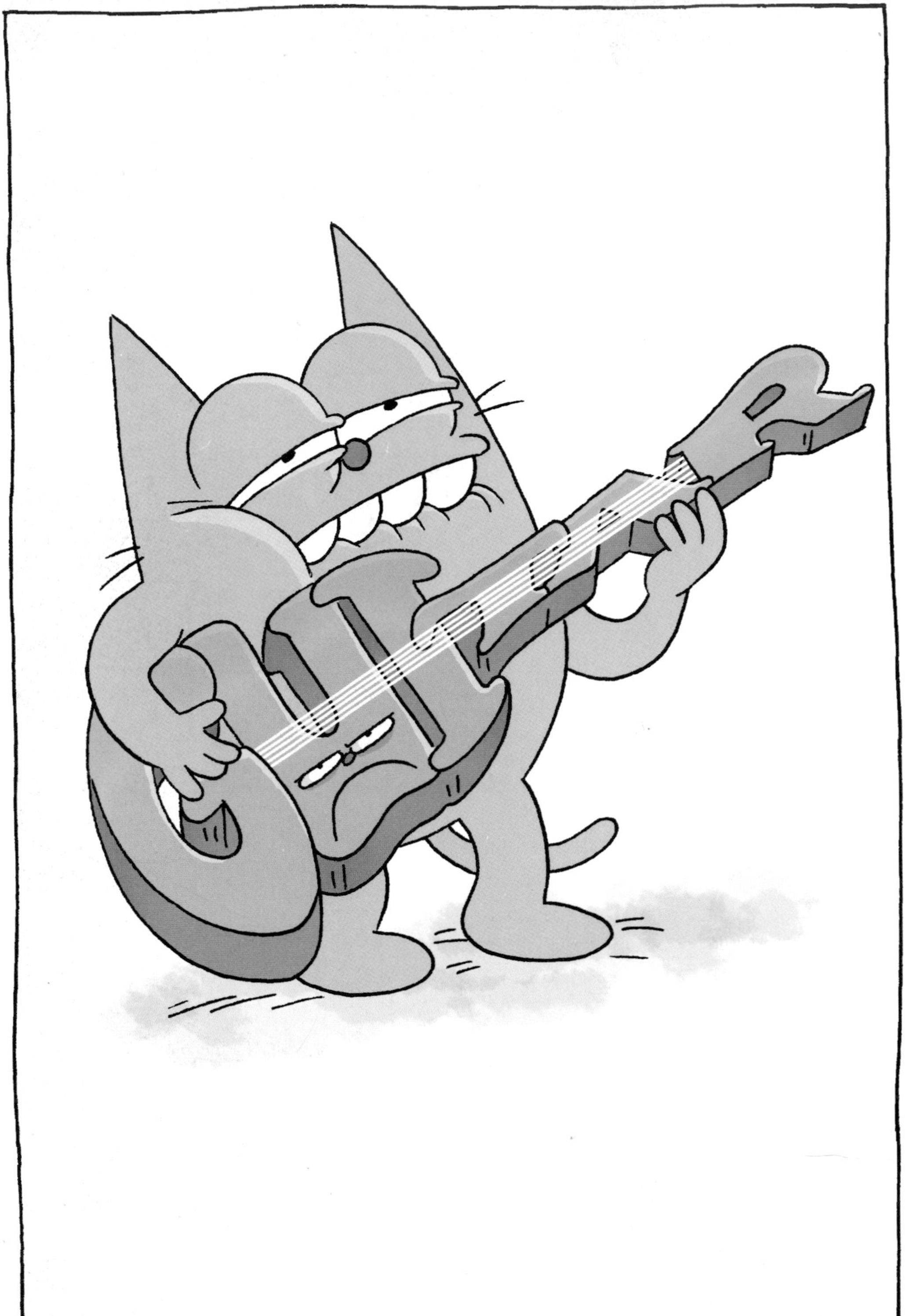

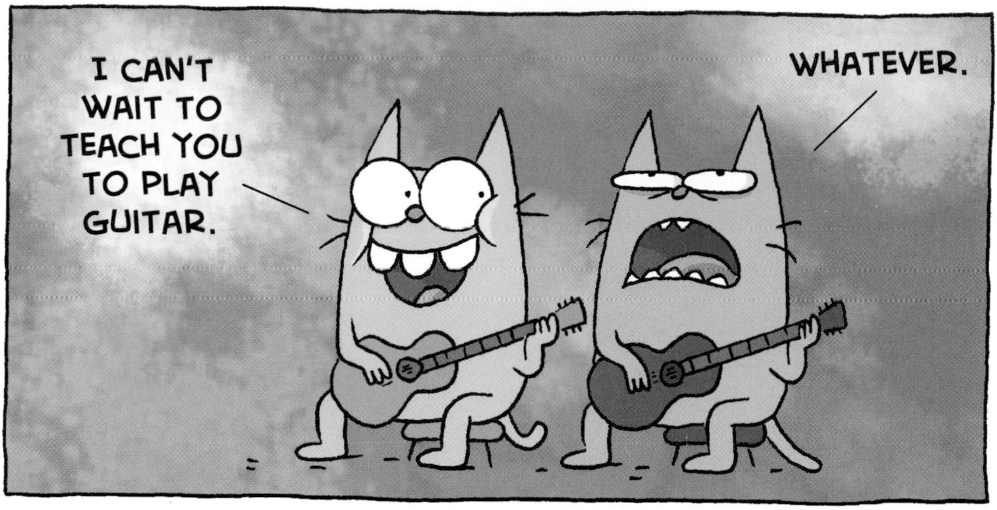
I CAN'T WAIT TO TEACH YOU TO PLAY GUITAR.
WHATEVER.

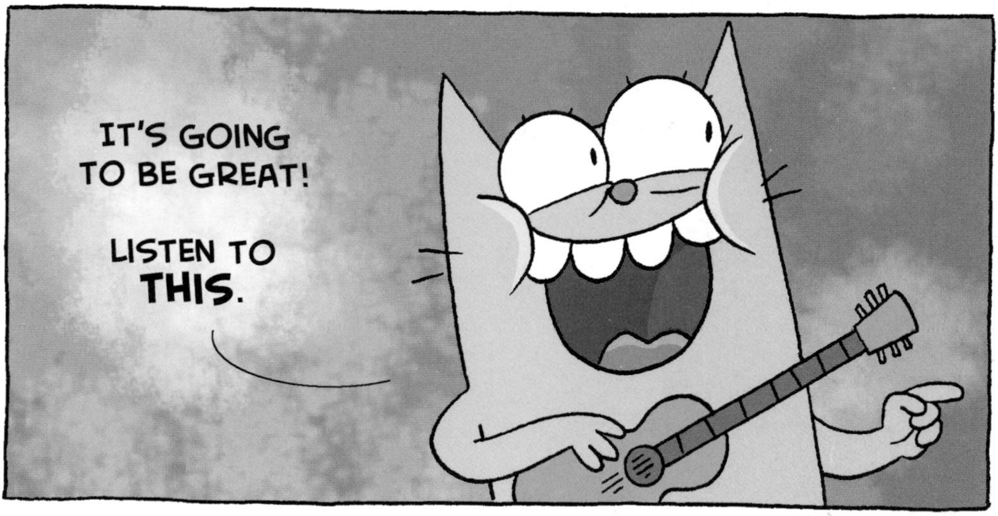
IT'S GOING TO BE GREAT!
LISTEN TO **THIS**.

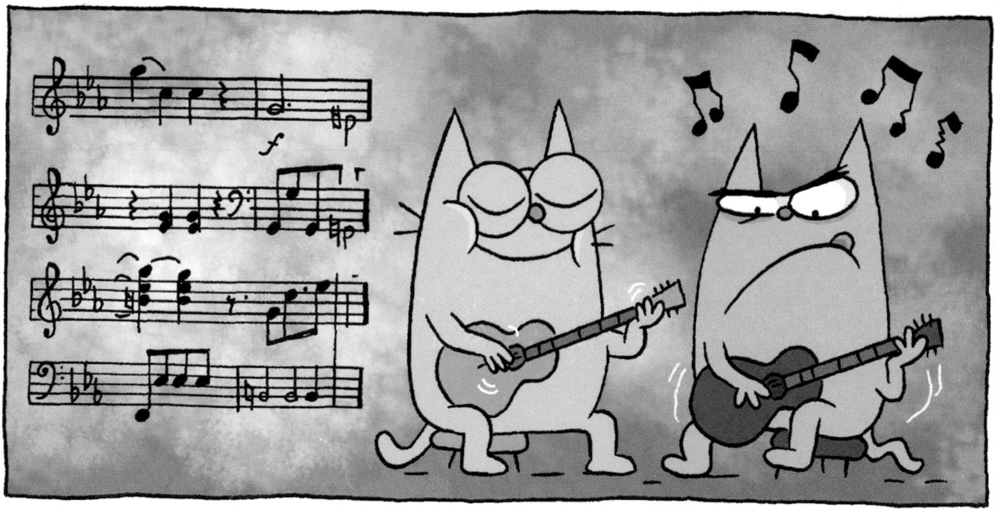

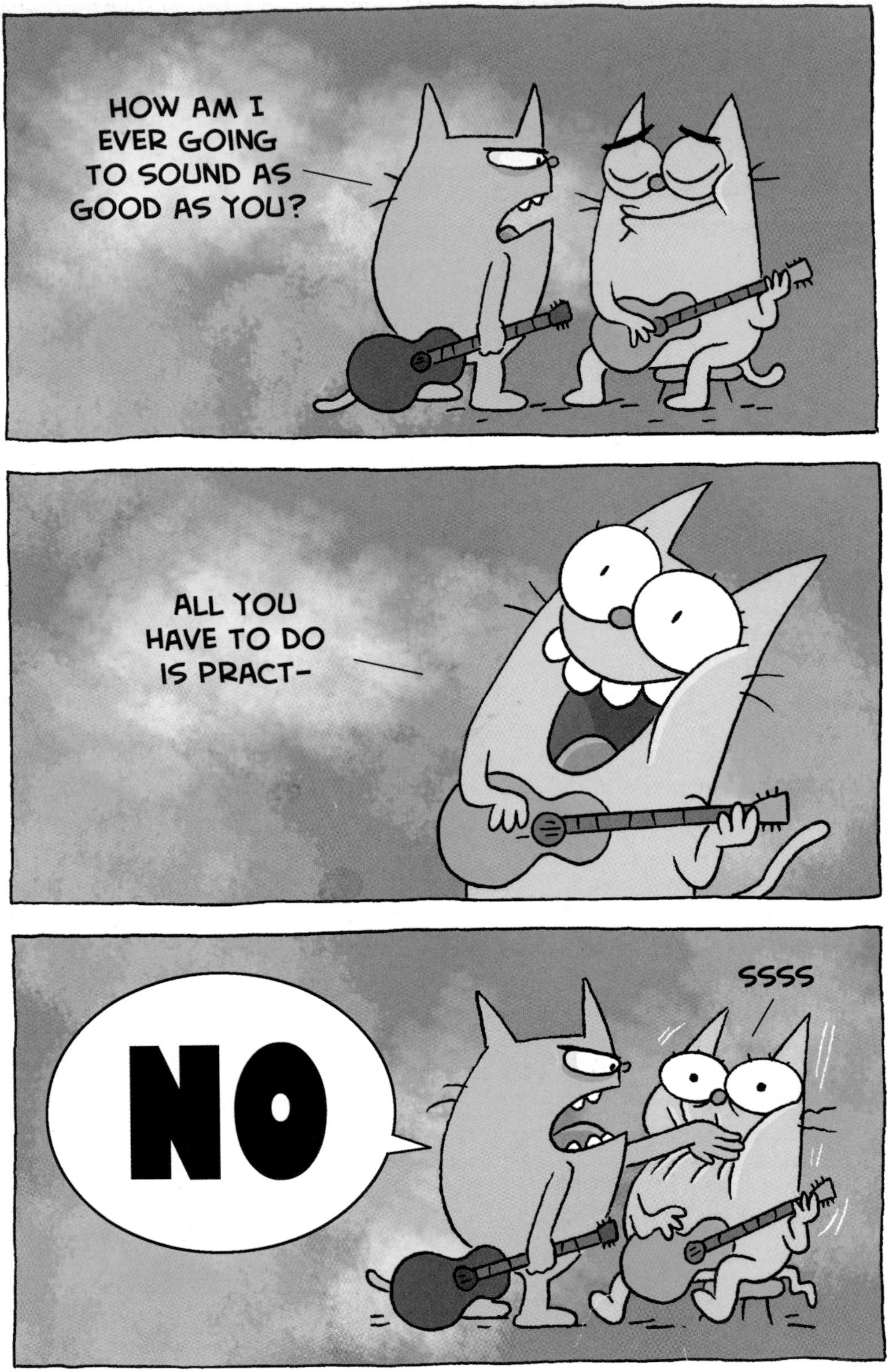
HOW AM I EVER GOING TO SOUND AS GOOD AS YOU?
ALL YOU HAVE TO DO IS PRACT-
NO
SSSS

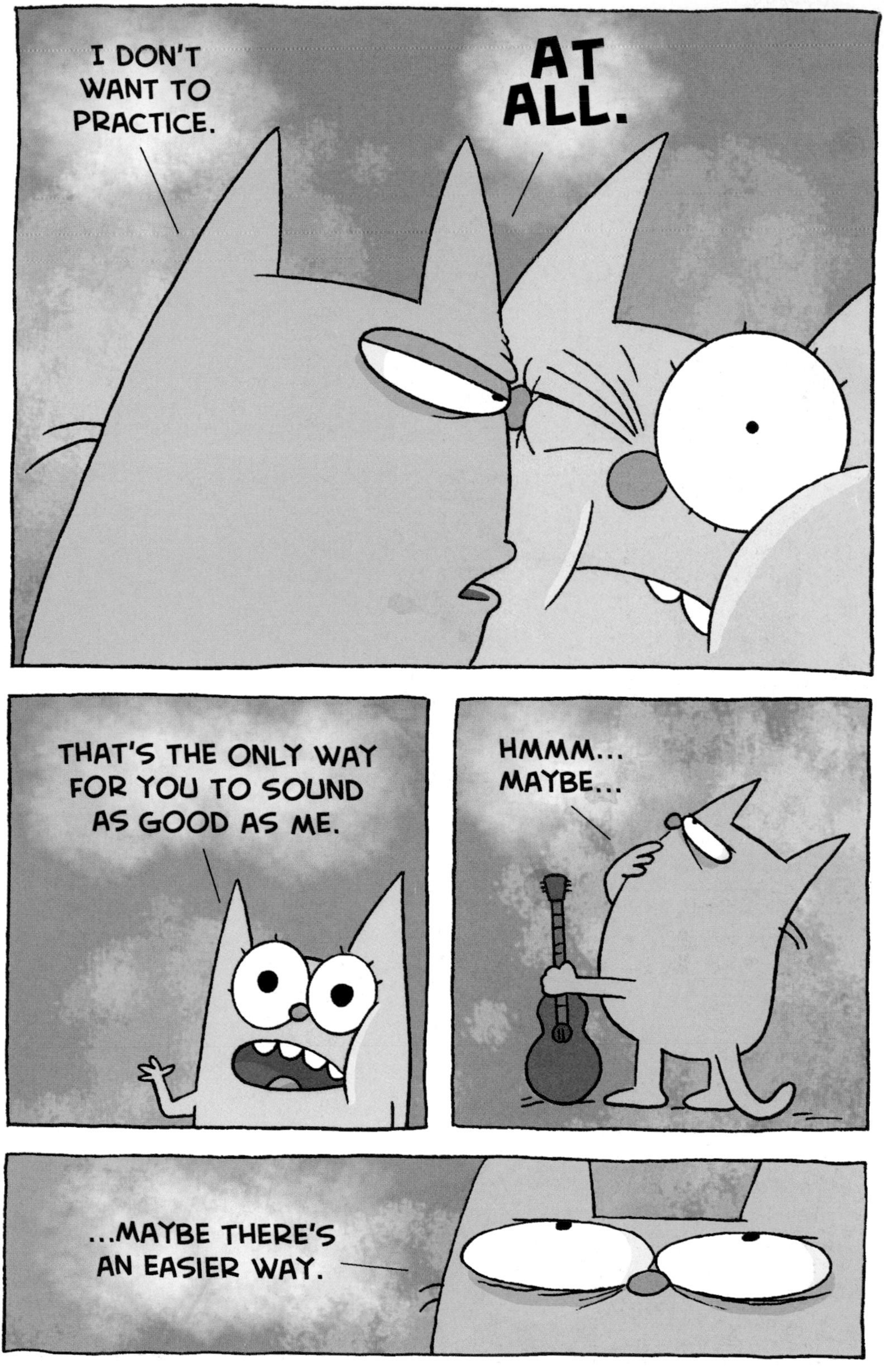
I DON'T WANT TO PRACTICE.
AT ALL.
THAT'S THE ONLY WAY FOR YOU TO SOUND AS GOOD AS ME.
HMMM... MAYBE...
...MAYBE THERE'S AN EASIER WAY.

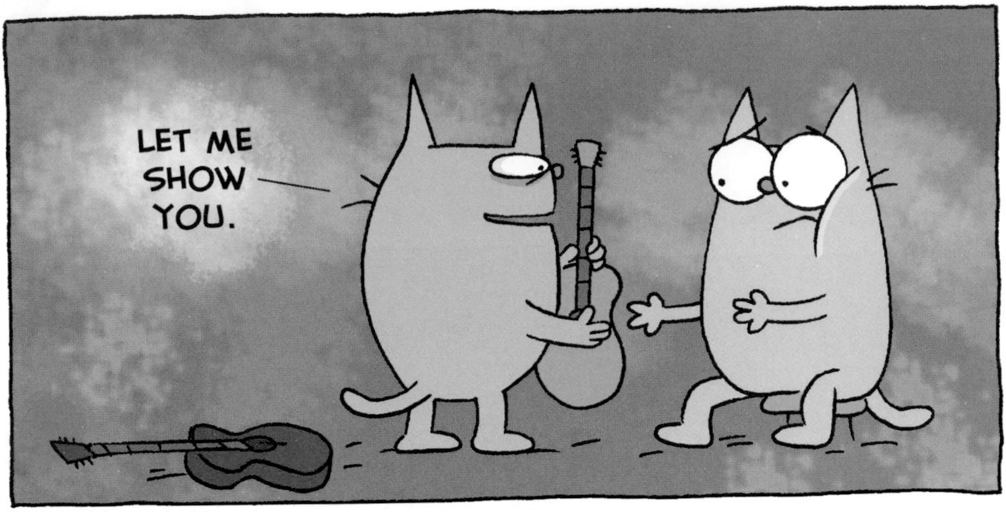
LET ME SHOW YOU.

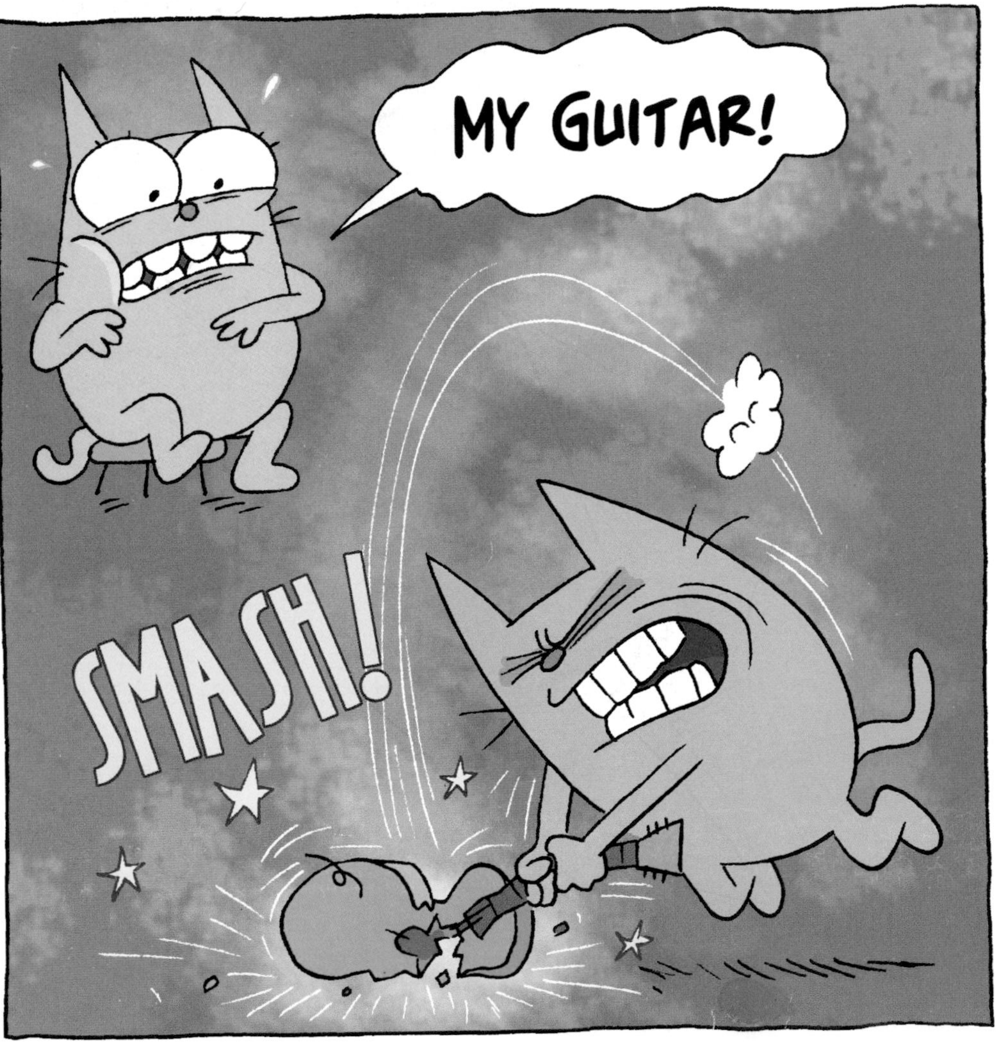
MY GUITAR!
SMASH!

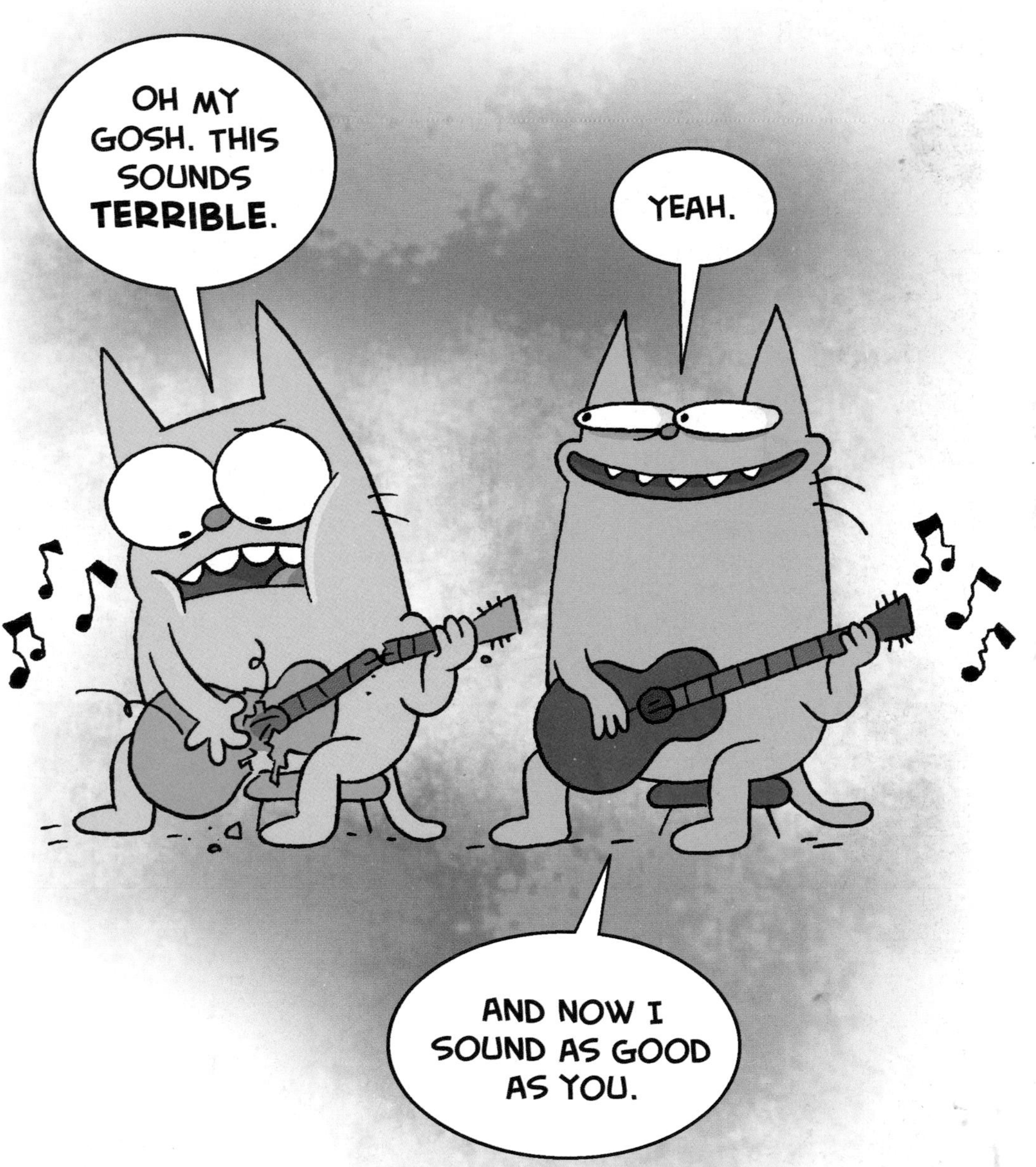
OH MY GOSH. THIS SOUNDS **TERRIBLE.**
YEAH.
AND NOW I SOUND AS GOOD AS YOU.

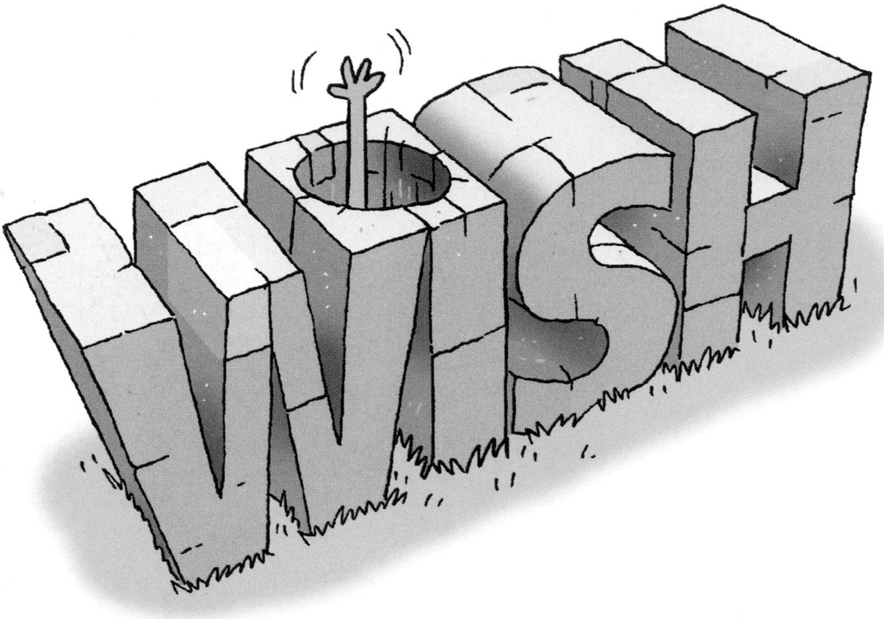
WISH

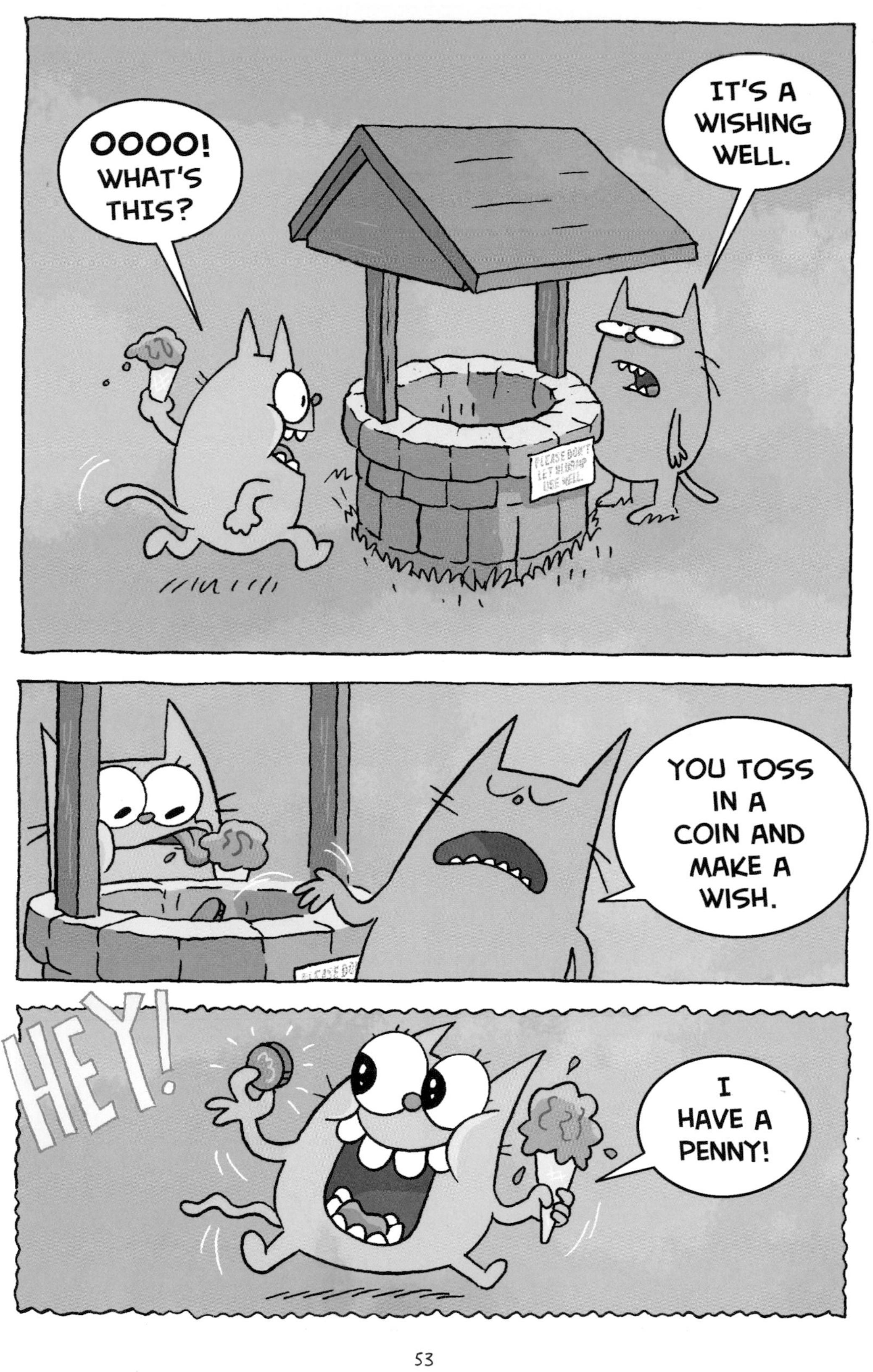
OOOO! WHAT'S THIS?
IT'S A WISHING WELL.
YOU TOSS IN A COIN AND MAKE A WISH.
HEY!
I HAVE A PENNY!

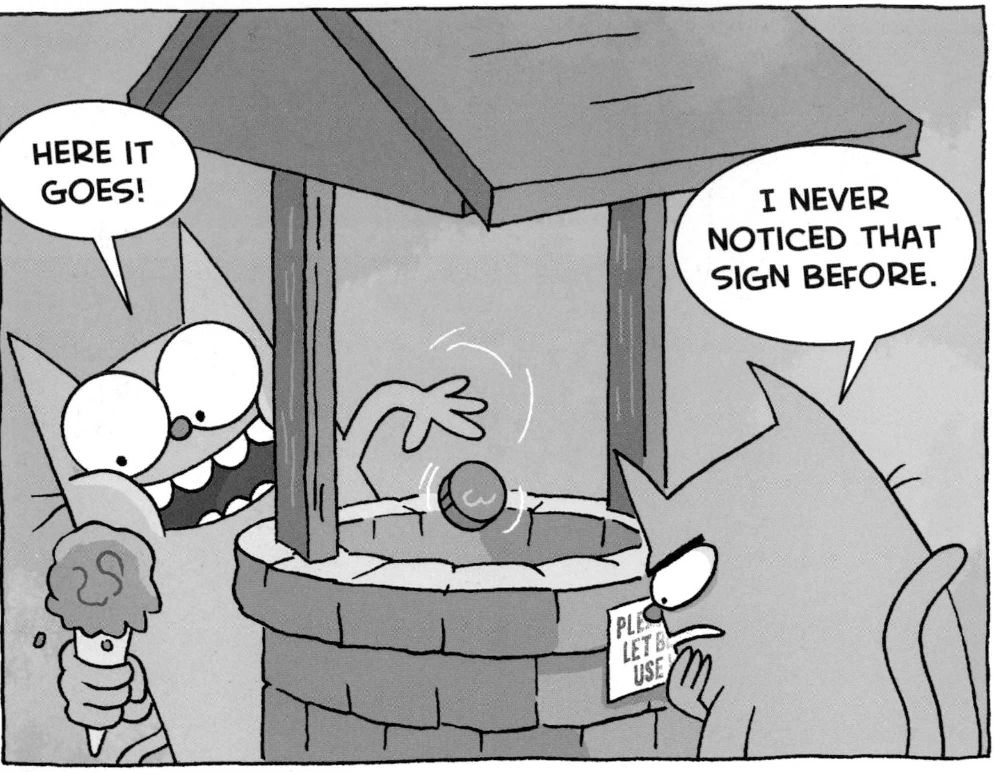
HERE IT GOES!
I NEVER NOTICED THAT SIGN BEFORE.

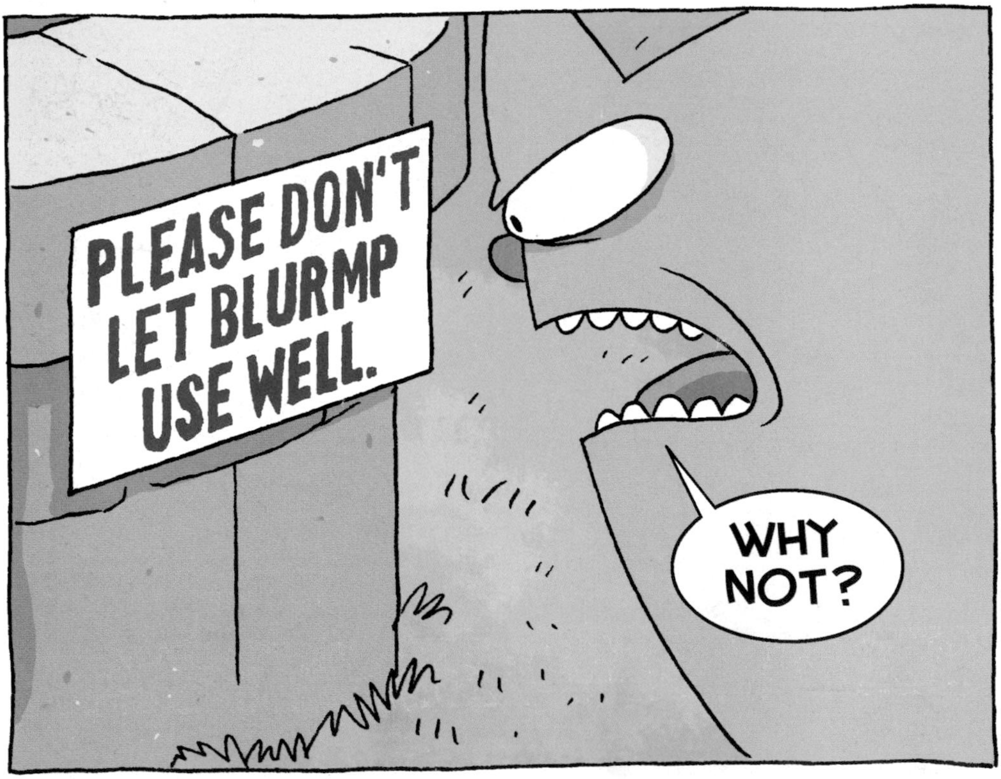
PLEASE DON'T LET BLURMP USE WELL.
WHY NOT?

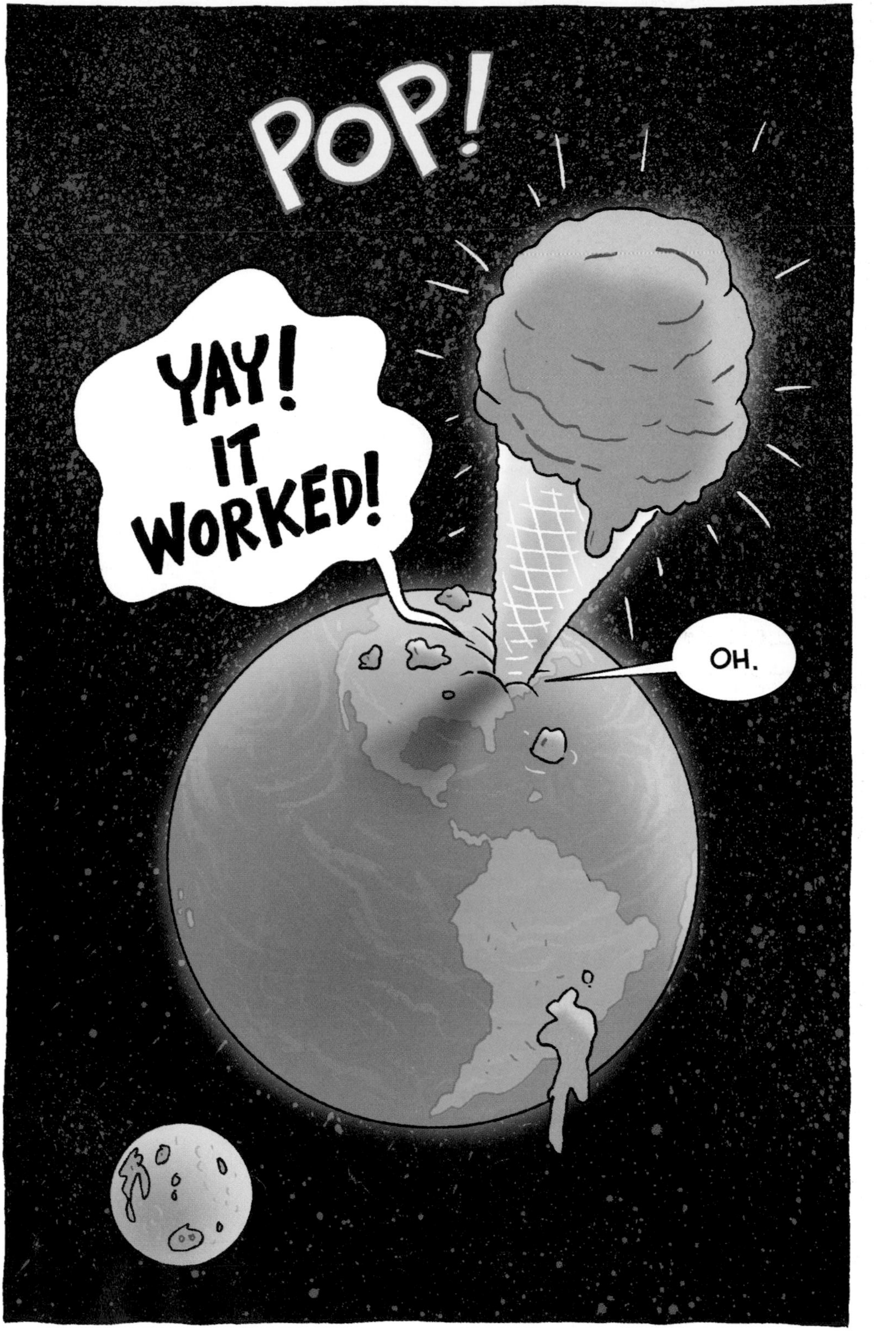
POP!
YAY! IT WORKED!
OH.

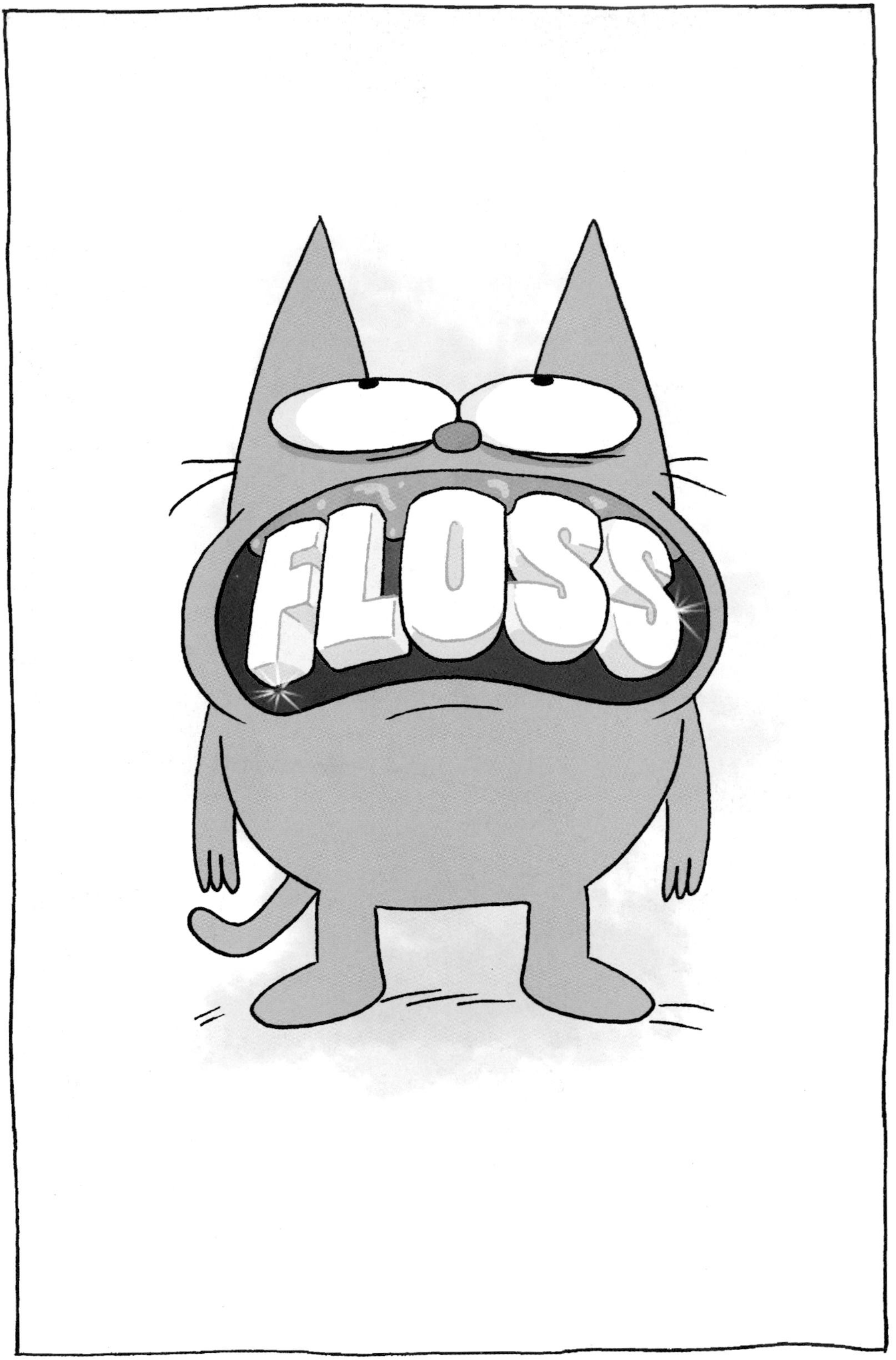
FLOSS

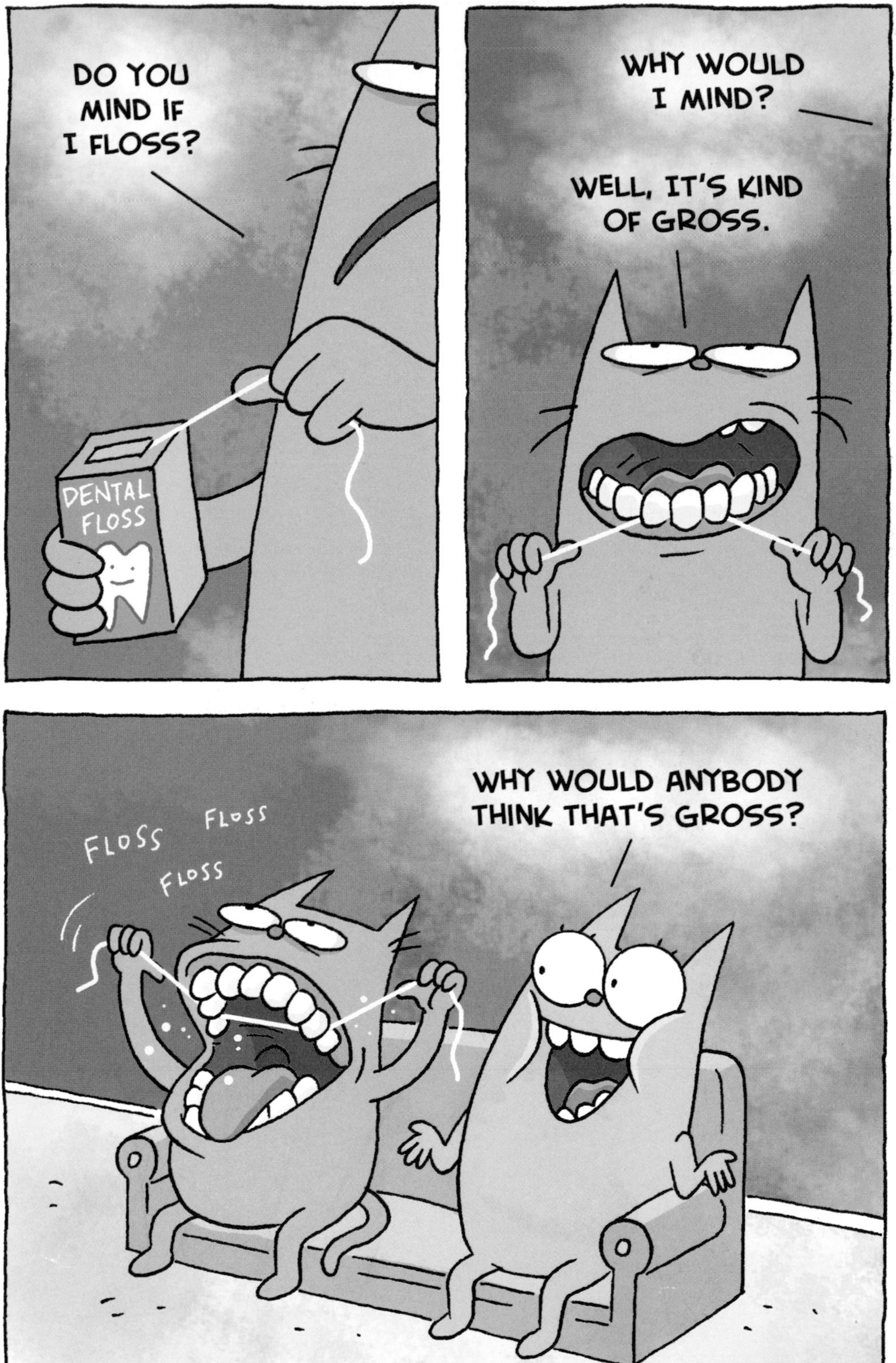
DO YOU MIND IF I FLOSS?
WHY WOULD I MIND?
WELL, IT'S KIND OF GROSS.
DENTAL FLOSS
FLOSS FLOSS
FLOSS
WHY WOULD ANYBODY THINK THAT'S GROSS?

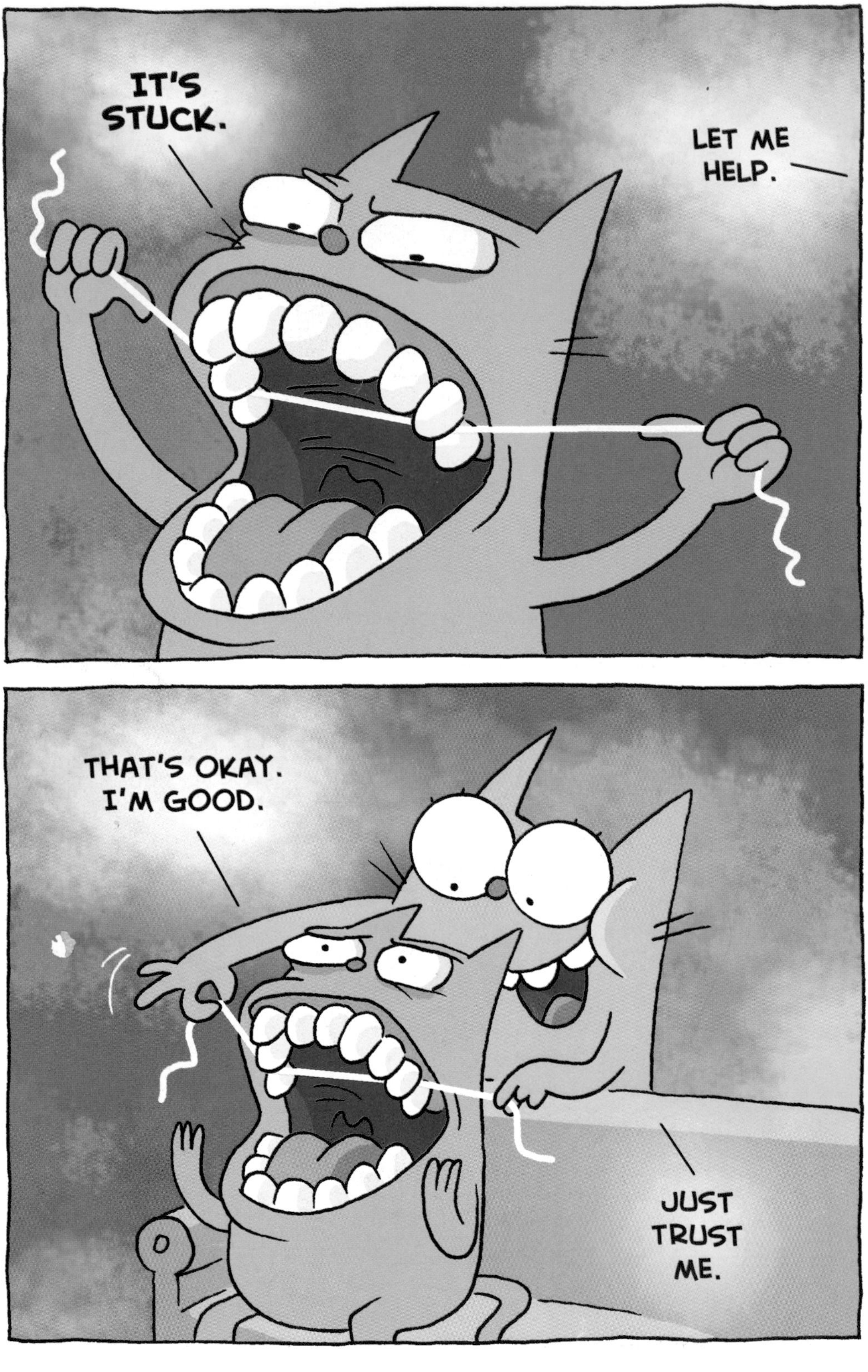
IT'S STUCK.
LET ME HELP.
THAT'S OKAY. I'M GOOD.
JUST TRUST ME.

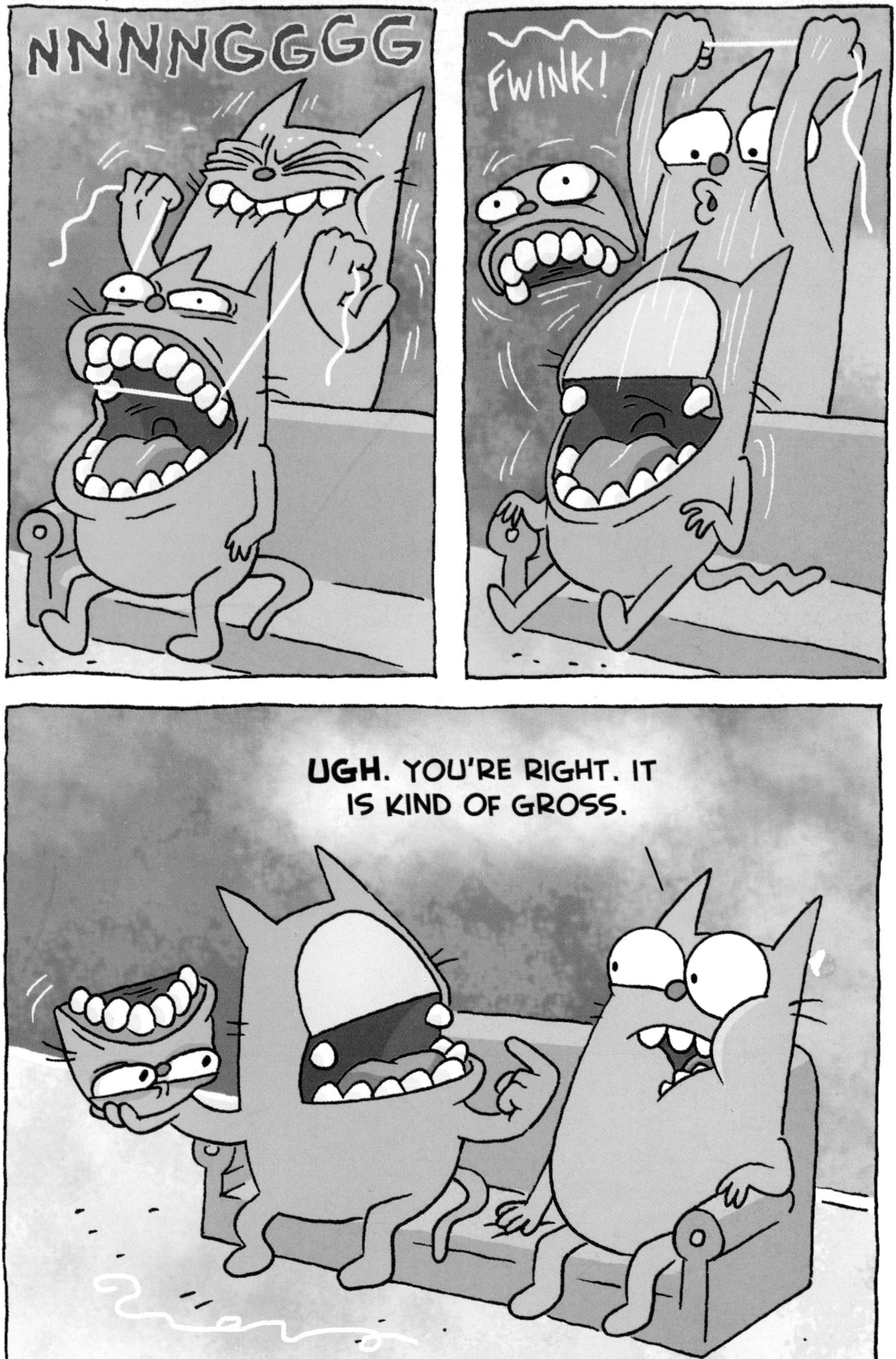
NNNNGGGG
FWINK!
UGH. YOU'RE RIGHT. IT IS KIND OF GROSS.

THE BUS

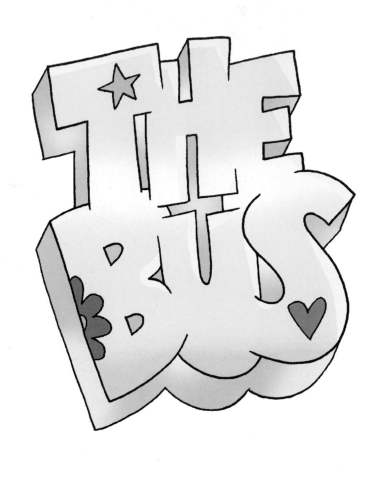

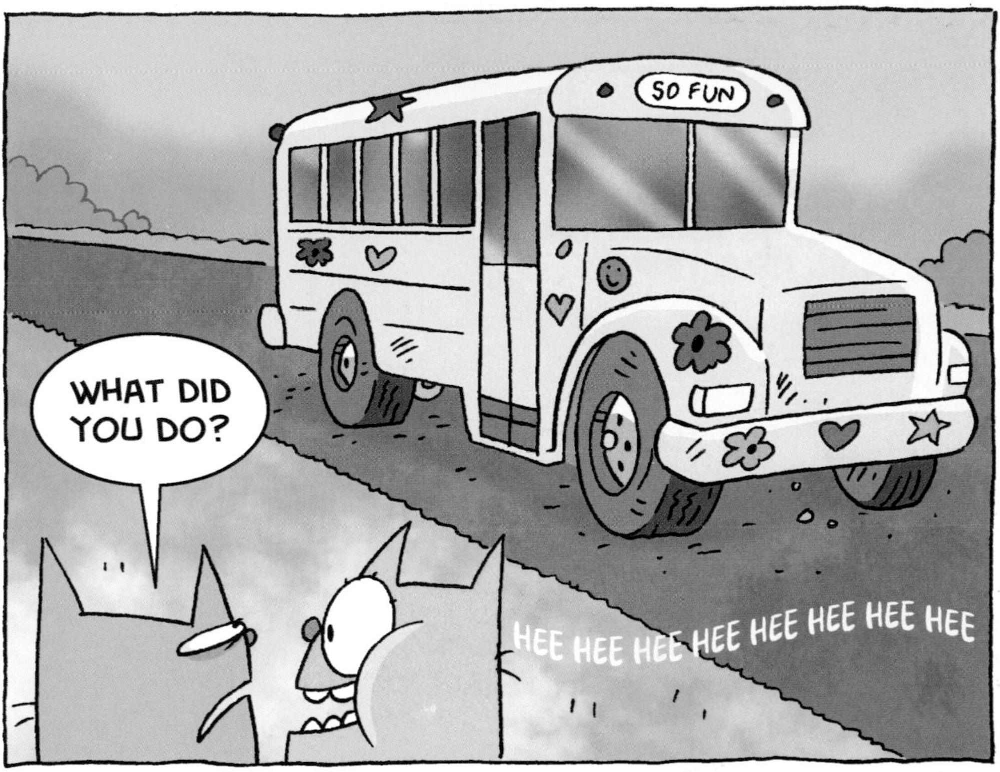
SO FUN
WHAT DID YOU DO?
HEE HEE HEE HEE HEE HEE HEE HEE

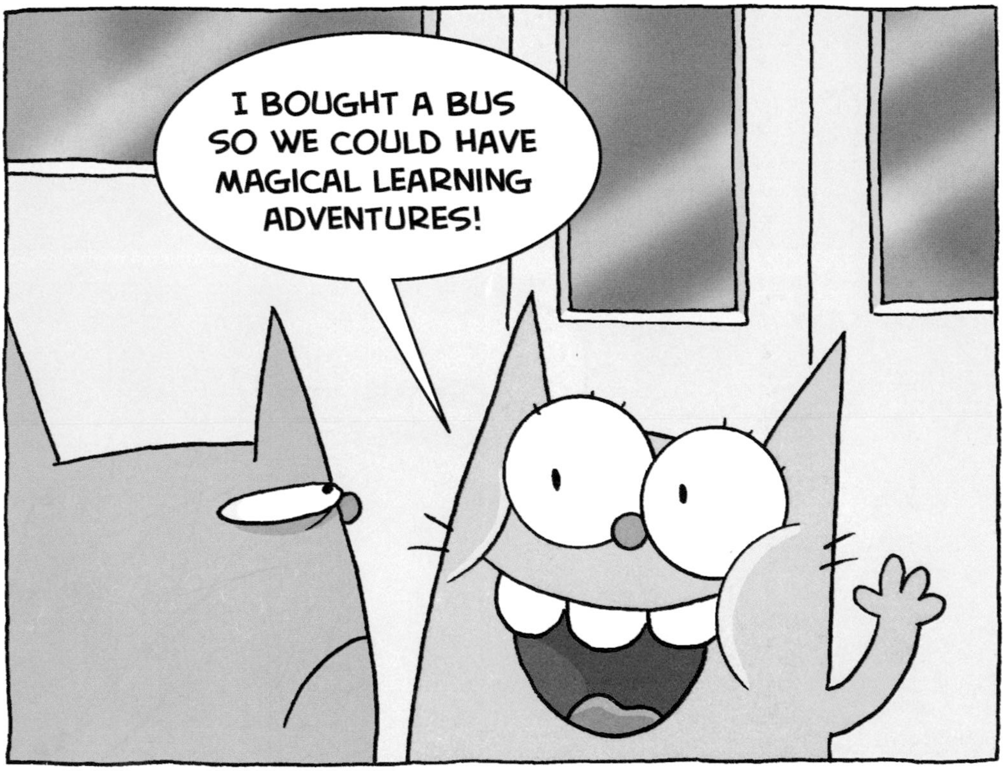
I BOUGHT A BUS SO WE COULD HAVE MAGICAL LEARNING ADVENTURES!

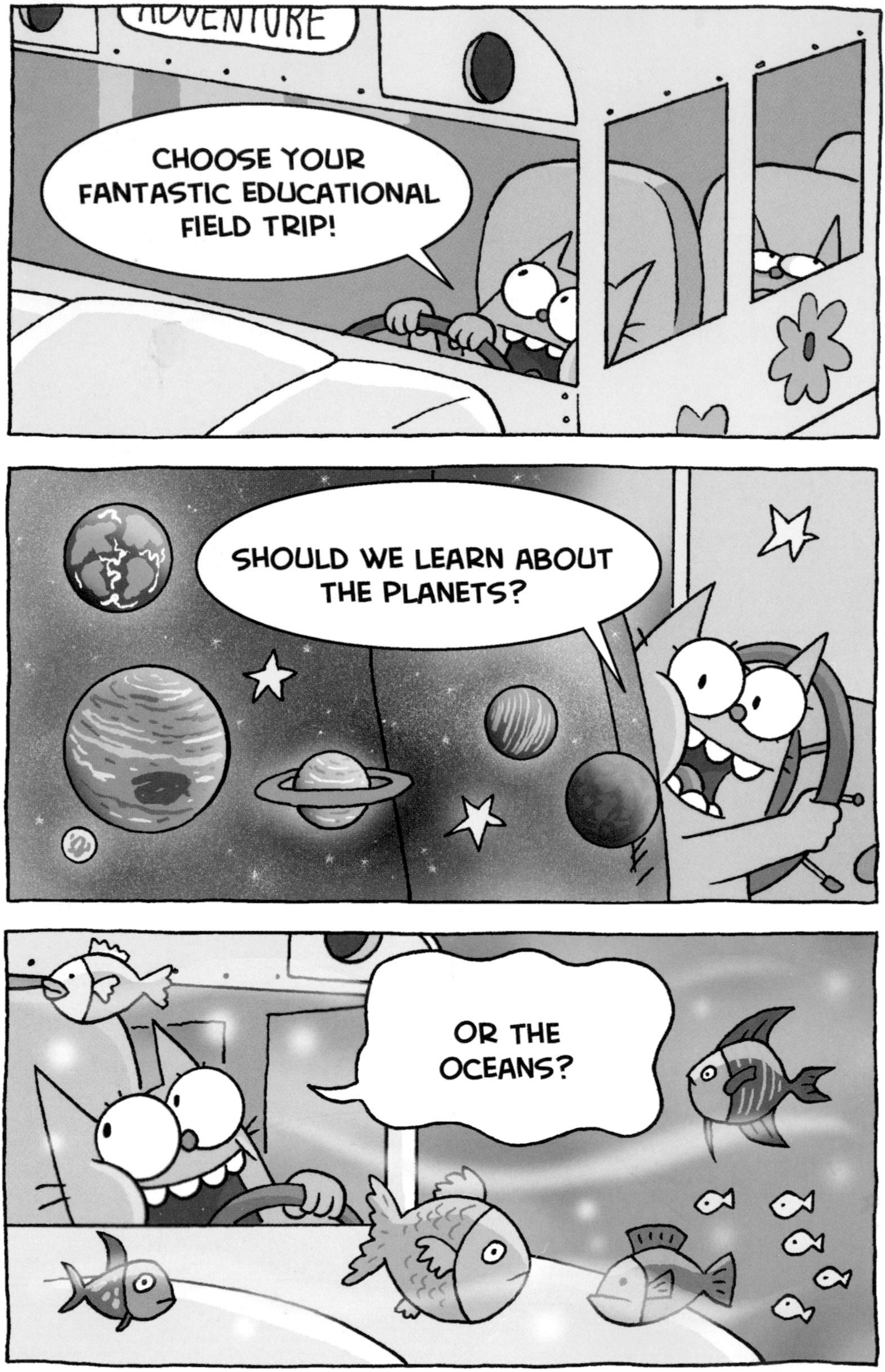
ADVENTURE
CHOOSE YOUR FANTASTIC EDUCATIONAL FIELD TRIP!
SHOULD WE LEARN ABOUT THE PLANETS?
OR THE OCEANS?

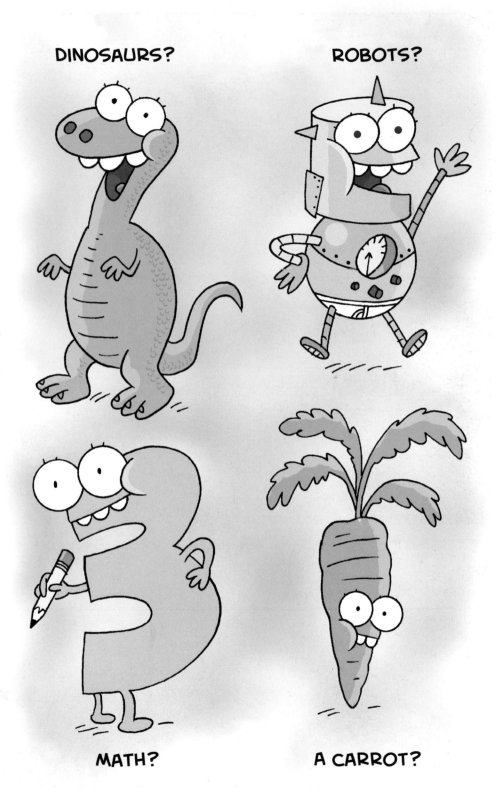

DINOSAURS?

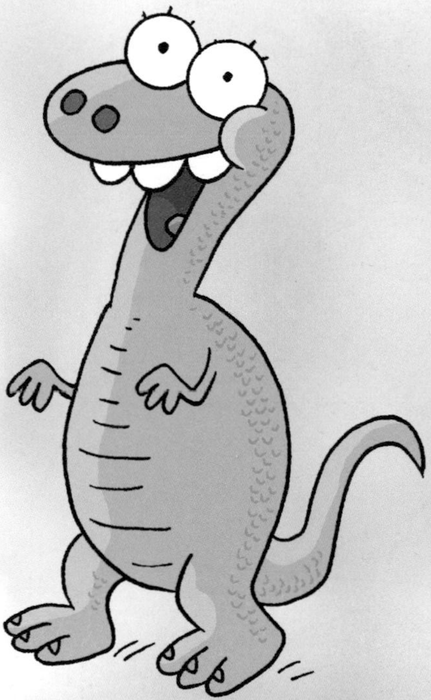

ROBOTS?

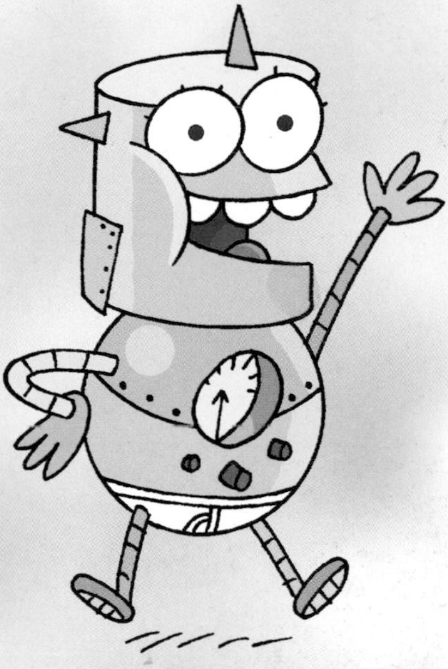

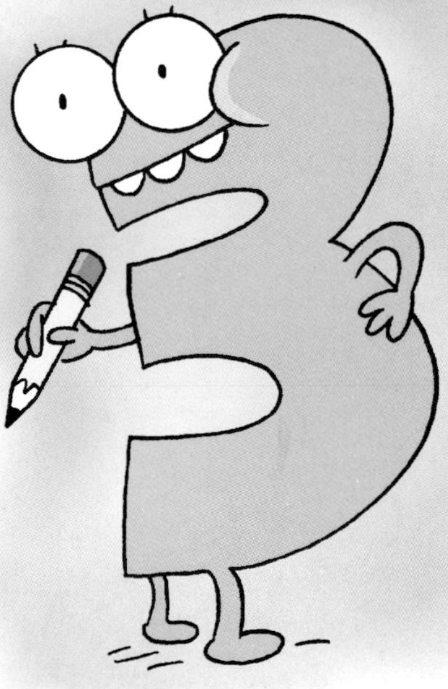

MATH?

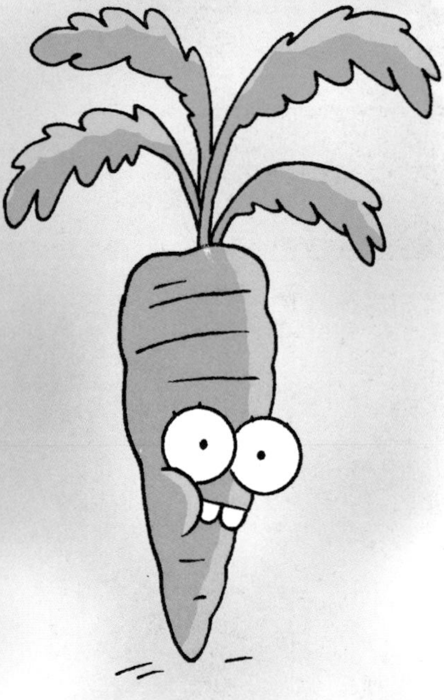

A CARROT?

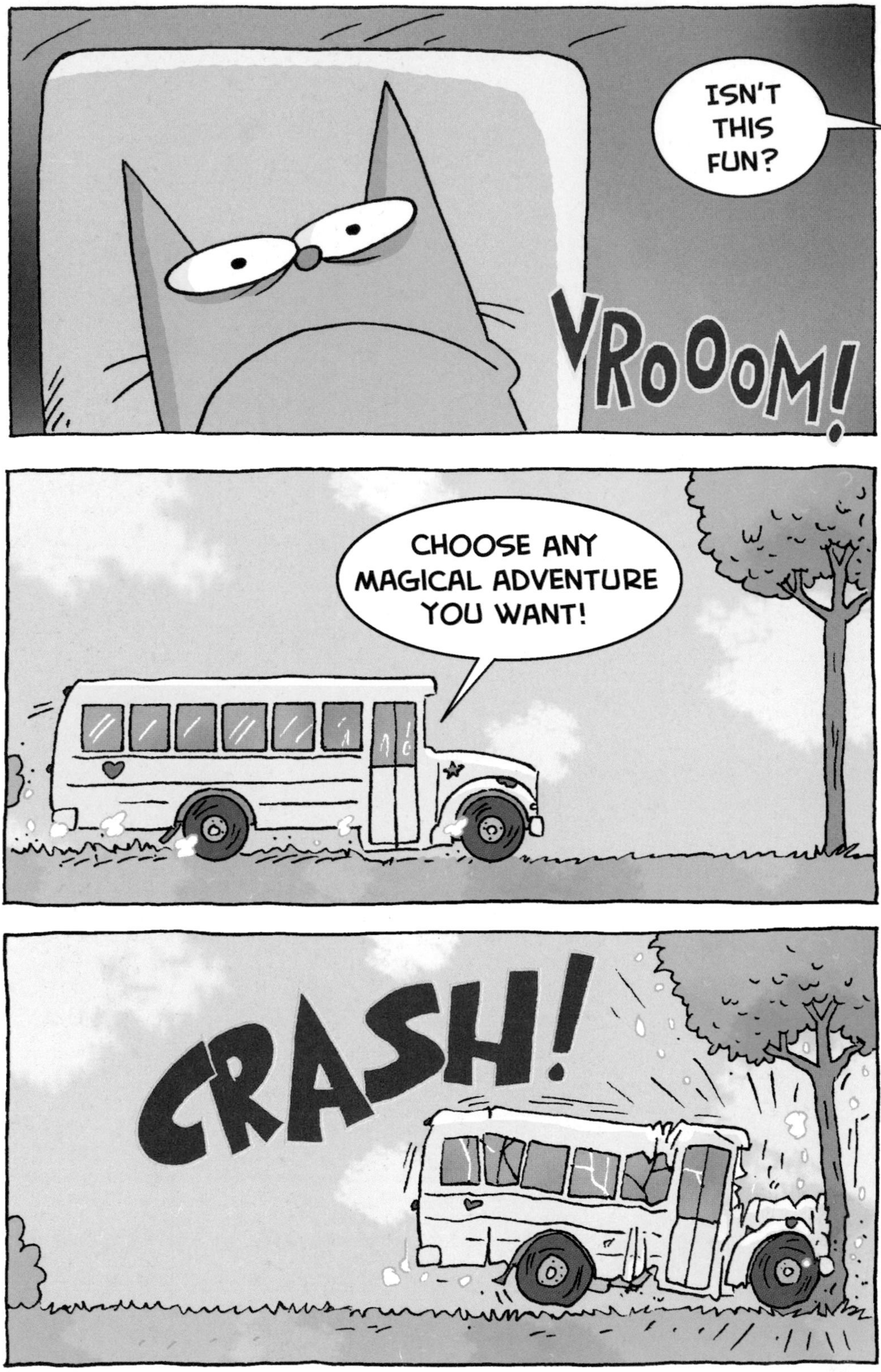
ISN'T THIS FUN?
VROOOOM!
CHOOSE ANY MAGICAL ADVENTURE YOU WANT!
CRASH!

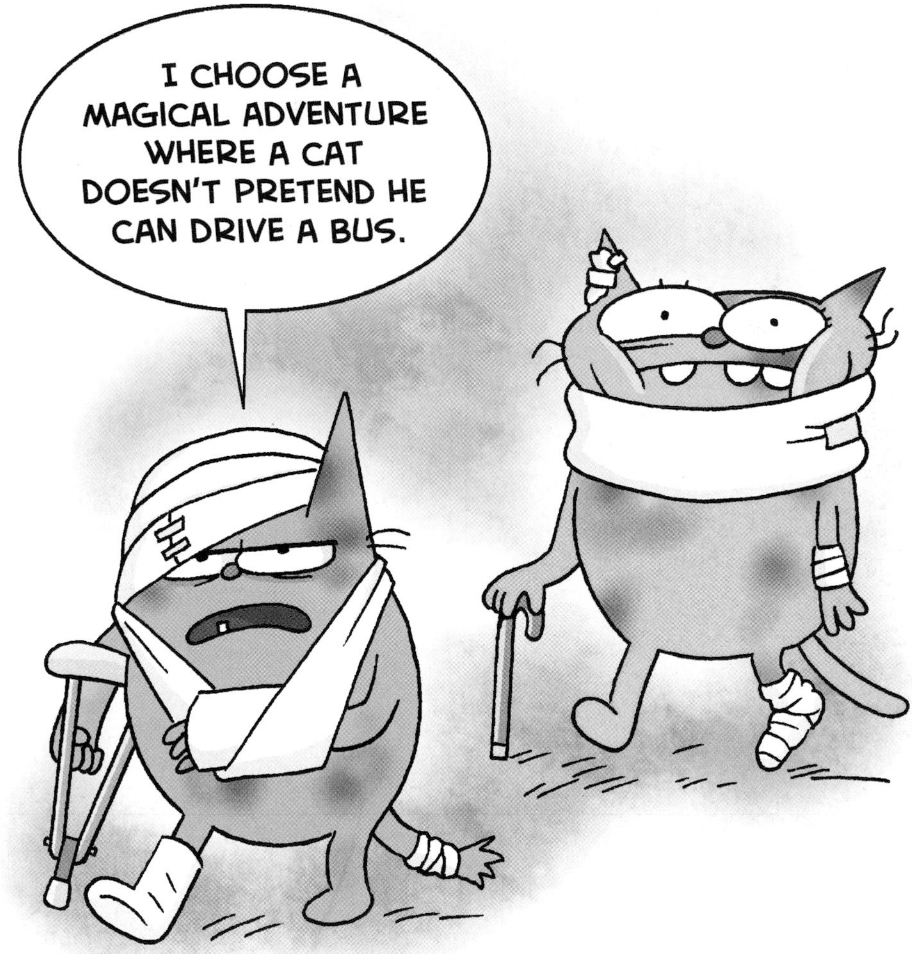
I CHOOSE A MAGICAL ADVENTURE WHERE A CAT DOESN'T PRETEND HE CAN DRIVE A BUS.

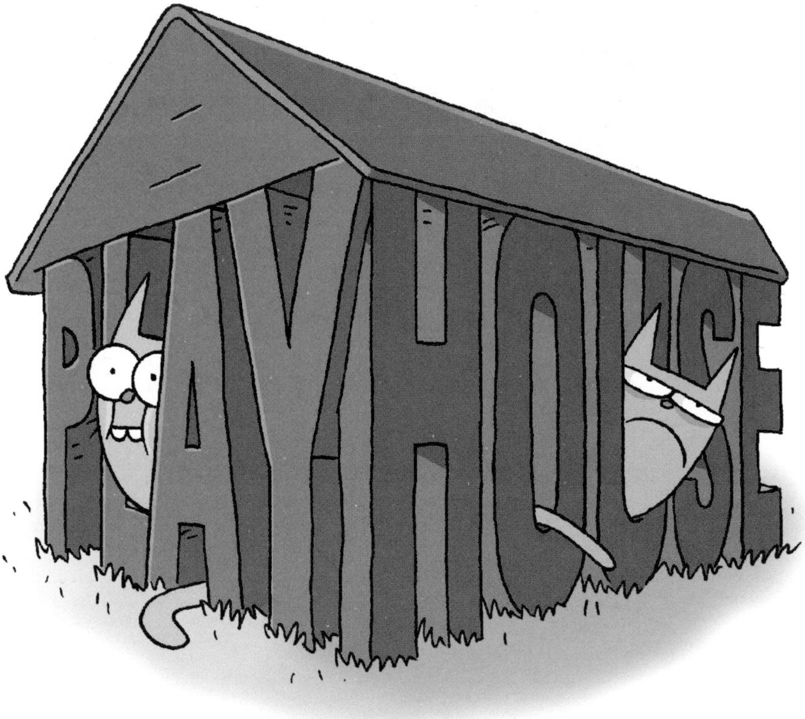
PLAYHOUSE

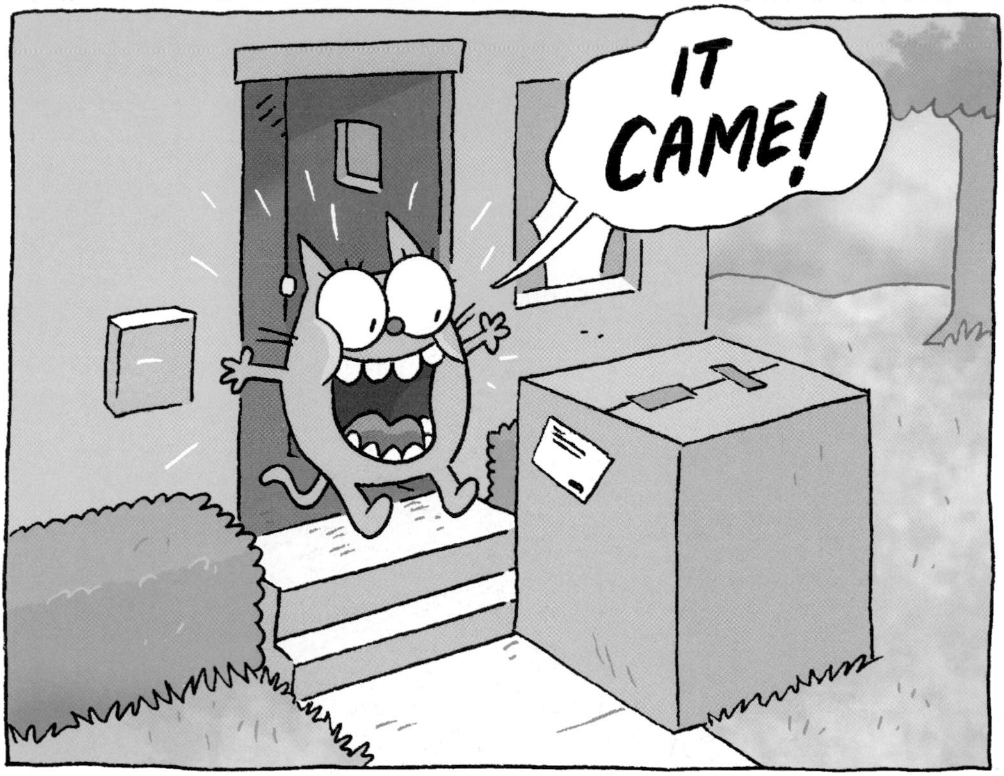
IT CAME!

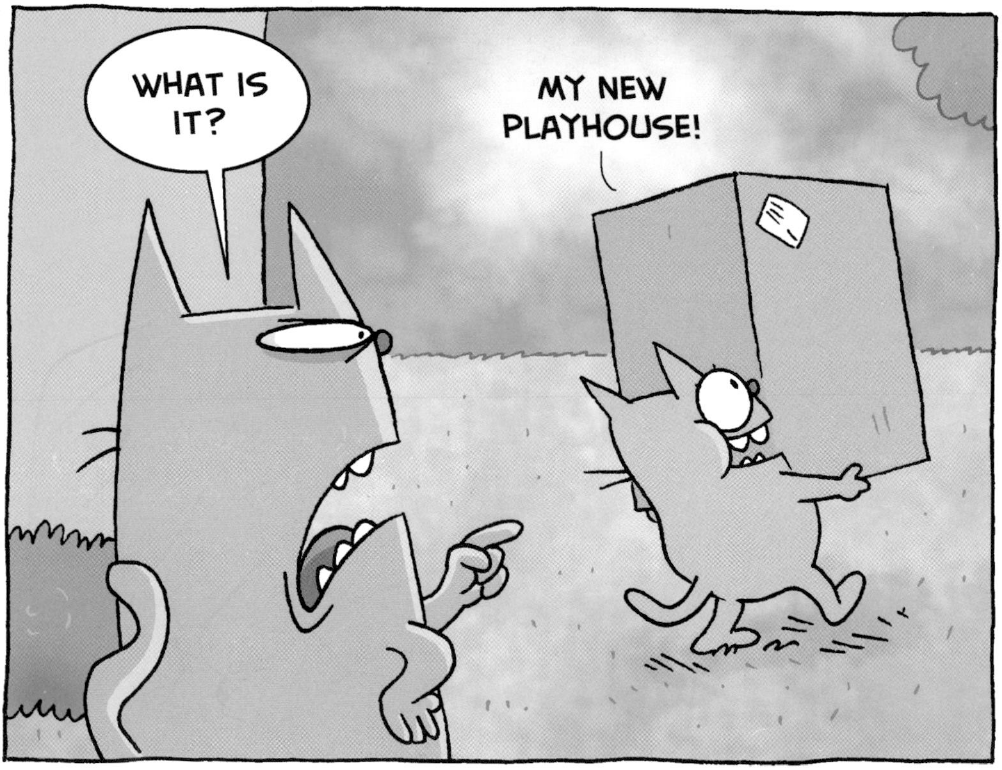
WHAT IS IT?
MY NEW PLAYHOUSE!

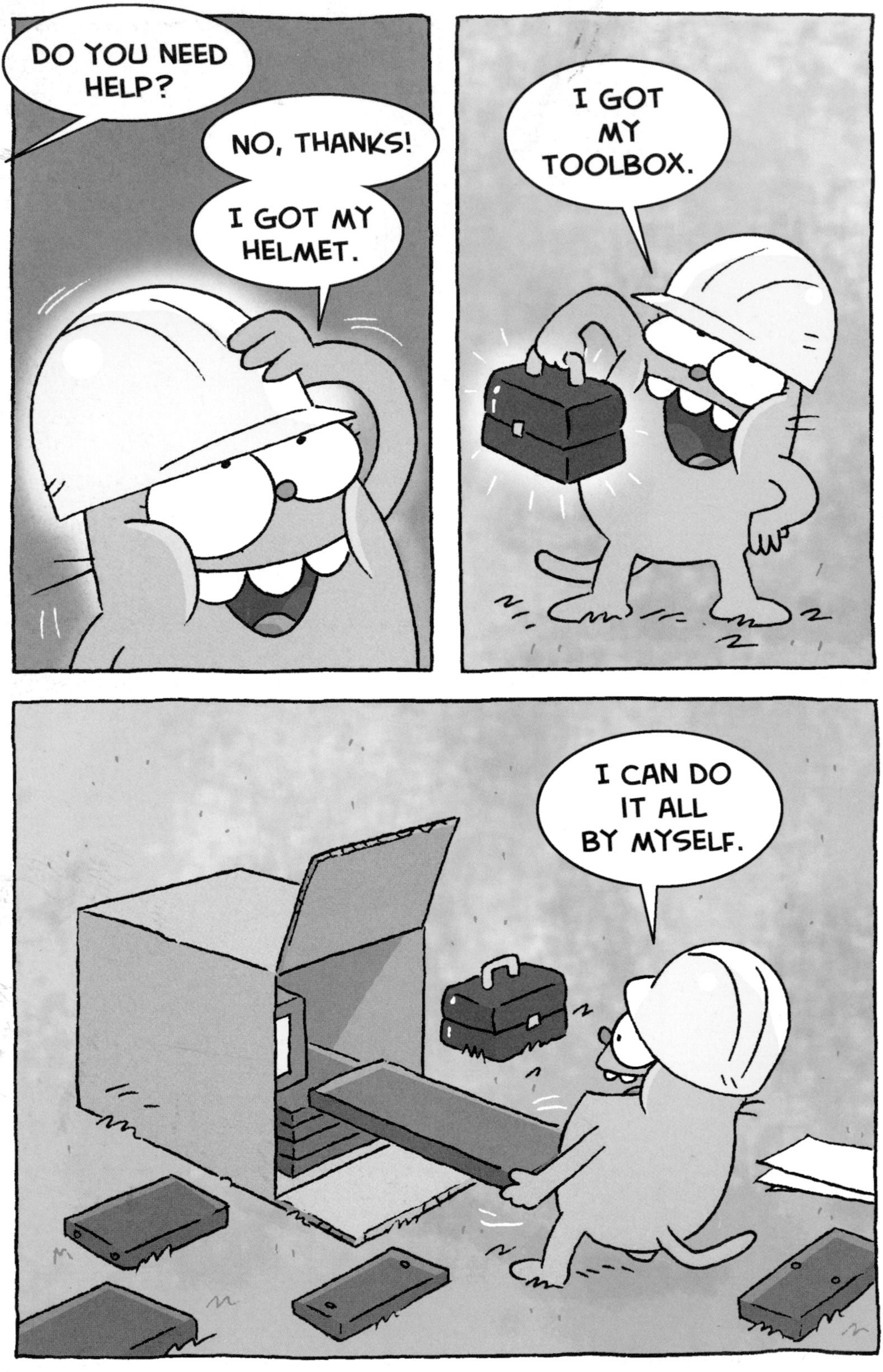
DO YOU NEED HELP?
NO, THANKS!
I GOT MY HELMET.
I GOT MY TOOLBOX.
I CAN DO IT ALL BY MYSELF.

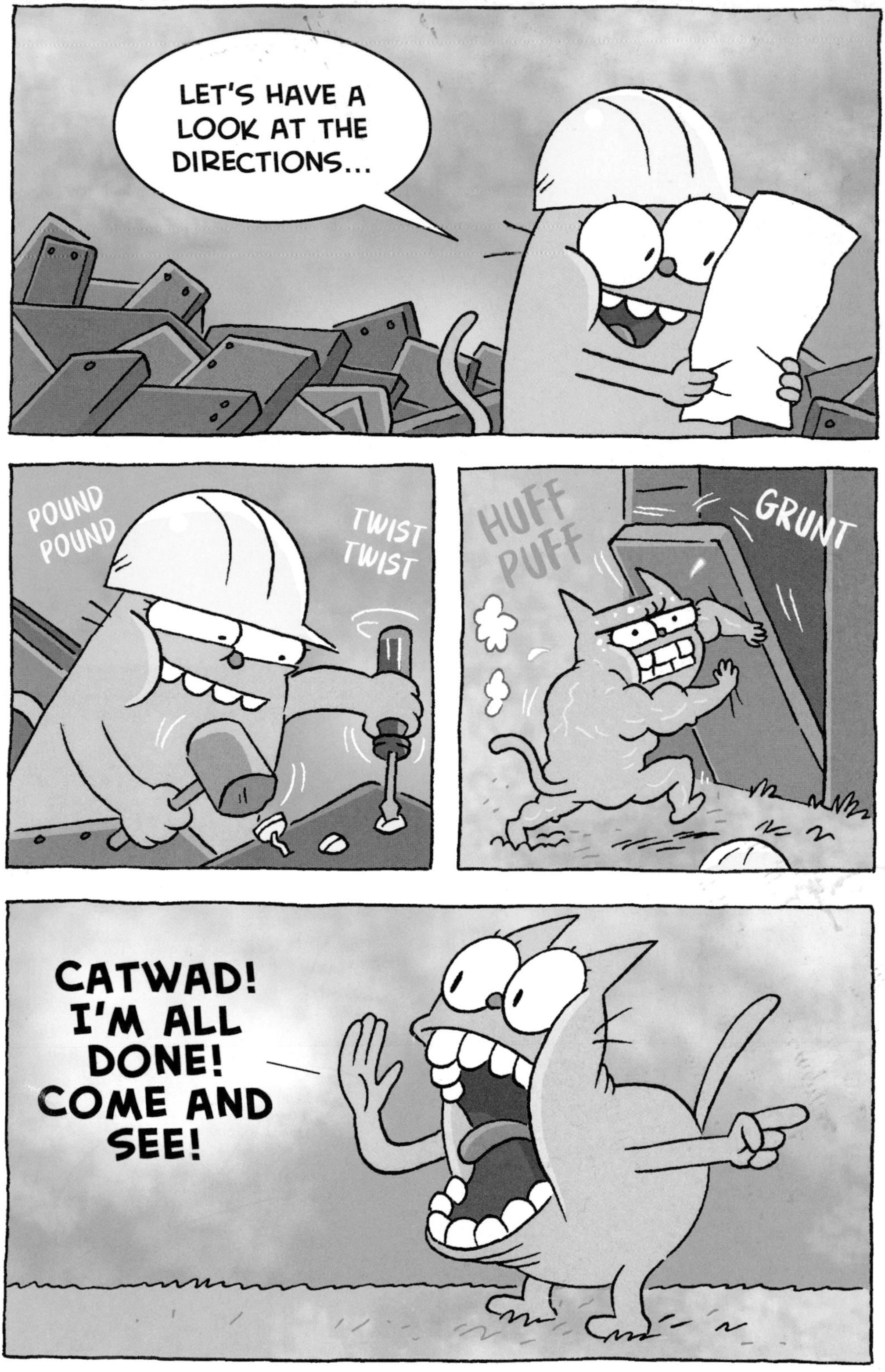
LET'S HAVE A LOOK AT THE DIRECTIONS...
POUND POUND
TWIST TWIST
HUFF PUFF
GRUNT
CATWAD! I'M ALL DONE! COME AND SEE!

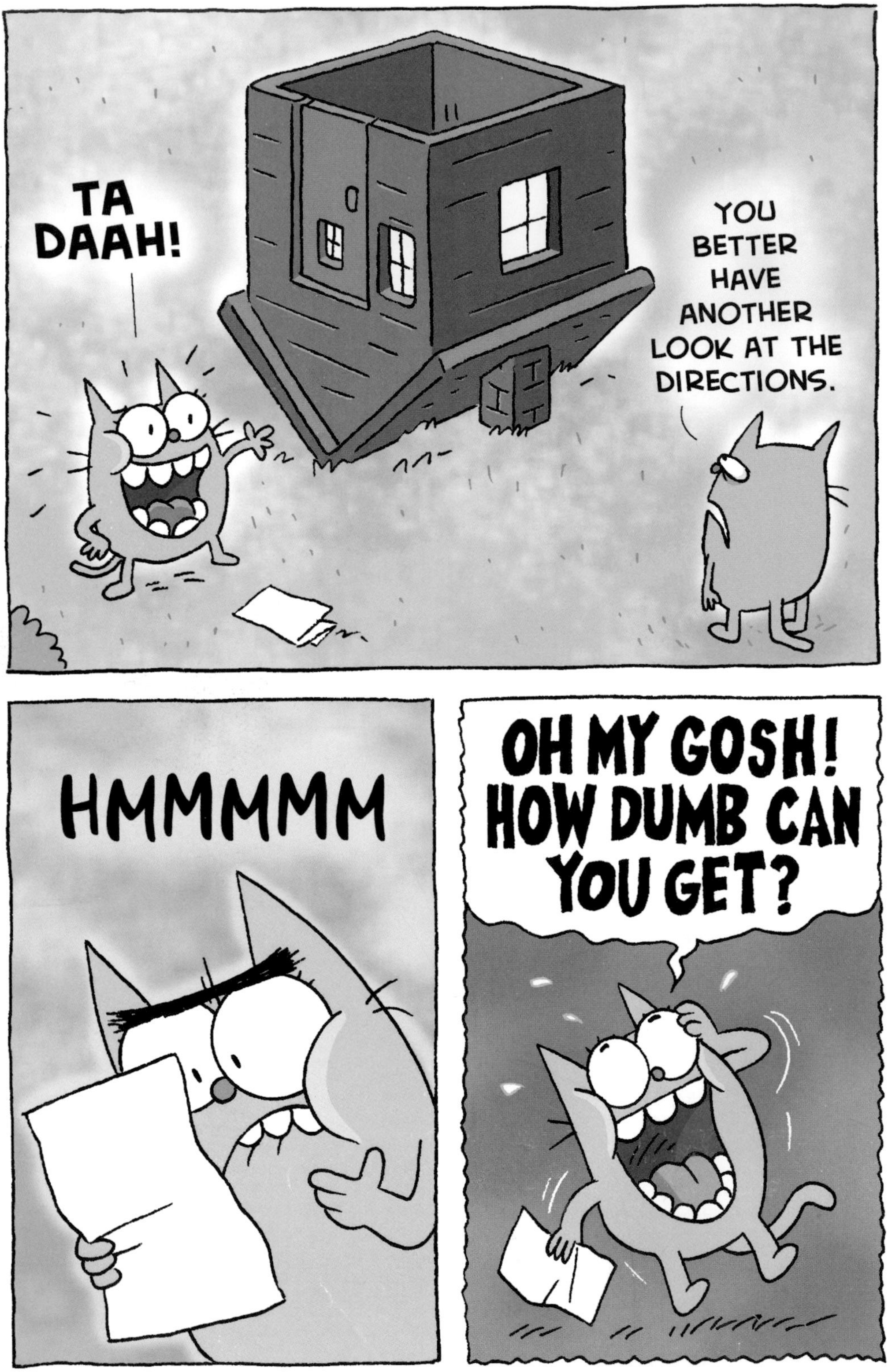
TA DAAH!
YOU BETTER HAVE ANOTHER LOOK AT THE DIRECTIONS.
HMMMMM
OH MY GOSH! HOW DUMB CAN YOU GET?

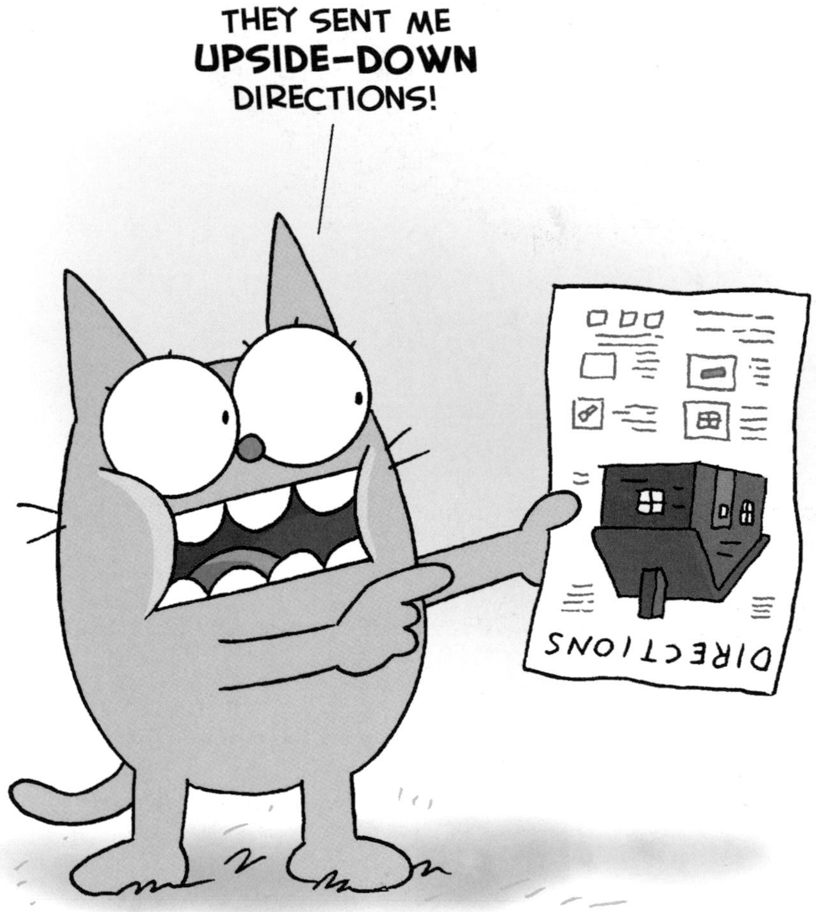
THEY SENT ME **UPSIDE-DOWN** DIRECTIONS!
DIRECTIONS

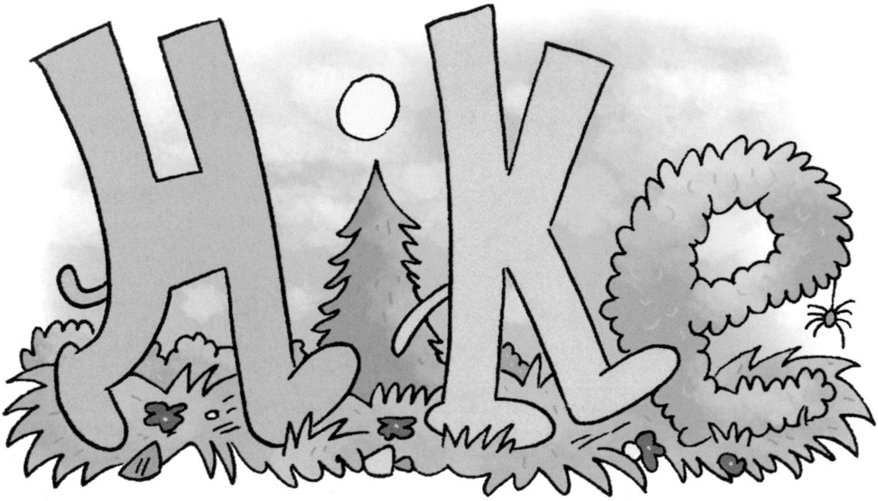
HiKe

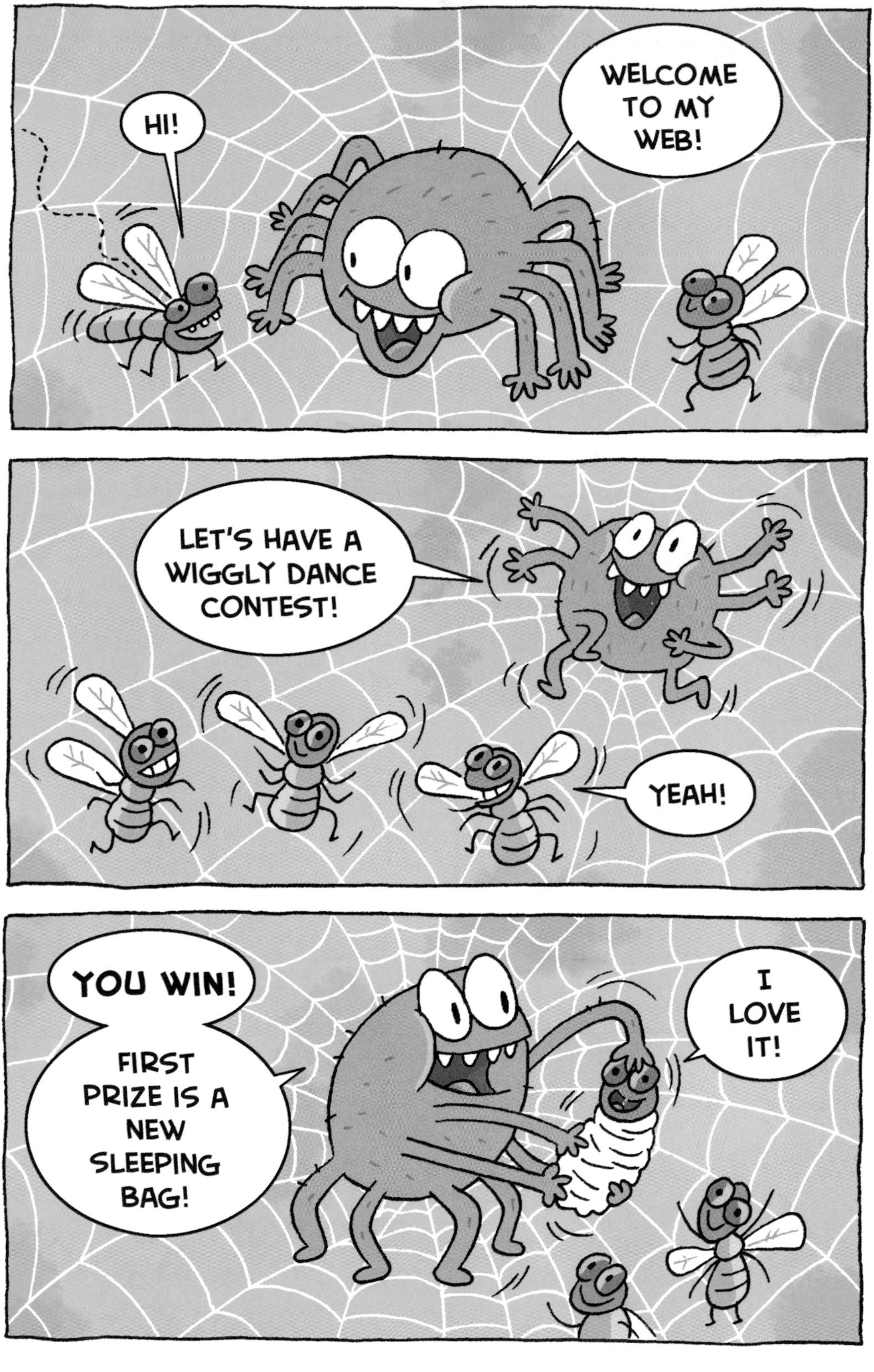
HI!
WELCOME TO MY WEB!
LET'S HAVE A WIGGLY DANCE CONTEST!
YEAH!
YOU WIN!
FIRST PRIZE IS A NEW SLEEPING BAG!
I LOVE IT!

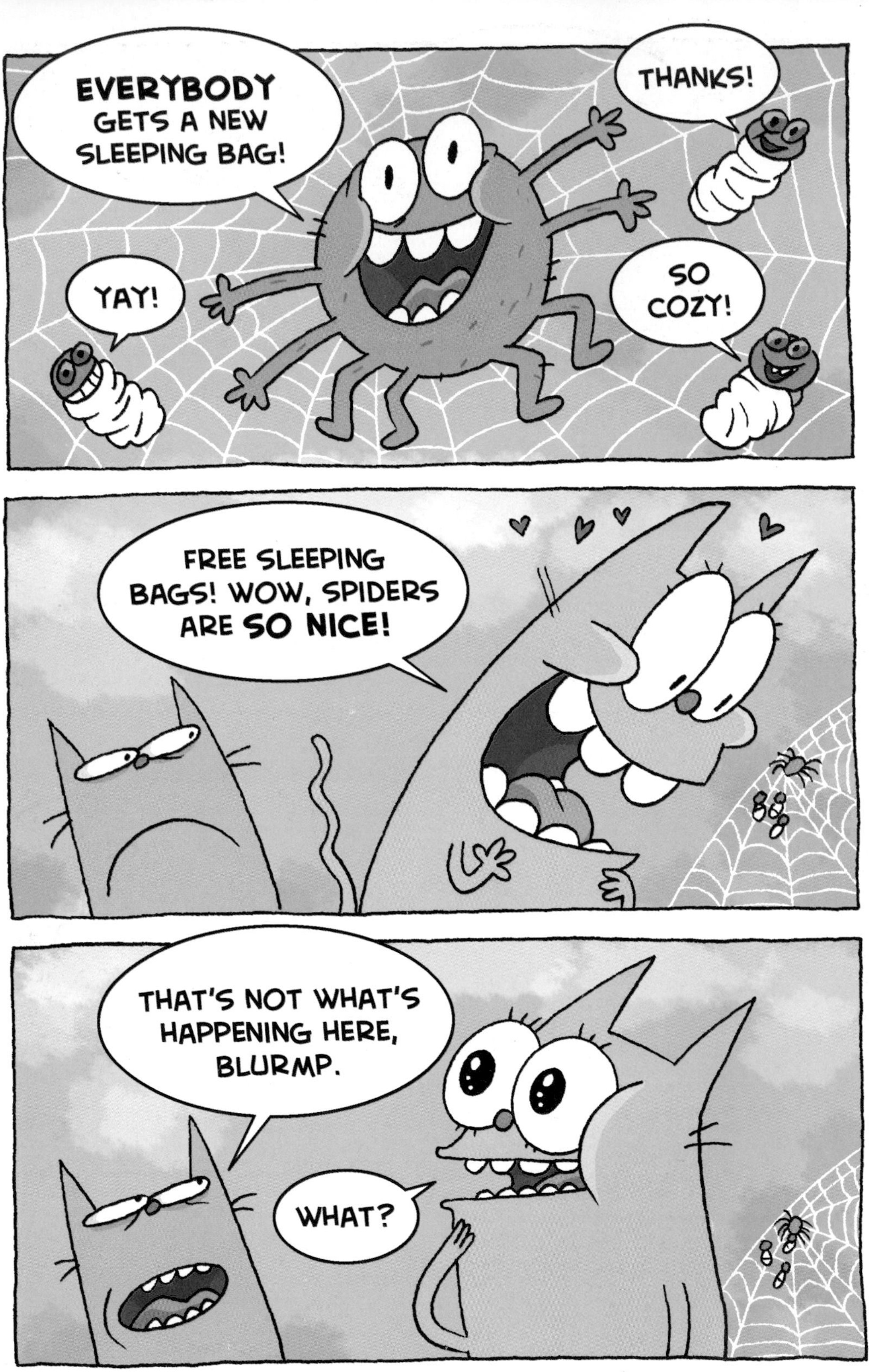
EVERYBODY GETS A NEW SLEEPING BAG!
THANKS!
YAY!
SO COZY!
FREE SLEEPING BAGS! WOW, SPIDERS ARE **SO NICE!**
THAT'S NOT WHAT'S HAPPENING HERE, BLURMP.
WHAT?

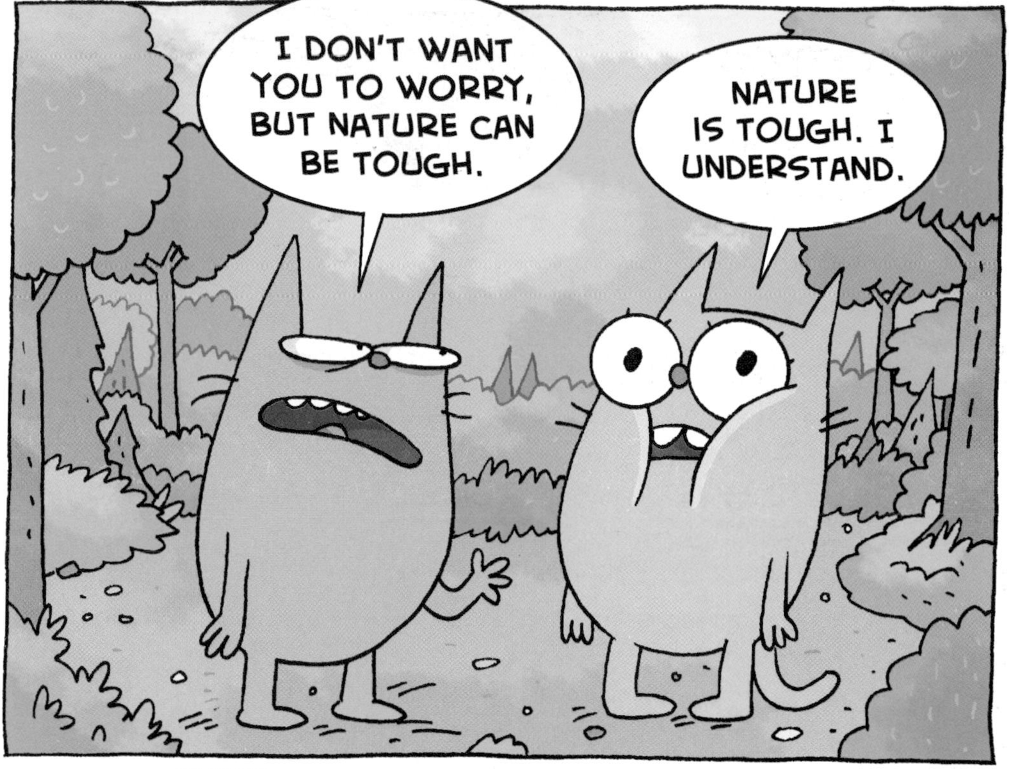
I DON'T WANT YOU TO WORRY, BUT NATURE CAN BE TOUGH.
NATURE IS TOUGH. I UNDERSTAND.

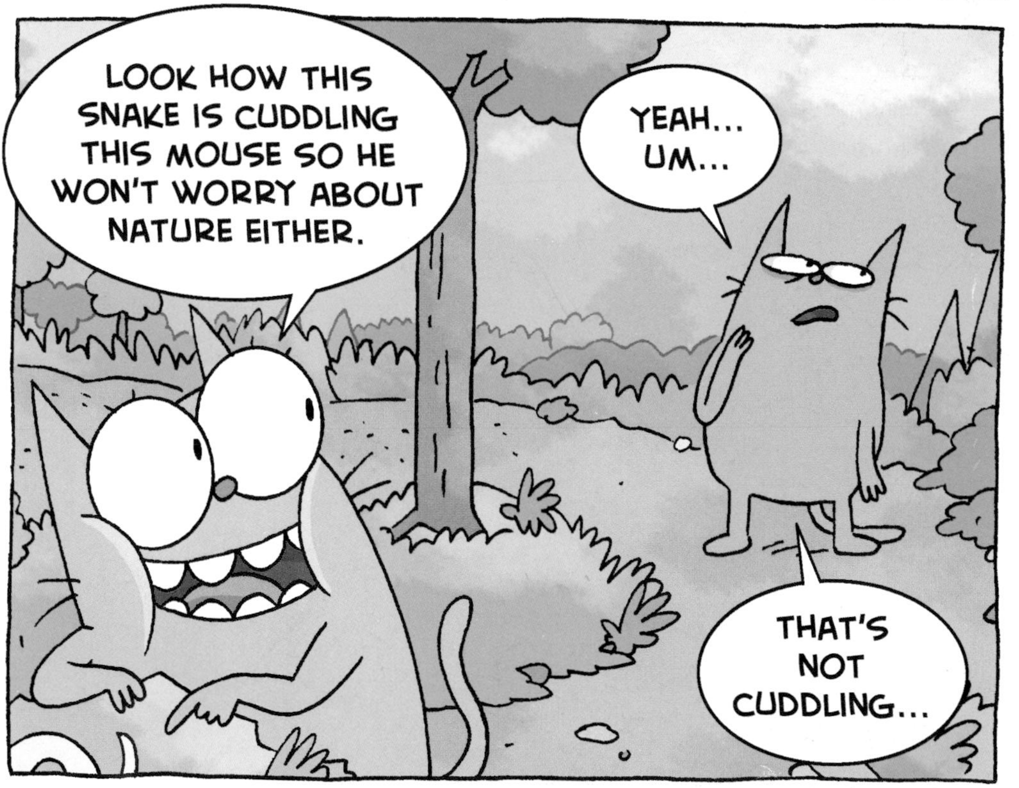
LOOK HOW THIS SNAKE IS CUDDLING THIS MOUSE SO HE WON'T WORRY ABOUT NATURE EITHER.
YEAH... UM...
THAT'S NOT CUDDLING...

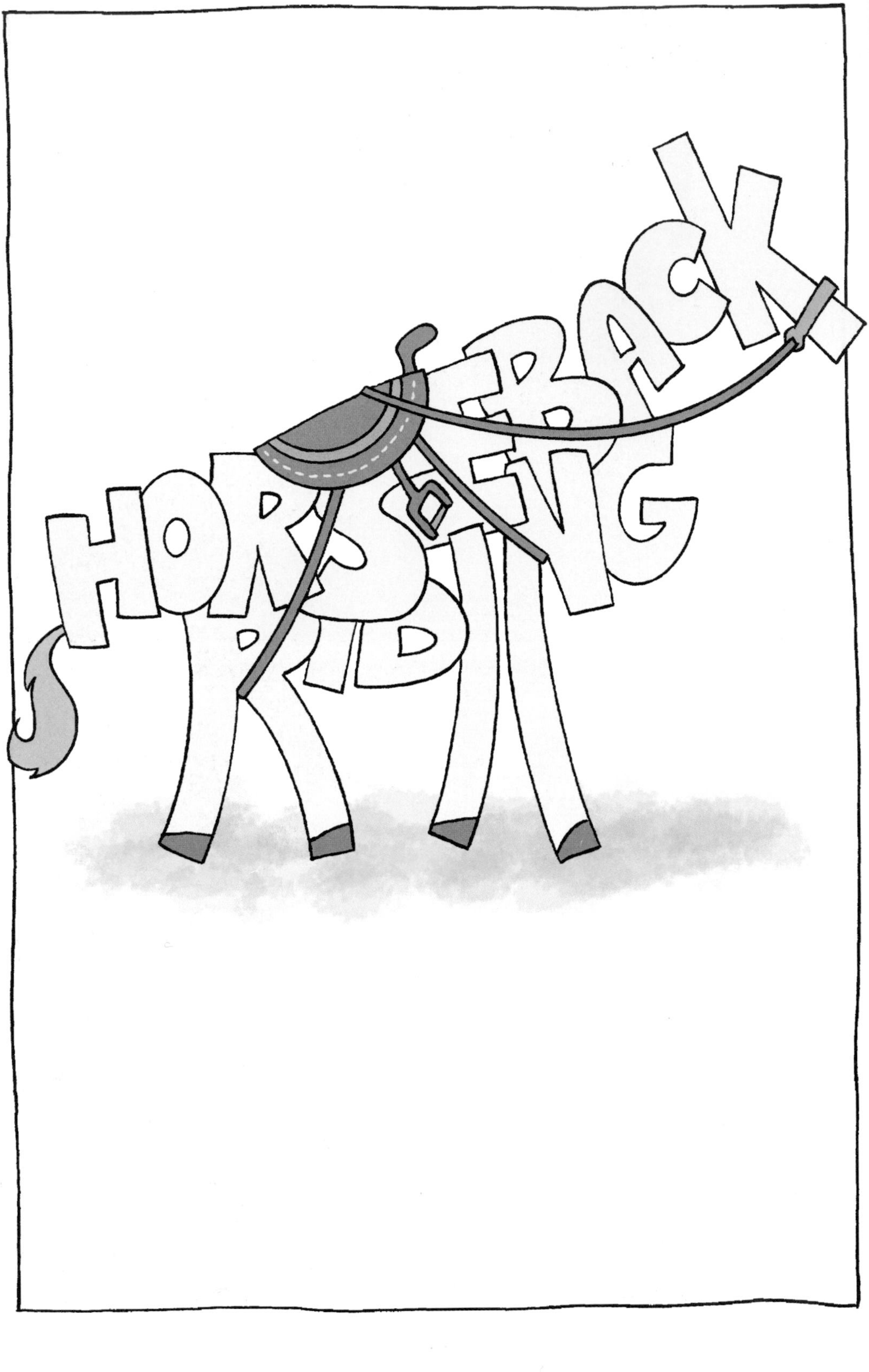
HORSEBACK
RIDING

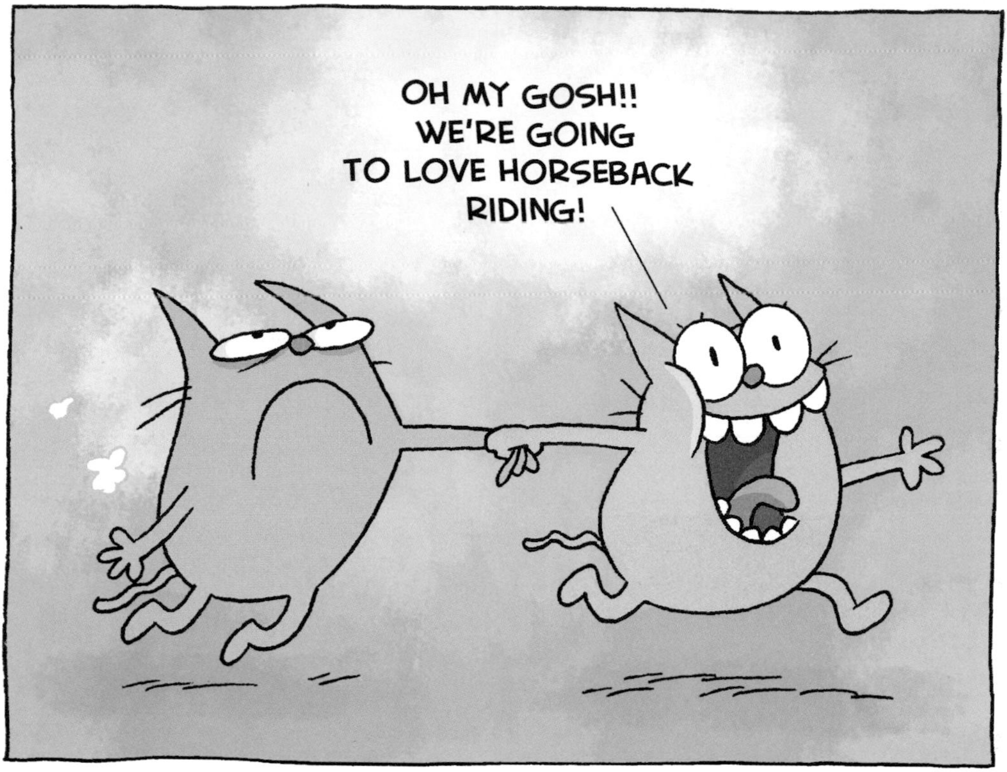
OH MY GOSH!! WE'RE GOING TO LOVE HORSEBACK RIDING!

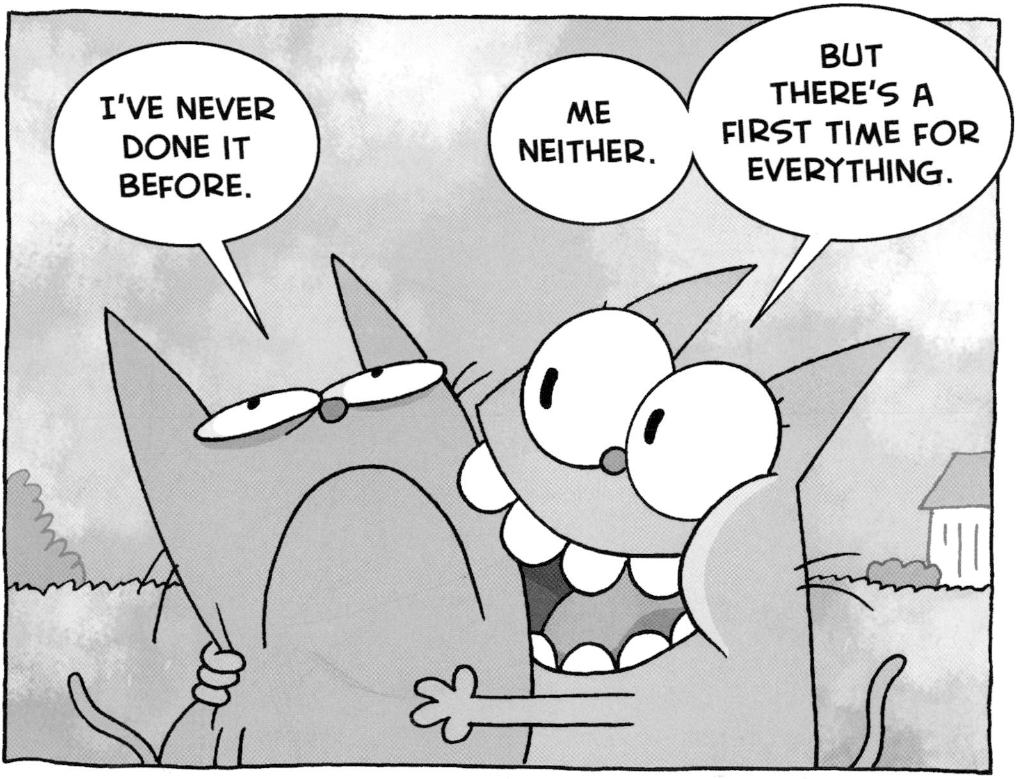
I'VE NEVER DONE IT BEFORE.
ME NEITHER.
BUT THERE'S A FIRST TIME FOR EVERYTHING.

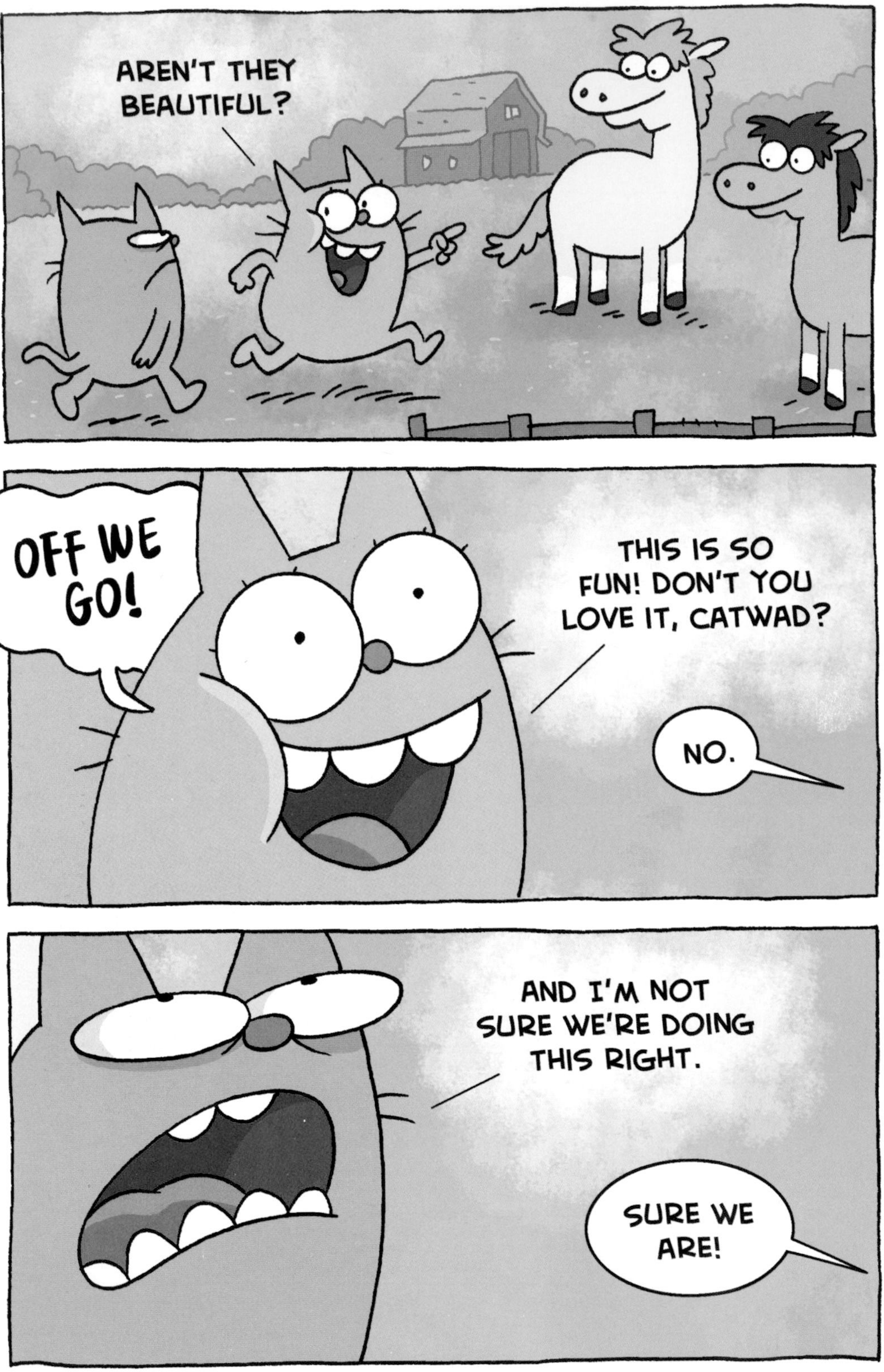
AREN'T THEY BEAUTIFUL?
OFF WE GO!
THIS IS SO FUN! DON'T YOU LOVE IT, CATWAD?
NO.
AND I'M NOT SURE WE'RE DOING THIS RIGHT.
SURE WE ARE!

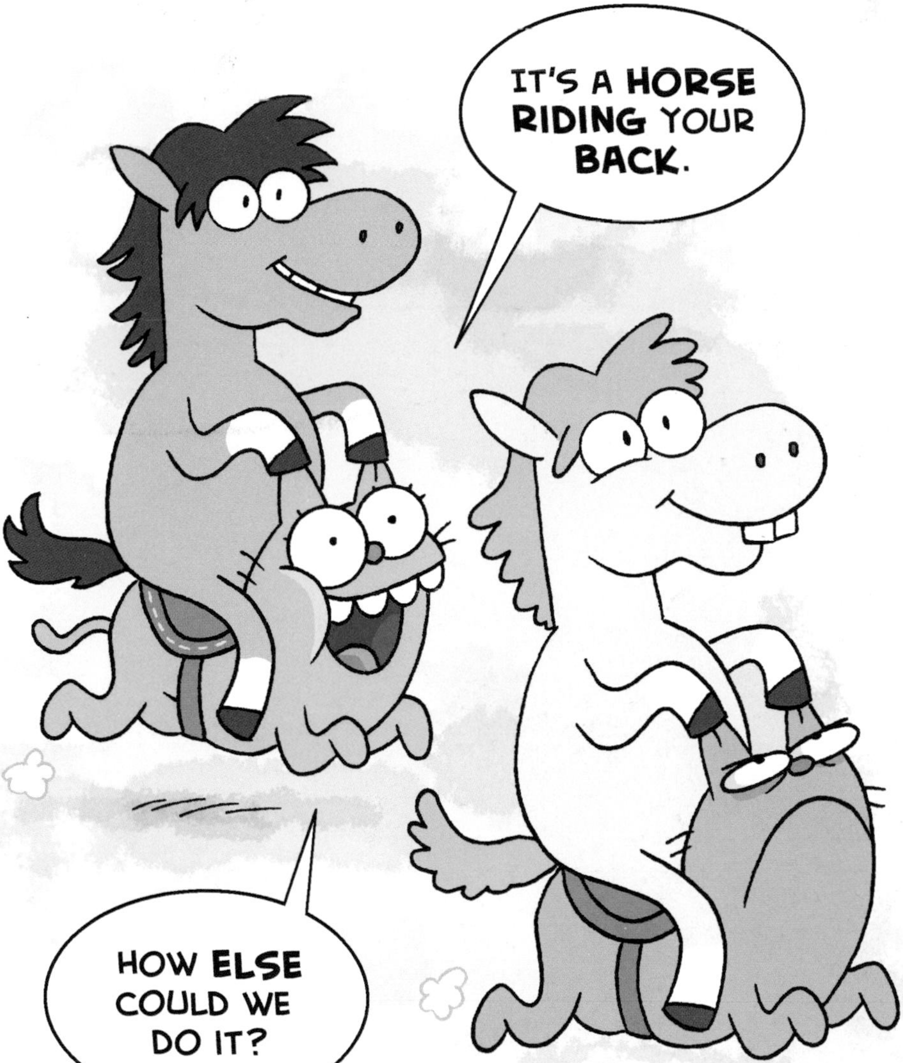
IT'S A HORSE RIDING YOUR BACK.
HOW ELSE COULD WE DO IT?

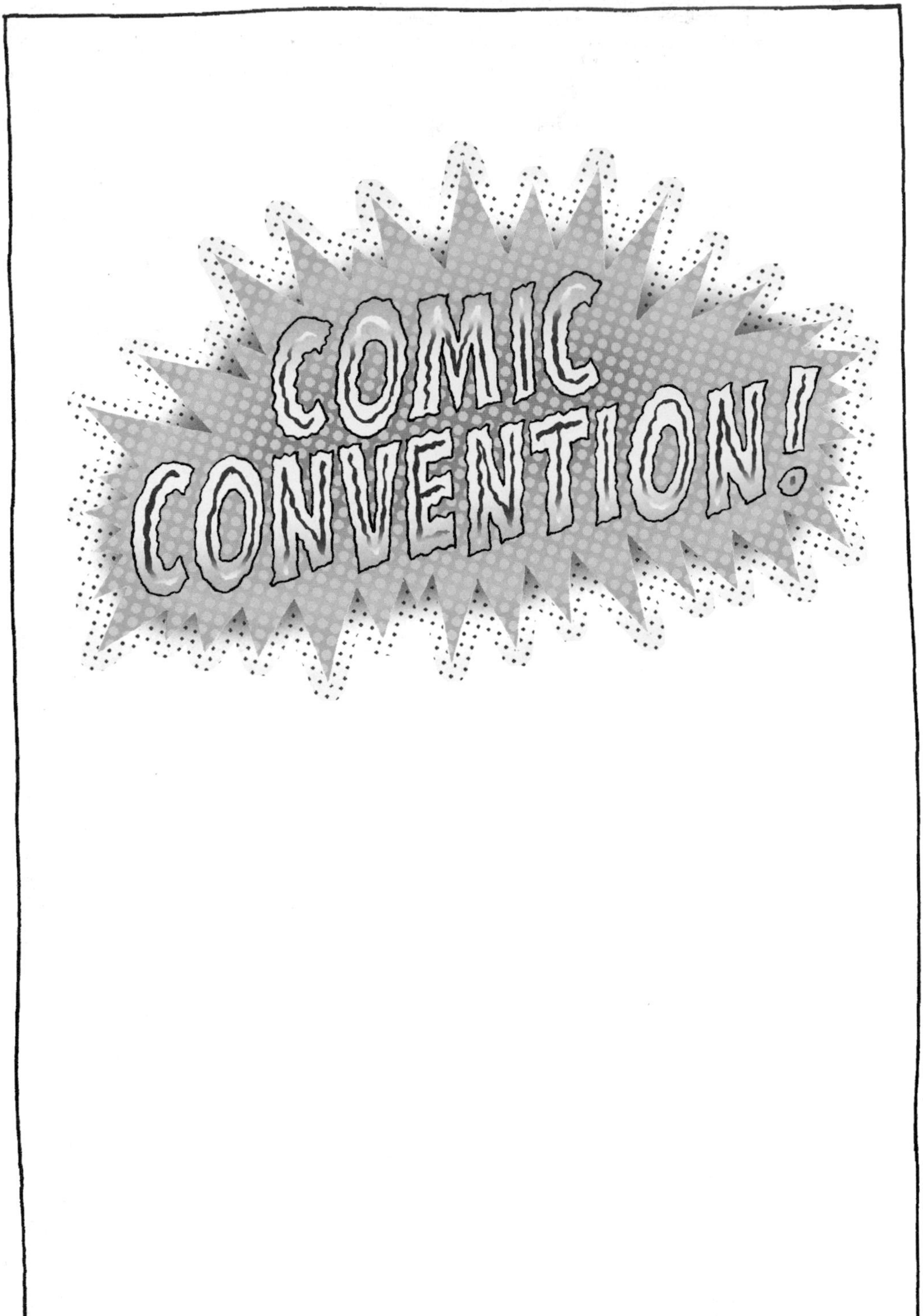
COMIC CONVENTION!

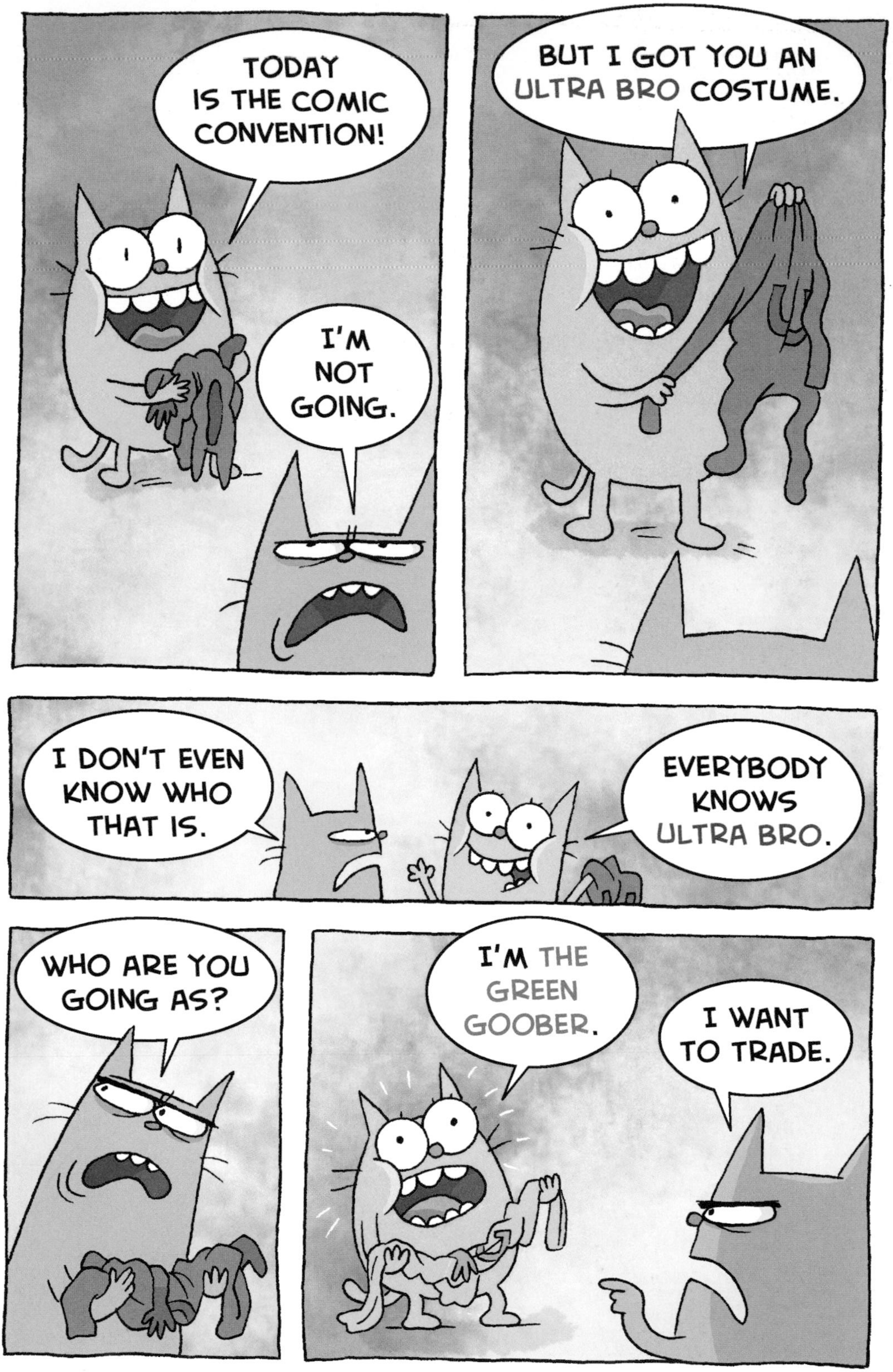
TODAY IS THE COMIC CONVENTION!
I'M NOT GOING.
BUT I GOT YOU AN ULTRA BRO COSTUME.
I DON'T EVEN KNOW WHO THAT IS.
EVERYBODY KNOWS ULTRA BRO.
WHO ARE YOU GOING AS?
I'M THE GREEN GOOBER.
I WANT TO TRADE.

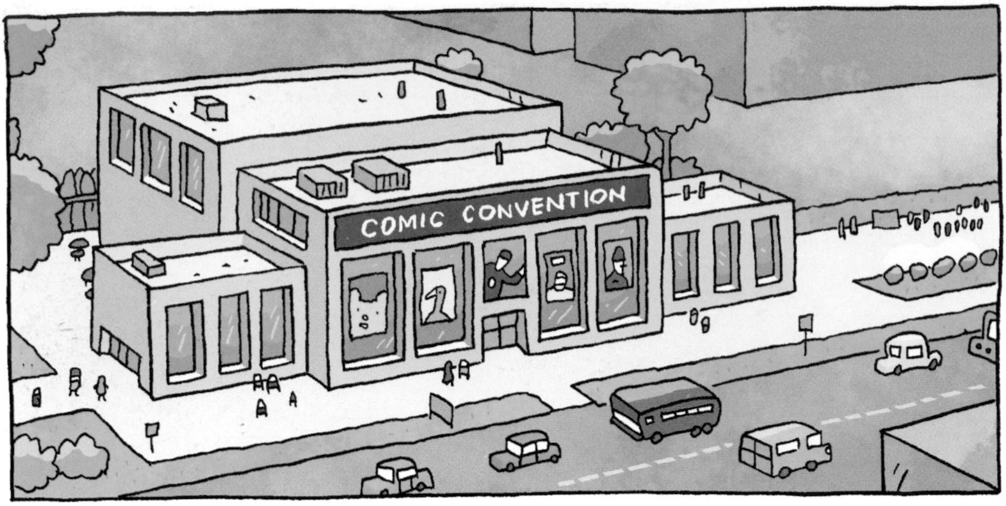
COMIC CONVENTION

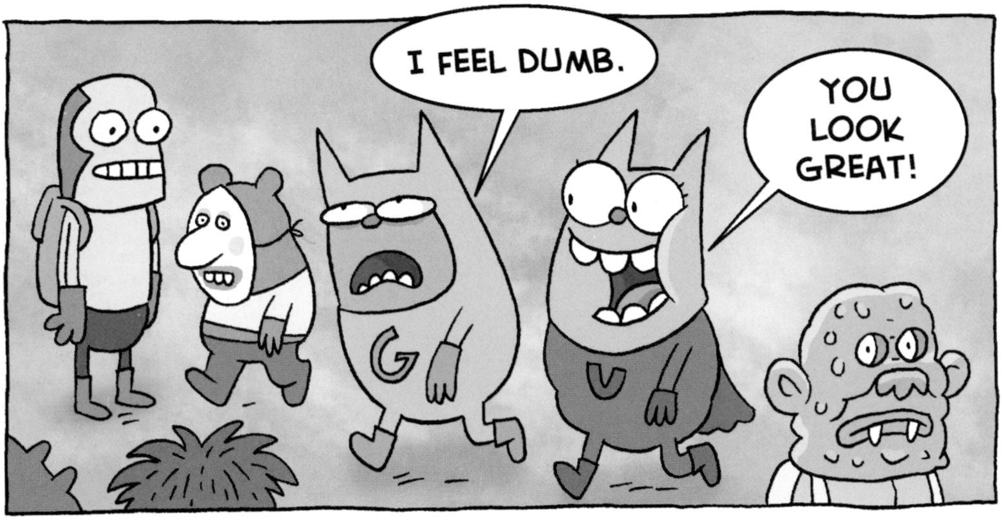
I FEEL DUMB.
YOU LOOK GREAT!

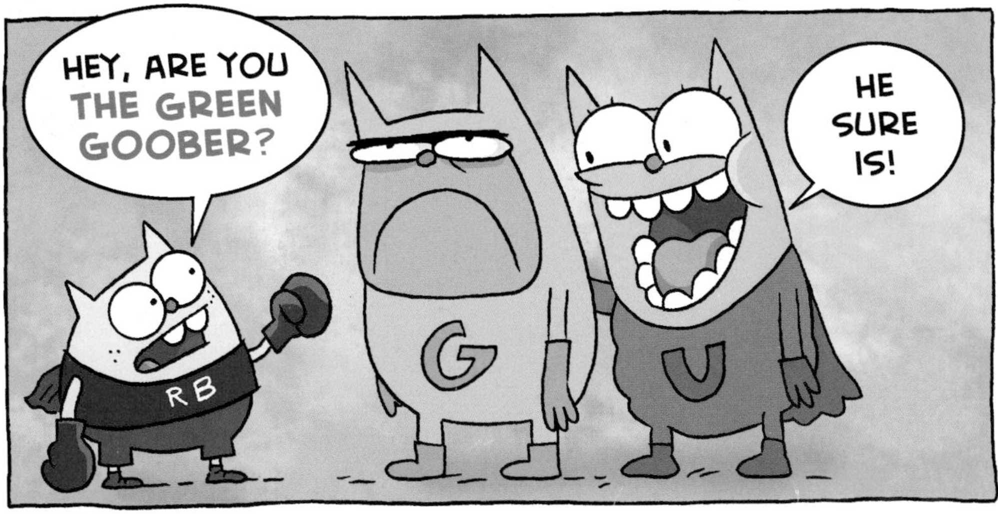
HEY, ARE YOU THE GREEN GOOBER?
HE SURE IS!
RB

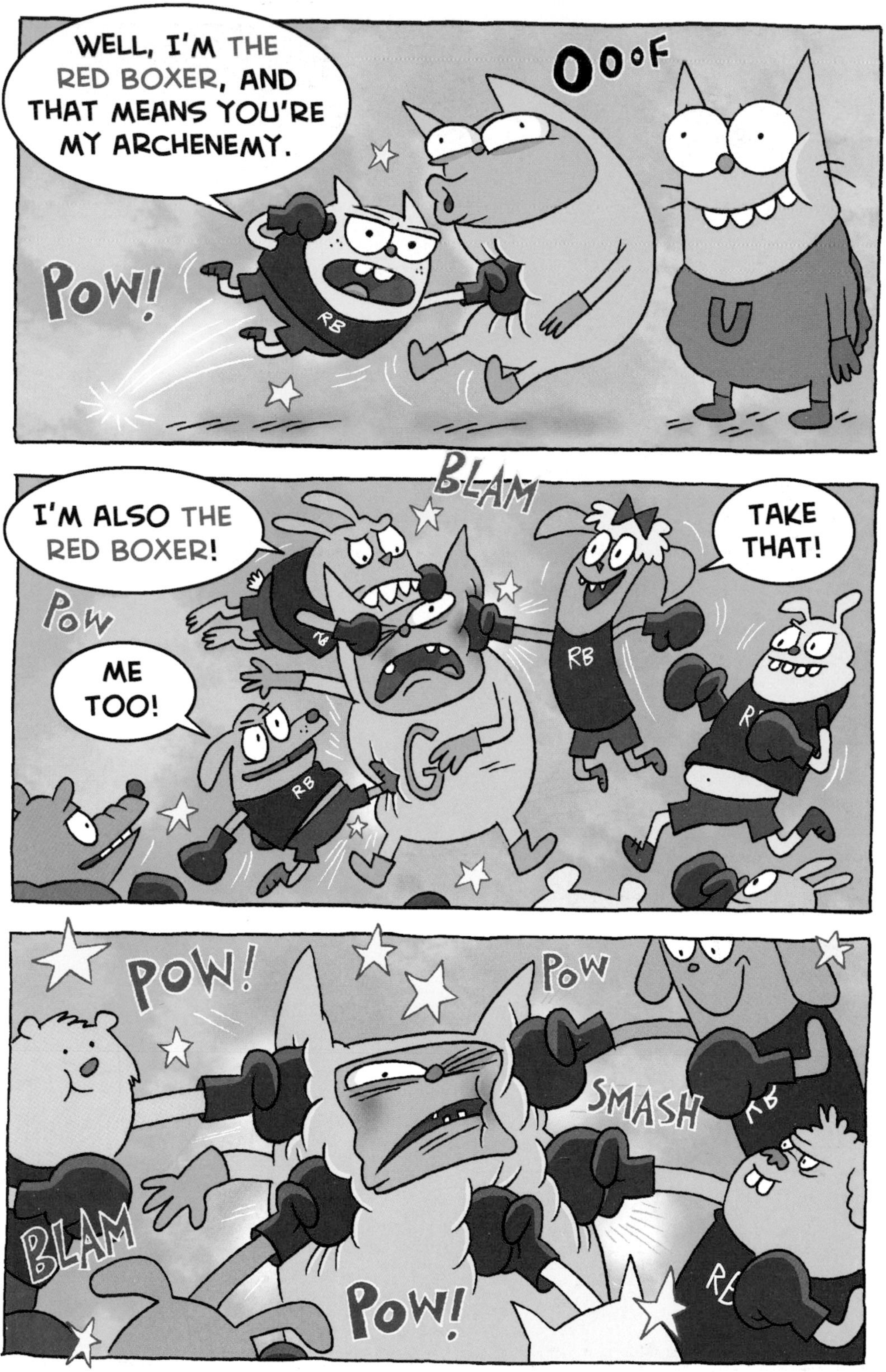
WELL, I'M THE RED BOXER, AND THAT MEANS YOU'RE MY ARCHENEMY.
OOOF
POW!
U
RB
BLAM
I'M ALSO THE RED BOXER!
TAKE THAT!
POW
ME TOO!
RB
RB
RB
G
POW!
POW
SMASH
BLAM
POW!

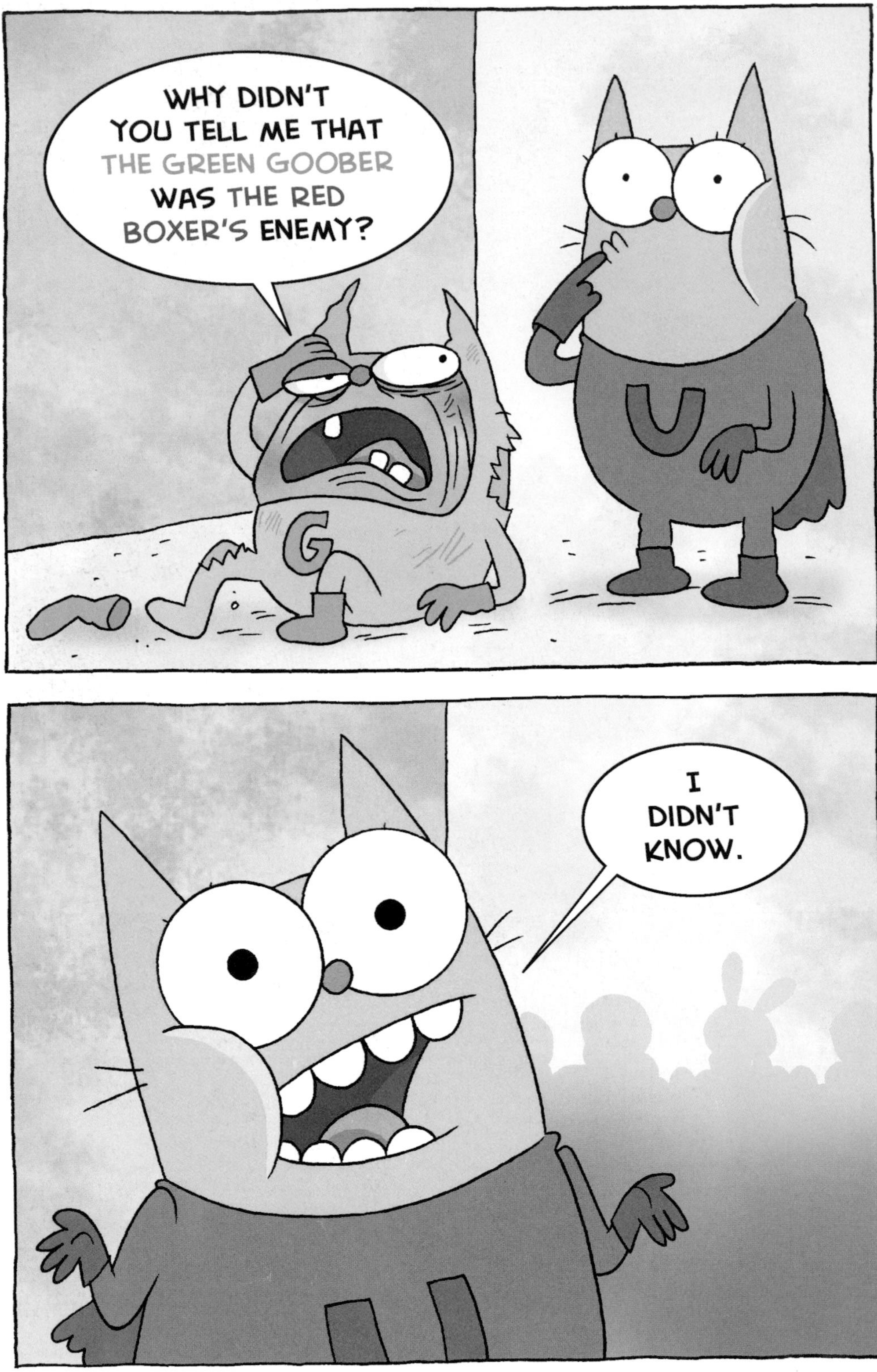
WHY DIDN'T YOU TELL ME THAT THE GREEN GOOBER WAS THE RED BOXER'S ENEMY?
I DIDN'T KNOW.

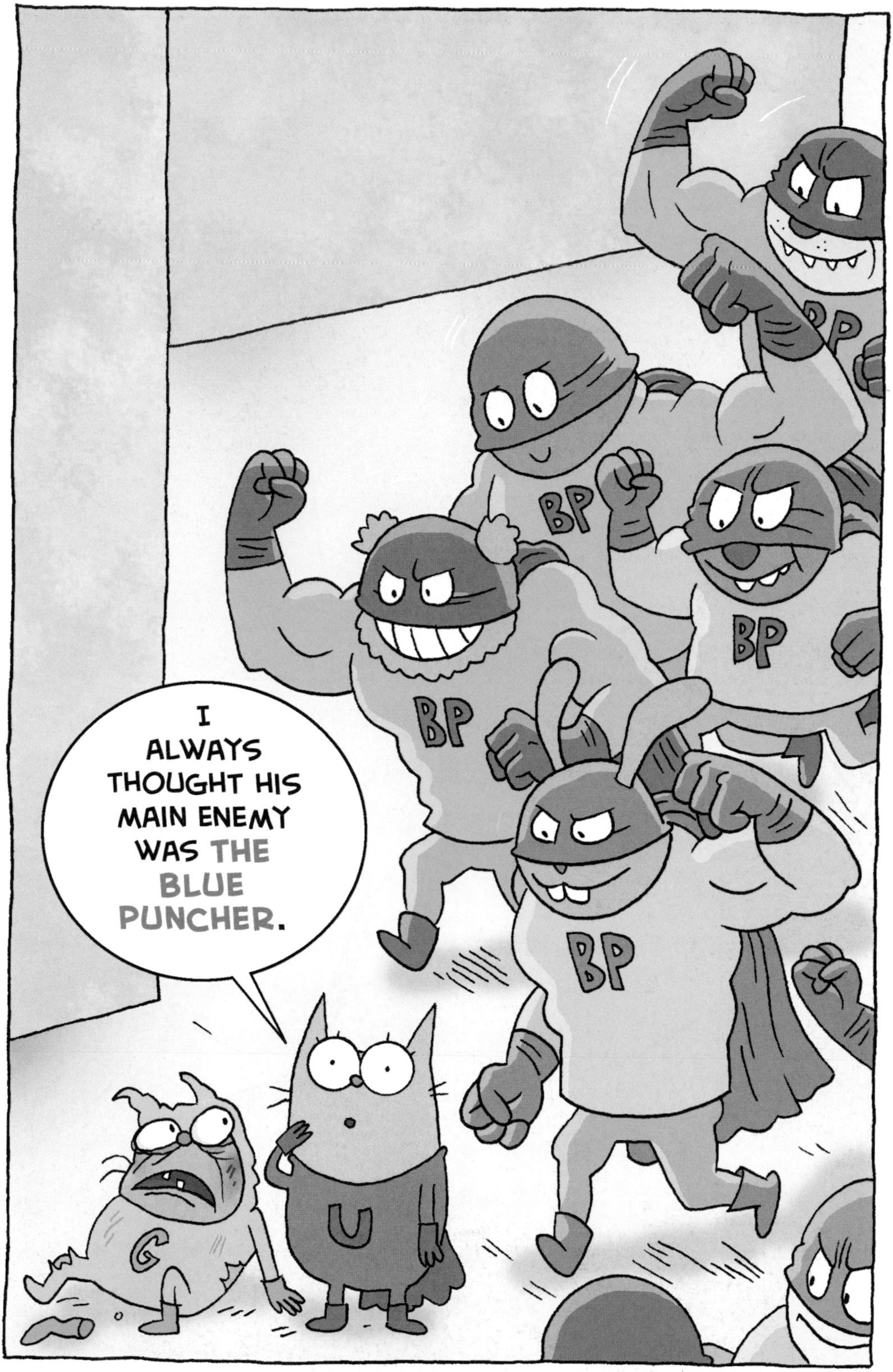
I ALWAYS THOUGHT HIS MAIN ENEMY WAS THE BLUE PUNCHER.
BP
BP
BP
BP
BP
BP
G
U

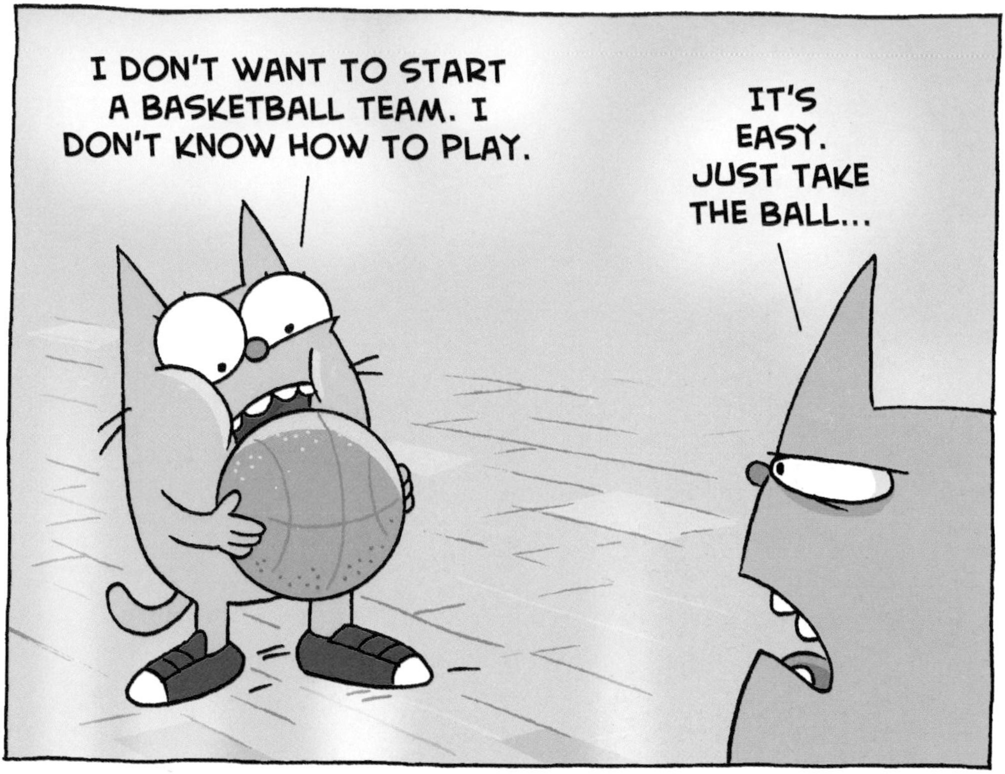
I DON'T WANT TO START A BASKETBALL TEAM. I DON'T KNOW HOW TO PLAY.
IT'S EASY. JUST TAKE THE BALL...

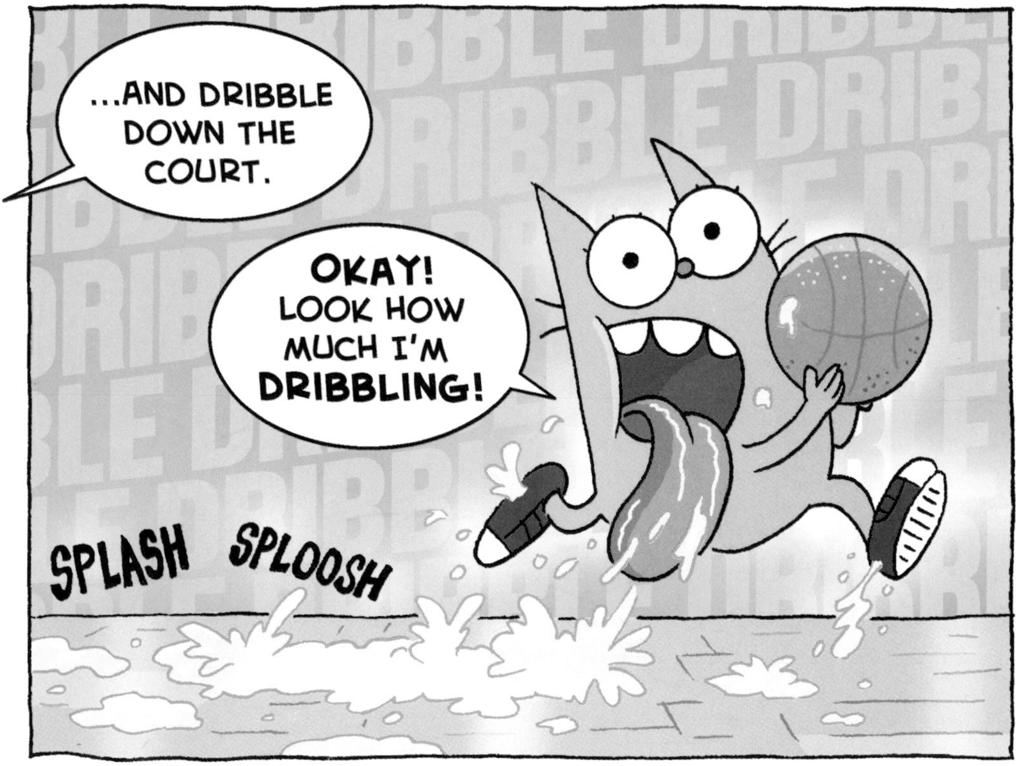
DRIBBLE DRIBBLE DRIBBLE
...AND DRIBBLE DOWN THE COURT.
OKAY! LOOK HOW MUCH I'M DRIBBLING!
SPLASH
SPLOOSH

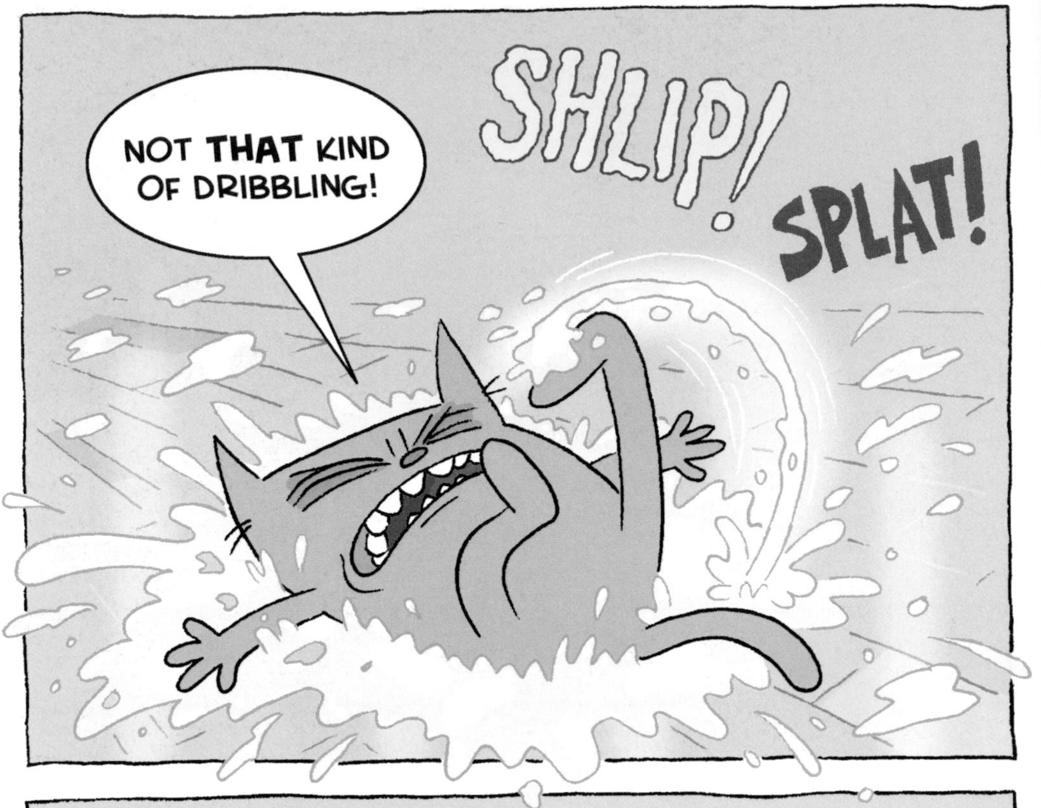
SHLIP!
NOT **THAT** KIND OF DRIBBLING!
SPLAT!

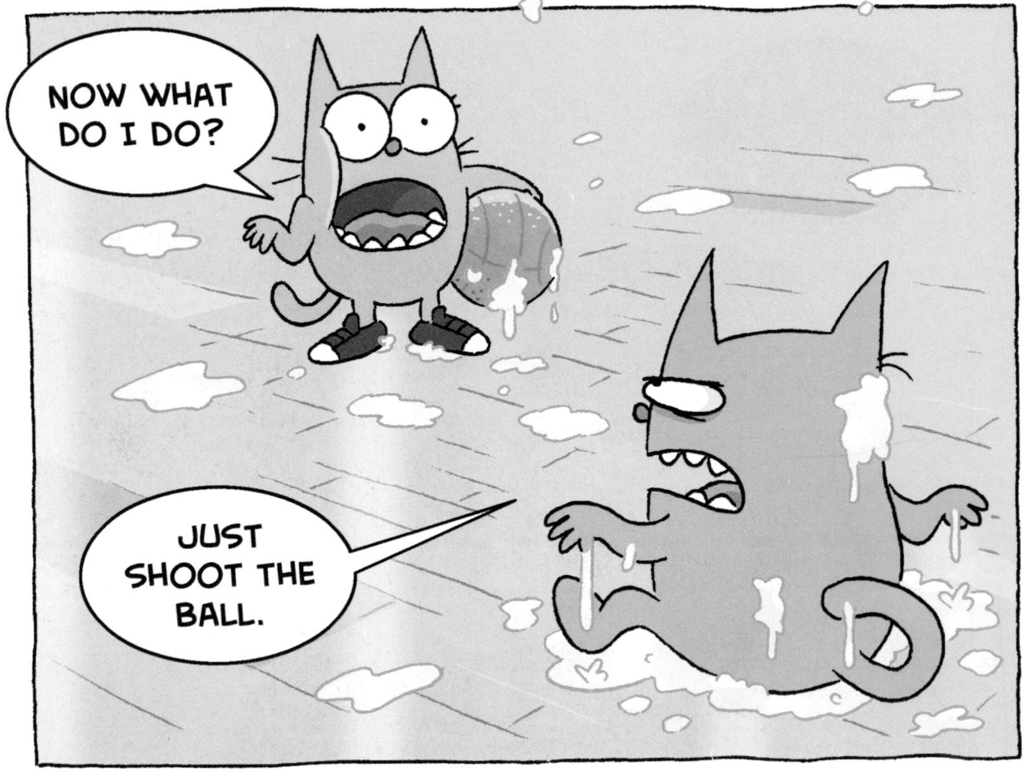
NOW WHAT DO I DO?
JUST SHOOT THE BALL.

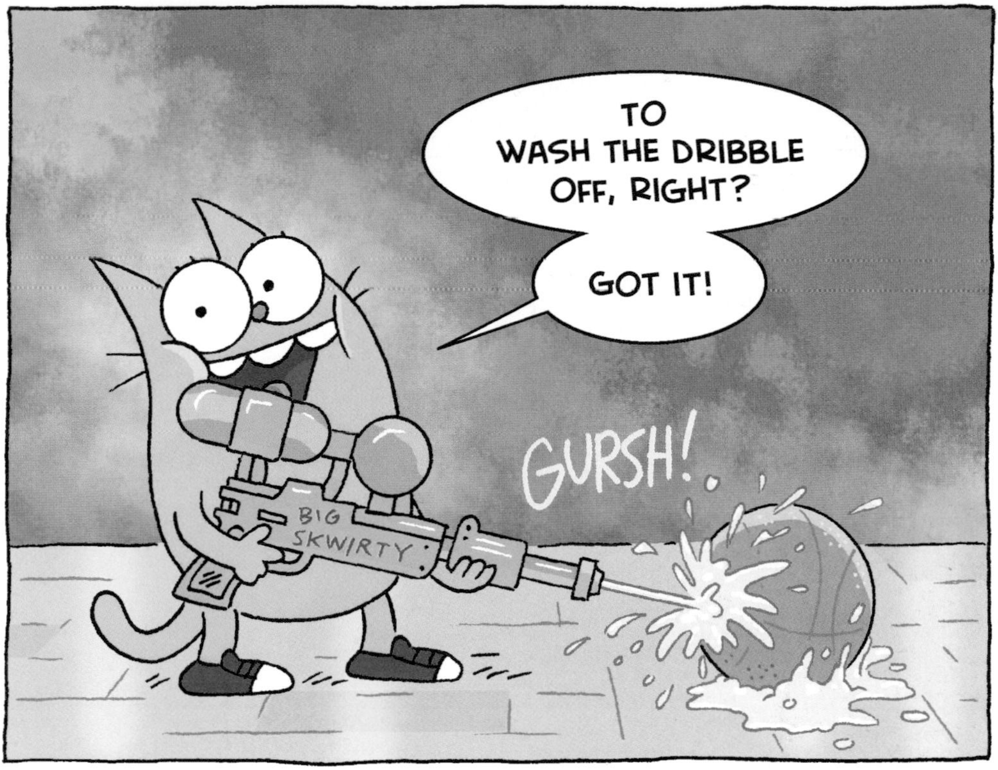
TO WASH THE DRIBBLE OFF, RIGHT?
GOT IT!
GURSH!
BIG SKWIRTY

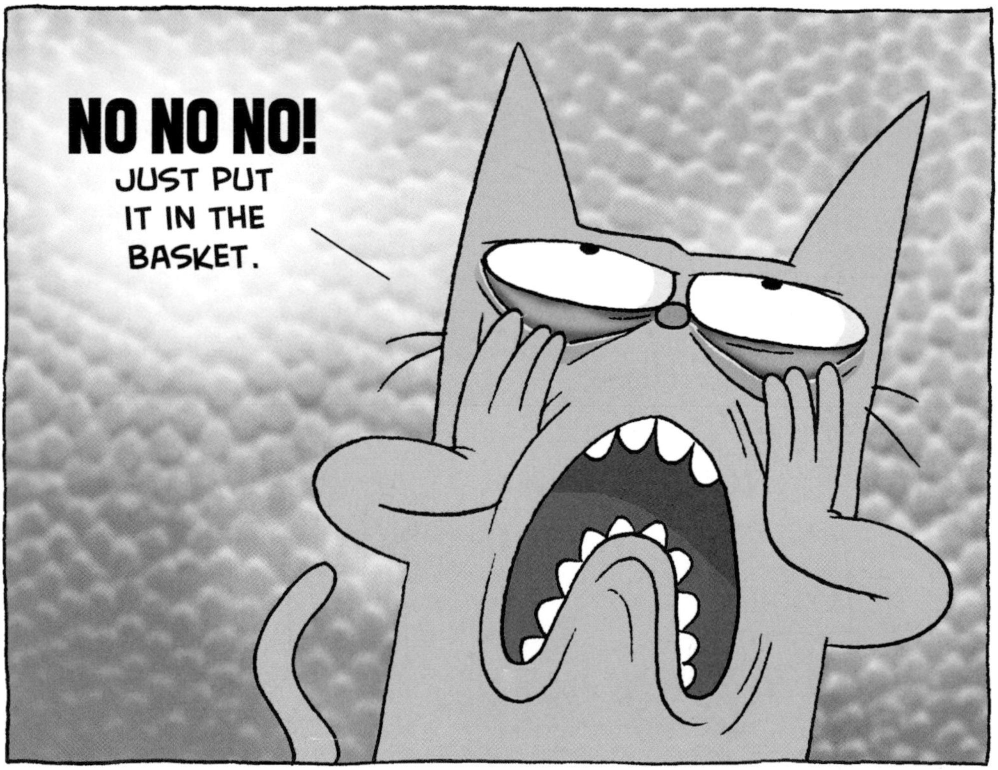
NO NO NO!
JUST PUT IT IN THE BASKET.

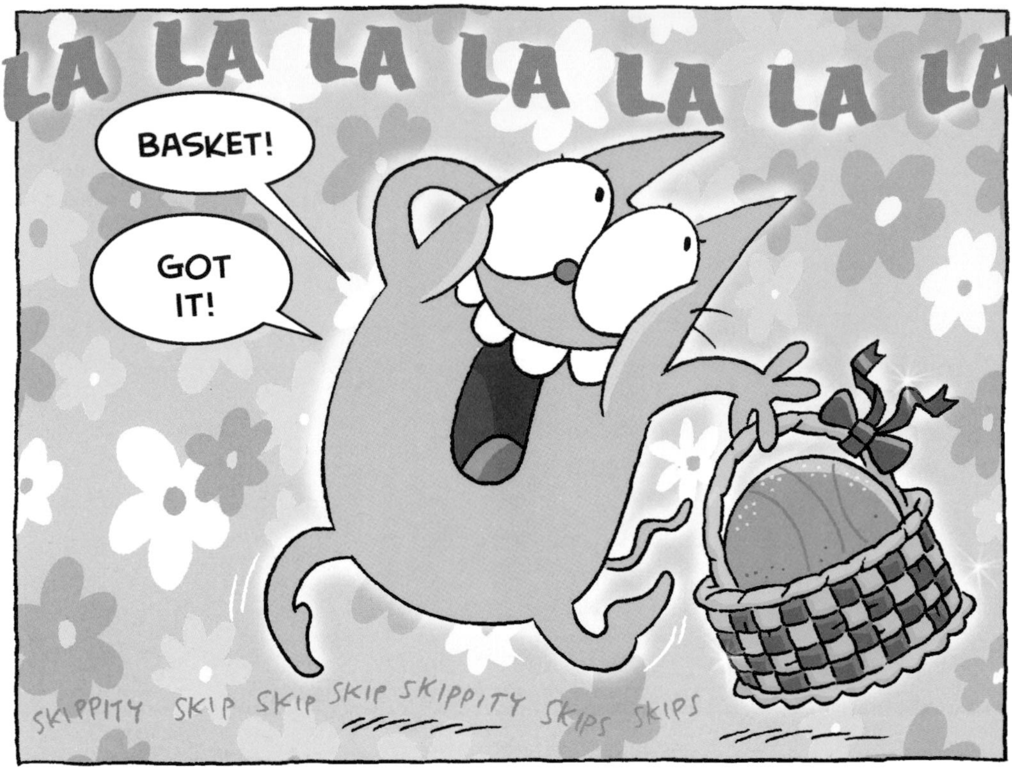
LA LA LA LA LA LA LA
BASKET!
GOT IT!
SKIPPITY SKIP SKIP SKIP SKIPPITY SKIPS SKIPS

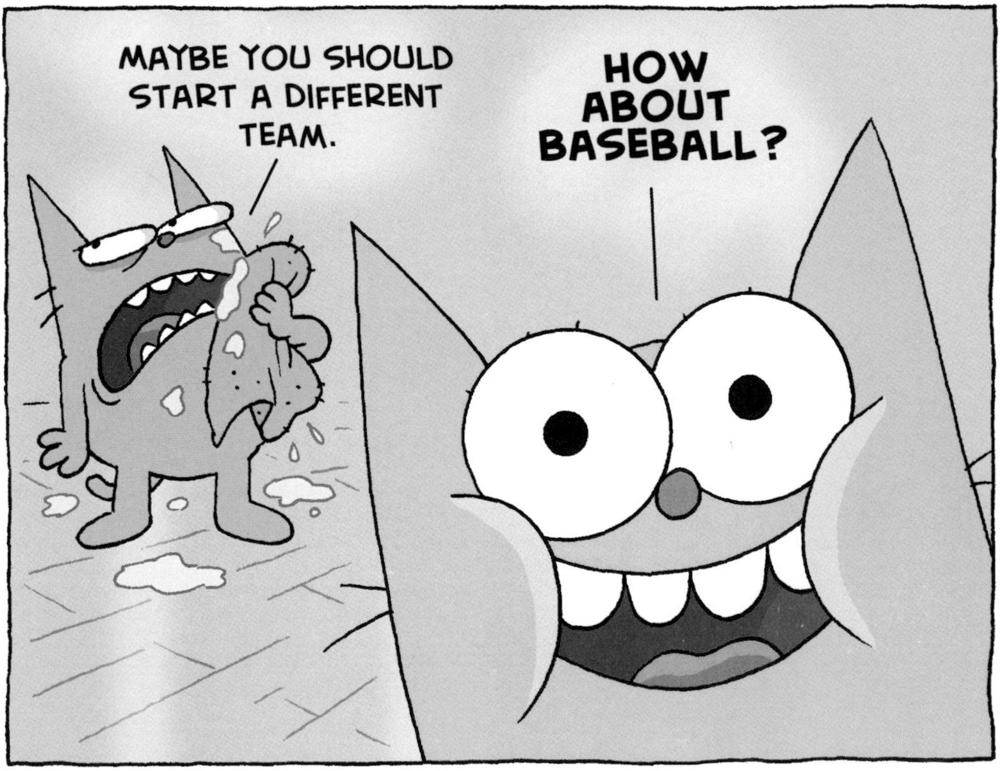
MAYBE YOU SHOULD START A DIFFERENT TEAM.
HOW ABOUT BASEBALL?

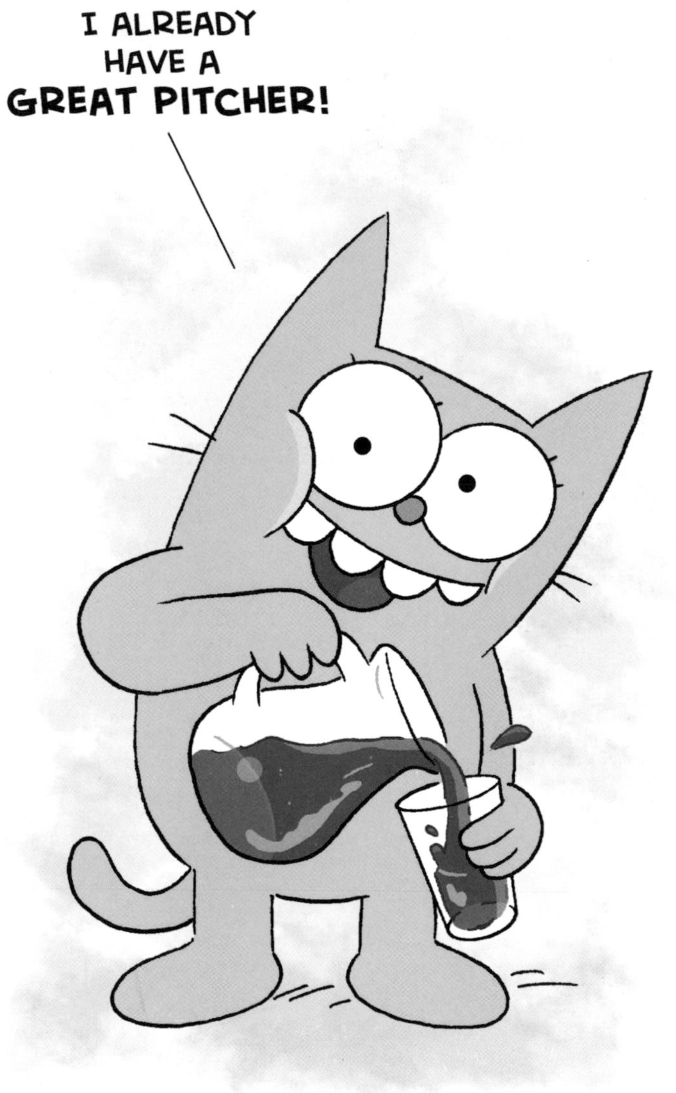
I ALREADY HAVE A GREAT PITCHER!

Water Sports

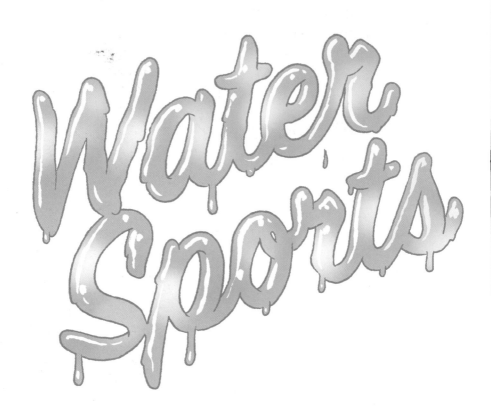

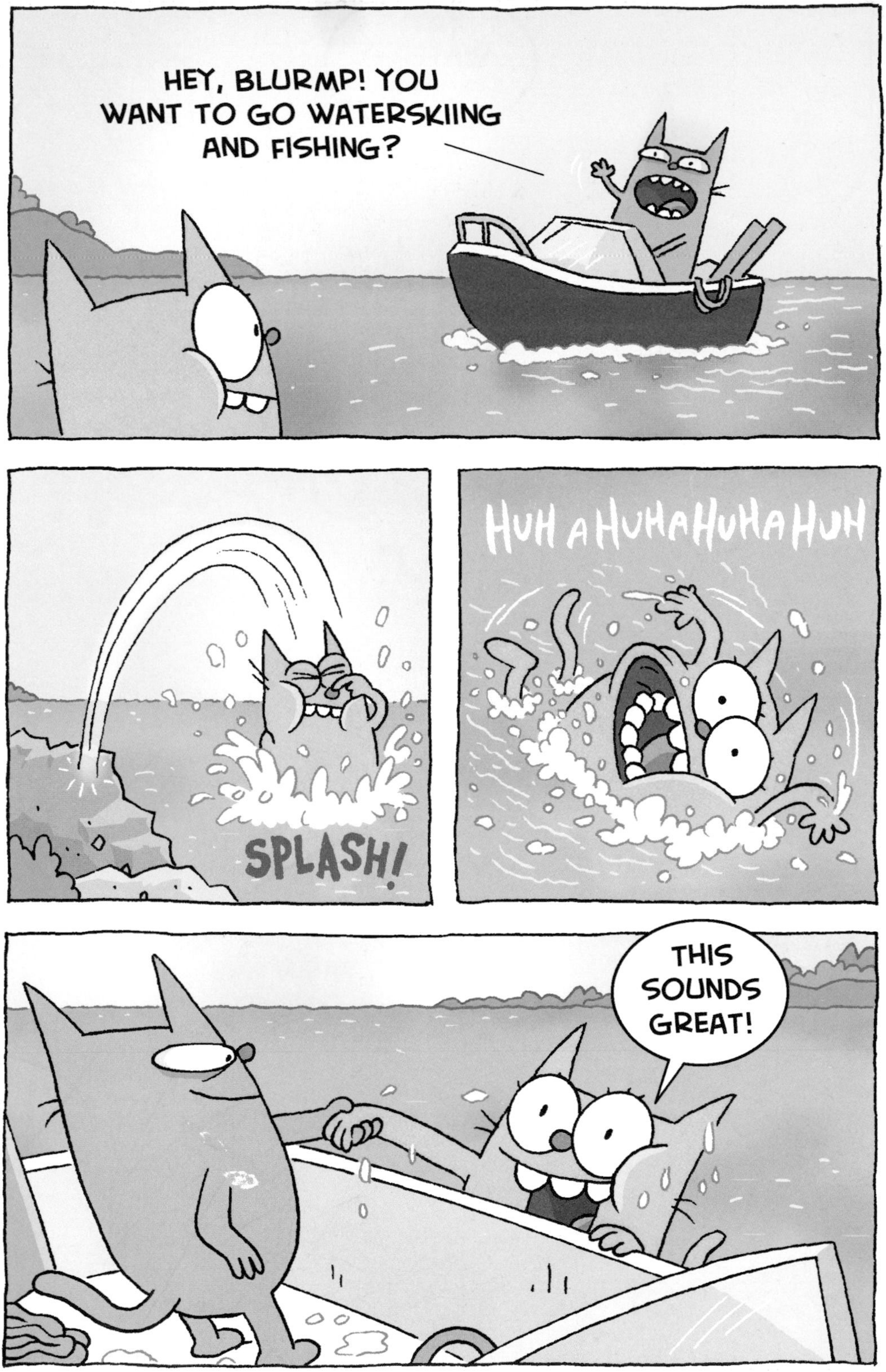
HEY, BLURMP! YOU WANT TO GO WATERSKIING AND FISHING?
SPLASH!
HUH A HUHA HUHA HUH
THIS SOUNDS GREAT!

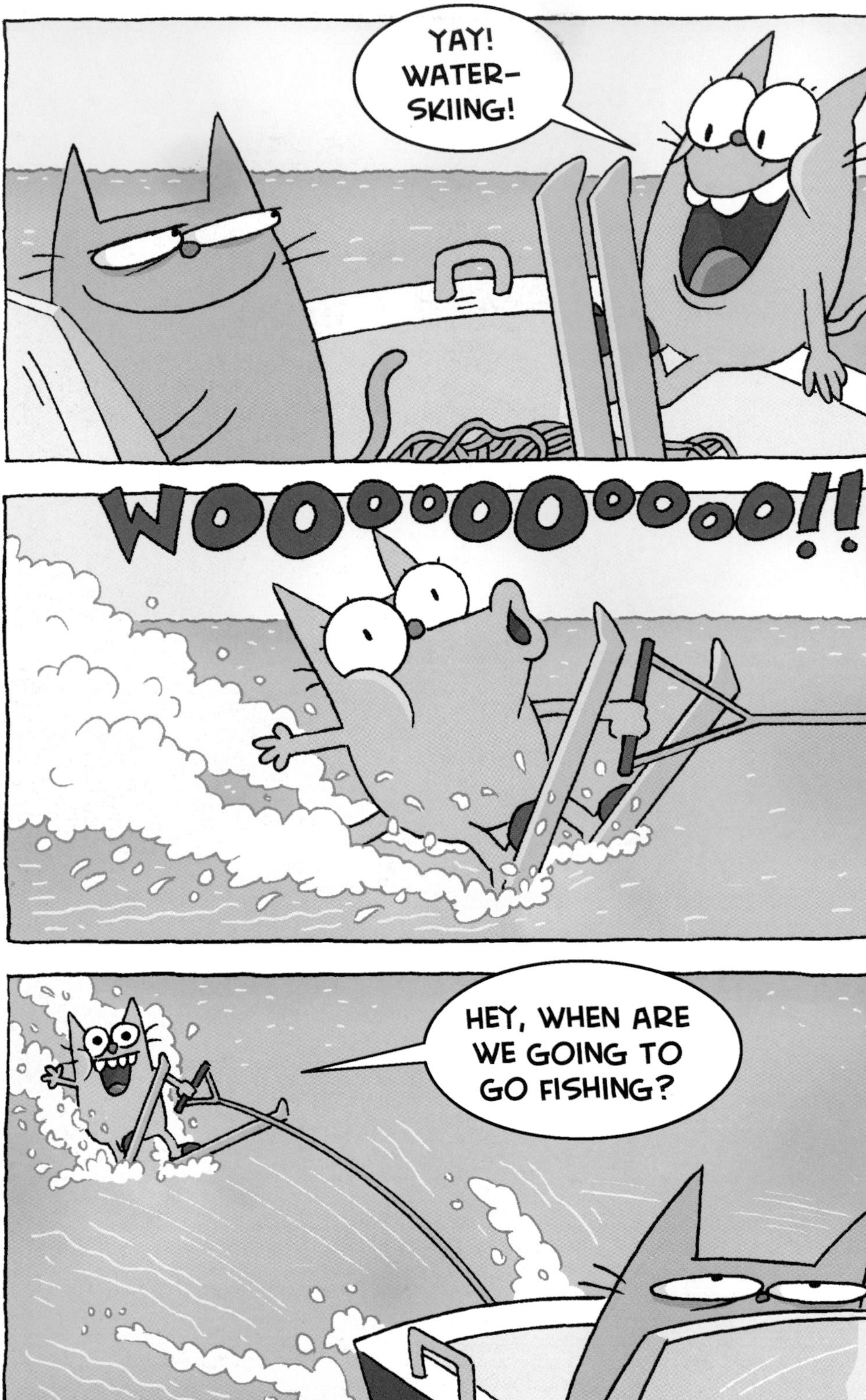
YAY! WATER-SKIING!
WOOOOOOOOOOO!!
HEY, WHEN ARE WE GOING TO GO FISHING?

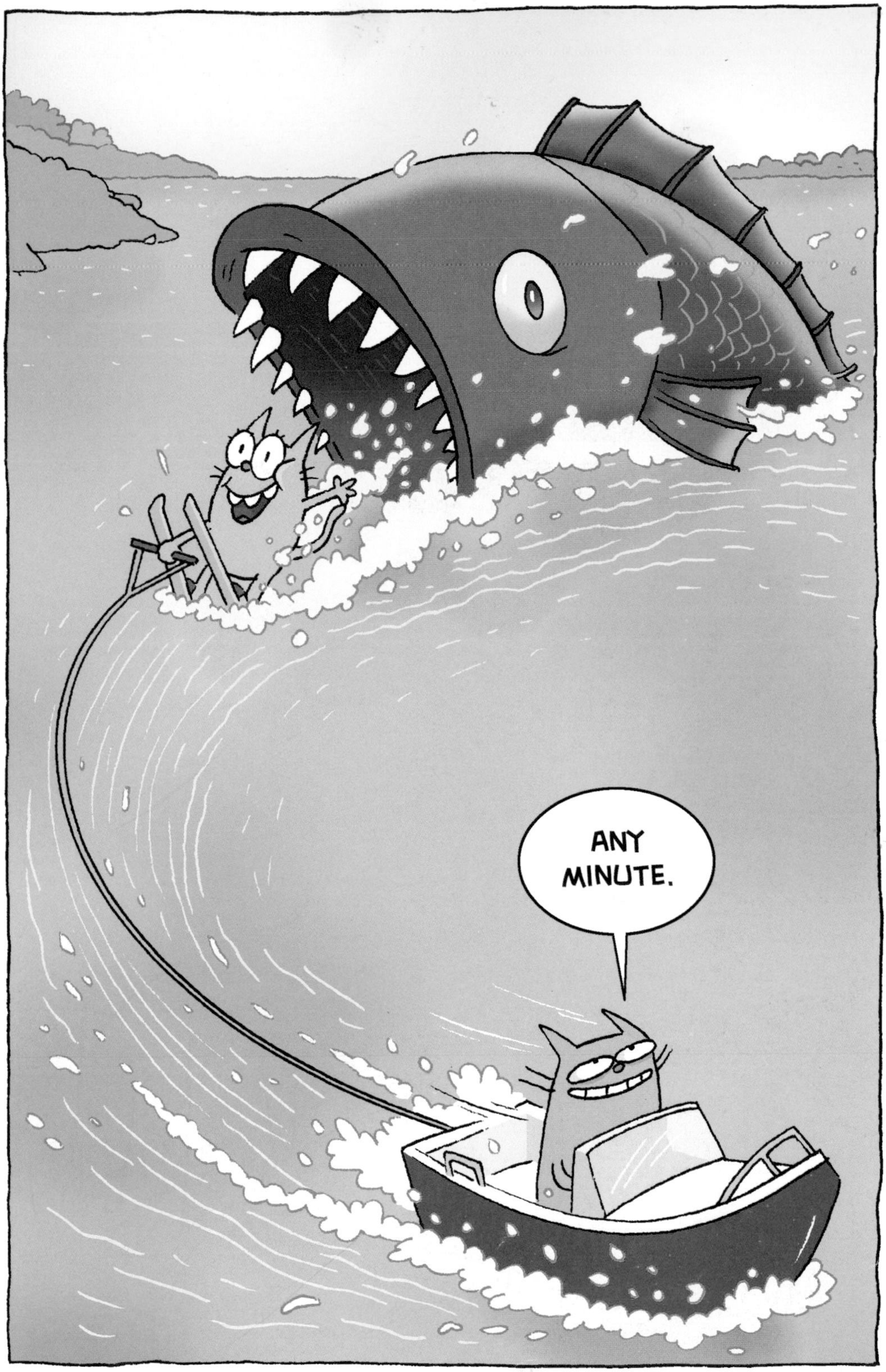
ANY MINUTE.

VISITORS

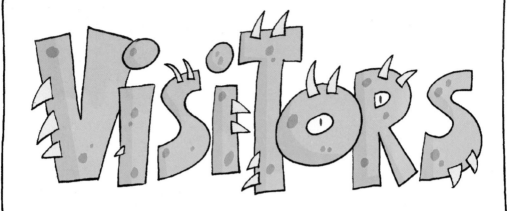

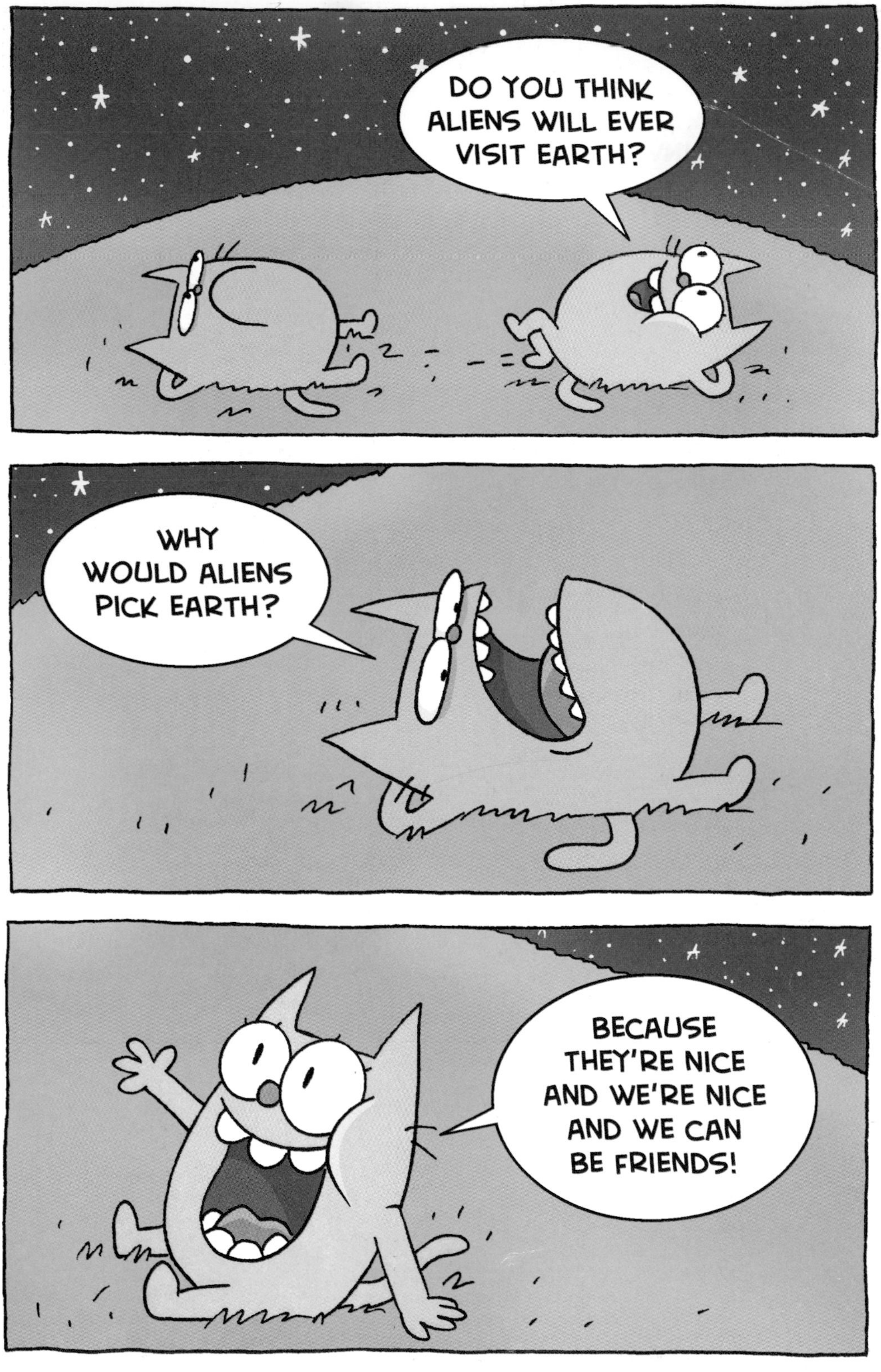
DO YOU THINK ALIENS WILL EVER VISIT EARTH?
WHY WOULD ALIENS PICK EARTH?
BECAUSE THEY'RE NICE AND WE'RE NICE AND WE CAN BE FRIENDS!

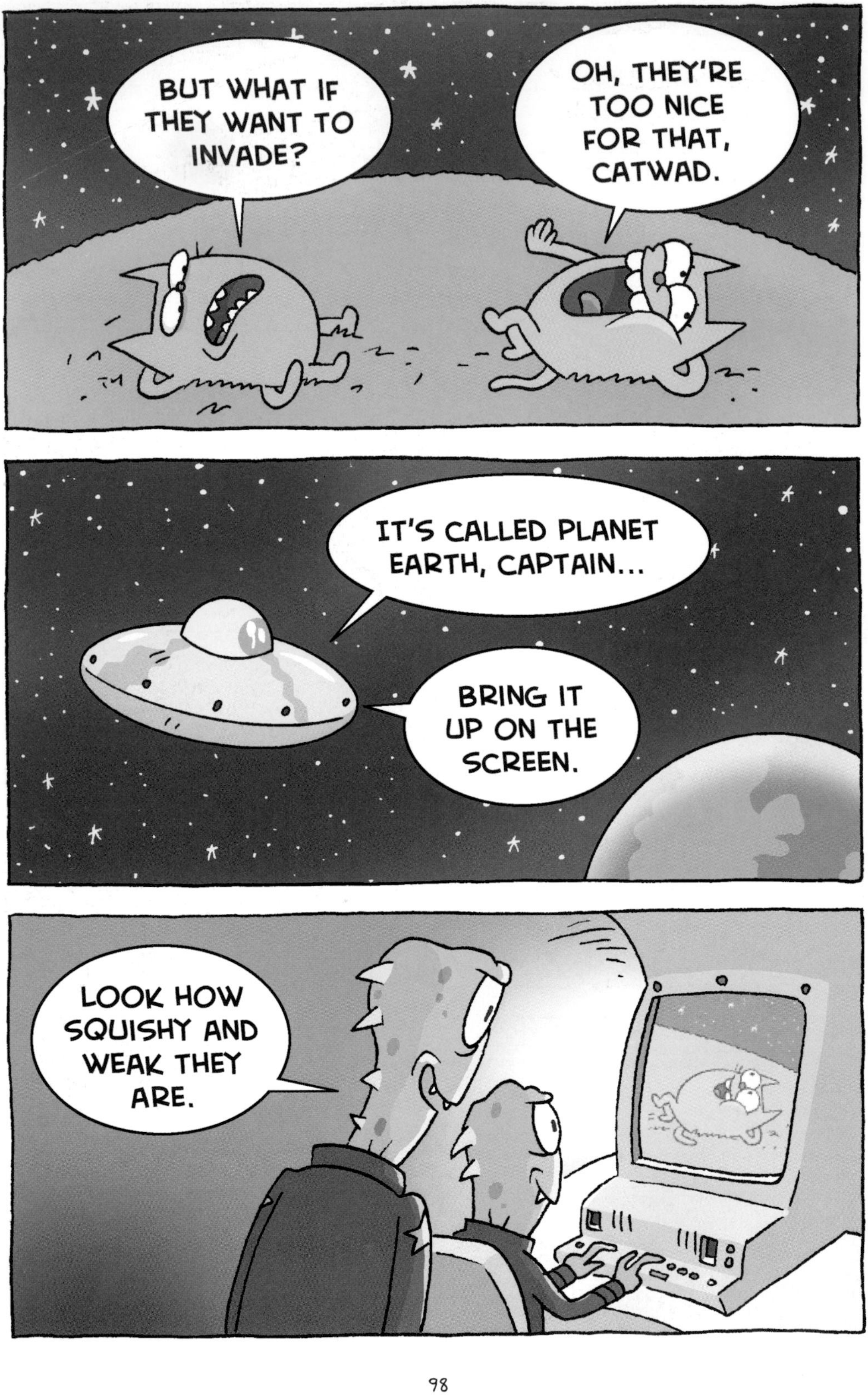
BUT WHAT IF THEY WANT TO INVADE?
OH, THEY'RE TOO NICE FOR THAT, CATWAD.
IT'S CALLED PLANET EARTH, CAPTAIN...
BRING IT UP ON THE SCREEN.
LOOK HOW SQUISHY AND WEAK THEY ARE.

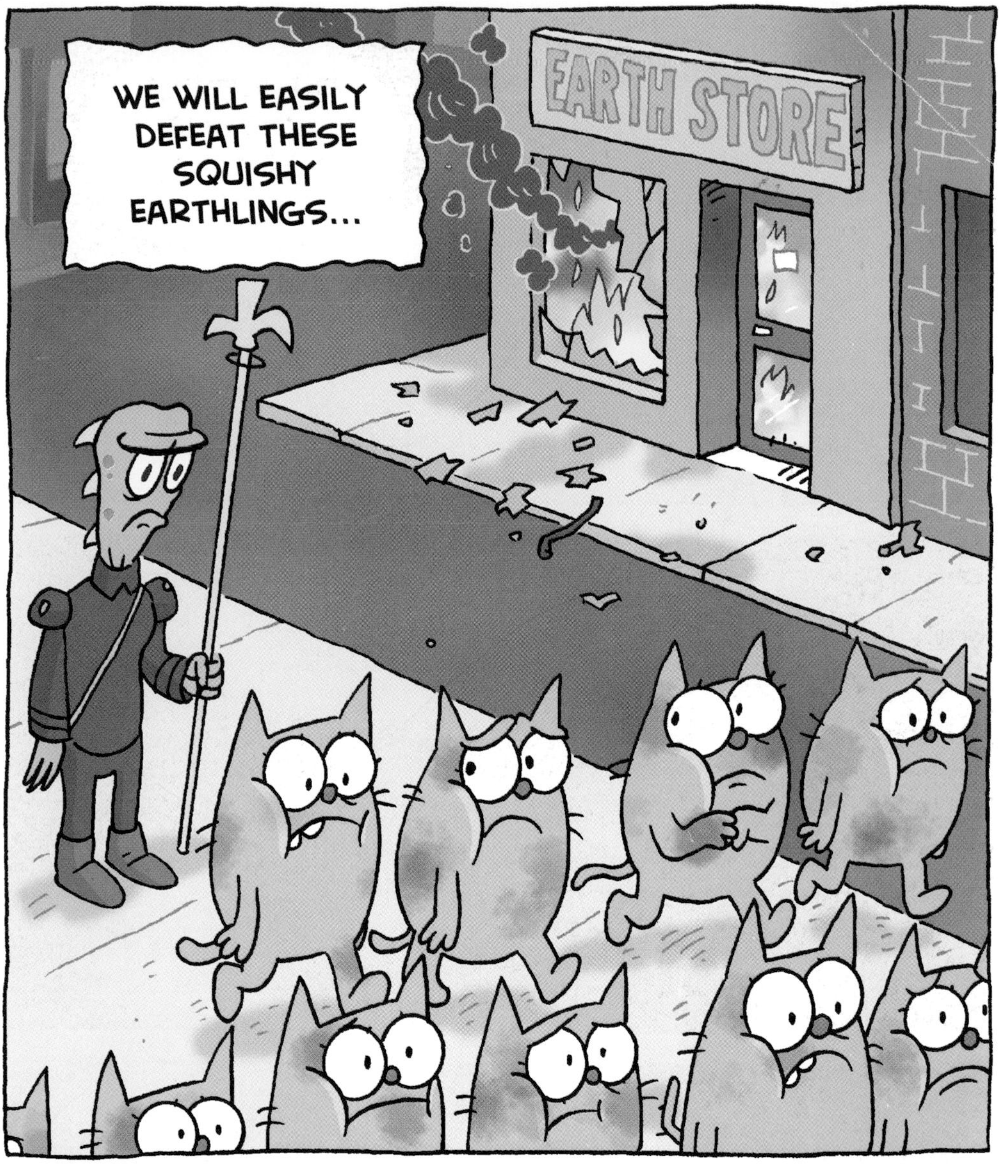
WE WILL EASILY DEFEAT THESE SQUISHY EARTHLINGS...
EARTH STORE

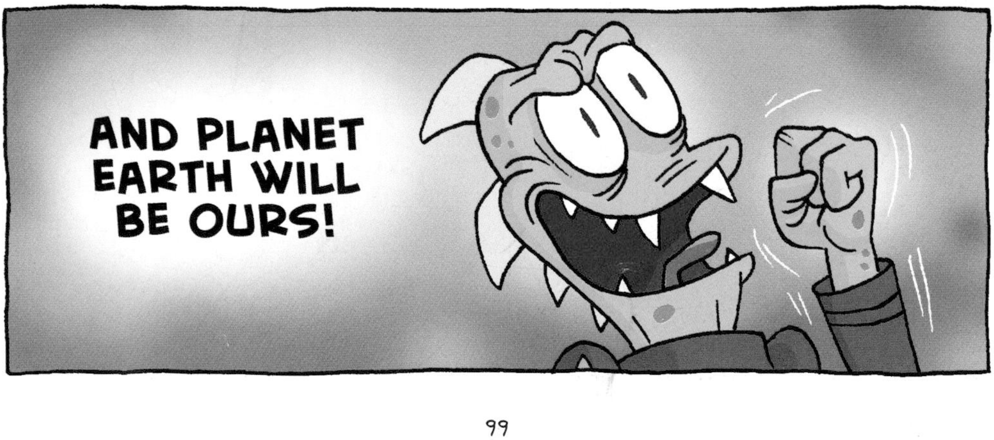
AND PLANET EARTH WILL BE OURS!

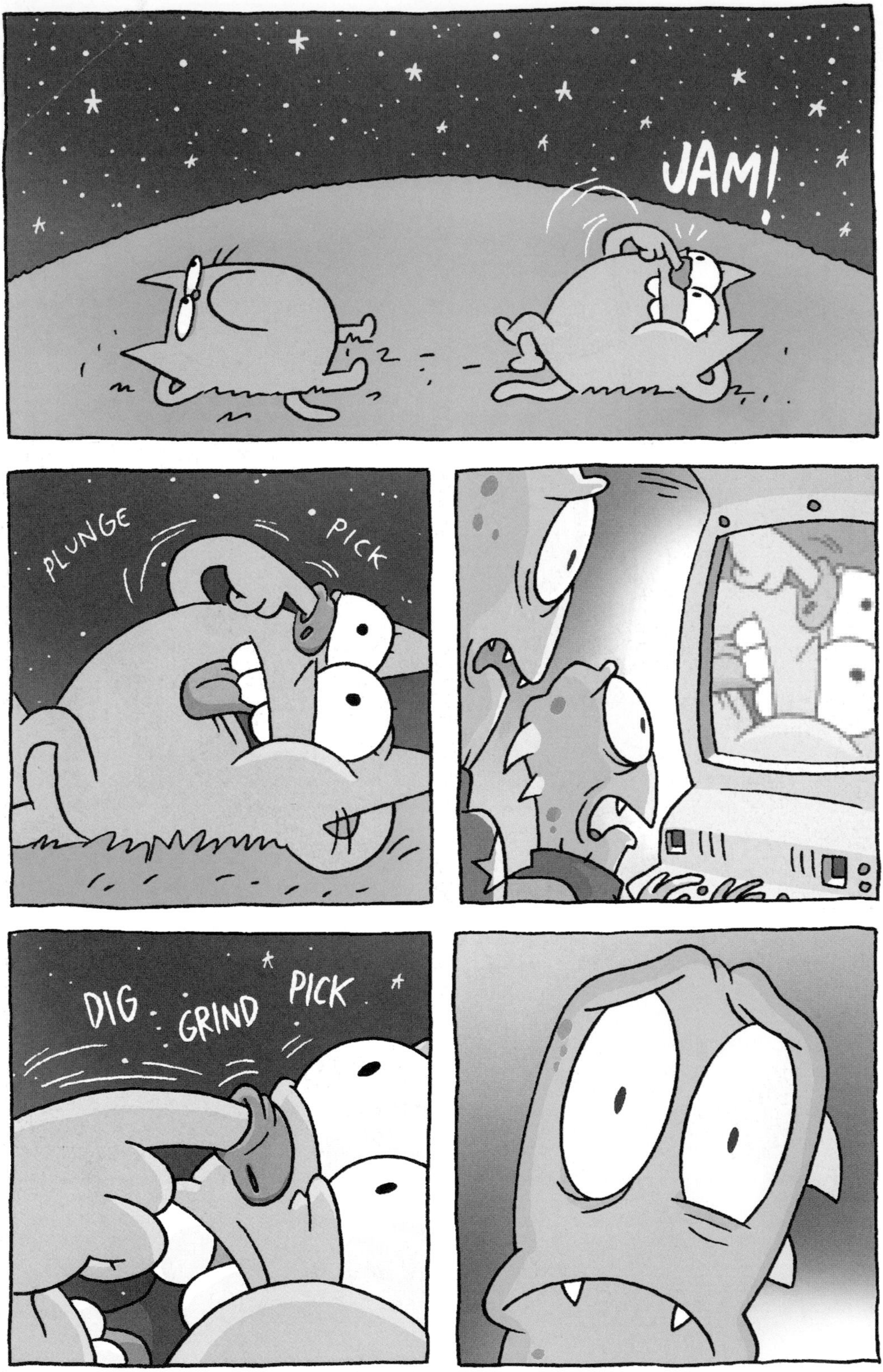
JAM!
PLUNGE
PICK
DIG
GRIND
PICK

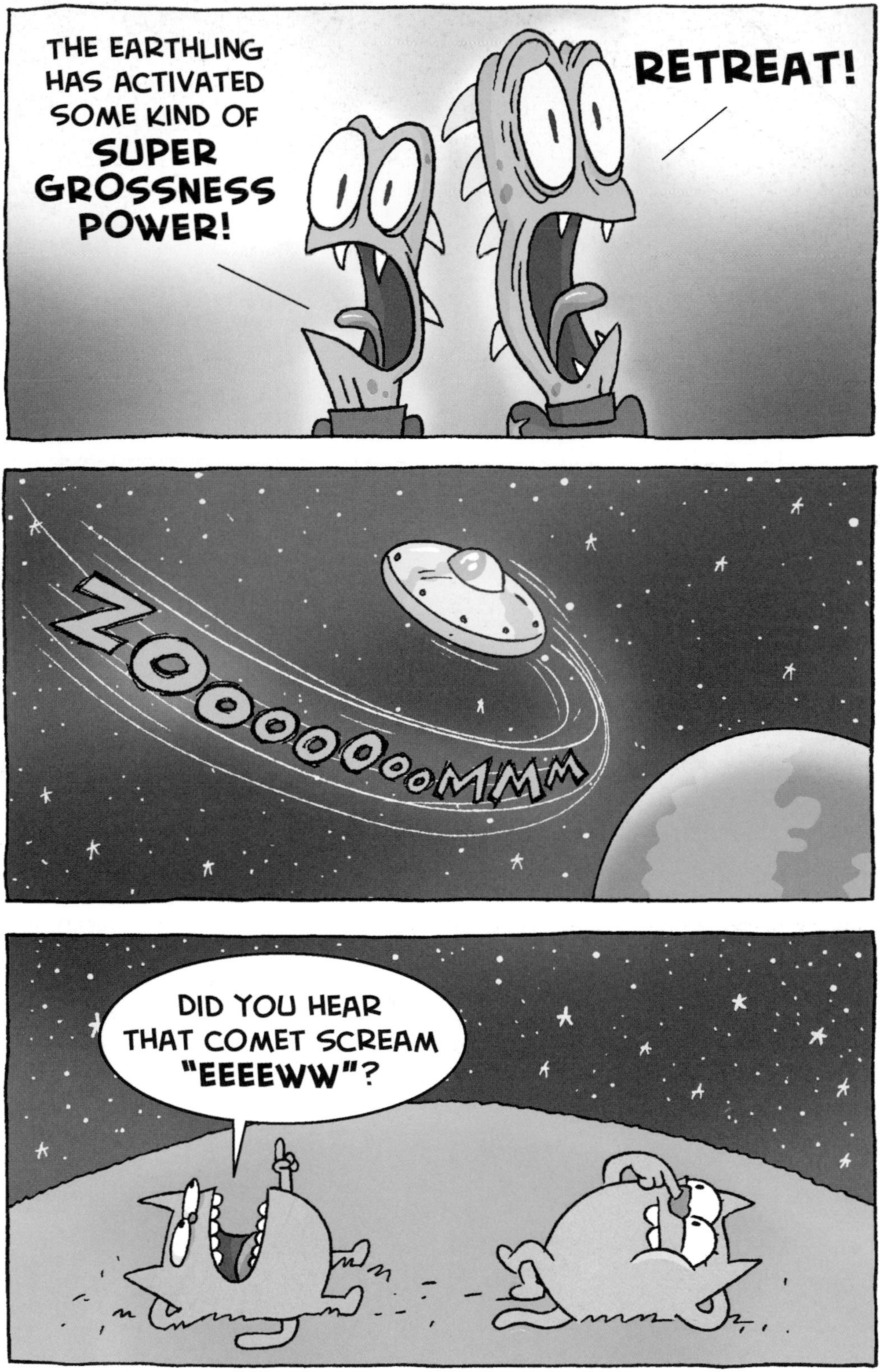
THE EARTHLING HAS ACTIVATED SOME KIND OF SUPER GROSSNESS POWER!
RETREAT!
ZOOOOOOOOOMMM
DID YOU HEAR THAT COMET SCREAM "EEEEWW"?

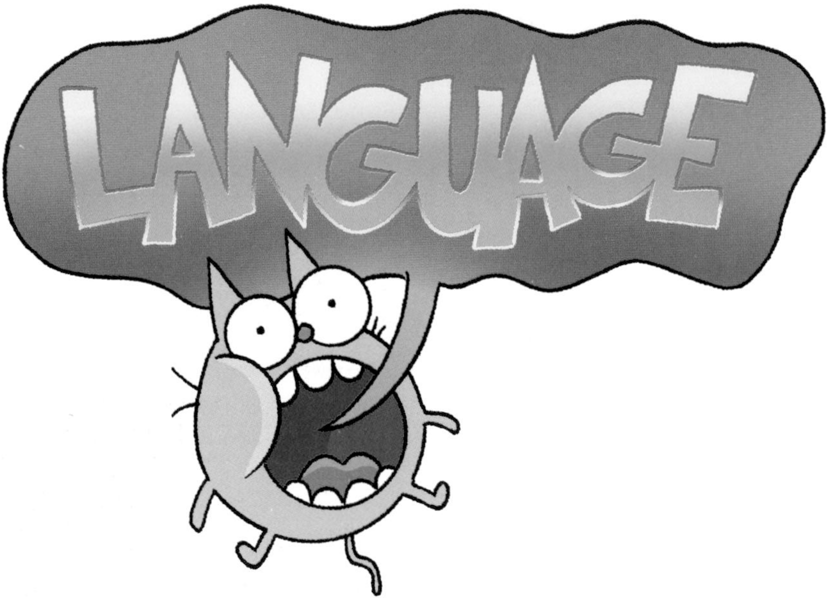
LANGUAGE

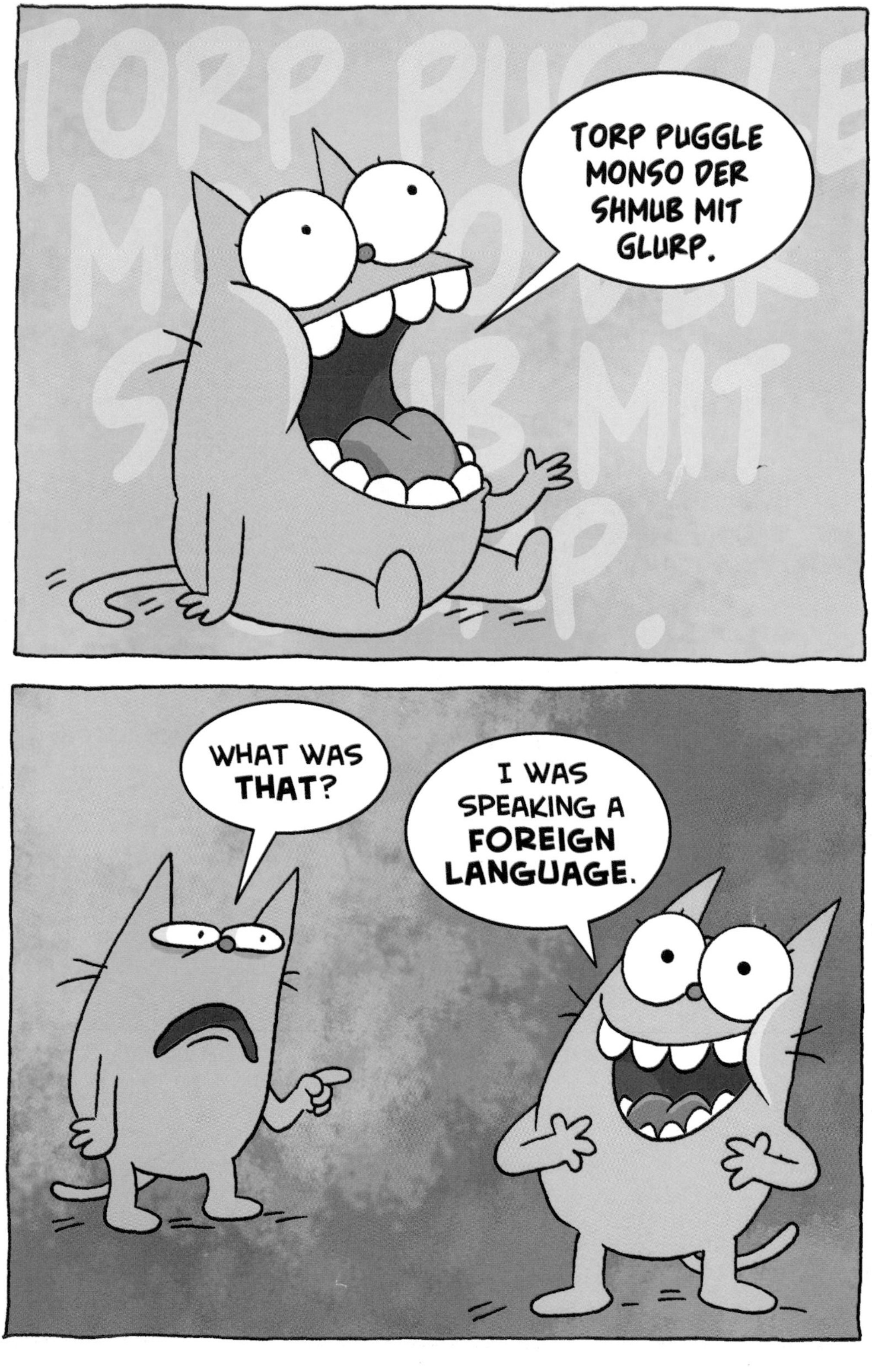
TORP PUGGLE MONSO DER SHMUB MIT GLURP.
WHAT WAS THAT?
I WAS SPEAKING A FOREIGN LANGUAGE.

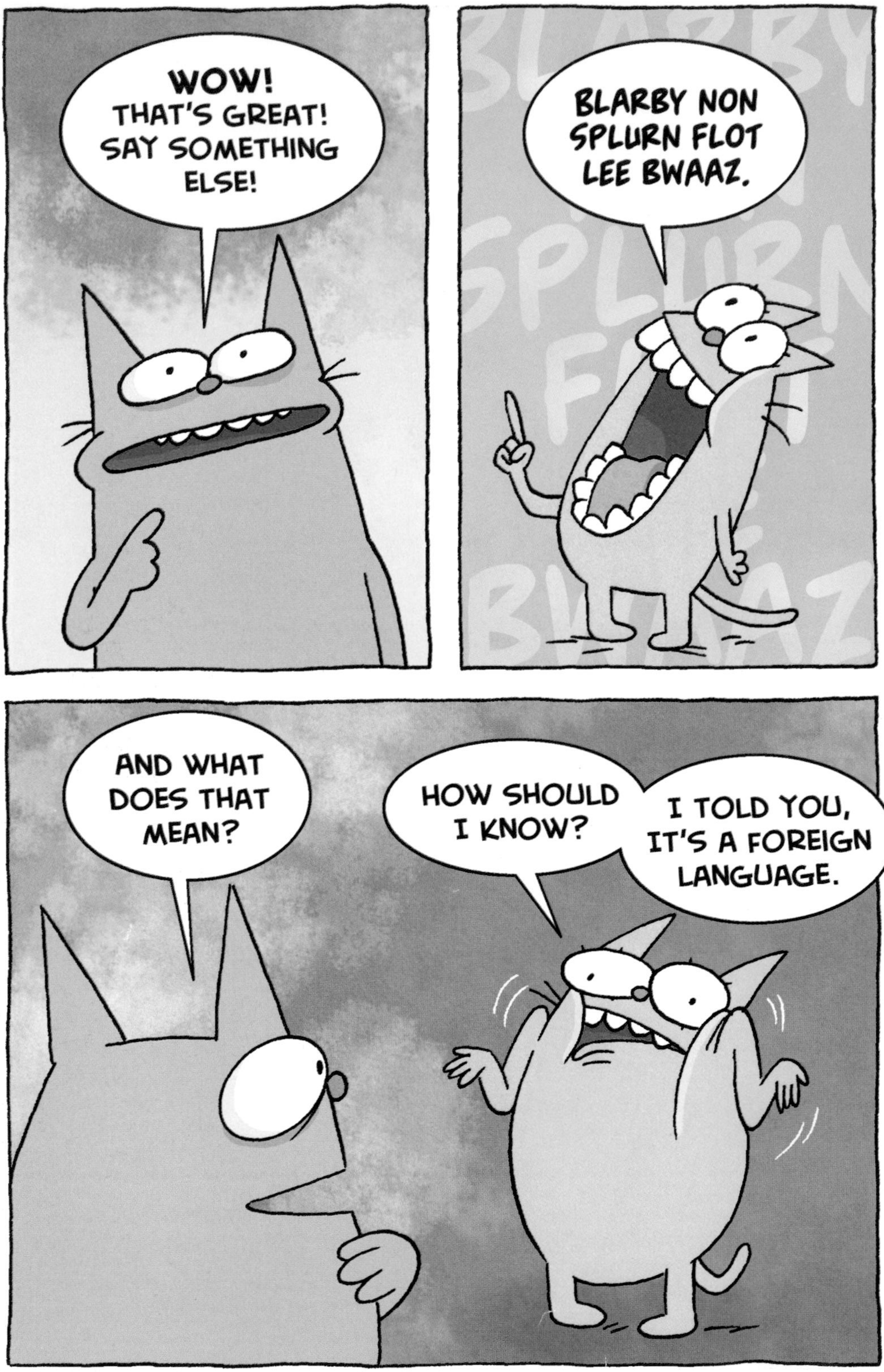
WOW!
THAT'S GREAT! SAY SOMETHING ELSE!
BLARBY NON SPLURN FLOT LEE BWAAZ.
AND WHAT DOES THAT MEAN?
HOW SHOULD I KNOW?
I TOLD YOU, IT'S A FOREIGN LANGUAGE.

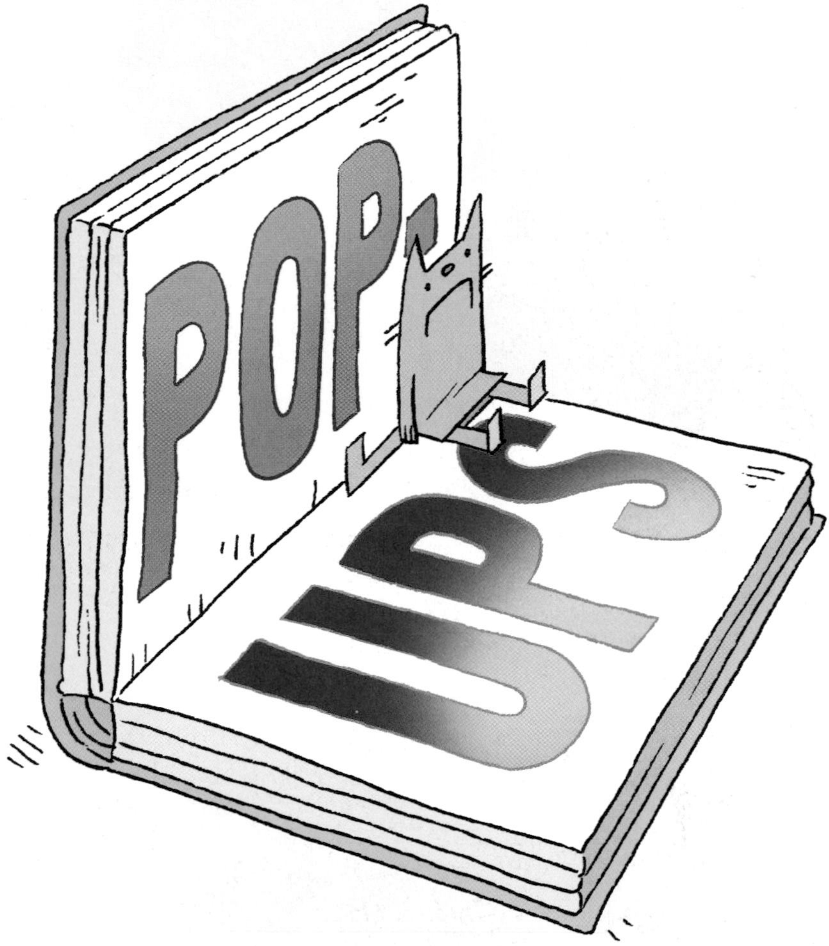
POP-
UPS

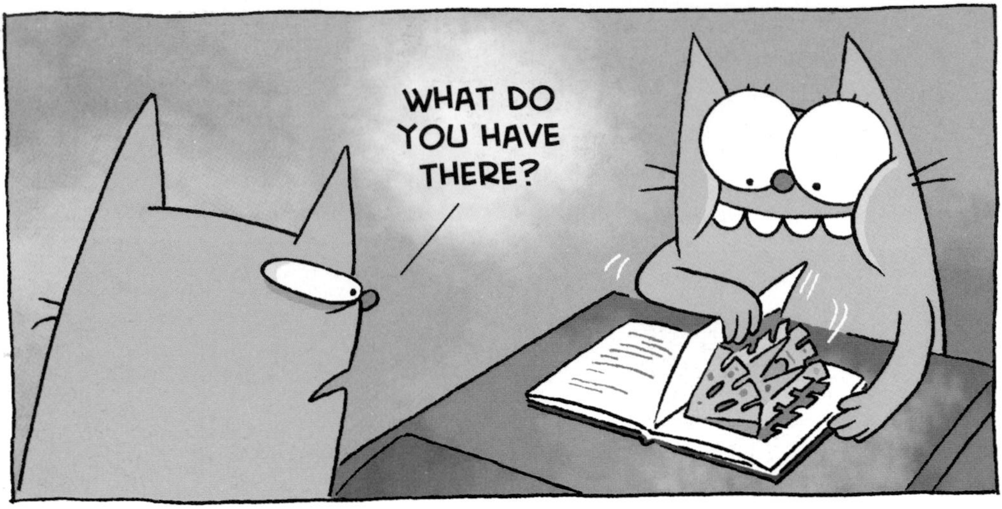
WHAT DO YOU HAVE THERE?

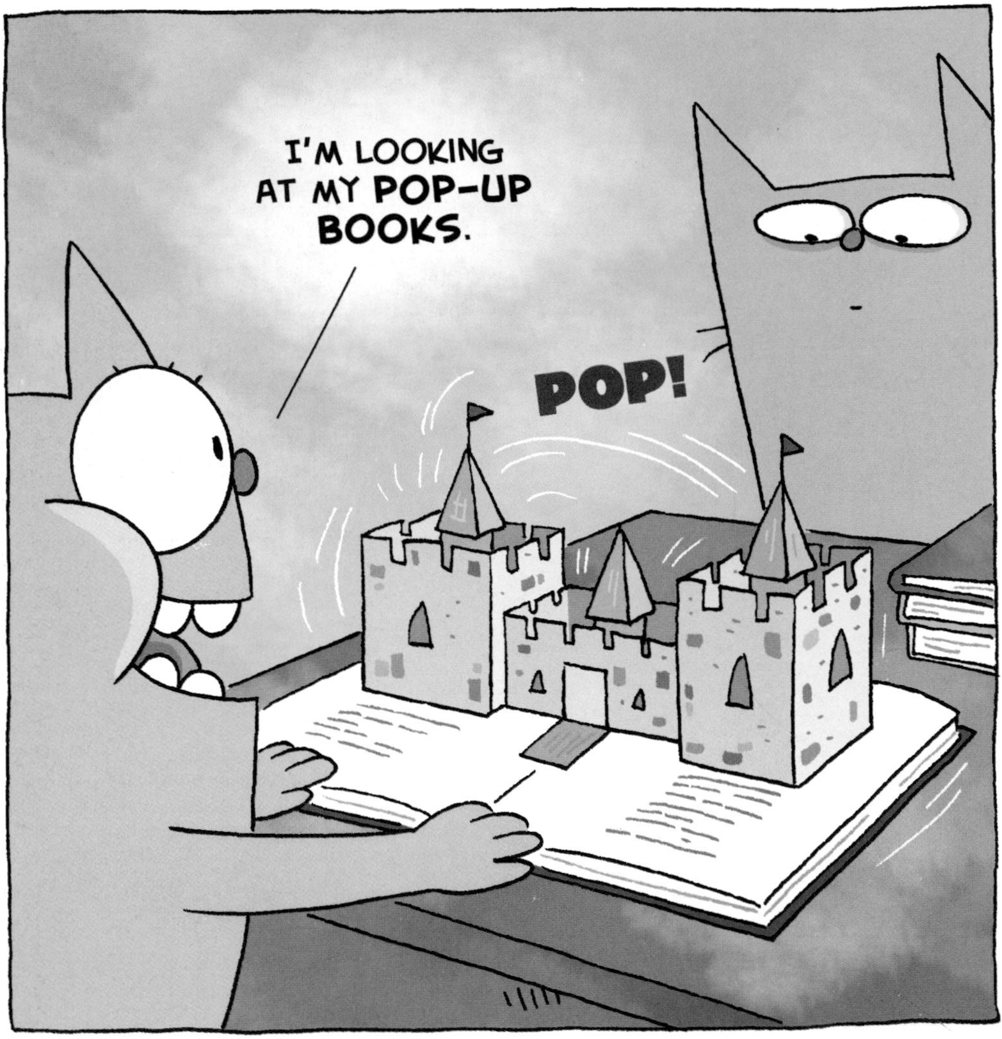
I'M LOOKING AT MY POP-UP BOOKS.
POP!

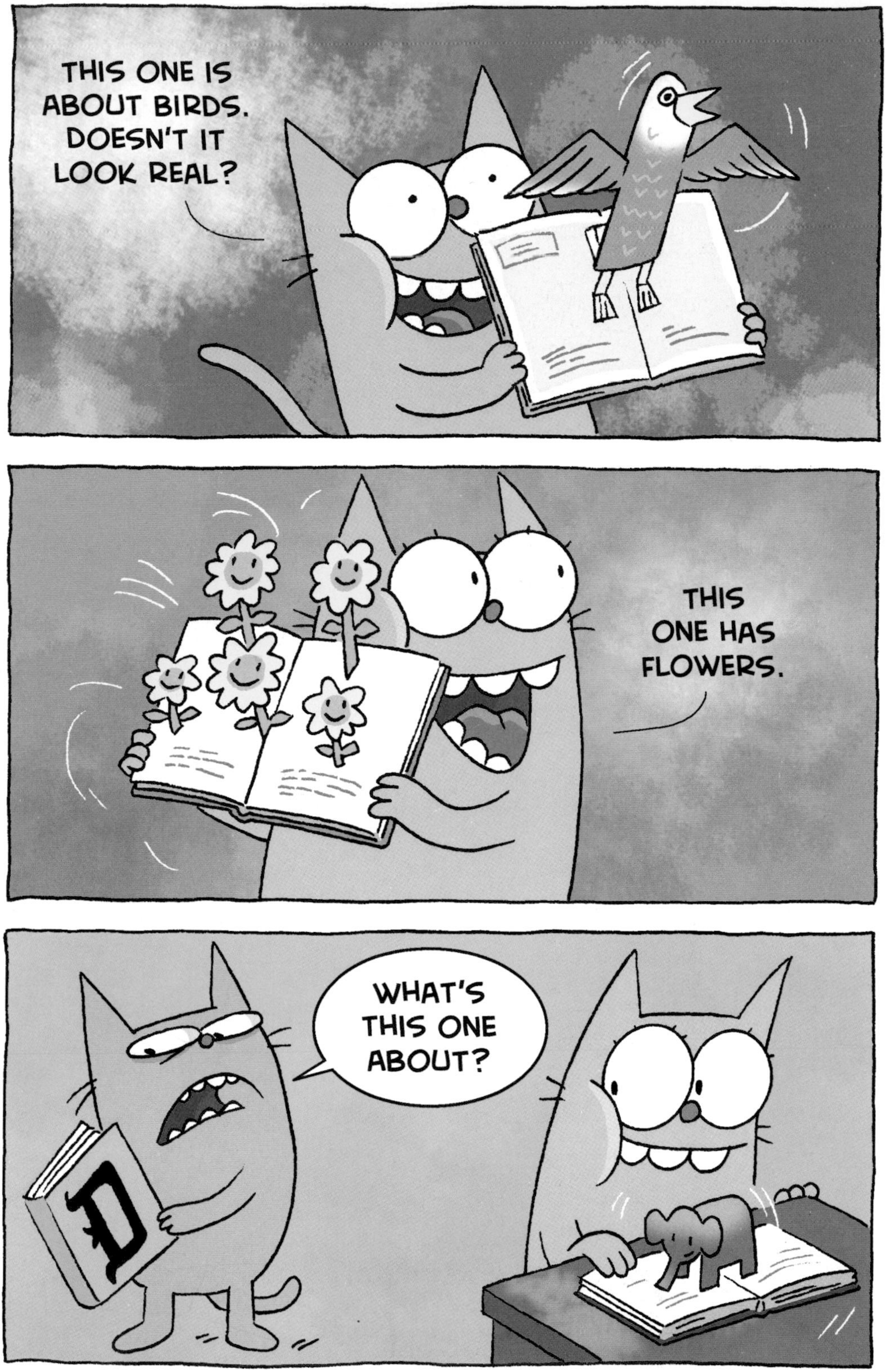
THIS ONE IS ABOUT BIRDS. DOESN'T IT LOOK REAL?
THIS ONE HAS FLOWERS.
WHAT'S THIS ONE ABOUT?

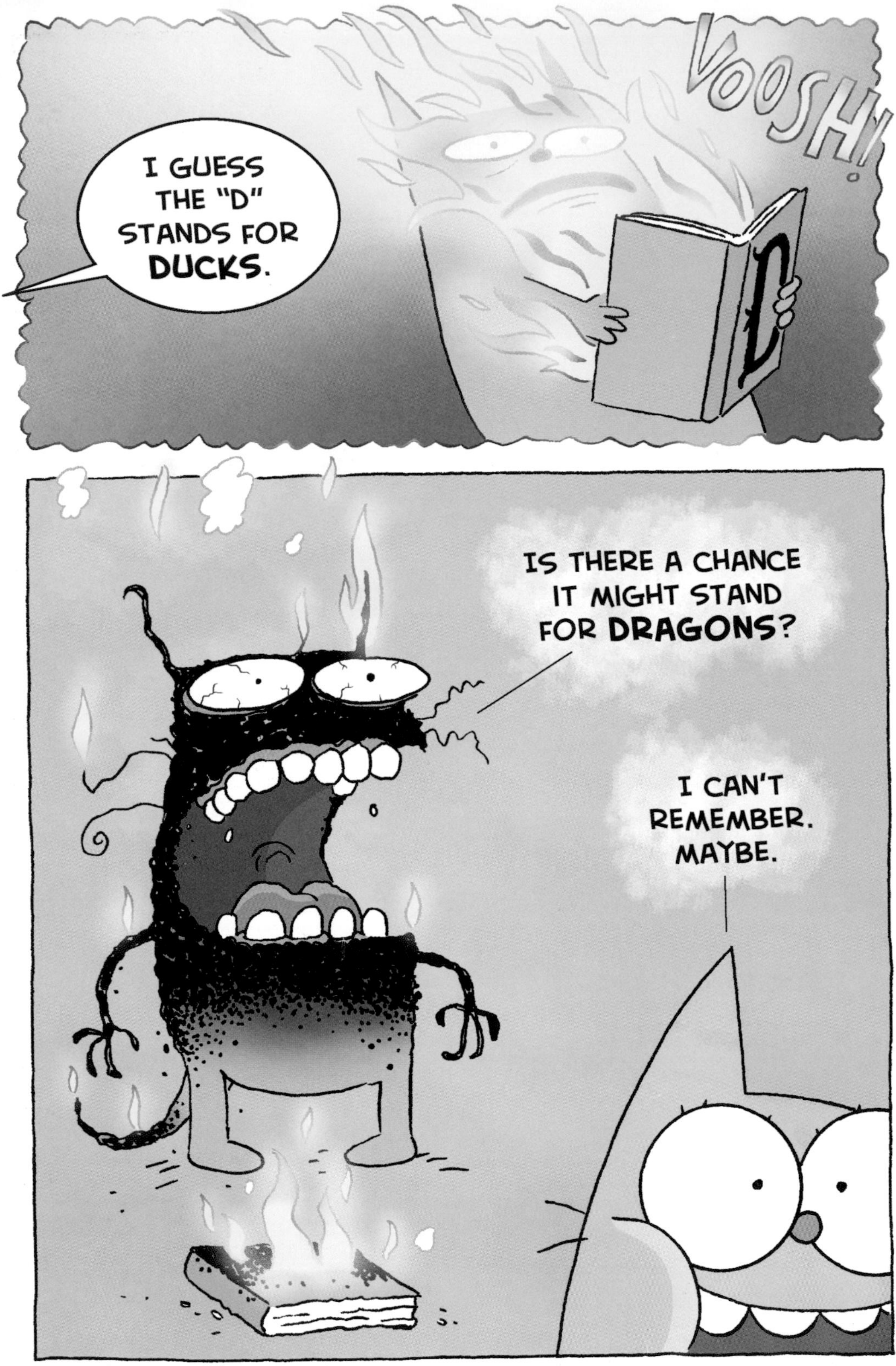
VOOSH!
I GUESS THE "D" STANDS FOR DUCKS.
IS THERE A CHANCE IT MIGHT STAND FOR DRAGONS?
I CAN'T REMEMBER. MAYBE.

SCIENCE FICTION

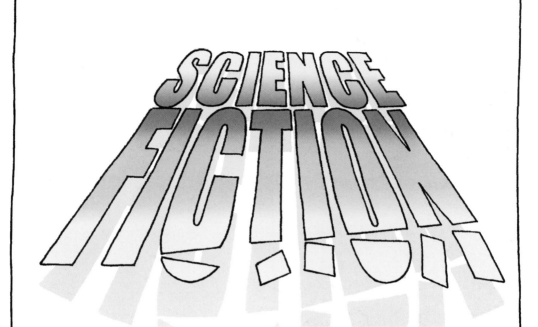

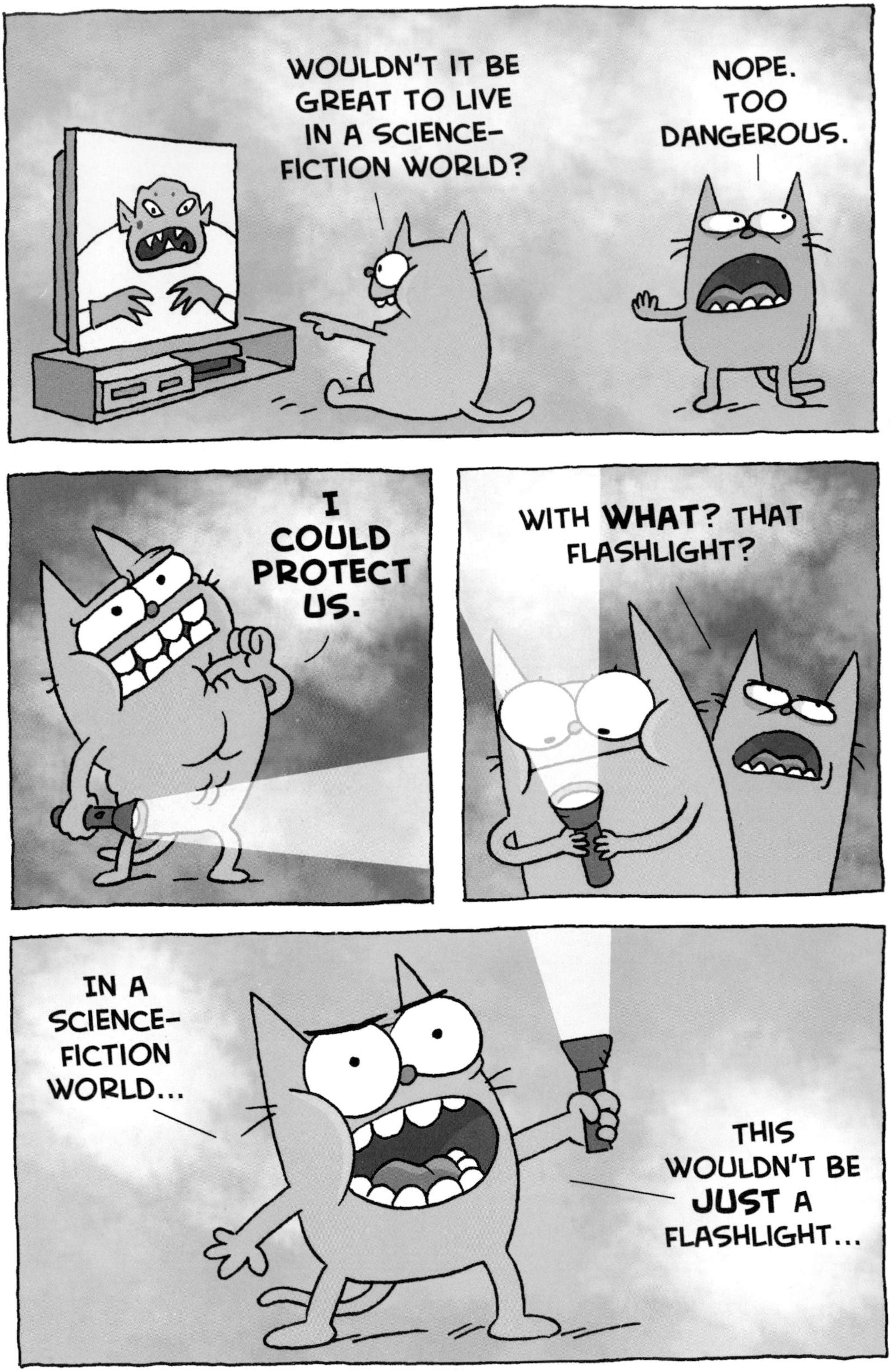
WOULDN'T IT BE GREAT TO LIVE IN A SCIENCE-FICTION WORLD?
NOPE. TOO DANGEROUS.
I COULD PROTECT US.
WITH WHAT? THAT FLASHLIGHT?
IN A SCIENCE-FICTION WORLD...
THIS WOULDN'T BE JUST A FLASHLIGHT...

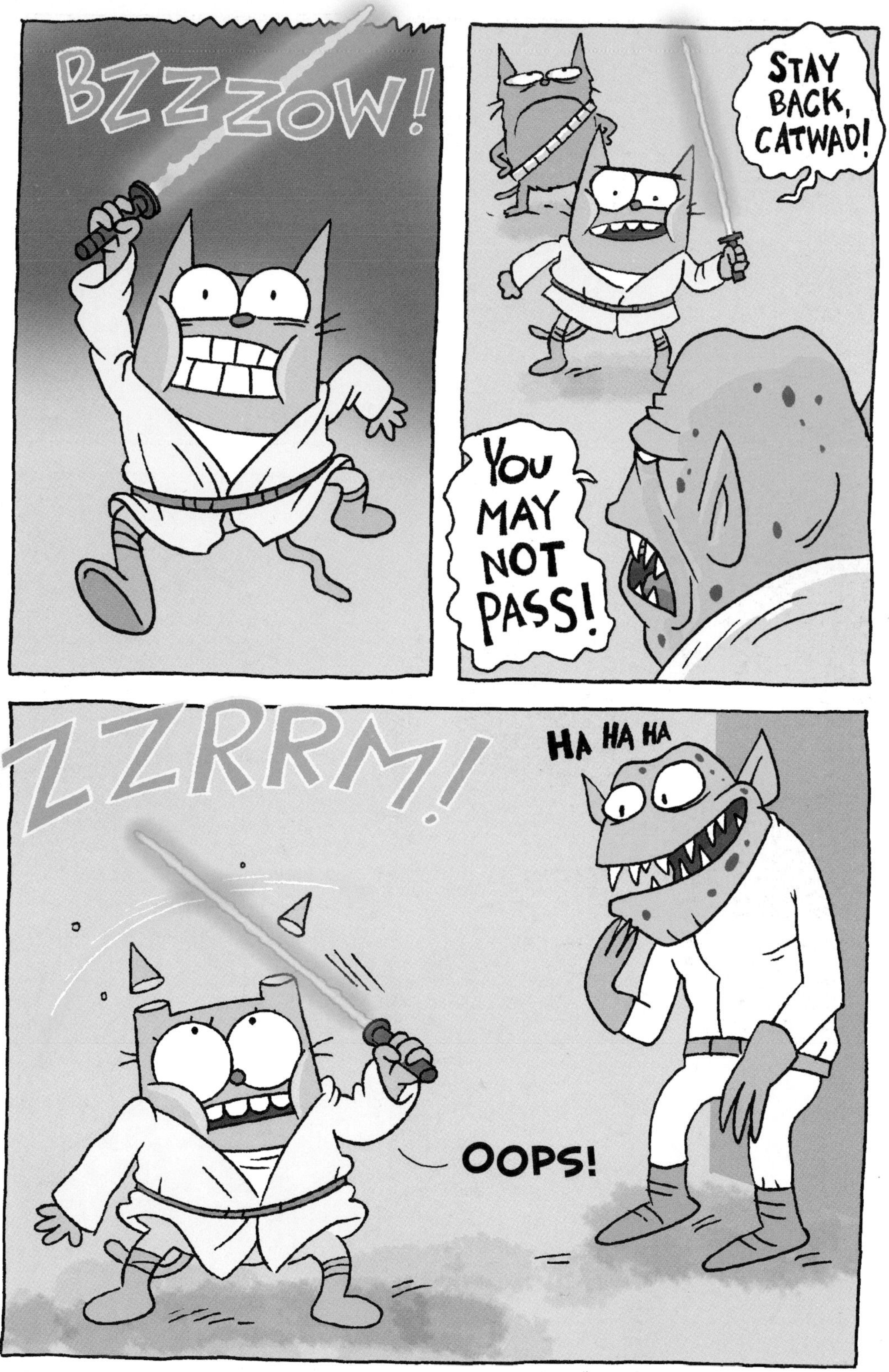
BZZZOW!
STAY BACK, CATWAD!
YOU MAY NOT PASS!
ZZRRRM!
HA HA HA
OOPS!

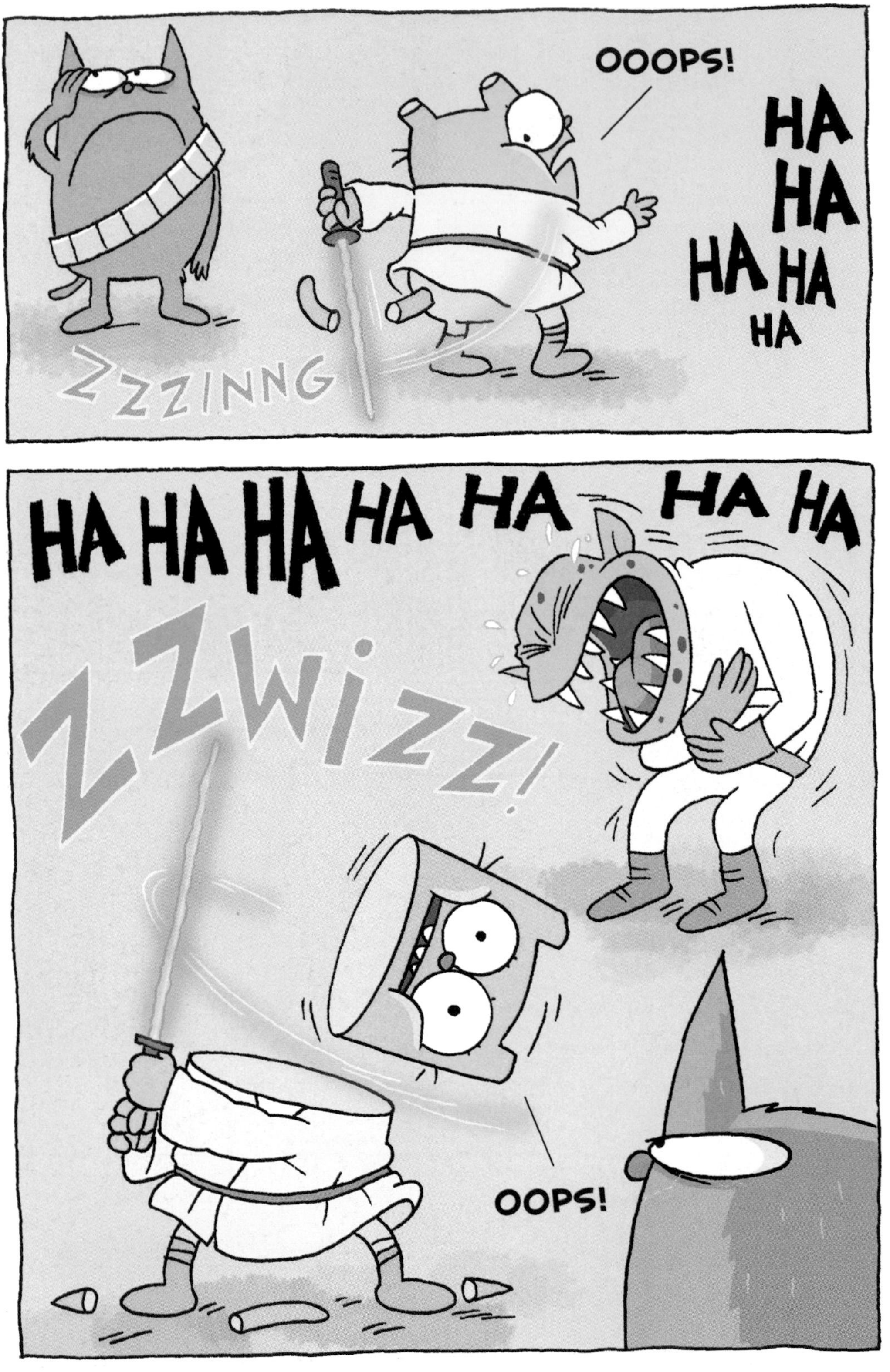

OOOPS!
HA HA HA HA HA HA
ZZZINNG
HA HA HA HA HA HA HA HA
ZZWIZZ!
OOPS!

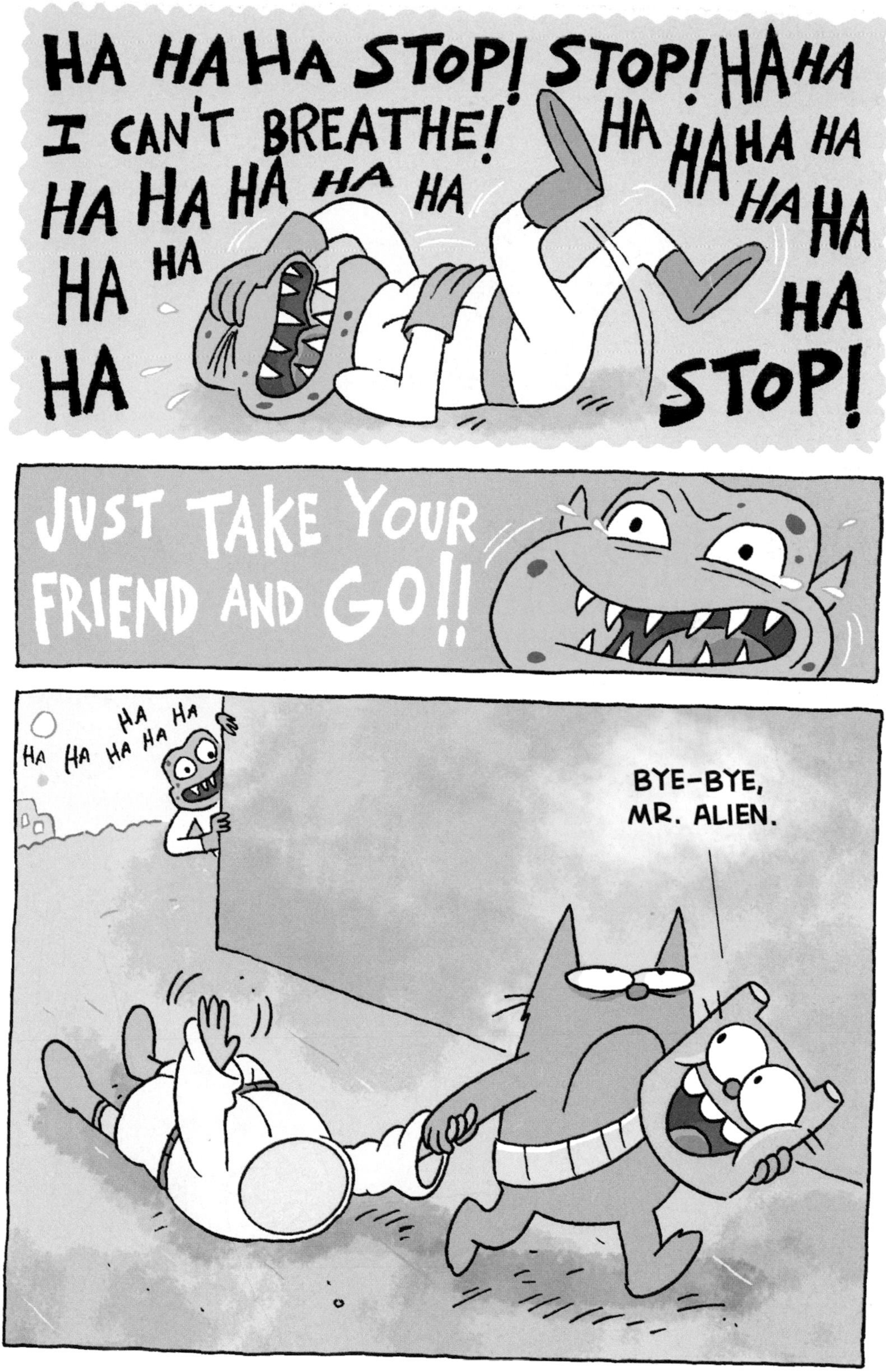
HA HA HA STOP! STOP! HA HA
I CAN'T BREATHE!
HA HA HA HA HA
HA HA
HA
HA HA HA HA
HA HA HA
HA
STOP!
JUST TAKE YOUR FRIEND AND GO!!
HA HA HA HA HA HA
BYE-BYE, MR. ALIEN.

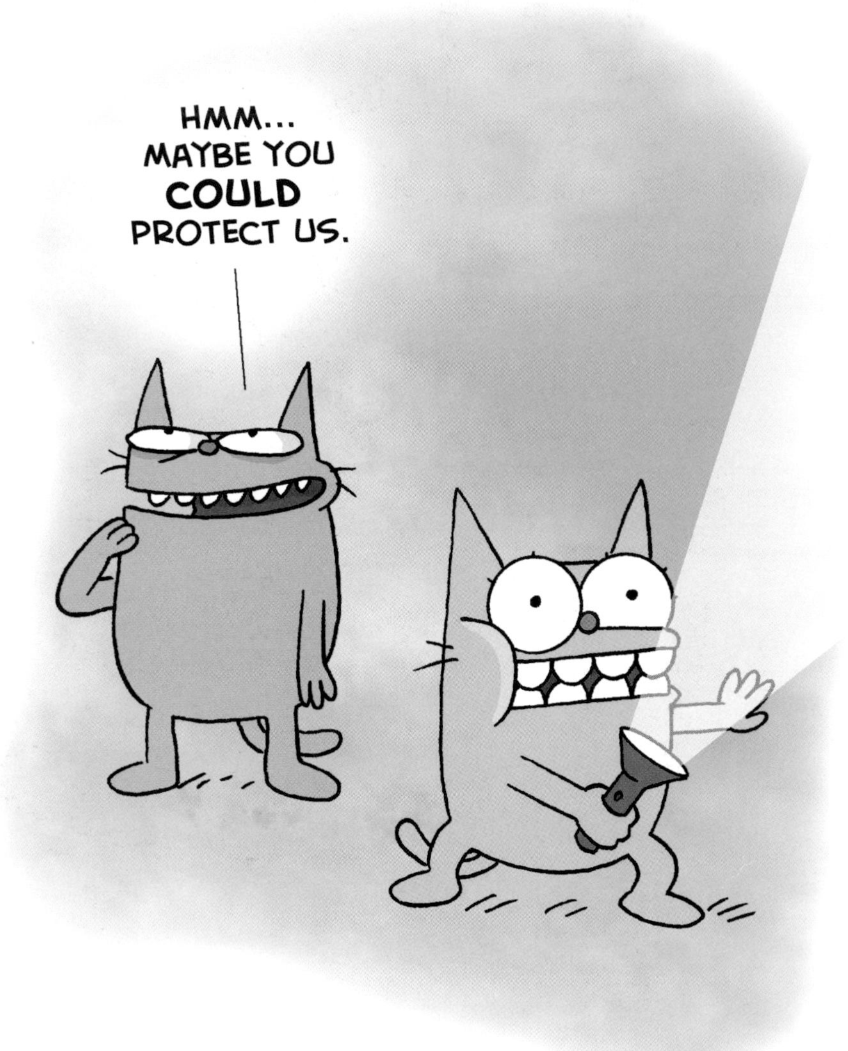
HMM... MAYBE YOU **COULD** PROTECT US.

The Bike Ride

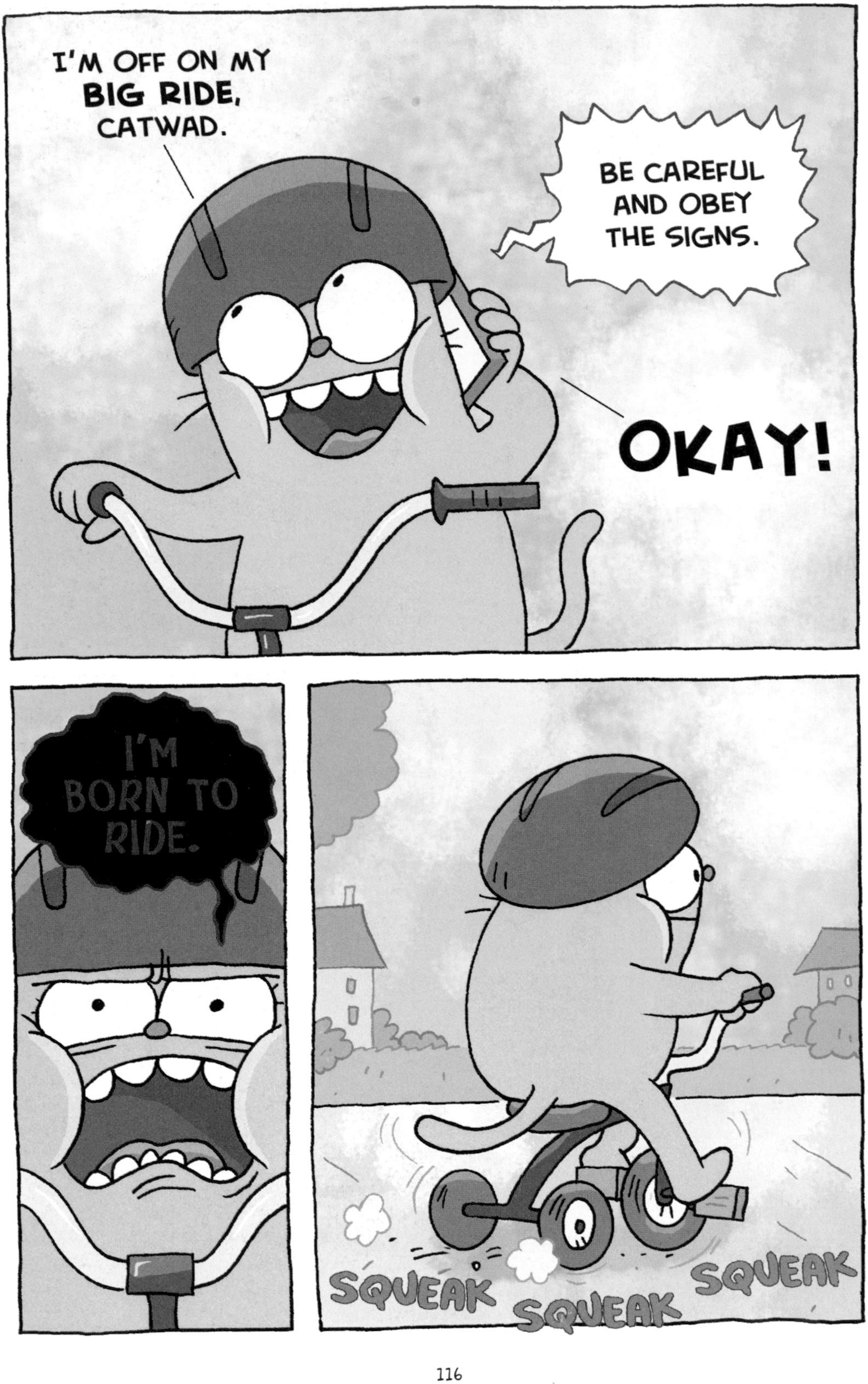
I'M OFF ON MY BIG RIDE, CATWAD.
BE CAREFUL AND OBEY THE SIGNS.
OKAY!
I'M BORN TO RIDE.
SQUEAK
SQUEAK
SQUEAK

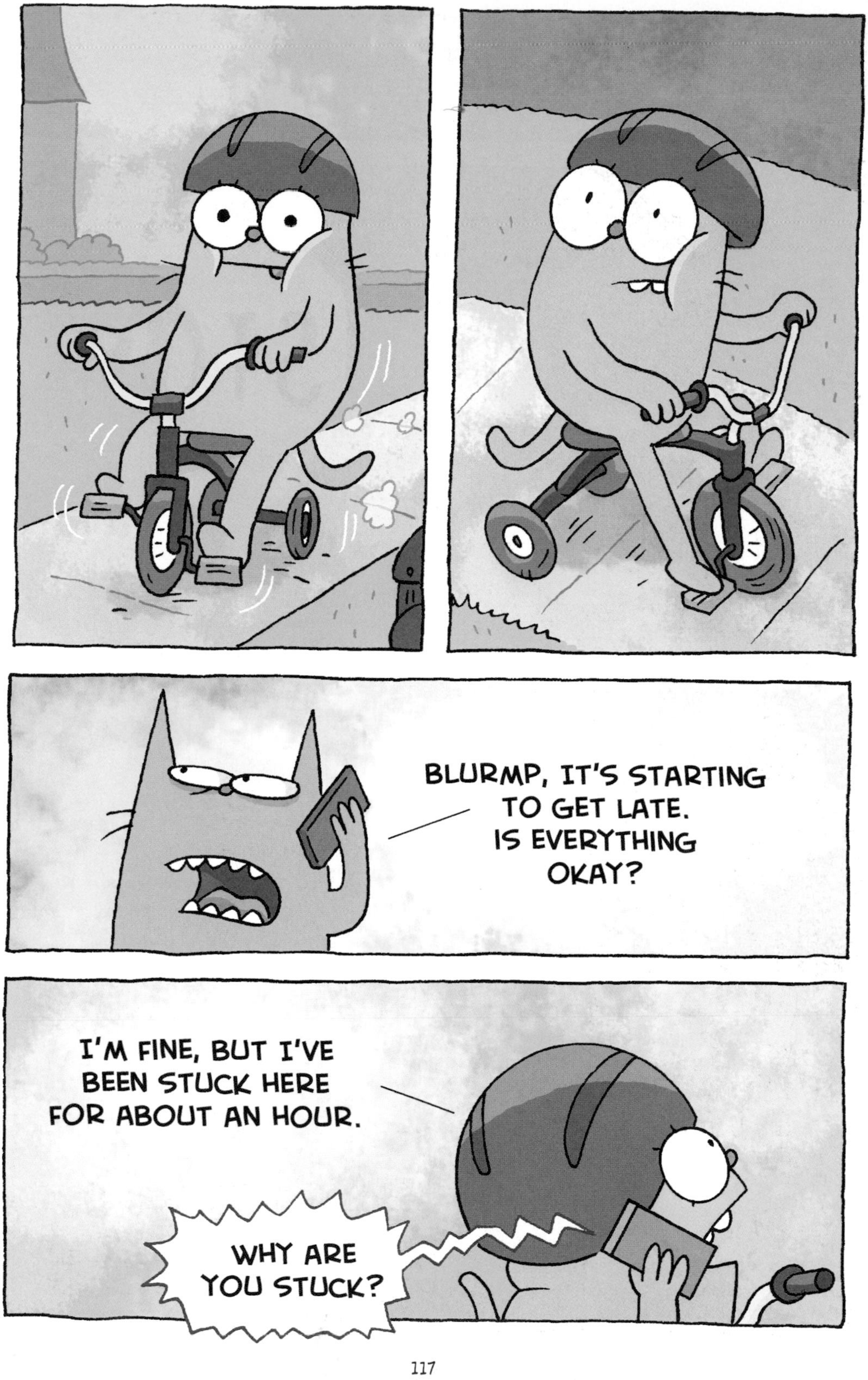
BLURMP, IT'S STARTING TO GET LATE. IS EVERYTHING OKAY?
I'M FINE, BUT I'VE BEEN STUCK HERE FOR ABOUT AN HOUR.
WHY ARE YOU STUCK?

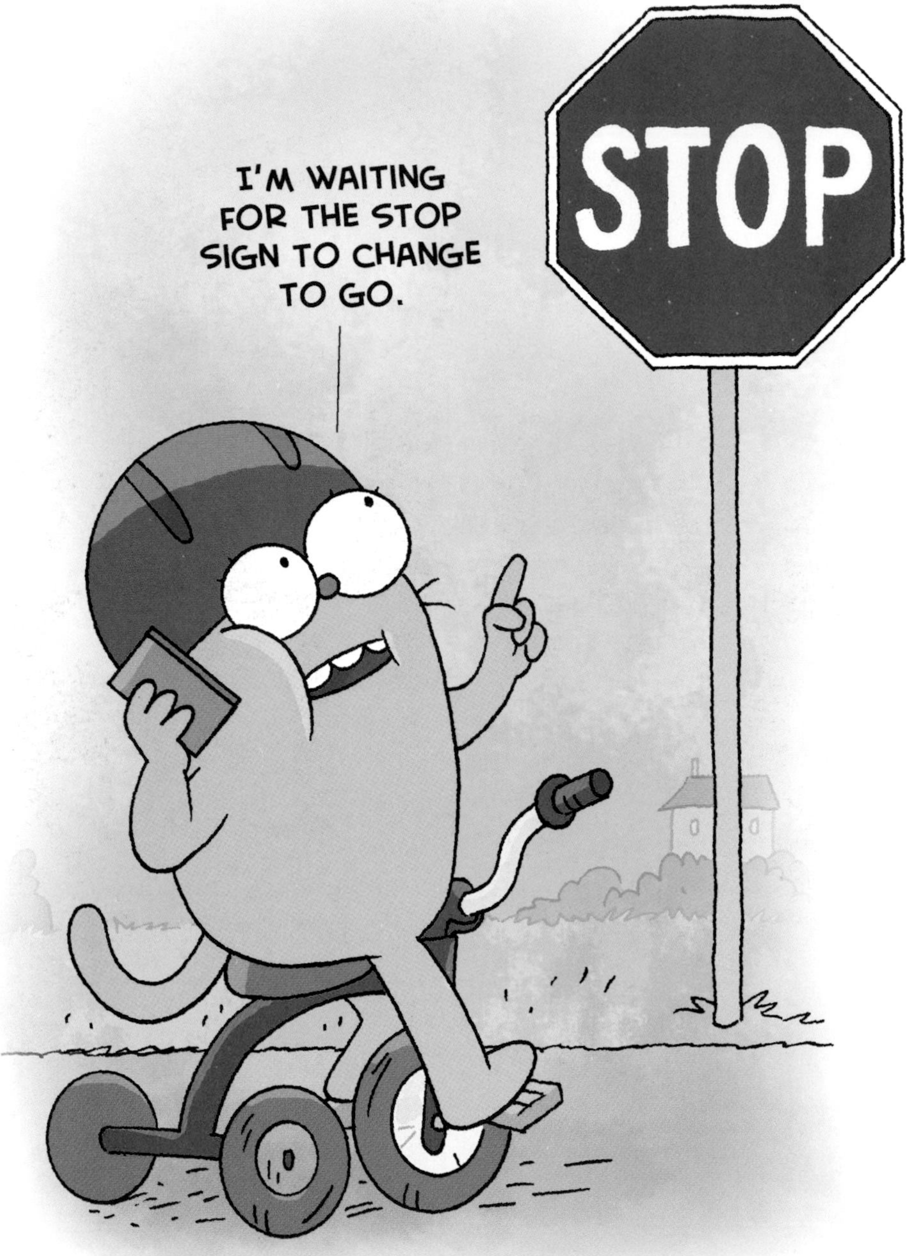
I'M WAITING FOR THE STOP SIGN TO CHANGE TO GO.
STOP

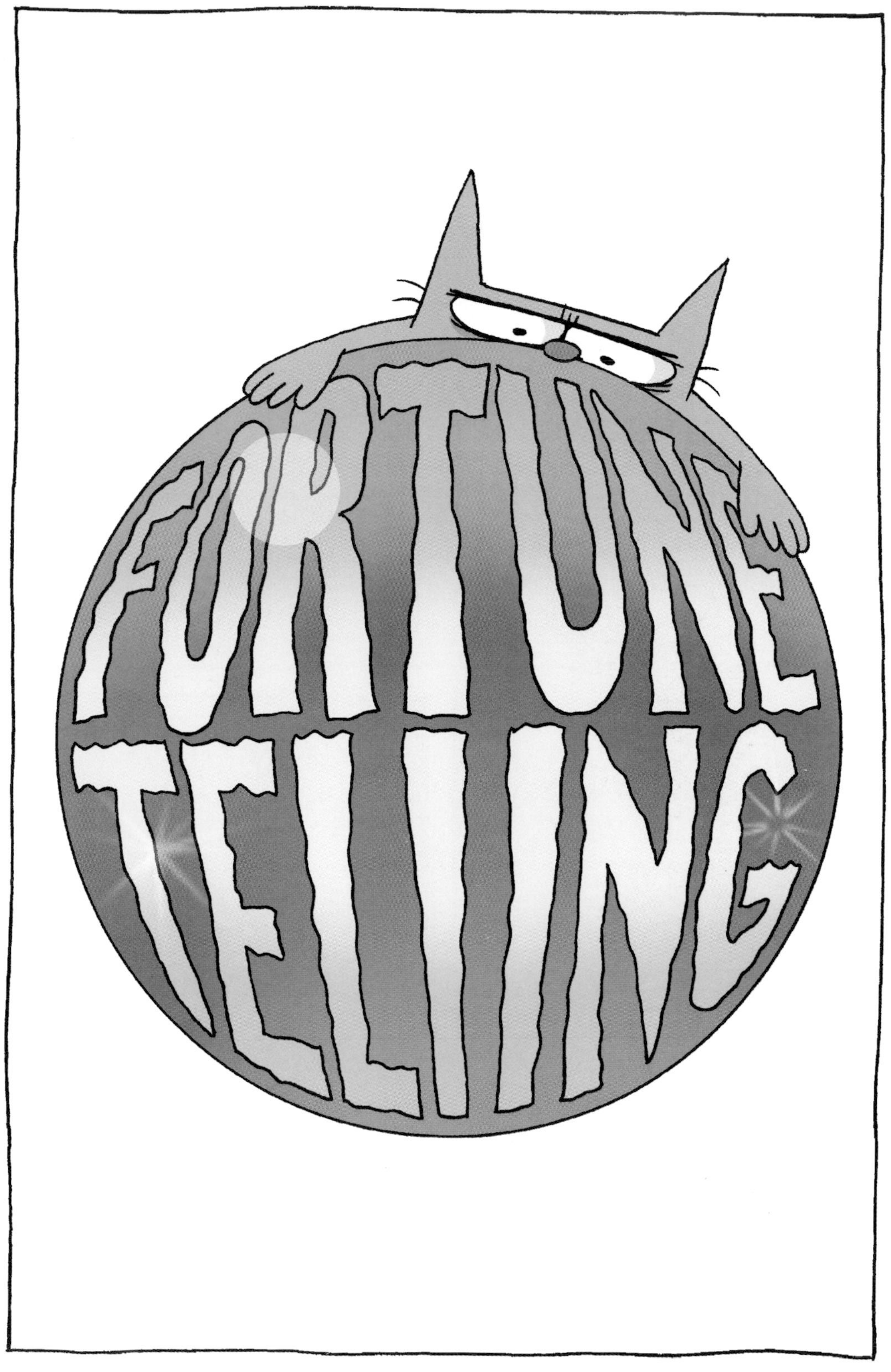
FORTUNE
TELLING

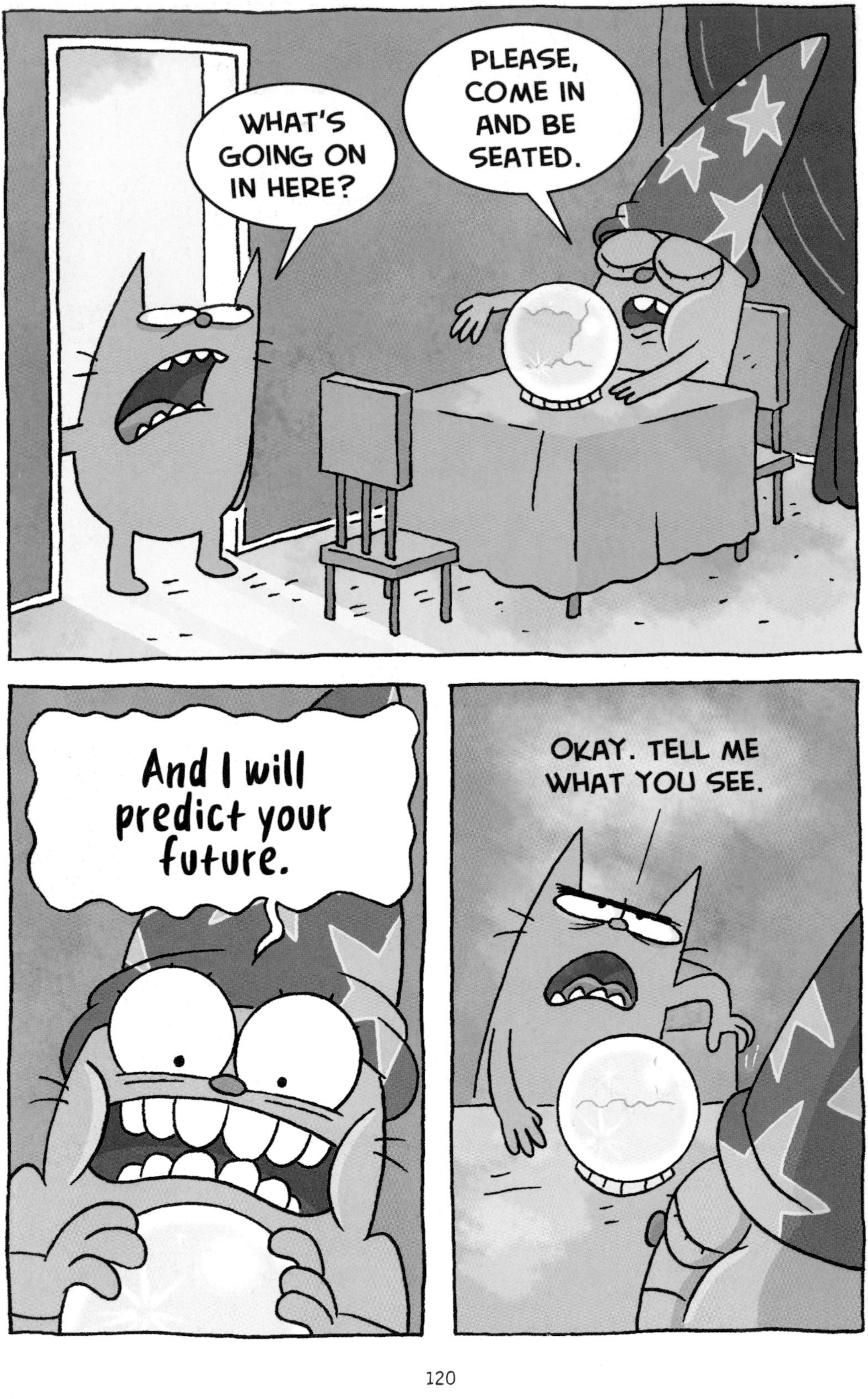
WHAT'S GOING ON IN HERE?
PLEASE, COME IN AND BE SEATED.
And I will predict your future.
OKAY. TELL ME WHAT YOU SEE.

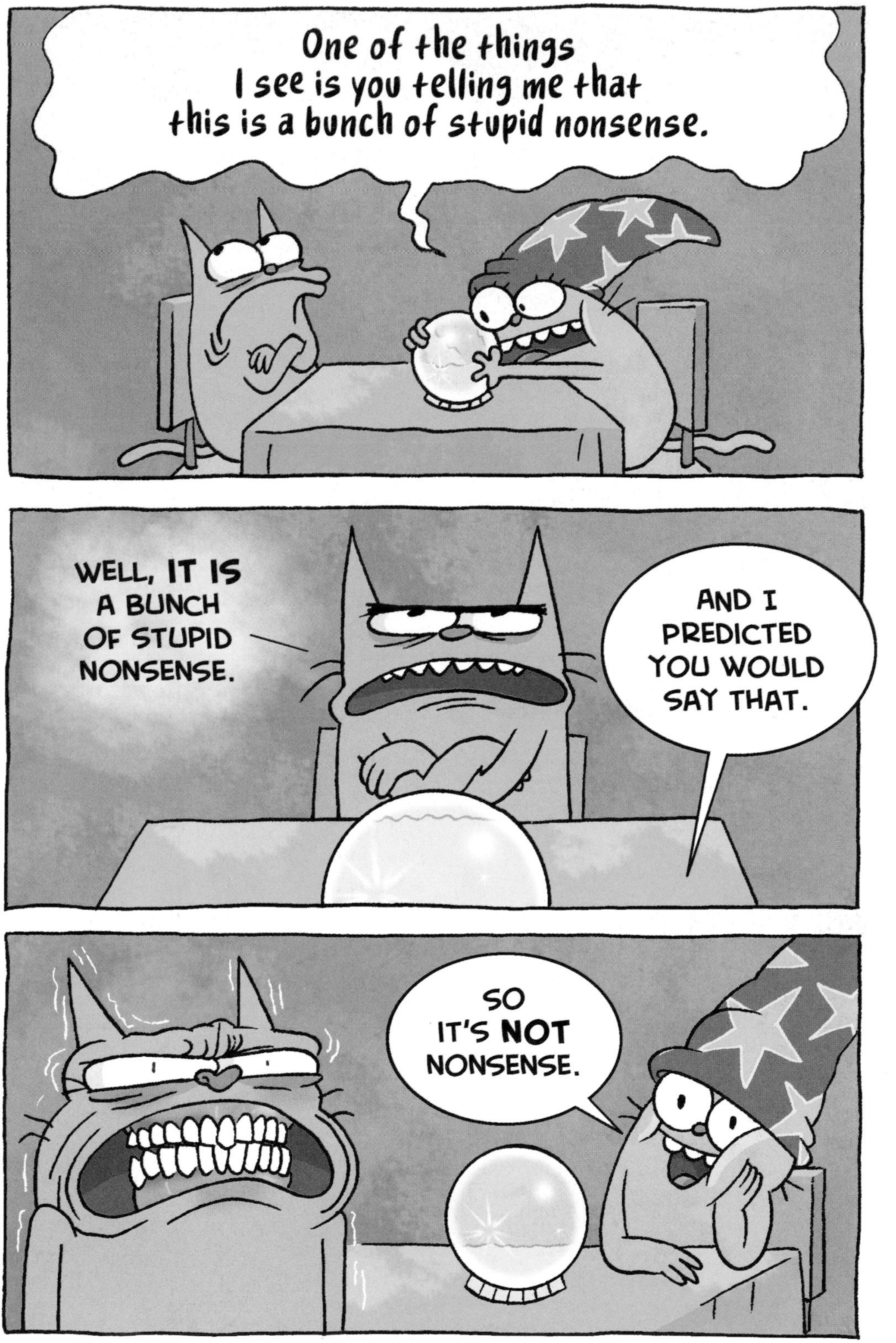

One of the things I see is you telling me that this is a bunch of stupid nonsense.
WELL, IT IS A BUNCH OF STUPID NONSENSE.
AND I PREDICTED YOU WOULD SAY THAT.
SO IT'S NOT NONSENSE.

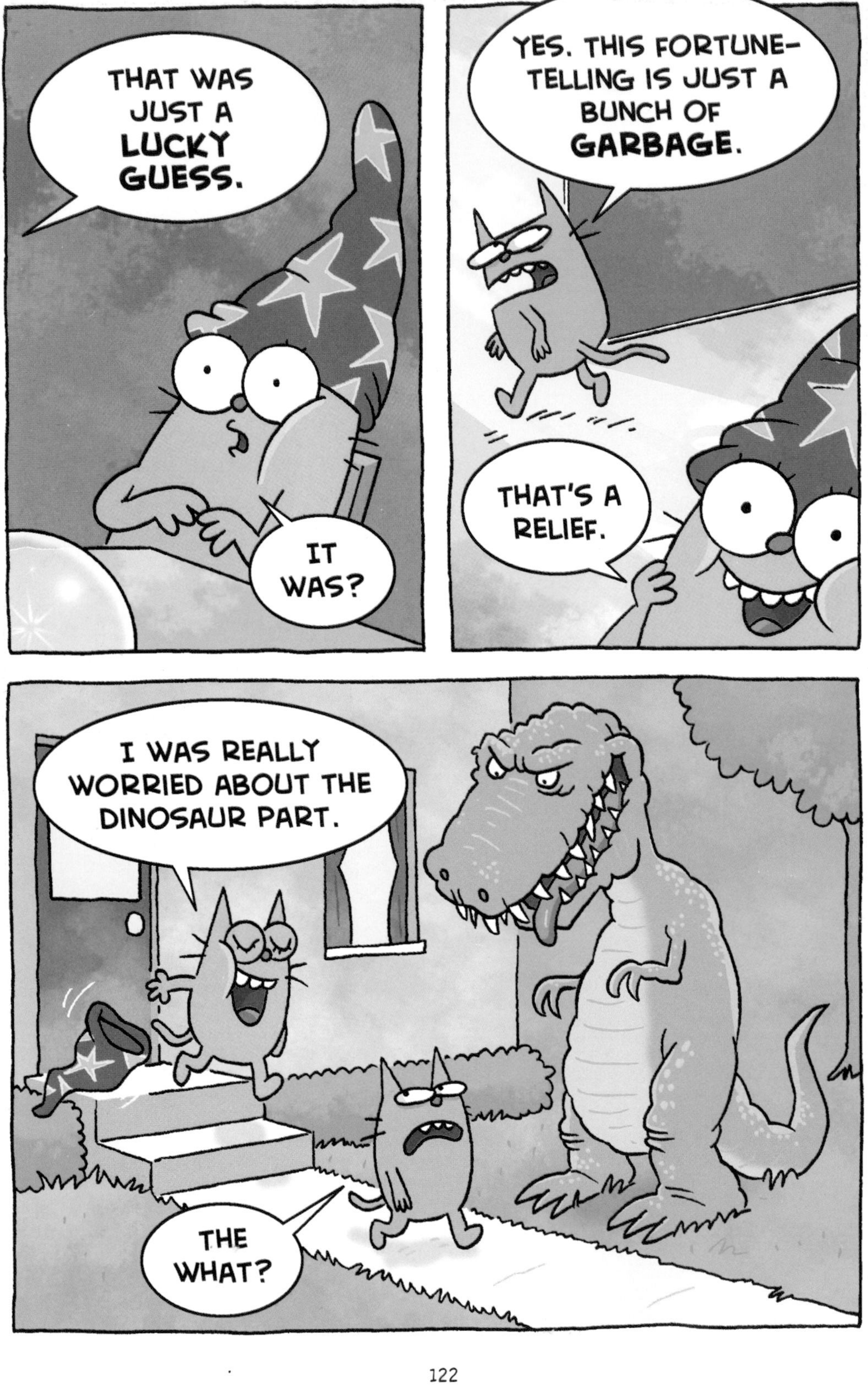
THAT WAS JUST A **LUCKY GUESS.**
IT WAS?
YES. THIS FORTUNE-TELLING IS JUST A BUNCH OF **GARBAGE.**
THAT'S A RELIEF.
I WAS REALLY WORRIED ABOUT THE DINOSAUR PART.
THE WHAT?

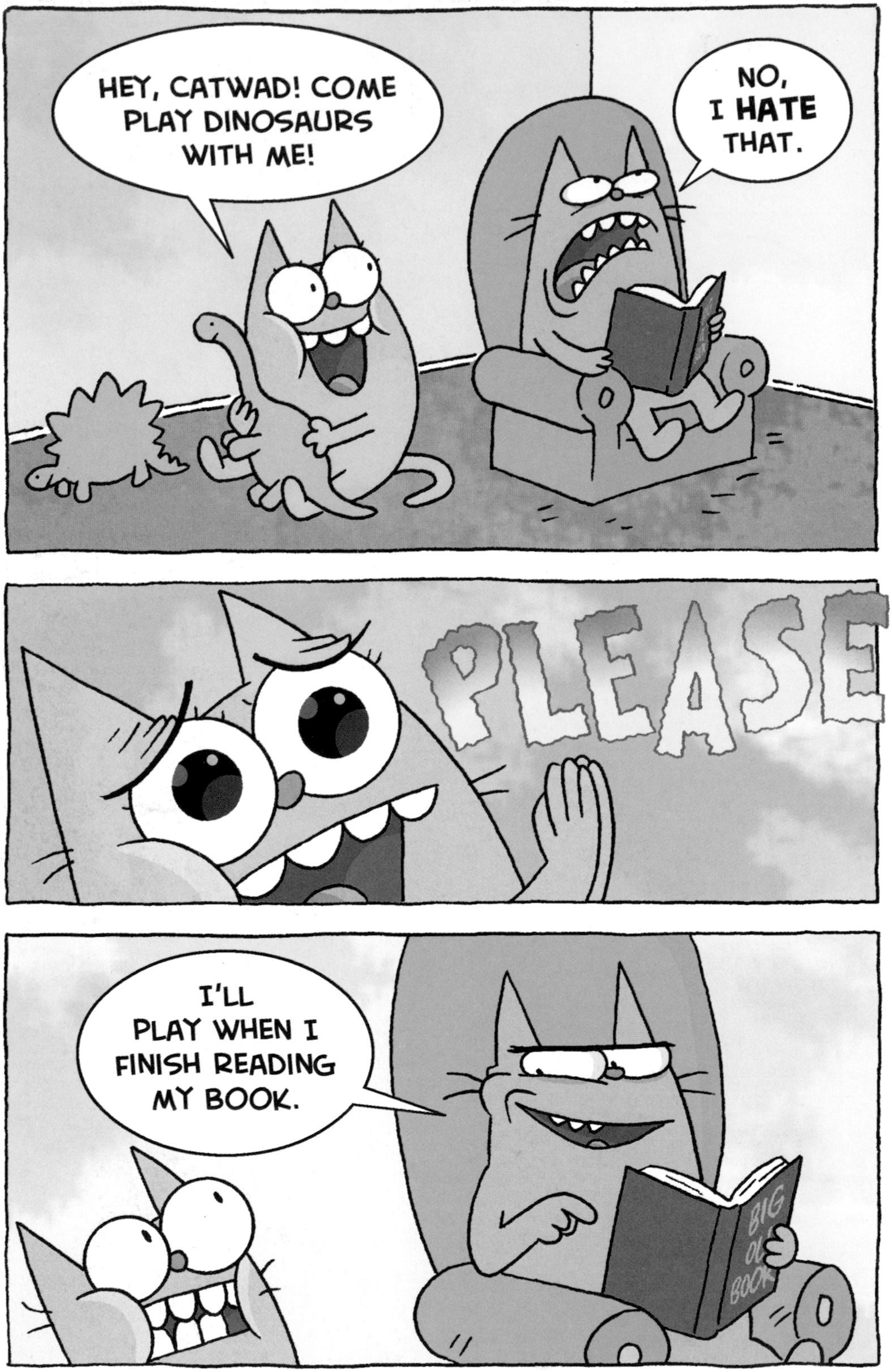
HEY, CATWAD! COME PLAY DINOSAURS WITH ME!
NO, I **HATE** THAT.
PLEASE
I'LL PLAY WHEN I FINISH READING MY BOOK.
BIG OL' BOOK

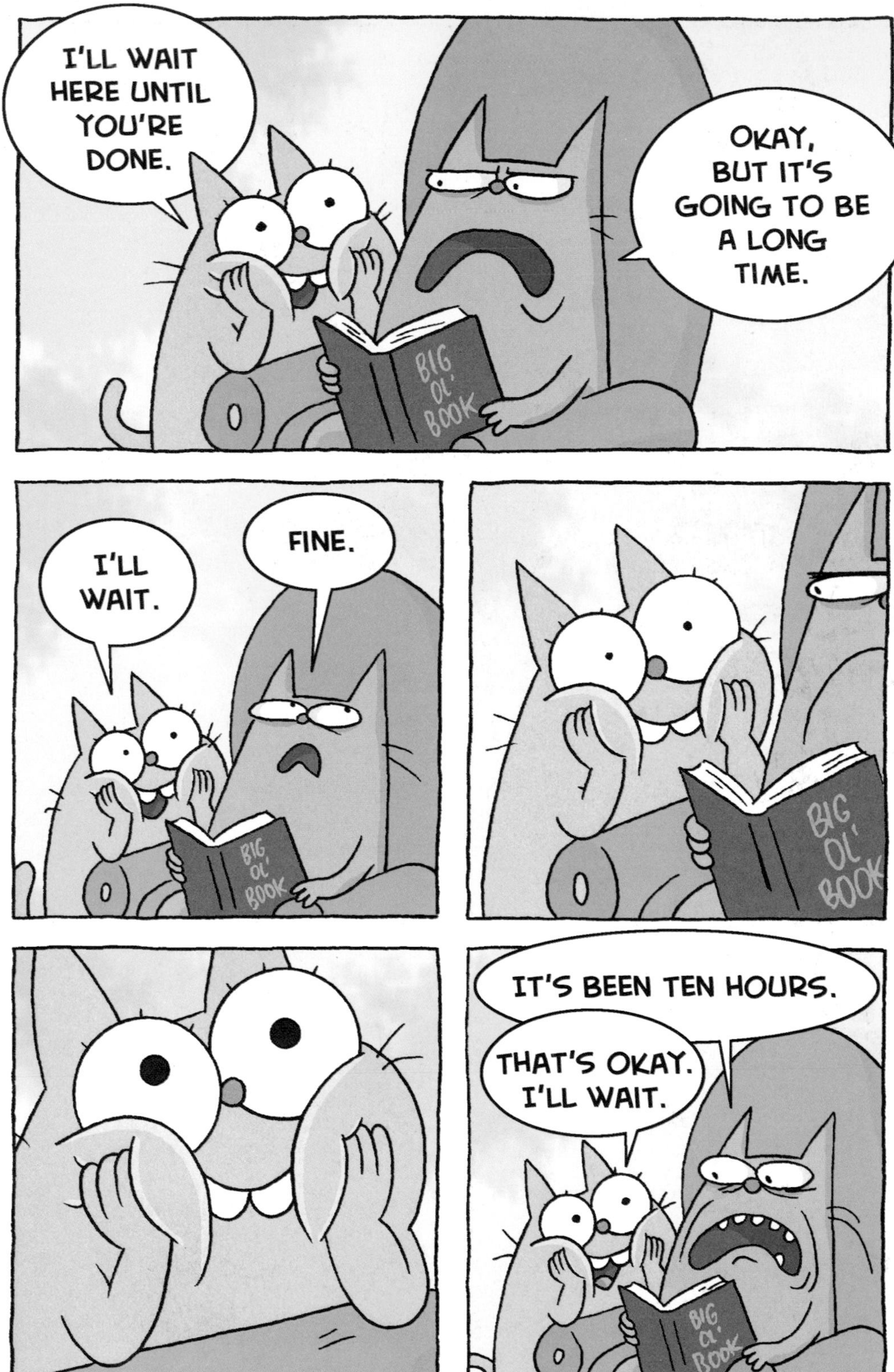
I'LL WAIT HERE UNTIL YOU'RE DONE.
OKAY, BUT IT'S GOING TO BE A LONG TIME.
BIG OL' BOOK
I'LL WAIT.
FINE.
BIG OL' BOOK
BIG OL' BOOK
IT'S BEEN TEN HOURS.
THAT'S OKAY. I'LL WAIT.
BIG OL' BOOK

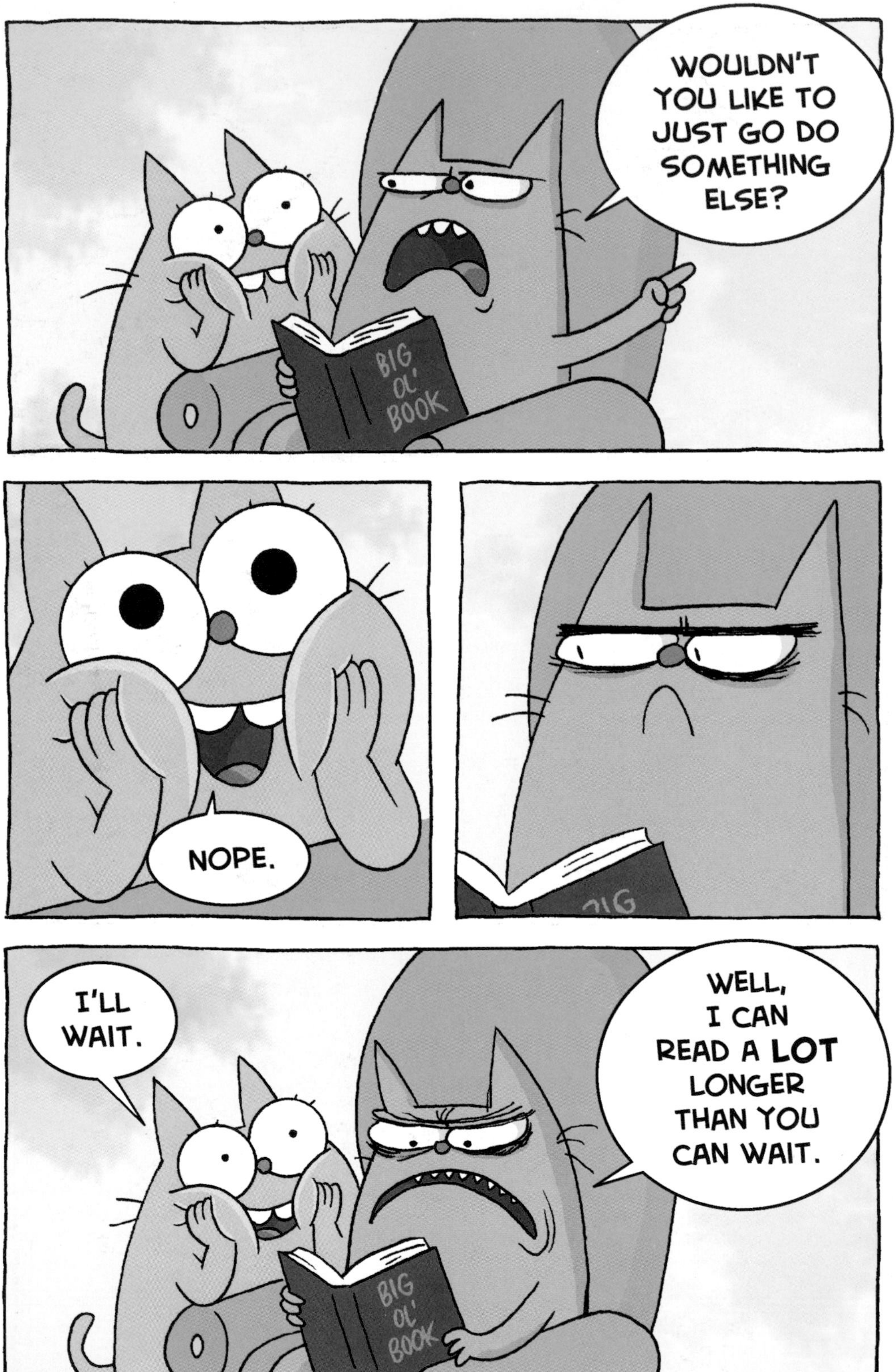

WOULDN'T YOU LIKE TO JUST GO DO SOMETHING ELSE?
BIG OL' BOOK
NOPE.
I'LL WAIT.
WELL, I CAN READ A **LOT** LONGER THAN YOU CAN WAIT.
BIG OL' BOOK

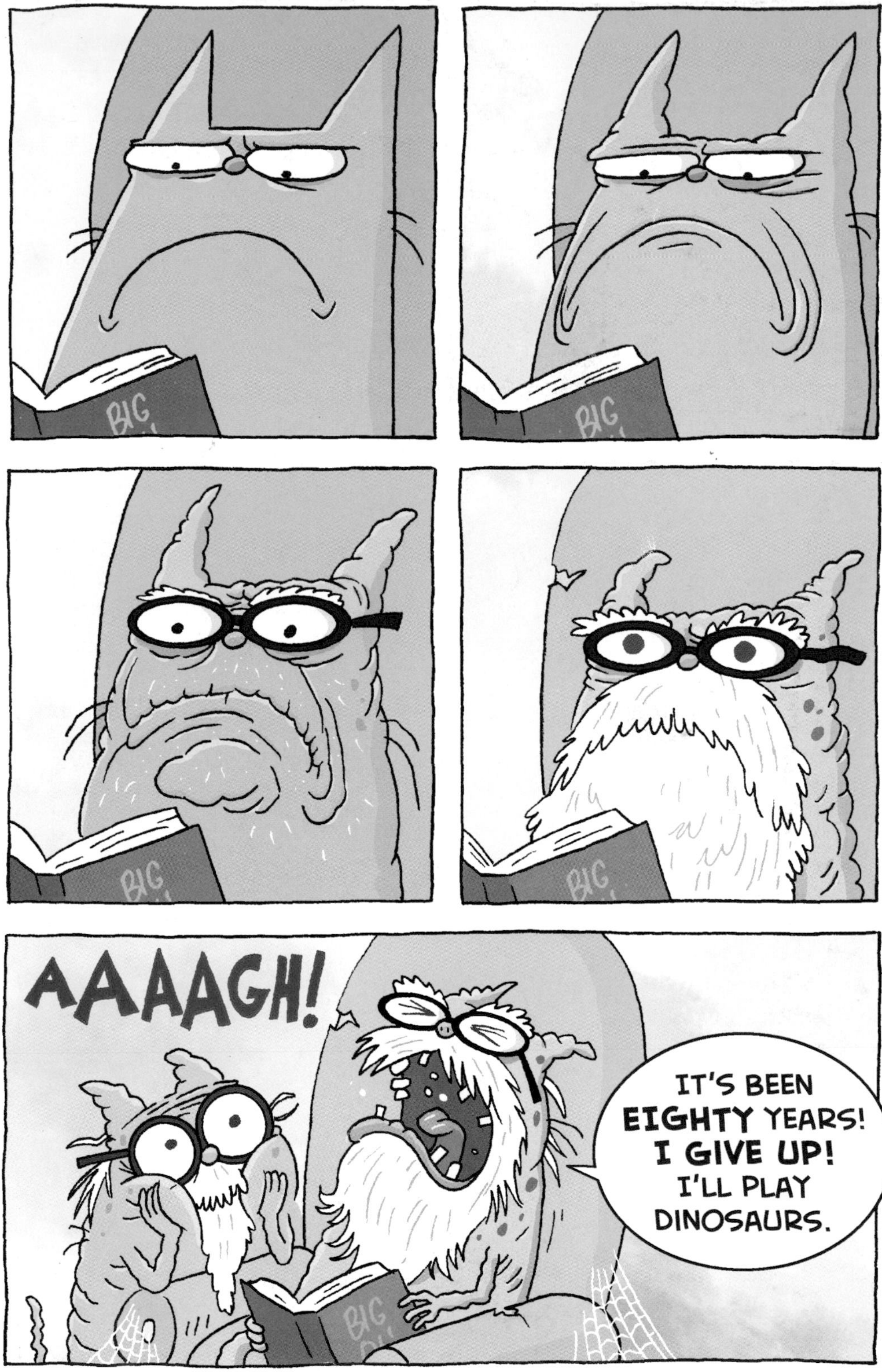
BIG
BIG
BIG
BIG
AAAAGH!
IT'S BEEN EIGHTY YEARS! I GIVE UP! I'LL PLAY DINOSAURS.
BIG

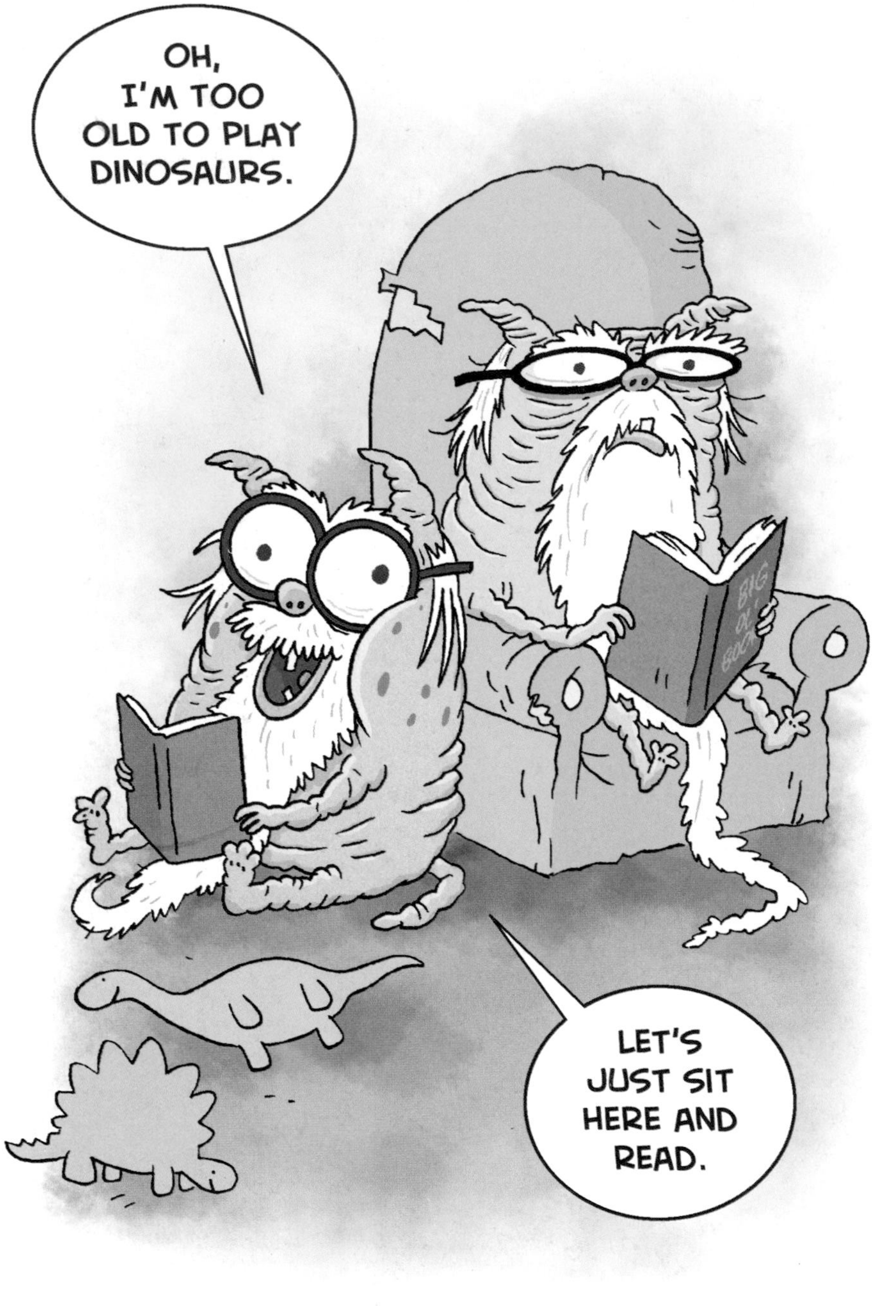
OH, I'M TOO OLD TO PLAY DINOSAURS.
BIG OL' BOOK
LET'S JUST SIT HERE AND READ.